GARGLING WITH TAR

JÁCHYM TOPOL is one of the best-known Czech writers of today. Famous in his youth as an underground activist, poet and songwriter, he was an early signatory of Charter 77, and published a samizdat literary magazine *Revolver Revue*. After the 1989 Velvet Revolution he co-founded the weekly newspaper *Respekt*. His first novel, *City Sister Silver*, was a huge success both in the Czech Republic and internationally. *Gargling with Tar* is his fourth novel. All his novels have been translated into many languages. Jáchym Topol lives in Prague.

DAVID SHORT has taught Czech in London since 1973. His translations include *Pirouettes on a Postage Stamp* by Bohumil Hrabal, *Notebooks from New Guinea* by Vojtech Novotny and *Dad Takes Goal Kicks* by Jiří Pokorný. He is currently working on a new translation of *RUR* by Karel Čapek.

GARGLING WITH TAR

JÁCHYM TOPOL

Translated from the Czech by David Short

Portobello
BOOKS

Published by Portobello Books Ltd 2010

Portobello Books Ltd
Twelve Addison Avenue
London
W11 4QR

The original Czech edition was published in 2005 under the title
Kloktat Dehet by Torst Publishers Praha © Jáchym Topol 2005.

The German edition was published under the title *Zirkuszone* ©
Suhrkamp Verlag Frankfurt am Main 2007.

English translation © David Short 2010

This translation was supported by the Ministry of Culture of the
Czech Republic.

A CIP catalogue record is available from the British Library

9 8 7 6 5 4 3 2 1

ISBN 978 1 84627 161 8

www.portobellobooks.com

Typeset by Avon DataSet Ltd, Bidford on Avon, Warwickshire
Printed in the UK by CPI William Clowes Beccles NR34 7TL

GARGLING WITH TAR

I
HOME FROM HOME

1

They called me Ilya

They used to call me Ilya, all the nuns, all our foster-mothers back in Siřem, because as a baby I would call out *iya, iya* to people, and since this is Czech for 'donkey', they called me Ilya.

I would call out whenever the faces of the nuns at the Home from Home began to break into my dreams of Shadowland.

Shadowland was my earliest childhood. I would sometimes find myself going there. Before the nuns arrived, I lived in the kitchen.

I matured rapidly in the Home from Home's prayer-filled, god-fearing atmosphere, and spoke Czech well. Monkeyface didn't speak at all.

The nuns called me Ilya long before their nerves began to shatter.

When I was very little they would even call me 'Ilya, our long-suffering little donkey'. They liked the way I fussed over my baby brother and 'wouldn't have a word said against him', as they put it.

After the kitchen, Monkeyface and I grew up at the Home from Home, because our parents didn't give a damn, not a shit, not one sodding shit about us. That's quite common here.

Apparently, our parents left us on a bus when they fled the country.

I'm not surprised they didn't want Monkeyface, but I've no idea why they didn't want to keep me.

The children at the Home from Home had all sorts of ideas about their real parents.

The only certain fact about them was that they had disappeared.

In Siřem, at the boys' home (as sisters Leontina, Alberta, Eulalia, Zdislava, Dolores and Emiliana called it), or 'this colony of louts' (as Commander Vyžlata called it), we all lived lumped together, boys of every imaginable nationality, including some Czechs, such as Dýha or Karel.

To keep us free from scabies and lice the nuns would scrub us with coal-tar soap.

The tar water, grey with the grime of us boys, splashed all over the black gowns and white caps of the sisters. The suds, whipped up by the washing process and constantly in motion, looked like the delicate lace trim on Sister Dolores's underwear, for often it was she who bent over us with the scrubbing brush. She would scrub us so vigorously that her gown was soaked right through. It was hot from the steam of the wash-tub and tiny beads of sweat would break out on Sister Dolores's forehead, then drip into our tub. Sometimes she found the heat so oppressive that she would loosen her gown and bare her shoulders. We used to sit in the tub in twos or threes. Sister Dolores didn't know that we could see her lace. She didn't know that inside her lace we could see her breasts. The nuns were not allowed to wear lace, just like we were not allowed to smoke.

The nuns had lots and lots of coal-tar soap. Sister Alberta had crates of it piled up in her closet. The coal-tar soapsuds killed our head lice.

We boys had a plentiful supply of lice. In return for a handful of lice – caught and killed or squeezed out of our bitten skin – we would be given a piece of fudge. It melted in our mouths with all the sweetness of the world. That sweetness stayed for a while, even after the fudge had slipped down.

We collected our dead lice in matchboxes. Sometimes we joined forces and put them in the same box. Then we would share them out. Sister Alberta would hack at the fudge on the kitchen table with the sharpest of the bread knives – *chop, chop!*

Sister Alberta was a nun like all the others, although she wasn't quite like the others. I'm pretty sure she loved both the Virgin and Czechia.

Even the smallest longshirts who had caught just one louse would get a lick of fudge. Some tried sucking up to us, offering us flies, spiders, midges, anything they could grab, anything that was too slow to get away. Sometimes we let them have a lick.

We used to steal full matchboxes from each other. Anyone caught thieving would get their knuckles rapped with a ruler. It hurt, but it was a mild punishment.

If anyone lied that they hadn't stolen a matchbox, they had to gargle soapy tar-water. It made great bubbles, but it was better not to get caught.

We had to gargle tar for other lies as well. It burnt and it got worse as the bubbles travelled down your throat or up your nose. Even a tiny bubble grew into a gigantic, scratchy bubble that hurt a lot. Even just thinking of telling a lie made you feel that burning sensation in your throat. Everyone wondered whether the pain was worth it.

In the dining room-cum-classroom of the Home from Home there was a painting of Jesus. When I was tiny, I thought it was the long-haired St Czech and his virgin mother. Then I thought about it more and decided that it was a portrait of my parents, but that was clearly nonsense. The idea had come to me during the Lord's Prayer! It was nonsense.

That rubbish stuck in my head, though, because sisters Leontina, Alberta, Eulalia, Zdislava, Dolores and Emiliana taught us all that we were the children of God. We weren't, of course, and the nuns paid dearly for lying to us. We weren't the children of God. We were vermin, bastards, psychopaths, sons-of-bitches and foreign scum. Later, Jesus would be replaced by Private Fedotkin from Stalin's Flying Brigade.

I was fine. Once we got to the Home from Home, I grew up fast. I learned to talk and get about.

Me and Monkeyface, we were from the same litter.

I used to find the idea terrible, but the truth is we had the same parents. That was one of the reasons why the nuns kept on stressing that the world was a vale of thorns and that life was full of tears. You can say that again!

Monkeyface would lie around in his cot and – if the walking exercises that sisters Leontina and Alberta, or perhaps Eulalia and Zdislava, and sometimes Dolores and Emiliana did with him bore fruit – he would shuffle through the corridors of the home, provided the nuns held him up. Best of all Monkeyface liked being with Hanka. Me too.

But most of the time Monkeyface just lay around.

Sometimes I lay down with him. He would immediately start squealing with joy, smiling all over his face. I would laugh back at him, as if into a mirror. But he never spoke.

Hanka was allowed to come and visit me and Monkeyface. Her hair bounced as she skipped up and down the stairs of the home. The nuns were glad to see her looking after Monkeyface. They had their hands full with the healthy boys. Hanka's mother, Mrs Kropek, did the cleaning at the Home from Home. She had Hanka to help out. Later, Commander Vyžlata put a stop to this. Hanka's hair smelt nice, she didn't smell of the Home from Home. She and I grew close. Cuddling in bed, how could it be otherwise? Hanka wasn't at all put off by Monkeyface. I sometimes wondered whether maybe she had brothers like him to look after at home as well. I fell in love with her, but it came to nothing.

Siřem was our home. There were two floors full of boys: the snotty-nosed 'longshirts' on one floor, and the older boys in shorts, we called them 'shortpants', on the other. What we required was a firm hand, plenty of food and warmth, and to learn Czech, or so the six nuns used to say.

We were rabble and needed a rod of iron to make strong men of us, Commander Vyžlata used to say.

We came from all over the place.

Whenever a new boy arrived, especially to join the longshirts, the older ones would look him over and weigh him up. A darkie stuck with the darkies, a Chink with the Chinks. Czechs would join Dýha, and when they brought someone in who was from nowhere and couldn't speak Czech, but just some gibberish, he'd sit in a corner for a while and blub, until the nuns took him in hand and taught him Czech and he became a child of God and started to get clothes donated by Czech children, and went to church with us, ate with us, stole lice and grew in size.

Every child of God – any new arrival, whether a longshirt or a boy already old enough for shorts – always got a bit of a working-over from the older boys, so that he knew for certain he had arrived at the Home from Home.

Above the two floors with the dormitories were the old upper storeys, which were always under lock and key. Below us was the cellar and on the cellar floor, water.

I was never once put in solitary confinement in the cellar. That was where boys were sent as a punishment or to 'cool off', as Sister Leontina used to say, because now and again one of the shortpants would go mad and throw a tantrum and have a fit as we were all psychopaths.

It was a Czech home for foreign kids, neglected kids, bad kids – boys, the sons of foreigners who couldn't give a fuck for them or had died on them or were in prison or had disappeared. That's why there were so many half-castes, darkies and Chinks among us. I wasn't a darkie, but I wasn't a Chink either, nor was Monkeyface.

Some boys spoke their own unintelligible language, though the nuns didn't allow it. You had to gargle tar for that. Any foreign words were washed away from their throats with bubbles of pain, then the boys were topped up with Czech. Baby longshirts arriving at the home spoke many different languages, the languages of savage races. What a mountain of textbooks that would make, I thought to myself. Yet even the tiniest longshirt spoke Czech in a few weeks, in just a few weeks of godly, church-going Sundays, because he had to.

After they turned up, in between crying, they would still babble a few foreign words. They were only little. Then they learned to recite a prayer and how to say good morning and thank you, and it went on from there.

Now and then, after lights-out, when the boys were asleep and there was a strict no-talking rule, you could hear lots of different languages in the dorm. The little ones talked in their sleep and shouted out in their sleep and cried in their sleep. Then a nun had to come running in, the nun on night duty, because as soon as one longshirt started talking or whining in his sleep another would strike up. They were afraid of the dark, and once they were awake and they were all screaming there was nothing you could do to silence them. So the nun who happened to be on duty would run in at the first sign of trouble, the first scream or sob, and she would try to calm them, saying, 'Come, come,' or 'Shhh, sleep now...' and Sister Eulalia would sometimes sing a low, soothing lullaby: 'Sleep, little angel...' In the night the nuns didn't punish anyone for speaking in foreign languages. They waited until morning. Mostly they had to punish the darkies, because they had their own language and used it so that no one could understand them. The nuns would punish us for saying certain words: 'shit', 'arse', 'crap' and the like. Anyone heard using words like that would be dragged off by Sister Alberta to the punishment cell in the cellar to sleep with the rats. I once got 'dickhead' and 'thickhead' mixed up and received such a caning from Sister Leontina – but I was still very small then. I only ever spoke Czech, and the nuns never ever punished Monkeyface. There was no point.

Monkeyface's bed was in one corner with a net over it, and I made sure that his nearest neighbours were gentle longshirts. I also chose two choirboys, Šklíba and Martin, to take care of him. They had to put up with Monkeyface's whimpering and they had to empty his potty and keep him clean, wiping his bottom and the saliva and snot from his face. I soon put a stop to all the jibes at Monkeyface's expense, and trained Šklíba and Martin to be on their guard. I was small, but in the longshirts' dormitory I was the biggest, though I didn't have to move upstairs yet. The boys upstairs would jerk themselves off, but that meant nothing to me. I didn't want to go upstairs, because I'd be away from Monkeyface, and who would have looked after him then?

I also taught the longshirts how to comfort Monkeyface when he was afraid, when he cried. The choirboys made a good team, having practised singing together. Because I sometimes didn't have the time to see to him myself, like when Sister Leontina's ordered me to dust her office... and I was the only one allowed to do that! After tidying her office I would sometimes stay behind and drop onto the kneeler under the Cross. It hurt my knees, but it was a good, strange pain. And I would stay rocking backwards and forwards on the kneeler so long that I'd be overwhelmed by the place I called Shadowland and I never got anywhere else when I was on the kneeler. Then I would go back downstairs and crawl into bed beside Monkeyface. None of the longshirts disturbed us. They wouldn't dare. And shortpants weren't allowed in our dormitory. That's what the nuns had decided. Only the nuns, me and Hanka were supposed to go anywhere near Monkeyface. Though Hanka spent a lot of time at her mother's in the village. Everyone else found Monkeyface disgusting.

I think it was because of Hanka that I abandoned Shadowland. The nuns themselves were amazed at how long I could remain there. I wasn't even aware how many boys – or what boys – passed by me in the Home from Home, following their own path in life. When I was in Shadowland the nuns would feed me, and I would open my mouth. Sometimes Shadowland gave me a headache and I would hear a rumbling and a buzzing sound long after I came out of it.

Cuddling with Hanka was better than Shadowland. Cuddling with Hanka was the most beautiful thing in the world. The boys might be busy studying, but I would stay with Monkeyface waiting for Hanka to come. She crept into bed beside me, and while Monkeyface was quiet we lay there, cuddling, each listening to what the other was saying. Monkeyface liked us being together. Czechia couldn't have been more beautiful than Hanka. One time Hanka grabbed me down below and said, 'This thing isn't just for peeing with, you know.' But she was laughing, happy. Or she would say, 'You don't go too far, so I'll let you do... this. And this!' More than anything I'd like to have lived with Hanka. But that proved impossible.

Sister Alberta was a nun like the rest, but she was also a local Siřem girl. Before the home became the Home, when it was just the kitchens of the manor house, she had been saddled with me in the kitchen, and also had her hands full caring for Monkeyface.

Before the home became the Home from Home, the Centre sent Sister Alberta lorryloads of beds and brooms and cutlery in boxes, and endless boys' tracksuits and tracksuit tops, and dinner-trays and sheets and mountains of soap in crates. It was only then that the nuns arrived in Siřem, with their hymns and their holy crosses. They came under the command of Sister Leontina, who had the entire Home from Home obeying her orders. The nuns had been driven out of their convent by the Communists. They were snatched away from their prayers and ordered to take care of us orphaned thugs, bastards, retards and juvenile delinquents. The nuns did look after us, until the Communists put a stop to it.

I don't know when I came to Siřem. I have memories of hearing squeaking snow. I know: it was Mr Cimbura carrying me into Sister Alberta's kitchen. Before that I was in Shadowland, where there was lots of noise and my mum and dad.

Sister Alberta and Mr Cimbura lived together as man and wife, until Sister Leontina put a stop to it. Sister Alberta wasn't repulsed by Monkeyface. Towards the end of the war, her own children got lost in a concentration camp somewhere. It seemed to me that if they looked anything like Monkeyface, she should count herself lucky. The truth is, she didn't mind Monkeyface at all, even if he yelled and crapped himself all the time. Mr Cimbura did mind. He minded me, too. I would listen to the fairy stories they told to get Monkeyface to sleep, even before I got stuck into *The Catholic Book of Knowledge* under the guidance of the nuns. Even before I attended Father Francis's homilies on a Sunday. Mr Cimbura didn't like Father Francis.

Sister Alberta would tell us about the wolves in Chapman Forest that gobbled up runaway orphans. And about the wicked fairies who lay in wait for boys on the run and would bite them between the legs. And the elves on Fell Crag, who would catch a boy and make him dig a tunnel into the mountain. Most of all, Sister Alberta liked telling us about Czechia.

I used to lie in my bed made from empty soapboxes, all fed and bathed, and Monkeyface, who in those days fitted nicely inside a single soapbox, would belch and fart, and Sister Alberta would read us to sleep with a fairy story about Czechia, who protected this wonderful Bohemian land from its enemies. Mr Cimbura used to come in quietly and sometimes cover the kitchen table with little parcels of goodies for us and for Sister Alberta, and he would listen attentively as Sister Alberta told us stories of how Czechia vanquished the devil's warlocks with their yellow, vulpine eyes, or some such tale. He often brought a little flask with him, and he and Sister Alberta would take sips from it, and they carried on talking until we were asleep. All of which I saw and heard before I dropped off.

Because she cared for Monkeyface, the nuns let us stay with Sister Alberta, even after the home became the Home and Mr Cimbura had to climb into the kitchen through the window. But not for long. It happened right in the middle of the tale about Czechia... Sister Leontina flung open the door and interrupted the story just as the virgin Czechia had closed the eyes of the last heroic defenders of Bohemia, and was riding out against its enemies, brandishing aloft her blazing sword... Seeing Mr Cimbura, Sister Leontina shouted 'A man!' and, as he left shuffling on his unsteady legs, she grabbed the flask from the table, sniffed at it and shouted 'Alcohol!', then immediately ordered Sister Alberta to tidy up the kitchen. That was the first night I slept in the longshirts' dormitory. Monkeyface too. Not in his box. He slept on a bunk, as if he were the same as the other lads. Then they fixed the net over him. Otherwise it wouldn't have worked.

Our nuns brought us up and cared for us day and night, and told us we were the children of savage or motley races, carried to Siřem on a whirlwind of bad times, when the world was a vale of thorns, but that none of this mattered because God had us safe in the palm of His hand, as did our guardian angels. But we were not to be naughty or act crazy or lose our tempers or fight or steal, or we would be consumed by hellfire. And we had to speak Czech.

At Siřem, the boys who were best at speaking Czech were the Czechs, who were scattered among both the shortpants and the longshirts. They were here because they had done something wrong, like Karel, or for stealing or running away. Even Dýha had run away from his parents or whoever he'd been with before.

It would be our last winter with the nuns, although we didn't know it.

The days passed and clearest of all I remember that last winter, when the nuns' nerves began to shatter; when some of them began wandering around on both floors of the Home and in the kitchen-cum-classroom in tears; and when they were on night duty they would fall down on their knees in the corridors, next to the holy pictures; and Sister Alberta would smoke a sneaky cigarette out of sight of the others, though we could see her and afterwards some of us would fight over her dog-ends.

That last winter, the youngest nuns, especially sisters Eulalia and Dolores, had tears in their eyes and stopped punishing us, even for pushing and shoving on the way to church, and laughing and deliberately falling down in the snow. And one morning Sister Dolores said to Sister Leontina, 'Five kilos! Oh God! They'll only let us take five kilos! What an awful place that re-education centre must be! Oh dear! What's five kilos of books and underwear?'

Sister Leontina frowned and told Sister Dolores, 'And how much underwear and how many books did the sweet young Mary take with her to Bethlehem?'

And Sister Dolores blushed, as we could easily tell, because she was standing against the pure-white snow. She nodded and we walked on.

Just like any other morning on the way to church we sang hymns as we went. I only really remember the frosty mornings and this was one of them. But Monkeyface never had to go to church, because he couldn't, and sometimes I didn't have to because the nuns allowed me to keep him company; so me and Monkeyface, we'd often be left all alone in the longshirts' lower dorm, all alone, and everything was silent.

I would go *iya, iya!* and tell him, 'Say something, you ugly mug, you bugger!' That's what I called him, but he didn't care and he went *gru, gru!* and laughed back at me, and poked his hands through the holes of his net. He wanted one of the nuns to come and walk with him. They wouldn't let me, because I couldn't hold him up. He would also have liked Hanka to come. Sometimes Sister Alberta or Leontina, Eulalia or Dolores, Emiliana or Zdislava would look in on us, whichever nun was on kitchen duty, and she would bring us some bread and butter and milk, and to me she'd say, 'It's so sweet how you look after your baby brother...', and she'd pat me on the head and think I was a long-suffering little donkey.

After the nun had gone, Monkeyface would gobble up all the bread and drink all the milk, then loll back in his cot and start farting. Sometimes I lay next to him, and before falling asleep I would think about Shadowland. The nuns didn't know about Shadowland. It was just for me and Monkeyface. I thought about Shadowland, where the shadows would hold me up high and stroke my head, coo over me and feed me something deliciously gooey, and they would laugh with me... I thought about these shadows and remembered them. The first people I saw were at Siřem, but by then I knew enough not to give a shit about this earth, because this earth is the earth of those bastards, my parents.

Cuddling was better. If we cuddled for a long time, Hanka smelt more. We put our arms around each other. 'Do you like this?' she would ask. I liked it a lot. Hanka didn't mind what I was like. I told her once it might be nice to do cuddling with Sister Dolores as well. Hanka gave me such a smack that I saw stars. She didn't want me cuddling anyone else. Her breasts were much smaller than Sister Dolores's. When Hanka was in bed with me, Monkeyface was usually calm and quiet. Maybe he was thinking that she was in bed with him as well, which she almost was. Because of the way she cared for Monkeyface the nuns wanted Hanka to be a nun one day. So did I. Then we'd always be together. But it didn't happen. It wasn't possible.

The church services were taken by Father Francis, and because his altar boys were lads from the village, the shortpants, led by Dýha, Páta and Karel, always made for the front pews. While Father Francis and the nuns were praying or telling stories about the saints and not watching us, the shortpants and altar boys would wave their clenched fists and make faces at each other.

The altar boys stuck close to Father Francis, because left alone among us somewhere in the church, they would have got a good thumping. Father Francis went on about love being the sweetness of the world and that those who have no love have nothing. The nuns kept an eye on us while blowing on their frozen fingers, and we listened to Father Francis because we had to, and whenever he talked about love and loving, the boys would giggle, but after a while we stopped nudging each other and pulling faces, and a chill came over us, because we had had a snowball fight outside the church and our wet clothes made us cold. Among the locals only the old women from Siřem went to morning mass. They loved Šklíba's singing and the other choirboys from the Home, and they would book Šklíba's choir for their funerals. I remembered some of the old women from the olden days, before the home became the Home, and before the nuns were in charge, and I thought the old women didn't remember me. But I was wrong.

There was a time when I was chosen to join the funeral processions as well, but then it was decided that only Czech boys should accompany the dead as it looked better that way. In exchange for crying a lot they got heaps of extra sweets and soup and other goodies, but they always had to surrender some to the shortpants, who refused to cry at the villagers' funerals and called the boys who profited from funerals crybabies... But that's not how it was! No-one wanted the shortpants at funerals, because they were wilful and cheeky and stole anything that wasn't nailed down, and nobody ever wanted me at funerals either and I never sang... but I didn't care!

The singers called themselves the Circle. They were led by Sister Eulalia, and Šklíba was the head choirboy. But the choirboys' voices hardly ever rang out in winter. Even Father Francis's teeth chattered in the cold, like ours, and so he would 'storm through the service', as the old women put it, the ones who came to early mass with us, and outside the church gave us the apples and walnuts that the older longshirts lost their milk teeth on, and if anyone lost a milk tooth it meant he was big enough to join the shortpants... So I was very careful when eating nuts, because the last thing I wanted was to join Dýha in the upper dormitory, where the lads kept wanking and going on about it, which didn't interest me at all.

When we walked to church in the morning, we always had to line up, us longshirts going first because we were slower and wouldn't be able to keep up with the shortpants. But in the frost and snow the shortpants went ahead to tread a path for us. The only thing I remember is those freezing mornings as our column of God's children passed the village pond on the way to church, and the village was empty except for the dogs that barked at us... The villagers didn't know us then, because Commander Vyžlata, who would hire us out to do odd jobs for them, hadn't arrived yet. The dogs didn't know us at all and they barked at us, a procession of children, wrapped up in the scarves and caps and clothes donated to us by Czech children.

The walk back was different, because by then the village had come alive, no matter how fast Father Francis had stormed through the service. And on the way from the church to the pond snowballs and chunks of ice whizzed through the air... Not on the village green, though. There we fell into lines with the nuns at each end, and we all sang 'Closer My God to Thee', so the village could hear us. But further on, where no houses lined the path, we formed a huddle. The village boys would be waiting for us, and they'd pelt us with lumps of ice and stones, and the shortpants would form a wall around the tiniest long-shirts, cursing and swearing, and catching the ice and stones and hurling them back. They made sure the lumps of ice didn't hit the heads of the smallest boys, throwing them back into the faces of the village louts. And the nuns were powerless to prevent it.

'You're all delinquents and syphilitics! Darkies and gippos! Losers and scumbags!' the village lads would taunt us. 'And you're bog-trotters and yokels! Peasants and churls and clodhoppers!' the shortpants shouted back. And Dýha, Chata and Karel and the other shortpants took no notice of the nuns' pleading and drew out of their trouser legs the sticks that they had got ready for the village dogs, which the locals sometimes set on us. It was all a scream and great fun, despite the bruises and the nosebleeds and the odd torn ear. And although the journey to church on those freezing-cold mornings seemed endless, on the way back, with all the mayhem of fighting and trying to dodge the whizzing ice and rocks we were inside the Home in no time.

Then the nuns would put iodine on our bumps and dress our wounds, and that day the youngest one, Sister Eulalia, was sobbing because a dog had frightened her and torn her habit. And that day Sister Leontina railed against the locals, calling them Philistines and comparing us to the holy infants of the Crusades, and that day the hero was Dýha, because his forehead had been cracked open by a stone, and all the boys who were limping or had their hands bandaged were heroes too, and they bragged about their injuries, and those who didn't have any pretended they did, and we began thinking up all sorts of traps and tricks to play on the village lads, and we shouted and cursed and swore. And that day in the dining room-cum-classroom Sister Alberta roared, 'Shut up, the lot of you!' and hurled a ladle to the floor.

Straightaway, one of the darkies grabbed it and licked it clean. Dýha kicked the darkie, but the darkie's brothers weren't going to stand for that, not even from Dýha, so Dýha received a gash on his thigh from a piece of broken plate to add to the cut on his forehead. The older boys started a fight, and the longshirts ran in and out among them, knocking each other down, and before long everyone was fighting, and those who had their own languages shouted and swore in their own languages, though they swore in Czech as well.

Sister Alberta sat on her chair, plates and cutlery flying over her head, and in the fracas someone overturned the milk jug and knocked a tray full of sandwiches to the floor, and Sister Alberta lit a cigarette and, in the middle of all the mayhem of fighting, crying and the sobbing of longshirts who'd got trampled on, flicked her ash on the dirty, greasy floor.

I got to the sandwiches and shoved one under my shirt, sticking the buttered side to my belly. I just had time to wolf down a couple more before Sister Leontina bounded into the room with a broom, followed by sisters Zdislava and Dolores with buckets of water. Sister Leontina bashed the brawlers over the head, while the other nuns sloshed water over them. Then Sister Leontina stood in front of Sister Alberta and gave her such a slap that the cigarette shot out of her mouth. 'Forgive me, sister,' said Sister Leontina. 'Our nerves are beginning to crack.'

And Sister Alberta said, 'Why won't the parish council send us a policeman for walking through the village?'

'Because they're godless,' said Sister Leontina. 'It's an ignorant Communist village!'

We all heard her, for silence reigned in the dining room, aside from the odd snivel.

The shortpants squeezed round the overturned tables and desks, and some of the longshirts were still rolling about on the floor in a state of disarray.

Sister Dolores, who was almost resting her back against a painting of Christ, cried out, 'What is to become of us? Oh God! What is to become of us?' Sister Zdislava put her arm around Sister Dolores and said, 'Calm yourself, sister, and consider what is to become of them, the little ones.' And when Sister Dolores heard her, she shrieked and fell back against the wall, banging her head, which made us all gasp.

Then Dýha stepped forward from one of the groups and stood opposite Sister Leontina, and although he was almost as tall as her, he stuck out his chin and said, 'I'm a Communist too!' And Sister Leontina said, 'So, you can spend the night in the cellar! And anyway, because of the fighting, I'm sending you all to bed without lessons, and there's an end of it!'

'Now, now, sisters!' Sister Leontina clapped her hands and the nuns lined us up in the direction of the door. They also clapped and sang to the longshirts to set the pace: 'One, two, three... "There was a little mouse, stealing grain about the house, but He understood her need and let her hold on to the seed!"' But it wasn't like that after teatime on other days. That day we were all battered and wretched, and nobody was showing off any more, and nobody said much either. Dýha stayed where he was, in a rage. Sister Alberta approached him, jangling some keys on a ring. It was her job to drag wayward boys down to the cellar, because she was the strongest. Sister Dolores was leaning against Christ on the wall and mumbling. Sister Leontina went up to her and grabbed her by the arm. Then they both joined Sister Zdislava to kneel before Christ and pray, all of which I saw and heard, as I was the last to shuffle out of the room.

Then I was alone in the corridor outside our dormitory.

And through the door I could hear the soothing voices of Sister Eulalia and Sister Emiliana.

The smallest longshirts had been terrified by the fighting. I could hear them crying here and there, but I could also make out Monkey-face's contented *gru, gru!* One of the nuns was probably trying to soothe him and lull him to sleep, so I didn't have to worry. I didn't feel like going in and joining the little ones. As the nuns left the dormitory, I hid around the corner, and I was pleased to discover that the bread I had concealed under my clothes had survived intact. The whole home fell silent as the boys slipped into sleep, while the nuns were probably lingering over their prayers.

I ran downstairs and stood by the big front door. It was locked. I tried the handle on the kitchen door, but that was locked too. Then I stood on the steps to the cellar, where it was almost dark. I could hear a voice coming from down below, so I set off down the stairs and along past the bend in the corridor... I knew it was Dýha shouting and singing, and that he was down there alone with the rats, and I thought I'd take a good look at him. He was behind bars, so if anything happened he couldn't get at me.

I followed the bends of the cellar passageway. It was almost dark. Here and there water dripped down, and because I was frightened of the rats I ran through the vile water making it splatter. I approached the punishment cell, past cubicles stuffed full of old papers. I knew that above our two dormitory floors there were more floors, but the nuns never went up there. The floors above us were kept locked and barred, and were said to be full of papers as well. Through the bars of the cellar cubicles I could see bundles of paper tied up with string, like little cities for mice... and then I was standing in front of Dýha and staring at him.

In the punishment cell he had a bucket and a blanket. A single bulb gave him light. He was leaning against the bars. I didn't know whether to say something, because longshirts never spoke to shortpants unless they were spoken to. I wasn't a longshirt, but I didn't really belong with the shortpants either... I waited for him to notice me.

'Wow, a rat!' said Dýha. 'I thought you was a big rat coming for me. And it's you, you rat.'

'Rats aren't this big.'

'They are though. Down here there's rats *this* big!'

'No way!'

'You're a bit small for a boy, but big enough to be a rat.'

'What do you do down here?'

'Nothing. Got a fag?'

'No.'

'There's a Communist uprising going on outside. So nip out and find Karel and get me some fags.'

'What?'

'Listen, why don't you sleep with us lot upstairs?'

'I'm staying with my brother.'

'Look here, Ilya. You're small, but old. You should be up top. How long've you been in the Home?'

'Since for ever.'

'Listen, if you get me some fags, we might take you with us. *Might.*'

'Where?'

'Foreign Legion. We're going: me, Karel and Páta. Chata as well. We've got knives and torches. You can come with us. We're the Bandits.'

'Can Monkeyface come too?'

'No way! Monkeyface is useless!'

'Then I'm not going, either.'

At that point Dýha shot his arm through the bars and hit me on the chin. The blow sent my head backwards, then he stuck his hand up my shirt and stole my sandwich.

'You just want to stay behind and stare at Dolores's tits, eh?'

'Idiot,' I muttered, gazing at my sandwich.

'I've had nothing to eat yet,' said Dýha, stuffing the bread into his mouth. 'Stop gawping and quit snivelling, will you, you big crybaby? You hungry?'

'No.'

'I haven't eaten!' said Dýha.

'Stupid idiot!'

'Ilya, you really are crying! Here!'

He handed a bit of the bread back to me through the bars. I popped it in my pocket.

'My old man's an airman,' said Dýha. 'He'll get me and some of the other lads into the forces. He sends me reports about the Communist uprising. How about that, then?'

'My old man's an airman too,' I said.

'Bollocks! They chucked you away! You and that little shit. No airman would do that.'

'Bollocks! He would!'

'You gonna fetch them fags?'

I was going to go, but we both froze and tried to grasp what we were hearing... It was the midday silence, and anyone who broke it was severely punished, but we both heard it. The front door had creaked noisily, we could hear voices and the tramping of feet, people shouting... It was as if a lot of new boys had come into the Home. Yet we could hear their voices and they were the voices of grown-ups. And now grown-up feet were pounding the stairs to the upper floors.

Dýha tried to poke his head through the bars, probably to hear better, but he couldn't. He was twisting, comically.

'They're supposed to walk quietly,' I said. 'I'm off to get them fags.'

I turned and went back through the cellar. I tried to go fast, to get through the gloom as quickly as possible and be out in the corridor.

'Wait, rat! Don't go!' shouted Dýha, but I wanted to see those people.

2

Previously

The manor house was at the bottom of the hill. From the house you went uphill to the village. At the edge of the village was the cemetery, and in it the family vault of the manor's previous occupants. When it was the manor house we lived in the kitchen. We never went to the upper floors. Mr Cimbura said that when the Czech nobility, like everything else Czech, came to an end, the Nazis put a soldier in the house. Mr Cimbura said that Hitler personally chose the best man for the job. 'Had a rifle to guard the locked upper floors with, he did. He never drank, not a dram,' said Mr Cimbura. 'He was human enough, though. Even lived in the village. When Holasa and Kropáček were sent to work in the Reich, and Moravčík and Kropka were in a concentration camp for poaching, he used to lend a hand in the darkened houses with no men in them.' Mr Cimbura winked at me and drank straight from his flask, while Sister Alberta tried to stop him. 'Of course, when the blokes came back, they sorted him out in no time. Yeah, there were any number of them, them Jerry soldier boys, knocking about in Chapman Forest in those days, I can tell you,' said Mr Cimbura, and he went on to tell me all about it.

'Then our bloodstained bourgeois government put a different soldier in, don't you know? A Czechoslovak lad. The very sort as had been shooting at the hungry masses during the uprising. Hanging's too good for the likes of them,' said Mr Cimbura, who went on to regret that I was too little for him to send me out for another bottle in such foul weather with snow on the ground. Mr Cimbura said nothing about Monkeyface. 'Yeah, guarded the upper floors, he did, that bloke with his tin hat and his little gun. Then he disappeared as well – to Hell I expect. But it was all still locked upstairs.'

He was right. The third floor was locked. Padlocks hung on the door, black and huge.

'But the rule of the people's yet to come,' said Mr Cimbura. 'It'll be some while before the new order reaches us all the way from Prague. But it will, you can bet on it, sonny.'

Mr Cimbura called me 'sonny', even though I wasn't his son. My mum and dad were in Shadowland. They had no faces. I taught myself to go back and visit them. It worked if I moved. I would rock backwards and forwards and Shadowland would start to come down over me. I used to do it when I was little. I used to do it before I met Hanka.

Previously, I had known only grown-ups. No boys, just Monkeyface. He grew bigger. He wouldn't have fitted in his old soapbox any more. Sister Alberta and Mr Cimbura finally realised he was never going to change.

'They used to stick little sods like him under the ice,' said Mr Cimbura. Sister Alberta was working on Monkeyface over by the stove. He was yelling and the shit came flying out of him.

'Just shut it, will you?' said Sister Alberta.

'Sods like him get born out of black eggs,' said Mr Cimbura, leaning on the kitchen table, unsteady on his feet.

'Shut it while the kid's around,' said Sister Alberta.

She meant me, of course, not Monkeyface.

It was cold. We were in the kitchen. I was sitting by the stove. I was waiting to see if Mr Cimbura would leave or sit down. If he sat down, he'd be with us for the evening. I wanted Sister Alberta to myself.

'And black-egg sods always cut their mothers,' said Mr Cimbura.

Well, if Monkeyface cut our mum, I'm not surprised she wanted rid of him, I thought.

'And they cut themselves on the eggshell as well, on their way out. That's why they turn out to be sods,' added Mr Cimbura, then he sat down.

'But he's a baby, for goodness sake!' said Sister Alberta. 'There, there, my ugly little duckling,' said Sister Alberta to Monkeyface. 'Isn't that right, little sausage?' He was washed clean now. Then he fell asleep.

But why Mum got rid of me too was puzzling. Mr Cimbura said he didn't know.

'But I ain't surprised, lad, I ain't surprised at all,' he kept nodding as went out to the woodshed with an axe. It was freezing cold and Sister Alberta sent us to the woodshed time and time again.

We used to live in the kitchen before the home became the Home. We lived in the kitchen and went outside to the woodshed. Because of Monkeyface we used to go to church.

Mr Cimbura led the way to church, trampling a path through the snow, because it had been snowing. The pond on the green was iced over. Our path linked up with other trampled paths. Till then I hadn't a clue what a pond was or what a green was, so I stared. Mr Cimbura went first, stamping down the snow, then I came next, and I also stamped. We were followed by Sister Alberta. She had Monkeyface in her arms. Those days anybody could have lifted him. We went to church to have him made better.

Mr Cimbura didn't come inside with us. He didn't like Father Francis.

There were lots of people in the church. The women came and stood around Monkeyface, smiling at him. They made signs of the Cross on his forehead. Mine too. He didn't cry. He obviously wanted to be made better. They poured water on him. Me as well. Even though he was the sod who'd cut his mother. Not me. All the way through their making him better I held on to Sister Alberta's skirt. People were singing all time. They were happy. So was Father Francis. He told the people what to do – kneel, get up, wave their arms – he ran the whole thing, smiling. In the church I was amazed how many things there were. I didn't know that later a painting of Jesus Christ would be on the wall at the Home from Home as well.

Afterwards everyone came from the church to our place. They ate in our kitchen. They drank alcohol from little glasses. Every now and then, someone stuck a finger in their glass and made a Cross on Monkeyface's forehead. He never squawked, just gaped. Everyone took care of Monkeyface. I slipped away to the woodshed.

I tried to reach Shadowland. I could stay in Shadowland from morning dark to the dark of night. I bet I could have stayed there from the first day of snow to the last. But Mr Cimbura came in. He couldn't have me taking naps in odd corners, he said. He said my tongue was hanging out of my mouth and I was out of it. Mr Cimbura spat. 'I ought to be on hand to help Sister Alberta,' he said. And he also told me to be ready, because before long I was going to have lots of brothers. That's what they'd decided at the Centre. What else was a stately home good for? The Germans had got rid of the last aristocrat. Mr Cimbura sat down on the chopping block. 'Did I ever tell you, lad, that he left it too late to fly away and escape 'em? He was, like I say, a keen flier. Now he's got a nice tomb in the cemetery,' said Mr Cimbura. 'Under the new order a tomb's the best place for toffs, I reckon. And their house is going to be a home for poor boys. And that's as it should be.'

'What boys?' I asked.

'Right little shits, mostly,' said Mr Cimbura. 'You'll see.'

He stood up and we went back to the kitchen. And now they all turned their attention to me. 'So let's drink to the firstborn as well, eh?' said Mr Cimbura. And people stood up or leaned towards me from their chairs and knocked back their shots in a toast to me and me alone. They were all gawping at me. Then they started chatting among themselves. They were all being nice to each other. But Monkeyface didn't get any better.

Then it wasn't quite so cold. I used to go to the front door. I would stand on the steps looking out for Mr Cimbura. He always came.

Then a lorry arrived from the Centre. Men in overalls carried beds and mattresses into the hallway. The men dashed all over the first two floors upstairs with wires and hung up light bulbs, while other men from the village followed them around and made a right pigsty of the place. Mrs Kropáček, Mrs Moravčík, Mrs Holý and Mrs Kropek came in with brooms and buckets and floor cloths. Every day they washed bits of the corridors and bits of the upstairs.

The men from the village and the men in overalls brought bundles of paper and piles of mouldy old books down from the first and second floors. They threw them on the lorry. The men in overalls trampled the piles of papers on the lorry, and Mr Holasa, Mr Dašler and Mr Moravčík opened the second-floor windows and, using pitchforks, tossed even more bundles of paper down onto the back of the lorry. When it was full, the men came down and drank some hard liquor with the blokes in overalls. They slapped hands and clapped each other on the shoulders. It wasn't that cold any more, but they made a bonfire outside the manor house. They warmed their hands at it. The lorry kept coming and going.

Sister Alberta also begged Czechia to help Monkeyface. She showed me a painting of Czechia. I liked her bare breasts. So maybe I wasn't quite such a kid any more. Or I was. I dunno. I wanted to keep looking at Czechia, but Sister Alberta took the picture away.

Whenever Sister Alberta talked about Czechia and Mr Cimbura turned up in the kitchen late in the day, a bottle in his hand, he sat down and listened quietly. When the story got to the great feats of Czechia, he didn't argue with Sister Alberta like he did at other times.

When *he* told stories, it was terrible.

The thing is, Sister Alberta sometimes needed to pop out for a chat with the girls, meaning great big Mrs Kropáček and great big Mrs Moravčík, so she didn't spend the evening with us.

Mr Cimbura scared us. He told us about this horrible black egg and how the fair Czechia took a gulp of stinking water from it and died. Monkeyface used to scream. Mr Cimbura would sit on his chair with his hands pressed to his ears and go on with the story at the top of his voice. You couldn't tell if Monkeyface was just making a noise or crying. I cried for real. Mr Cimbura didn't care.

At other times, Mr Cimbura talked about Chapman Forest. It was spread all around Siřem. 'There's wild animals in the forest,' he said. I believed him, because Sister Alberta had told us the same thing. I was glad to be sat in the kitchen by the stove and that I didn't have to share the fate of wayfarers lost in the forest.

'When a wayfarer falls asleep, he dreams of faraway places, and when he wakes up, he gets drawn to them places! The fate of them as can't stop is terrible – horrible – so you just listen!' Mr Cimbura would wake me if I fell asleep by the stove. If Monkeyface fell asleep, me and Mr Cimbura were glad. We stared at the wall and the creeping reflections of the flames from the stove, and we imagined faraway places. But best of all Mr Cimbura liked telling stories about Czechia.

He would spit on the floor, because there was nobody to tell him not to, and start: 'If Czechia is ever destroyed, then the hardworking, diligent sons of the Bohemian Basin will be exterminated. I hope you understand that, my lad. But Czechia's protected by intrepid warriors. They've vanquished everybody from the Tatars to the Krauts. Other enemies have hardly been worth their bothering about. They can swat 'em with their hats. One day you'll be an intrepid warrior too, laddie. I'll make sure of that.'

And Mr Cimbura promised that when I was older he'd get me a portrait of Czechia for me to keep as my very own.

Mr Cimbura told us that when he gave away pictures of Czechia to the newly confirmed outside the church, Father Francis reported him, and Mr Cimbura had been horsewhipped by the lord of the manor. But that didn't matter. When he got back to his cottage after the whipping, the newly confirmed who hadn't got a picture came knocking at his window in the night. 'Girls,' said Mr Cimbura, 'want to be like Czechia, and boys want to have her, but her not being around, they lie on top of the girls and make babies with 'em, so the seed of the Czechs shall not perish! Czechia dealt with that toff in a roundabout way, it seems. Anyway, he's long been resting in his tomb. He tried to take off in his plane, but the Communists hanged him, the collaborating Jerry bastard,' said Mr Cimbura, although he had said something different earlier.

He also told us how Czechia's intrepid warriors would lay traps in the forest for the Krauts and Tatars. How they would carve images of Czechia into the trees with axes dipped in the putrid matter of black eggs. Some warriors would cut her image into their own skin. She was their protection. And an enemy soldier would go mad in a wood full of images of Czechia cut into the trees, throwing down his weapons and equipment and becoming a wanderer. And he would walk on and on, never stopping, until he died.

Mr Cimbura liked telling that story. It amused him.

When Sister Alberta told stories, I stuck it out through the nasty parts and fell asleep, feeling happy, because Czechia was victorious and everything turned out all right. But Mr Cimbura didn't like happy endings.

I remember all that. In fact I don't remember anything else at all.

That's how we lived before the nuns arrived.

And then someone else came.

I was standing in the corridor. I might have been able to hear Dýha if I craned my head towards the cellar steps, but I wanted to see who these new people were.

3

The nuns. Mayhem. Quiet outside. He did it himself!

I ran up the steps, almost crashing into a soldier. He had a rifle, but no helmet.

'Where do you think you're going?' he shouted. I shot past him like a rat, ran into the dining room and crouched behind the door. You wouldn't have spotted a whisker, or even my rat's tail... Standing in the dining room were sisters Zdislava and Alberta, Eulalia and Emiliana, and Sister Dolores as well. They had little bundles in their hands and wore travelling coats. Soldiers or cops from the Communist uprising were standing around them and one Communist said, 'Five kilos each, I said!' The nuns stood there in a huddle, looking like chickens in a book of nursery rhymes or like naughty schoolboys who hadn't learned something they should have. Then one of the nuns said, 'Yes, sir.' And the Communist said, 'There aren't any sirs now,' and laughed. Then the Communists poked the nuns with their rifle butts, and one of them roared, 'In line!' and they set off, out through the door of the dining room into the corridor. I was hunched down behind the door. The nuns didn't see me. Not even Sister Dolores, who was the last out. I never saw her again, ever. Sister Eulalia suddenly ran towards the door of the smaller boys' dormitory, but the Communists dragged her back into line.

The Home was silent. The boys were probably pretending to be asleep, making good use of the midday calm for a nice nap. The Communists led the nuns down the stairs, and Sister Zdislava gripped the banister and said, 'What will happen to them?' and one Communist said, 'Come on,' and pulled her away. Then downstairs the door slammed as the nuns and the Communists went out to the front of the Home. 'Where are they taking them?' I wondered. Then the door of Sister Leontina's office flew open and she fell through it. She didn't have her dark cape on, that came flying through the air afterwards, tossed from the office by a Communist. Sister Leontina fell to the ground. She was wearing a funny white shirt, and if I hadn't been able to see her head, I might have thought one of the taller longshirts had fallen down... For the first time I saw Sister Leontina's hair. It was grey and lay flat against her head. She got up slowly and kept touching her hair with one hand. Two Communists came out of the office. They didn't have rifles, just pistols, and the one who had thrown the cape had his gun in his hand. He said, 'You should have had kids yourself, bitch!' Now Sister Leontina was standing, wrapping her travelling cape around her body. She lifted her head back to stare at the Communists, just like Dýha when he spoke to her, and she said, 'God can see you...' 'Sure, you old prayer-bag,' said the one with a pistol in his hand. 'Get moving!' said the other, and he pushed Sister Leontina so hard that she almost fell, then shunted her along the corridor. Then Sister Leontina walked on by herself, the Communists behind her. I didn't even wait to hear the door bang. I jumped to the window like a rat. Outside the sun was shining. The five nuns were standing in the snow in their travelling capes, the Communists standing around them. Then Sister Leontina came out of the Home from Home, and the gaggle of nuns surged around her. A lorry drove up and the nuns, one by one – sisters Eulalia, Zdislava, Dolores, Alberta, Emiliana and Leontina – climbed onto it. The Communists were laughing, prodding them. I bet they felt Sister Dolores's tits. That's why they were laughing so much. The lorry drove away slowly, and the Communists lined up in twos, like us boys on the way to church. Behind me I heard a noise in the corridor, voices. Longshirts were creeping out of the dormitory, one after the other, their mouths open. From above I heard the tramping of feet... the boys in the other dormitory running to the window. They were all around me at once, and they crushed and shoved at the window, pushing me aside, but I still saw the nuns waving to us. I glimpsed them. Six nuns raising their arms, waving to us, then the lorry picked up speed and they were driven off up the hill.

Someone asked, 'Where are they taking them?'

Somebody replied, 'Dunno.'

And one longshirt started blubbering. It was cold by the window and maybe someone had trodden on his foot.

I went to see Monkeyface, to tell him what had happened.

Then mayhem broke out all over the Home.

Monkeyface was trying to scramble out of bed. He was surprised that the midday calm was so full of noise and shouting. His net was over his bed. I didn't let him out. I went to see what was going on. Monkeyface gawped at me through the net. I came back and gave him some bread. The whole bit that was left. He wanted more.

'I could go and join the Legion as well, you know,' I told him. 'The lads want me to go. So watch yourself!'

And I went and found the others.

Mayhem had broken out on both floors and in the dining room. I'd hardly left the dormitory and in the middle of all the hullaballoo – with all the lads whooping and shouting and laughing and running up and down the stairs – I heard *bang! bang!* coming from downstairs. And when I got there, I saw that the shortpants had grabbed a big bench and were hammering away at the kitchen door – *bang! bang!* – and the door flew open and they broke in, laughing and shouting. Pushing in behind them went the little longshirts, clambering over the bench, and I jumped over it too, and landed in the kitchen and got a shock to see it was snowing... The shortpants were hurling bags of flour at each other, and their faces were all white, and they'd also opened all the cupboards, big and small, that weren't under lock and key. First we ate the fudge. Anyone who could get hold of it crammed it in his mouth and chewed away. No-one cared about ruining their teeth. There wasn't all that much fudge, so in the hurly-burly we stuffed ourselves with gherkins too. There were huge jars of them and one fell out of a cupboard and smashed. So, laughing and shouting, we hunted the gherkins all over the floor. They slipped out of our hands. And if anyone had felt like it he could have stuffed his mouth with butter. There was a great pile of it in little cubes. Then Karel announced, 'And who wants some bread?' and with a huge kitchen knife he hacked at the loaves and handed out bread to anyone who put up his hand. In a cupboard we found jars and jars of jam and plum curd, and everybody's face was sticky with the goodies, and we swapped bread and gherkins and jam among ourselves. Then Karel called out, 'Pick up the glass, dammit!' because some of the little ones had dropped their jam jars, which smashed on the floor, and the sticky sweet glass lay among the glass from the gherkin jars, and the little ones were wading up to their ankles in flour and laughing, playing tag and smearing butter over each other's faces. Then finally someone kicked or smashed open the door to the pantry, but inside were only boring things: scrubbing brushes, buckets and floor-cloths and boxes full of coal-tar soap... And the noise! The lads kicked the bars of soap all over the kitchen and the corridor, aiming them into the corners... There was a huge washer drum in the kitchen for doing the dirty linen, and one little boy climbed inside and the others set it turning, laughing as they stood round the drum. They all wanted a spin inside. They got hold of the tub we used to bathe in too. Someone climbed into it and the others dragged it around. Then some of the older boys found some salamis. They cut them into little cubes and anyone who wanted some got some. The longshirts left the drum and the tub and begged for salami... Then no-one could eat any more, so we started throwing it at each other.

I put some bread and salami in my pocket.

I went out into the corridor and there was just one longshirt there, sitting on the overturned bench, gripping his belly and snivelling.

'What's wrong?' I asked.

'Ow!' He just crumpled up on the bench.

'You mustn't eat glass!' I said, but by then I was standing by the front door of the Home and I took hold of the handle and the door opened.

It had been snowing. I could see the footprints of the nuns and the Communists, and the deep tracks of the lorry.

The snow was still falling, so the tracks looked as if someone had sprinkled flour into them.

I watched. The slope went off into the distance. Towards the village. I took a step, then another – and I was outside.

It was quiet. The noise and mayhem had calmed down. I turned and saw the others standing in the doorway.

First to come out was Karel, then Páta, and in a moment even the little ones were outside, plastered with jam and with flour in their hair; and some of them didn't have shoes on, having crawled out of bed barefoot or in their socks. Now they were standing in the snow, and suddenly Páta roared 'Yippee!' and jumped in the air. They all started shouting and hopping up and down, and the snow outside the Home was suddenly full of footprints and tracks as we ran around, snowballing and chasing each other round and round in the snow... Then we stopped and suddenly the silence was massive outside, like a great blanket. In the Home you could always hear someone talking, shouting, stomping around or at least coughing... but here it was silent and no one was laughing. We turned back, one by one, and went inside, and the last one closed the door.

I went to see Monkeyface.

I walked up the staircase. The lads had knocked the holy pictures off the walls and the dining room was a mass of overturned tables, but it was still quiet. The door to Sister Leontina's office was ajar, as was the door to the longshirts' dorm. And Monkeyface wasn't in bed.

That had never happened before.

The net had been torn down. He couldn't have done that by himself.

During the riot downstairs I hadn't spotted Martin or Šklíba.

The silence upstairs was filled with my breathing. I came out into the corridor. I pushed at the door to Sister Leontina's office and said, 'Where are you, you buggers?'

Papers were scattered about the office and the kneeler lay on its side. The only light came in through a chink in the blind. The nuns stood there in the gloom. And the nicest, most beautiful of them, Sister Dolores, came towards me, raising her arms... So I raised mine... Then a great rumpus broke out, and shrieks and high-spirited laughter, and suddenly I saw the lads from the Home leaping around me and shouting, 'Iya! Iya! Stupid Ilya!'

They had dressed up in the clothes they had found, putting on the nuns' bonnets and even their black capes. Amid the shouting I heard crying and whimpering. It was Monkeyface calling to me for help. They had tied him to a bed and jammed a bonnet on his head. He was trying to get it off, but was making himself choke. He was crying and snot was streaming from his nose. I wiped his tears and saliva away with my sleeve, and Monkeyface let out a big puff and a huge glob of snot landed on my face. Now the lads were laughing their heads off. I tried to untie Monkeyface. My fingers were shaking. Then someone bashed me on the head. It was Šklíba and he was shouting, 'Watch the dummy yourself, dummy!' Then someone else thumped me, and they kept pounding away at me. It didn't hurt much. I just wanted it to stop.

The door flew open and Karel and Mikušinec came in. 'Is Ilya here?' said Karel, and the longshirts fell silent and grabbed at me from different sides, and Karel said, 'Get out of that clobber now, you faggots!'

The longshirts started stripping. They felt silly now. Karel stamped his foot. 'Beat it, scram!' and they fled.

I untied Monkeyface at last. He grabbed me around the neck and wouldn't let go. He was overjoyed that I'd found him.

Karel stood over us and said, 'When you're done with him, come down to the cellar, okay? We're having a meeting, okay?' Then he left with Mikušinec.

I knew I couldn't carry Monkeyface by myself, and I didn't want to ask Karel and Mikušinec. Monkeyface made all the boys feel sick.

I picked up a sheet and tied him to the bed by one leg. He couldn't undo it.

And I had a bright idea: I would get the tub from downstairs. I could push him around in it. And when Dýha and the others invited me to join the Foreign Legion with them, I would tell them we could easily push Monkeyface along in the tub. He would be able to come with us. But then I realized there was snow all around the Home. I wouldn't be able to get the tub through it. We would have to stay behind. The lads could go and join the Legion. But how were we going to live at the Home?

I wished the nuns would come back. Then I could lie down next to Monkeyface and drop off to sleep.

I gave him all of the bread and salami.

He looked pleased.

I was on my way to fetch the tub when I met Karel and Mikušinec. They were waiting for me. So I had to go down to the cellar.

In the kitchen, the bigger longshirts had swept up the glass and the little ones were fooling around with the washer drum. I looked around for the tub... two longshirts were pulling a third around in it.

Then we went through the gloom of the cellar and from the bend in the passage I saw candles flickering, which was strictly prohibited in the Home. Some shortpants sat or squatted outside the grating of the solitary-confinement cell, smoking cigarettes. Dýha was standing, leaning against the bars.

If one of the lads moved, his shadow on the wall moved as well.

'Did you get 'em from the kitchen, the candles?' I asked Karel.

'Yep,' he nodded.

We walked through the gloom, splashing in the cold cellar water, the line of boys standing and sitting there rippled as they made way for us, along with their candles. Now we were standing in front of Dýha, the bars of the cell between him and me.

Dýha pushed an arm through the bars and grabbed my ear.

'Arsehole!' he said. 'You didn't obey orders!'

I tried to duck, but I couldn't, because of my ear.

'I was gonna get some fags,' I said, 'but that lot turned up!'

'My orders count!' said Dýha, and tugged my ear so hard that my head banged against the bars. Then he let go.

'Whose orders?' said Chata, standing beside me and making my shadow a head taller. Then he said, 'Dogshite to you, you cellar Communist arsehole!'

And the lads laughed.

'We're the Bandits,' said Karel. 'We agreed to go and join the Legion. But now some of you wanna join the Communists. So what are we gonna do?'

They all started gabbling and asking questions: 'Where are the nuns?' 'Where did they take them?' 'Will they be coming back?' 'What are *we* going to do?' and nobody listened to Dýha. That was okay.

Then Chata said we ought to sort ourselves out and go to the village, and some wanted to go and some didn't... As they got up, waving their arms about, and sat down again, the shadows on the wall got all mixed up, sliding into each other. They were all out-shouted by Dýha.

'Listen up, guys!' he shouted. 'Belt up, I tell you! My dad'll be here in a couple of days and he'll get this place organized. For now, you find the key to this cell so I can get out. My dad organized the Communist uprising.'

'Your dad, eh? He's always in the slammer!' Karel cracked up. He laughed and pointed at Dýha, who was now careering round and round the cell in a rage.

'At least he ain't dead!' Dýha bellowed at Karel. 'Least he ain't pushing up daisies, is he?'

'You shuddup!' shouted Karel and leaned towards the bars. 'You're locked up.'

'And you're a psycho,' said Dýha, shoving his face up against the bars so that it was only inches away from Karel's.

They stared at each other, then gobbed at each other, and Karel hammered at the bars with a knife, making a terrific racket. Then he stuck his arm through the bars and, stretched out on tiptoes, stabbed and slashed at Dýha with the kitchen knife, but Dýha just dodged out of the way, and now it was his turn to laugh.

'Cut it out,' said Chata. 'I reckon we should go into the village.'

'Ha, ha!' (It was Dýha again.) 'Go to the village then, darkie. They'll have a welcome waiting! Off you go, gippo, and grab us a chicken while you're there!'

The lads started to laugh, and I was smiling and Chata also laughed.

Karel sat down and the other lads got up, and the shadows on the wall rose and fell.

I didn't know whether to join the Communists or the Foreign Legion. I realized that the first thing me and Monkeyface needed was the tub. Once that was sorted, we could think about which side to join.

Then I heard a *vroom-vroom* noise, like when the old washing machine was running. 'They've started the drum!' someone shouted, and Mikušinec said, 'You take charge of the little brats, Dýha, they're messing up the place!' Then we all started laughing again, and the washing-machine drum above our heads went *vroom-vroom...* until the cellar ceiling shook. The youngsters must have plugged it in and didn't know how to switch it off. 'Washing detail at the ready... wash!' roared Dýha and we all laughed. Then Páta bellowed, 'Shitty shorts at the ready...' and we all roared 'wash!' then fell about laughing. *Vroom-vroom*, the drum above us shook and rattled all its metal parts; the plaster came off the ceiling in bits, falling into our hair, then someone came running into the cellar... longshirts! They were screaming and splashing through the cellar water. Šklíba ran up to us out of breath, and covered his head when he saw me.

He was protecting his head. The moment I saw him I guessed what they'd done to Monkeyface. The dreadful noise kept making the cellar ceiling shudder... *vroom-vroom...* I sprinted down the passage and shot up the stairs, and the further up I went, the louder the *vroom-vroom* became. I burst into the kitchen and yanked the plug from the socket. It was high up, but I jumped. There was a broken chair on the floor. They hadn't been able to reach, because it had snapped under them. The noise stopped, but the drum kept turning. Martin was standing there with blood on his hands. He'd tried to stop the drum, but the metal had cut into him. I tripped over a sheet lying on the floor. Aha! That's what they had used to carry Monkeyface!

The drum was still turning. With Martin's help I stopped it. I flipped the iron lid back and heaved Monkeyface out. He'd always been too heavy for me, but now I pulled him out by myself. He didn't make a sound. I carried him upstairs without help. His head was dangling and his little face was all squashed.

The inside of the drum was covered in spit and shit. He had it all over him. I hauled him upstairs to our floor. I had to stop for a rest, propping him up against the frame of the window opposite the dining room. Now he was whimpering quietly. I held him tight.

I heard the slap of bare feet and the clump of boots. It was the boys. I pressed my face into Monkeyface's, not caring that it was covered in sick. I'd never been bothered by his spit either. We were always together... He was heavy. I think he wanted to walk. His legs were shaking. He was kicking and fighting, and I was shaking as well, and Monkeyface flopped against the window, banging his knees at the glass, thrusting his knees out in front, fighting to get away from me, slipping... He thrust me out of the way, and now he was top-heavy and banged his head against the window. I grabbed him by his feet, but he kicked out at me and flew headfirst through the glass. He fell, turning once or twice in the air, then thumped down, landing on his back in the snow, bits of glass showering down around him.

'Shit!' said Páta, who was standing next to me.

'It wasn't Ilya!' panted Karel. 'Monkeyface fell out by himself. I saw it.'

'He did it himself!' shouted someone who had just run up from the cellar.

'Yeah,' said Páta. 'I saw it too.'

Now there were lots of lads standing around. We looked down from the window at Monkeyface lying there. He wasn't moving.

I went downstairs. In the kitchen I looked for a tablecloth or something to put over Monkeyface. But I almost didn't care, now he was dead. I couldn't find anything anyway.

My head started to ache from being bashed on the bars when Dýha grabbed my ear. If my head were as soft as a cucumber and if the bars were made of knife-blades, they'd have sliced my head like salami. Similar ideas filled my head. I didn't want them, but unfortunately they kept coming. I was sitting by the washer drum. I didn't know if the blood on it was from Martin's fingers or from Monkeyface.

Chata, Mikušinec and Karel came in. They stood there in the kitchen and looked. We all had the same hairstyle. Mikušinec was gingery. The shortpants made fun of him. They said he had dirty hair. Karel and Chata were the tallest. Dýha was fat. Karel was bigger than Chata.

'Here, have a drink,' said Karel. 'You're a Bandit now, and we've decided to join the Legion.'

He handed me a small brown bottle.

'Give it here,' said Chata.

'Hey, let him have a drink,' said Karel. 'He's in shock.'

I was glad to be a Bandit. That was important. Chata reached out to grab the bottle, so I took a swig. My stomach heaved. It wasn't as disgusting as tar water, though. The horrible clammy taste stuck my lips to the neck of the bottle. I carried on drinking.

'You'll make yourself puke,' Chata told me.

I felt a bit like puking, but I had to laugh as well. I had turned up before them. Years before. The lads knew a lot. About how to do a runner. They knew a lot about Chapman Forest. But I was there when the Home from Home was a stately home. I started laughing again.

I emptied the bottle and dropped it on the floor. Someone opened the door. It was Páta. 'Come,' he said, 'all of you.'

I went, though I kept falling about in a funny way. Karel dragged me along by the shoulder. By the kitchen there was some blood on the floor. I wanted to tell the lads it was the longshirts' blood from when they were fishing for gherkins in the broken glass, but I couldn't speak. My tongue kept flopping about.

4

The cellar again. My watch. They arrive

Now there were lots of candles in the cellar and lots of lads, including longshirts, and lots of shadows.

We went to the solitary cell, and Dýha shouted, 'Is he blubbering?'

And Mikušinec shouted back, 'Nah, he's pissed!'

All the lads, crammed into the cellar next to the cell where Dýha was locked up, were laughing like mad, even the little longshirts, most of whom had pulled sweaters and anoraks over their nightshirts... But Šklíba and Martin weren't laughing. They were shut up in one of the cubicles. They sat on a pile of papers and underneath them was a mouse kingdom, and the mice could come and get at them through all the little tunnels and runways they had dug, and they could get out through the bars too, because mice can... but the boys couldn't.

They didn't have a blanket or a bucket or a light bulb.

Šklíba was kneeling on the piles of paper, like you do in church, saying a Hail Mary... Martin said nothing, he was blubbering.

'We're gonna sentence them now,' Karel whispered in my ear.

'Quiet!' shouted Dýha. 'I declare this meeting of the Bandits open, because they stuck Ilya's Monkeyface in the washer drum. Šklíba, shut it!'

But I never heard whether Šklíba stopped praying, and none of the others could have heard either, because the front door banged again, and voices and footsteps echoed through the Home from Home. Someone was pounding up the stairs, and suddenly I felt elated that things were back, back the way they had been! The others also thought the nuns were back, because the little longshirts let out a cry; they were all shouting now and suddenly thrusting their way out of the cellar. The youngsters pushed me and Karel to one side as they sloshed their way out through the cellar water. We ran after them, though I was a bit unsteady. I was the last and our shadows kept jumping. Mikušinec and Chata blew out the candles. After all, no-one could even imagine having candles in the cellar – it was forbidden! In the dark I could hear Šklíba mumbling something religious. I was the last to haul myself out of the cellar. There was no-one anywhere. Slowly I went upstairs, leaving the cellar behind me... and then I opened the front door. I was going to fetch Monkeyface, but I got a surprise!

Outside there was a little horse harnessed to a sleigh, and on the sleigh there was a pile of blankets. They'd come by sleigh! The villagers... I peeked under the sleigh, but Monkeyface wasn't there. I kept looking for him! I craned upwards and saw the broken window, and I was trampling on the broken glass in the snow... There were no footprints any more; instead the snow had turned into black mud and everybody had been trampling in it. I went round to the little horse and then I got this stupid idea... the idea that the horse had been sent to me by Monkeyface, since he wasn't lying there. But that was impossible! Sent for me to get in and let the sleigh take me to Shadowland, and my little brother would be waiting there for me... And then I heard, 'What about that then, sonny?' and I looked up and there in the sleigh sat Mr Cimbura, wrapped in blankets. He was looking at me, but I don't think he recognized me. I always recognized him, though he was much older.

'Some surprise, that, eh? When they took them penguins away, eh? Well, it had to come. I'm from peasant stock, sonny, and I served 'em for years. But now the people's rule's reached even us, here in Siřem, and the worker and the peasant shall eat from the nobleman's plate. Listen, where did the silly bitches hide their gold crosses and pyxes? Their vestments and stuff? The valuables? Do you know?'

'They didn't take them with them,' someone somewhere behind me said. It was Mr Holasa, and behind him was Mr Kropek. I don't think they recognized me. When the Home was the manor house I was little, and the villagers couldn't tell one child from another if it wasn't their own. But I knew who they were.

From lying in his blankets Mr Cimbura sat bolt upright, looking silly, and he said, 'I'm interrogating this youngster here, see.'

'Is that you?' Mr Holasa asked me, so I knew he had recognized me.

'I'm Ilya, sir.'

'What sort of a name's that? You some sort of little Russky?' Mr Holasa punched me in the shoulder.

'Little Russky be damned!' Mr Cimbura croaked. 'What's in a name?'

Mr Kropek was also looking at me. He put out a hand and tapped me on the shoulder by way of saying hello.

'Otherwise they're all little Russkies, Asians, and lots of gippos!' said Mr Holasa, and he rifled around in the blankets on the sleigh, Mr Cimbura shifting out of the way.

Mr Holasa got some wire-cutters and a hammer from under the blankets and handed them to Mr Kropek. Then he fished out some wire-cutters and an axe for himself, and they went inside the Home from Home.

'I'll finish interrogating this youngster,' Mr Cimbura called, but they ignored him. The little horse looked straight at me. I dodged, but his head still followed me...

'Don't worry, I'll tell them,' I said to the horse...

'I knew it!' said Mr Cimbura. 'You know where those holy cows hid it all, don't you, sonny? We won't let on to anyone else. Here.' Mr Cimbura leaned out of the sleigh and handed me two squares of chocolate. I wolfed them down at once, and the vile taste of alcohol still in my mouth was sliced through by the fabulous sweetness. I ate it all myself. I wouldn't have to share things ever again.

'I can't help it that he's dead!' I cried.

''Course not, sonny. Just tell me where they put it.'

'He wanted to. He did it himself!' I said.

'Of course, sonny. I know. I'll testify for you,' said Mr Cimbura and he gave me another piece of chocolate...

'He wasn't any use and they didn't like him,' I said. 'All the time he wanted to die and he couldn't.' I swallowed and my belly was full of sweetness... and the little horse snorted and pawed the ground, raising his head and looking at me. Oh no. Tears started streaming down my cheeks, and I'd been so proud when Mikušinec had shouted down there in the cellar that I wasn't blubbing. Ha! And there I was blubbering. 'I don't think it hurt him much,' I said, and the little horse snuffled warmly at my ear.

'Ah well,' said Mr Cimbura, 'I'd give you some more, but that's all he had. Wanted to die, he did, mouldy old monk, and you can bet it hurt him. We stamped all over him... punishment detail. Red specialists come all the way from Prague to interrogate the counter-revolutionary Vatican maggot,' said Mr Cimbura. 'He wanted to die, sonny. You're right there. Then he did. And you know what, sonny? He got such a doing-over, that bastard of a priest, they had to toss him up onto the lorry. Then they threw some straw over him and the nuns sat on top of him, and how the stupid cows must've started squawking when they found their arses resting on their very own vicar... So towards the end I reckon he did want to die...'

'Like I said!' I said, moving my shoulder out from under the little horse's mouth. The horse breathed hot on me, then I went inside the Home from Home with Mr Cimbura calling after me. But I didn't stop.

Not in the kitchen, but in the dining room there were bits of paper everywhere, old yellow bits and blackened bits. They crackled when you touched them and fell apart, lying around the floor and even floating in the air.

Then from the shortpants' floor came a crashing noise – *bang-bang!* Longshirts were running around everywhere, gathering handfuls of documents and throwing them down the stairs, enjoying seeing them flutter. The large, studded door on the second floor, the door with the big black padlocks, had probably been broken open by Mr Holasa and Mr Kropek, busting them with iron bars. For the first time ever I saw the forbidden stairs leading to the upper storeys. We weren't allowed there, and the nuns didn't go there either... Now the longshirts with sweaters and anoraks over their long white nightshirts were chasing one another up and down these stairs and causing havoc, and in all the racket they were making the banging went on and on.

The men were smashing in all of the doors on the first forbidden floor. That was the noise I'd heard.

Piles of paper lay in and on the cupboards, some on top of each other in bundles, others any old how, and in places the stacks reached up to the ceiling.

Mr Holasa and Mr Kropek split another door in two, knocking it flat on the ground, then went inside in a cloud of dust, and we followed them, we Bandits... We stood in a huge room, the walls plastered white and in many places it was flaking off, and against one wall there were piles of linen baskets and suitcases with rusty padlocks, and Mr Holasa shouted, 'This is it!'

They started dragging the linen baskets away from the wall, then smashed them open straight away.

Mr Holasa and Mr Kropek turned the baskets upside down, and it was all just more paper. They covered the floor with it, waded through it, then kicked at the cases and swore.

Páta and Bajza climbed onto the mountain of linen baskets and started throwing them down onto the floor, and me and Chata were almost buried. They did it on purpose! They made the plaster dust swirl, and the dust from the masses of crumbling paper. Then Mr Holasa bellowed, 'That'll do now! Bloody kids!'

The men smashed their way to another floor, and Mr Dašler called,

'Come here!' and Mr Holasa and Mr Kropek went. Shortly after, we heard heavy footsteps above us.

I went over to the toppled linen baskets and saw a huge picture. It was leaning against the wall. It wasn't a religious picture. I wanted to call the lads over, but they were still having fun. Plaster and swirling dust were falling all around the picture. I waited for it to settle.

'Guys!' I called. We huddled around the picture. It showed a big man and a little woman and an aeroplane. The plane was quite small. I think the big man was the flying toff Mr Cimbura used to talk about. The woman was slitty-eyed with long black hair and a fat belly.

Looking at it, Páta spluttered with laughter. We kept pointing at the funny-looking woman with the belly and sniggering.

'It can't be from round here,' someone said. 'There's no forest. They're in some sandy, flat place.'

'That's a desert, idiot,' said someone else.

There was something about deserts in *The Catholic Book of Knowledge*.

We looked to see what a desert was like.

Then Chata started sniggering at the picture again, and laughing a squeaky laugh. Then he said, 'Idiots! That's Dýha's dad, the airman!' We all started laughing. Then we made to leave, but Páta stopped me. We stayed behind in the big room.

'We put him in the cellar,' he told me in a low voice. 'When you was pissed.'

'What?'

'We put Monkeyface in the cellar, so these buggers won't see him. We took him down in a sheet.'

'Aha,' I said.

'He's next to Šklíba and Martin, since they're the ones as did it to him. We was gonna put 'em on trial, but now we can't.'

'So what can we do?'

'Dunno.' Páta shrugged. 'Nobody knows.'

A little kid came up. He'd been wandering about the floor on his own. Now he stopped and stared at us.

'Are these people gonna take us away?' he asked.

'Where to?' said Páta.

'I wouldn't mind the village,' said the boy. 'I could live with some people and herd their goats and feed the chickens. I've done it before.'

'Don't be daft. The altar boys would eat you for breakfast!'

'But I never fought 'em. I never threw anything at 'em. And I'd fetch water and firewood.'

'Bollocks,' said Páta. 'They've got kids of their own to do that for 'em.'

'Us Bandits are off to join the Foreign Legion,' I told the kid. I stretched out full length on the paper. I lay on one of the heaps of paper and stared at the ceiling.

'I wanna get away as well,' said the boy. 'I keep dreaming about my mum and dad.'

We don't say anything. He's one of the youngsters.

'My parents were executed, see,' he added.

'You don't say!' said Páta.

'Honest!'

'By the Germans, right?' I wanted to know.

'Don't be stupid!' said Páta. 'That was ages ago. The Communists did it, didn't they?'

'I'm frightened of 'em,' said the lad.

'They can frighten the Germans or the... them others, but they don't frighten me!'

I was lying on the paper as if it were a gigantic bed. The ceiling was high up above me. Páta and the other kid were still chattering. I was thinking about the picture we had found, and other stuff. It was nice. I could even have fallen asleep on the paper.

I did fall asleep, and dreamed of Mr Holasa and the others putting the wire-cutters and the iron bars and the axes and the hammers onto the little horse's sleigh, and leaving only Mr Cimbura in the blankets, because he was old and his legs were wobbly, and the little horse heaved, straining every sinew, but only a little bit... the sleigh was light! – and it pulled the sleigh out through the gates of the Home from Home and trotted daintily up the hill, and the men followed the sleigh and they were arguing and cursing and swearing, because they hadn't found anything, no expensive goblets or cups, no vestments or gold candles, no precious ornaments... That's why the sleigh was so light! It wasn't weighed down with any treasure, so the little horse was carrying just Mr Cimbura and the blankets and axes and wire-cutters – but what's that to a little horse? Nothing. It's not heavy... It couldn't have coped with all the men and a huge treasure trove – that would have put its back out, they would have hurt him, and no-one wanted that... crippling a little horse with a heavy load. They wouldn't do that. It was a nice dream.

And then I woke up, because Karel gave me a kind of gentle kick... and handed me some bread and a frankfurter.

'Where did you get it?' I asked him. The dream and the food made me feel happy.

Karel flopped down on the paper heap next to me.

'They brought it on the sleigh – frankfurters and bread! They're afraid we might go knocking out their windows and scavenging around the village. I've come to wake you. It's your watch.'

'What?'

'The committee decided we have to take turns on watch, 'cos of the altar boys and Communists.'

'I see,' I said and got up.

'Look, the thing with Monkeyface was a bit off, I know, but at least you can come with us now,' said Karel.

'I know.'

'I saw it happen, little Monkeyface falling out of the window by himself, and Páta saw it too. We was there!'

At that moment we spotted a little light moving through the dark. It was Chata with a torch in his hand. He reached us and said to me, 'You're on guard duty, twat,' then sat down where I'd been and tucked into the bread and sausage. So I went.

Outside the moon was shining, the light flowed across the snowy slope up through the windows and was reflected off the white papers I was tramping over.

The piles of paper everywhere were spooky, there were so many. I almost tripped over two longshirts asleep in a heap of documents as if in a big mouse nest.

There were more longshirts up the staircase.

One was setting fire to the papers with a match. I stamped on the flame and told him to scram. He turned on the waterworks, as did the other longshirts squatting there on the stairs. The boy gave me his matches, and said, 'We're really scared!'

'Did you nick 'em from the kitchen, the matches?' I asked.

'Yeah.'

'We could've burnt to death. You mustn't set fire to paper.'

He started crying even more.

'Come with me, all of you.'

'Sure, we're coming,' said one of the ones sitting on the staircase, and he got up and grabbed me by the hand.

I led the longshirts down the stairs. As I did so I wasn't afraid. On the second floor one lone youngster was sitting on the ground, and when he saw us he started screaming... Then other feeble little voices piped up, more like those of giant mice than boys, and, just like mice, little longshirts came crawling out of all the nooks and crannies where they'd been sitting or lying, some possibly sleeping, others perhaps chatting together... Another two appeared at the top of the stairs and came running down towards us, and one of them had no shoes on and he called out 'Wait!'

So we waited. I took all the ones I found into the dormitory, and there, in Monkeyface's bed, someone was asleep, a youngster, and I let him be. I didn't care... The longshirts kept snivelling, and they crawled into the beds and one asked, 'Is Sister Eulalia going to come and sing about angels?' and I said, 'No.' And another asked, 'And we don't have to wash?' and I said, 'No.' Then the one who'd asked about Sister Eulalia said, 'Couldn't you sing it instead, Ilya?' and I said, 'Get into bed!' and he said, 'Okay,' and went straight to sleep. I was still on guard duty.

There was a pile of frankfurters on the dining-room table, so I had one more and went to stand guard in the kitchen. There was water sloshed about everywhere. I looked towards the washer drum and couldn't believe that so much could have happened in one day.

Then I heard the choirboys. From the cellar they sounded just like when Sister Eulalia used to practise hymns with them.

So I went down to the cellar to take my turn at guard duty.

Standing at the bend in the passage I could see the flames of candles, and the little songsters had stopped singing. The cubicle where Šklíba and Martin had been locked up had had its bars forced outwards, and the choirboys had chucked out bundles of papers and made room... I saw they had brought the kneeler down from Sister Leontina's office. They had also stolen her Christ on the Cross, and Sister Eulalia's six little songsters were kneeling on the ground, not at all bothered by the slimy cellar water. Šklíba was standing and Martin too, and both were wearing the nuns' quite badly torn and dirty gowns, which they had drawn tight at the waist with string somehow – of course, they were quite small... Šklíba was prancing around and waving his arms like he had seen Father Francis do, and Martin now handed him a fat book, and Šklíba said, 'Let us pray.' The heads of the ones who were kneeling dropped as they prayed... and then I heard a great roar: 'Let me out!'

I moved away from the wall and saw Dýha leaning against the bars under the light bulb, which was swinging like mad, probably because he had been hopping all over the place. I went closer... and what did I see? Monkeyface was lying on some papers in front of Šklíba, wrapped in a sheet. They had put lots of paper under him, so he wasn't lying in the cellar water. I went over to them.

Dýha saw me first. 'Ilya,' he said, 'tell 'em to stop!' Šklíba came stumbling towards me, tripping over his black gown, and raised his arms in a pious way. 'Look,' he said, 'we've washed him and got him ready. Now we have to bury him. We've said all the right prayers, but we can say 'em again: "Our Father", "Hail Mary" and "Sleep, Baby, Sleep" and all that... that's if you want us to.'

I wanted to say something to them, but I couldn't make my mouth work, and I was shaking. I didn't want to look at Monkeyface, but I did.

'We searched everywhere for you, but we couldn't find you,' said Martin. 'It was bloody dark upstairs.'

'I know,' I said. 'But now the moon's shining everywhere.'

Suddenly I went very cold, as if the chill of the cellar had gone straight to my bones. Monkeyface lay on the papers, through which the cellar water was starting to seep.

'Come on,' said Šklíba, and he took me inside the cubicle and past Monkeyface and past the kneeler, and there at the very back behind mountains of paper Martin bent down and lifted a half-rotten board from the floor, and underneath it was some rusty metal, a cover... Martin lifted it to reveal a drain, and from below came a droning noise, probably the wind.

I had stopped shaking, and I wasn't crying.

'Catacombs,' said Martin.

'Do you want to put him in yourself?' Šklíba asked.

'No.'

'Do you want to see him one last time?'

'No.'

'We're the Virgin's choirboys. Do you want to join us?' Martin asked me.

'No, I don't.'

'You don't have to sing.'

'I don't want to.'

So those six little boys picked up Monkeyface, carried him, sagging, in the sheet, and Šklíba made the sign of the Cross at the spot where his hidden head was dangling. Then they dropped him into the drain. There was no splash, so the loud droning noise must have been the wind.

Šklíba dropped the cover back and Martin replaced the board, and the little choirboys who had carried the sheet now joined forces to shove a heap of paper over the drain. I went up to Dýha.

'This is stupid,' he said. 'He's buried and any detectives are gonna find out sod all, and now we can't hold a trial for 'em killing him in the washer drum.'

'But it ain't clear who killed him,' Martin chimed in. He was standing behind me. Outside he would have looked ridiculous in his black smock. Anyone would have laughed at him. Not in the cellar though.

'We'll pray for him here and consecrate it,' Martin went on. 'Now we've made it a cemetery. The first saints and Christians also held requiems in the cemetery. Nobody wanted them. The nuns told us.'

'He fell out of the window,' I told them. 'Karel saw it happen, and Páta.'

'Some of us'll stay up all night to pray,' said Martin.

'Till the daystar appears,' Šklíba added. 'Now we'll help you,' he told Dýha.

To the bars he tied a washing line nicked from the kitchen. The little choristers grabbed hold of it. Me and Martin tried to work the grille loose.

We were tugging at the bars and the plaster started coming away. The Virgin's little songsters pulled on the line. Šklíba tried to prise off the grille from below with a plank. Dýha was also levering away with a plank. Just as I was about to say, 'I'll go and wake the Bandits,' the choristers got a grip and Dýha got a grip and I clenched my teeth and got a grip, and Šklíba yelped and dropped his plank, the grille came loose and fell out of the wall. A shower of plaster landed on Dýha and clouds of dust on the rest of us, but we were all chuffed... and Dýha came out and said, 'Now I'm gonna grab some of them frankfurters... if there's any left!'

'There is!' I cried, and off we tramped through the cellar water, and the choirboys called out, 'Wait for us!' and pushed the kneeler and crucifix on top of the pile of paper... Then we set off along the passage and up the stairs, and when we came up from the cellar and snuffed out all the candles, we went outside and one of the little lads said, 'Hey, it's light!'

And so it was! The sky was blue, but full of light. We looked up at it and high above us shone one pinprick of light, and Šklíba said, 'Lo, brethren, the daystar.'

But Dýha said, 'That's *Sputnik*, idiot!'

We stood outdoors and breathed the air, dusting ourselves off... and suddenly we heard, 'Well, my lads, that's what I like to see. Bright and early and already hard at it! Or are you exercising? That's fabulous! We're going to get on well together.' Outside the Home from Home stood Mr Vyžlata, our caretaker and carer and commander, though we didn't know that at the time. Behind him stood a boy pulling a cart, a kind of trolley thing, and when I glanced at him, I couldn't believe my eyes.

5

I swear! Work began. You can't do a runner in winter

The next day the first morning of our new life began, and Mr Vyžlata was everywhere.

And we set about clearing up.

And the Commander kept checking our home.

The youngsters even decided there had to be more than one of him, because Mr Vyžlata was in the dining room when we thought he was checking the first floor, then he showed up in the kitchen when we thought he was investigating the cellar, and when we sneaked off for a fag by the aeroplane picture on the third floor, suddenly he was there, as if he had been waiting for us among the piles of paper. He snatched Páta's fag end from him and threw it on the floor, but didn't squish it.

'What do you want to be, lad?' he asked.

Páta pulled a funny face and several of us sniggered, because whenever the nuns asked that question, everyone replied, 'An orphan', so they gave up asking.

'Most of all I want to be a cowboy on a cowboy ranch, sir.'

'No sirs now. Call me Commander. Understood?'

'I'd like to be a cowboy, Commander.'

Along with the rest of us Commander Vyžlata watched the wisp of smoke rising from the fag end in the pile of paper, but he didn't squish it, and he said, 'Ha, ha! Have any of you ever seen a gippo cowboy? You're a teeny bit of a gipsy, aren't you, lad?'

Páta was pissed off, you could tell.

'Attention!' Commander Vyžlata bellowed, so loudly we all froze, not just Páta. 'Just to clear up a few things here! You are the most neglected boys in the whole of Czechoslovakia. Understood? You're the sons of syphilitics, alcoholics and murderers, whores and foreigners. On top of that you've been ruined by an obscurantist education. But that's all going to change. Do you see that fire, lads?' And you can bet we were wide-eyed, because a little flame had shot up from the smoke. 'Do you suppose I'm afraid of this fire? Certainly not. I've come through worse fires. Have you read these documents?' Commander Vyžlata kicked more stacks of paper into the bonfire. ''Course not. They're written in languages dead to the future, and that's why they must go. But then you and I will get this place cleaned up, won't we?' the Commander suddenly roared, making us jump, and tossed another fistful of papers onto the fire. The crackling flames snaffled them up... They began to nip at his fingers.

'You boys, everybody else has thrown in the towel where you are concerned, but I picked the towel up! I used to be like you... abandoned, a hard nut, a wretched street kid, but I was found by soldiers from Stalin's Flying Brigade, who offered me friendship and made me a son of the regiment – *syn palka* – and I was saved, and you too shall be saved... You there, don't move until you're told!' and Dýha, who had meant to stamp out the fire, jumped back. The smoke was getting up my nose, so I let out an almighty sneeze.

'Boys,' shouted Commander Vyžlata, 'this fire between us is going to carry on burning until you give me your oath... You'll be given airguns, tracksuits, mess tins, compasses, provided you swear that we'll be friends... But if you don't, may we all burn to death!'

We stood there... Dýha, Páta and me... and there were others too, but it was hard to see, hard to see even the Commander, standing by the door, but the fire was between him and the door and it had begun to spread. Then I saw Commander Vyžlata's face right in front of my own. He had leaned across the fire and he said, 'Do you swear?'

'Yes!' I gasped, then I heard Dýha shout, 'I swear!' and Páta shrieked, 'Yeah!' and others called out 'I swear! I swear!' Then Commander Vyžlata's voice broke in and said, 'All right, lads, you can put it out.'

We jumped onto the papers, trampling them down, putting out the flames as best we could, then suddenly – *hisssssss!* – we were all splattered by a stream of something white. The whole of the third floor was full of smoke, and as we coughed our guts out and tried to flap the smoke away with our arms we saw Commander Vyžlata holding this small red drum thing, and out of it he was squirting a stream of white stuff to extinguish the spreading fire, and the Commander was laughing, 'I don't suppose you've ever seen the latest fire-fighting technology, lads, but that's something else that's going to change... run along and get outside.'

Half-choking, we staggered to our own floor and on down the stairs. Outside the Home from Home stood the longshirts, the choristers and the rest of the Bandits, goggle-eyed and staring at us. I was the last out, and I heard Bajza say, 'Hell, you look like ghosts,' and someone else said, 'We thought you was dead!'

'Yes,' said Commander Vyžlata, who was suddenly standing there in the doorway. 'They were dead, but they've given me their oath, so now they're boys with a new life ahead of them. And the same goes for all of you.'

And so our work began. Before we could set about clearing dead languages from the upper floors, we had to line up and be counted, so that Commander Vyžlata knew how many of us there were. We didn't mind.

Now we, the shortpants, had to catch all the stray, lost and hiding youngsters, and they were everywhere... Some were blubbering and calling out for the nuns, some had shat themselves and others were screaming with hunger.

We older ones got the kitchen stove going and washed the youngsters and ourselves, and Commander Vyžlata unlocked a cupboard with a key on a metal ring, and in it were heaped sackfuls of clothes donated by Czech children. So we chased all over the upper floors, catching the littlest boys and hauling them down to the kitchen... We dragged every weepy, shit-arsed, struggling longshirt over to the stove and washed their bottoms and faces, and then they got some clothes. Karel sliced some bread and Páta poured tea into mugs. 'Well done, lads!' Commander Vyžlata praised us, and perhaps because I was the smallest of the shortpants, and maybe also because I had the experience, I got the arse-washing job and I stank. We found a nest of three longshirts sleeping among piles of paper and shouted to wake them up, sending them down to get washed and eat, chasing them downstairs, where Commander Vyžlata was standing. 'There we are, lads,' he said. 'I picked up the towel others had thrown in, and I was right!'

Then me and the older longshirts pottered about the first and second floors, picking up the papers and bits of books that had fallen or been thrown down from higher up and making them into little stacks. And we had a good view of Commander Vyžlata in the dining room with the new boy, and of what the new boy was up to. 'He's going all over Christ with a damp cloth,' said Dýha, and Mikušinec said, 'Ilya, the new boy looks like you!' 'Hmm,' I said. 'Have you got more brothers somewhere?' Mikušinec asked. I shrugged to show I didn't care, but there was a tingling in my shoulders. We looked at the new boy, who had hair like mine and a nose like mine and eyes like mine.

Many of us were still washing and counting the lines of longshirts, while others of us went off with Commander Vyžlata to another cupboard, which he opened with another key on the ring. Then he handed out scrubbing brushes and floor-cloths... We scrubbed and washed the floors upstairs and peeked into the dining room... We saw the new boy painting over the face of the Lord Jesus.

Then Commander Vyžlata heard our report that the longshirts were filling up the kitchen and eating, and that some had fallen asleep, sprawled on blankets beside the stove – that the kitchen was gradually becoming a longshirt camp... Then we heard an uproar, and the Commander ran to the dining room and some of us ran after him.

In the kitchen Šklíba and Martin were fighting with the new boy, kicking over his pots, which contained white paint. There wasn't much left of the holy picture in the dining room: Christ and his Mother had almost been painted out... Commander Vyžlata grabbed Šklíba and Martin, each by an ear, and said, 'What's this then?' and Šklíba said, 'We want the sisters and Christ back!' and Commander Vyžlata clapped one hand around his own ear in a funny way, and bent down over Šklíba and said, 'What's that I hear?' and Šklíba stamped his foot and I could see he was about to burst into tears. Then Commander Vyžlata spoke severely, 'There are boys here who look after their little comrades,' and I almost yelped, because Commander Vyžlata suddenly leapt towards me and grabbed me by the shoulder and shouted, 'See! This boy is almost the double of the lad I've brought you. This boy washes the little boys' bottoms without complaining – and that's something out of which friendship can be forged! But we also have here victims of the obscurantism of the old, dying world!' Commander Vyžlata roared at Šklíba. 'Listen lad, before you and I swear to be friends, I want you to understand one thing: *there were no sisters here.* There were never any of them nuns here! Right?'

'There were!' Šklíba shouted back.

'You are a stupid, stubborn boy,' said Commander Vyžlata. 'Tell me again: were there nuns here?'

Šklíba shook his head.

'Were their sisters here?'

'Yes!' Šklíba shouted.

'But sisters are nuns, and no nuns were here. So they weren't here and there's an end of it. You'll get the point one day, my lad,' said Commander Vyžlata.

The first day of our new life ended with us sorting the longshirts into small and smaller. We assembled them on the first floor and Commander Vyžlata walked past their yawning ranks and pointed: you to the left, you to the right... We drove the ones assigned to us into the littlest ones' dormitory, grinning at each other and winking, expecting tears, screams and shouts! But Commander Vyžlata locked himself in with the youngsters. He was only there briefly, and when he came out there was no uproar. They were quiet and asleep. There wasn't even time to register our surprise. Commander Vyžlata nodded to us and we went into the dining room and sat at our places, as if for lessons.

'I know, lads,' said Commander Vyžlata. 'It's evening and you've had a hard day of it. But, believe me, I came here convinced that I could turn this home full of ne'er-do-wells in the middle of nowhere into a first-rate unit. The nuns stuffed your heads full of nonsense. Have any of them ever had to get a hut full of Russian street urchins to sleep? No. But I have. As a son of the regiment I was forged by Stalin's Flying Brigade. They sent me from the Centre to cleanse this place. We're going to cleanse it together! We'll sling out all those vile old papers full of nonsense! Together we shall cleanse it by fire, and that way we will forge a glorious friendship. And I, my lads, will prepare you for life in the new age. I, lads, have been seared by the fiercest fires of the twentieth century! Yes, I was forged on the anvils of the twentieth century! So now I'm prepared to nurture you for the new age. And in this new age I want you to become leaders and commanders. Understood? Together we shall lay the foundations. Agreed?'

We said nothing. He didn't want us to answer. That was obvious.

'Boys!' Commander Vyžlata shouted. 'Others threw in the towel, but I picked it up and, believe me, I take this challenge seriously. Listen closely!' Commander Vyžlata stood up.

'Many of you are orphans.' He started walking about, waving his arms around as he spoke. 'You've been neglected. You're morally defective. You're a bunch of sneaks and liars and petty thieves. You're scumbags. Village kids of your age are already slogging away in the fields, and the only thing you know how to do is say your prayers.

'I'm sure you're thinking, "This is all bullshit, I'm gonna run away"... Because that's all you've ever learned, running away... But you can't run away now. You'd die of starvation and hypothermia. But by the spring, lads, I'll have you forged... You've got just one hope, lads! That hope is *work*! And work is everything that I'm going to tell you to do! I've already ordered airguns and knapsacks and billycans and mess tins. Which of you wants to learn how to shoot and crawl and throw hand grenades at the enemy?'

We all shouted, 'Me! Me! Me!' and Commander Vyžlata nodded. Now the new boy, the one who looked quite like me, came up to him and the Commander smiled and placed a hand on his shoulder. 'This boy and I have travelled the world together,' he said cheerily. 'I met this boy in a faraway eastern land, where I snatched him from his dying family in the midst of combat.' The Commander was smiling... and we were glad he'd stopped calling us names and being so cross. We were always calling each other names, but it was never for real, and sometimes the nuns used to call us 'little demons', 'gallows-fodder' or 'scallywags'. And they'd call the youngsters 'sweetheart' or 'angel' or 'poor wee thing' or 'frightened little bird' and stuff like that... but that wasn't name-calling either. And Commander Vyžlata told us how he had snatched this boy from a horribly dysfunctional family – a drunken father who was a waste of space and a mother dying from an infectious disease – so that he could forge him into a future commander. 'Which is what lies ahead for you, too, my lads!' And the Commander would have us know that the new boy had an important task... in place of the religious painting in the dining room he was going to do a portrait of Private Fedotkin from Stalin's Flying Brigade! 'You'll be hearing all about Private Fedotkin and the son of the regiment. I can promise you that, lads,' Commander Vyžlata bellowed, and some of us shouted 'Yeah!' and 'Yes!' because that was the kind of thing that made the Commander happy.

'So I want to introduce this boy to you.' Commander Vyžlata pointed to the new lad. 'His name's Margash!' he said, smiling at us. So we laughed as well, and Bajza shouted 'Goulash!' and fell from his desk, laughing and kicking his legs in the air.

Commander Vyžlata raised his arms to command silence, but it didn't come. Pebbles and pencil stumps and whatever else anyone could find in their pockets started flying through the air. We created mayhem, banging our fists on the desks and stamping our feet, and the Commander stood there with his arms flung wide, listening to the noise. And Commander Vyžlata reached into his pocket and pulled out a big black pistol: *bang!...* and what a bang it was! And the bullet buried itself in the dining-room ceiling above our heads, and when a strip of plaster peeled away and fell somewhere among us, then there was total silence. Commander Vyžlata put away his pistol and said, 'Go to bed.'

We had stopped laughing. We were totally worn out. We tramped up to the second floor, to the shortpants' dormitory.

We flopped onto the empty bunks wherever we could, and the ones left over crept in with someone else, it didn't matter. Our heads were all drooping, but some of us were talking anyway.

'What did he mean, saying we're scumbags?' wondered Mikušinec.

'Nobody wants us,' someone said.

'Airguns could be fun,' Mikušinec whispered. 'It's like being in the Legion!'

'Look,' I said, 'let's do a runner. Let's go and join the Legion. How about it?'

'Idiot,' Dýha whispered. 'You can't do a runner in winter. He was right about that.'

'You can, even in winter,' someone said.

'But not in Siřem,' said Dýha. 'Listen, let's wait for them airguns. That could be just what we need. The altar boys don't stand a chance, and if Vyžlata starts buggering us about we can cut and run and shoot our way to the Legion.'

'And what did he mean about the sisters?' asked Mikušinec.

'You've just gotta act like they were never here, or he'll do his nut,' someone said.

'But they *were* here!'

'Forget it.'

'Okay.'

'Sod him,' said Páta, and someone started sniggering into his pillow and said, 'Ha, ha! A gippo cowboy! Ha, ha!' and from somewhere in the dormitory came, 'Yeah, that's a good one, a gippo cowboy... I just had this vision of a gippo cowboy and I had to laugh.' And Páta said, 'You're all stupid.'

Then I whispered to Karel, whose bunk was across the aisle. 'Karel! I'd still rather go and join the Legion.'

'It's winter, Ilya. Go to sleep.'

6

All about Fedotkin. Hanka. Cleaning out. The new lad

In the morning we lit the stove and washed in basins, as we always did in winter, and someone said, 'Do you reckon they've brought those airguns yet?' and Páta roared, 'Yippee!' Then we heard Commander Vyžlata: 'Weapons training will come later, lads.' He led us out to the front of the Home from Home and got us limbering up in the crisp, cold air... He was wearing just a vest and shorts and set the pace, and after the tiniest longshirts had collapsed in the snow, he appointed me and Páta and the new boy Margash to exercise with the littlest ones and look after them, and when any of them flopped into the snow, we picked them up... The youngsters enjoyed falling in the snow when it was down to me or Páta or Margash to catch them, so I reckon that us three got the most exercise that morning. Then Margash and I suddenly made a grab for one longshirt who had fallen down and our foreheads crashed. We picked ourselves up and I watched him in slow motion, and it was like looking in a mirror, and I said, 'Watch out!' and he said 'Okay!' So he did speak Czech!

Work began only after we'd limbered up. We began clearing the Home from Home of its mountains of paper. Fortunately, we started at the top of the house, because if we'd begun with the cellar, Commander Vyžlata would have discovered the grave in the cellar floor. I knew that.

Teams of us took turns at carrying out the old paper and burning it at a spot we had cleared of snow, outside the front door. We took turns so all the lads had their fair share of time in the fresh air.

We liked having a bonfire. We turned the burning heaps of paper with poles.

We spent each day clearing bundles of paper out of the Home from Home, passing them in a long chain, and we also picked up the various documents that had landed here and there, blown about in the draught. Inside the Home from Home there was a draught all the time now; the wind whistled along all the corridors and through all the upper floors, making the doors bang. We also knocked the holy pictures off the walls and added them to the fire. The Commander didn't want them in the corridors.

On the very first day, Commander Vyžlata informed us that we older ones didn't have to sleep at midday, which we welcomed with a roar. The nuns used to make us. We went to the dining room and watched Margash sketching, then painting, a picture of Private Fedotkin on a white patch of wall where a holy picture had been.

The days of our new life dedicated to work – and later to studying as well – passed one by one, and the portrait of Private Fedotkin was very quickly coloured in on the wall, and Commander Vyžlata used tiny brushes to add his own touches to it.

We no longer talked among ourselves at night. Commander Vyžlata would lull us to sleep, so we didn't waste our energy in the evenings, and got up in the morning well rested and eager for work and study.

Commander Vyžlata lulled us to sleep in the same way he had persuaded the waifs in the huts of Vorkuta to sleep at minus forty degrees. He told us about the son of the regiment.

He would walk up and down the dormitory and tell us the story of Private Fedotkin and an abandoned street kid, and I kept my eyes closed, holding on to the day's images under my eyelids: burning paper and floating shreds of scorched parchment dragged back to earth with poles; assembly in the dining room before lessons and at mealtimes; teams of boys moving from floor to floor; and our dusty hands passing bundles of documents from one to another all the way to the bonfire.

Sometimes I thought about Monkeyface. I didn't want to. It took the story told by Commander Vyžlata to overlay Monkeyface's image in my mind. So I probably waited more expectantly than any of the others for the Commander to come.

The voice of the storyteller was interrupted by the breathing and snoring of the ones who fell asleep first.

The Commander told us about the son of the regiment, who had not only been abandoned, but was also beaten and driven out and jeered at by villagers, and by people in the towns. His parents – whores and foreigners – couldn't give a shit about him. The boy trudged his way through the world until one day, having escaped from a fire, he saw a tank drive into the fire and on top of the tank stood Private Fedotkin of Stalin's Flying Brigade. Private Fedotkin reached out for the boy and they forged a friendship, and together they crushed lots of Jerries to a pulp with their tank and generally made mincemeat of heaps of wicked people, and the boy became the son of the regiment and Private Fedotkin made him a boy-sized uniform. Every evening the story was the same, and the lonely boy at the start of the story endured endless wrongs, beatings, slights and jeering among stupid people. But then his life was transformed by Private Fedotkin. They travelled the world together in triumph.

And how did it end? I really wanted to know what became of the son of the regiment, but I always fell asleep.

Commander Vyžlata told the story of Private Fedotkin in Czech and Russian, so we could talk about it among ourselves, and if anyone didn't know some word, somebody else would tell him. It was easy. We came from all over the place.

We swapped parts of the Commander's story among ourselves. Some had extra bits, because they'd been dreaming it, and others lost some words of the story in their sleep, so we all knew slightly different versions.

Mikušinec, say, fell asleep hearing about the tank driving into the fire... Others fell asleep earlier and others later. So it was ages before I pieced together the whole story of the son of the regiment... Dýha, for example, talked about Fedotkin being disgraced, and then he and Karel would always argue. Karel claimed Fedotkin was officially delegated to the hut at the Vorkuta camp!

'Delegated, you stupid prat! That means he was promoted!'

'Bollocks!' Dýha shouted back. 'If that's so, why was Fedotkin brought before the criminal tribunal of Stalin's Flying Brigade, eh?'

None of us ever heard the story to the end, because Commander Vyžlata didn't have just a pistol in his armoury. He also had a voice that made you sleepy.

So the days passed, and one day a van came up from the village...
and we were excited at the prospect of airguns. I hoped that Mrs
Kropek would show up with Hanka, but it was Mr Holasa bringing
salamis and smoked meats. He dropped off his load of crates and left.
And another day another van came, and we gathered round in expec-
tation... it was Mr Kropek with bread and jugs of milk and stock cubes,
but he had Mrs Kropek with him as well, and I went backwards and
forwards carrying the jugs of milk ever so carefully so as not to spill
any. I spotted Hanka, too, but it was just as we were being given our assignments. We formed into cleaning details, details to watch over the
youngsters and mopping details... There were no more classes with the
nuns, no more praying or singing (and only the choirboys were sorry
about that), and no more geography or bible stories or homeland study
and we were glad, because we didn't give a shit about learning by heart
all the rivers and forests of some bloody homeland.

Every day our teams struggled with bundles of ancient documents
and heavy old books, and the strongest among us would rip them from
their bindings and we burnt everything, but there always seemed to be
plenty more... So far we hadn't cleared out a single floor. Great
mounds of ash piled up around the spot where the fire blazed, but we
couldn't dig them into the ground because it was frozen solid.

So the days passed, one after another, each one much like the next,
like pages torn out of the same book, round and round in a circle, days
turning at their centre, which was always the evening, when we fell
asleep to the story of Fedotkin.

During the day, thoughts of Monkeyface were driven from my
mind by work. It was a good thing that I could look forward every day
to the Commander's story.

Me and Hanka did see each other, on the day the van came from the village, but they split us up straight away.

I was taking out a full ash pan from the kitchen stove and bumped into her in the doorway. Bleary-eyed from sleep and half-blinded by the ash that the wind kept blowing in my face, I put an arm around her, because I was falling over. She put an arm around me too. The smell of her hair was gorgeous. She hugged me to her. The weight of the ash pan nearly toppled us over. I accidentally placed a hand on one of her breasts. It was soft, firm and warm. Unfortunately, my other hand was holding the ash pan. I tried to tell her everything quickly. I was sure she was looking for Monkeyface. But her hair was in my mouth. We had our arms around each other, but only for a moment. I had to let the ash pan go, so I could put both arms around her. It clattered off down the cellar steps. We stood there in a cloud of ash and started coughing. Then it was over.

Some of the lads came running out of the kitchen. The noise had broken in on their morning ablutions. Billows of steam followed them out. They whooped and shouted. Dýha, Karel and the others. 'Wow, look at that! Ilya's groping Freckleface,' shouted Mikušinec... And now they were right by us, and Dýha touched Hanka. Then they were all touching her. They shoved me away with their elbows, backs and bottoms and formed a huddle around Hanka. I couldn't get through to her. For a moment I couldn't move at all.

She tripped, she was on her knees. I caught only glimpses of her face between the boys. It was bright red now. In the steam they were all going bonkers, as if they were hidden in a cloud. Some longshirts also came out into the corridor, squeaking and shouting.

And suddenly there was the Commander. In an instant he had

opened the front door and there he was. And did he lash out! The lads fell away from Hanka, fleeing from the Commander. Mrs Kropek also came indoors, and started screaming and shouting and raging. 'Filthy beasts! Wretched little idiots! And you, you silly tart, stop gawping!' That's how she spoke to her own child, and she pushed Hanka outside. Suddenly they were all outside. Mrs Kropek stayed behind with me, leaning against the door and breathing so fast that I thought her heart was going to burst.

'Don't stare, you poor mite!' said Mrs Kropek ever so softly. After all the shouting I quite liked her soft voice. She turned and went outside. So I went too.

I pottered up and down outside the Home from Home. Where had the Commander chased them all off to? I followed the wheeltracks of the Kropeks' truck around the corner.

And there I saw Hanka again. She was sitting huddled in a blanket and staring ahead. I tapped on the window. What did I want? I dunno. I tapped the glass again. I dunno what she was thinking. The Kropeks never came again. Later on they couldn't.

And every day we stood by the bonfire and poked at the piles of pages and documents with our poles and rakes to make sure they were thoroughly burnt. And sometimes a flame shot up high and a wall of fire whooshed up and over and hung in the air, then slid hissing back to the ground. Some of us danced and shouted, especially when the Commander ordered us to burn the books the nuns used to teach us: *The Catholic Book of Knowledge* and *My Jesus ABC*... and other books. The lads hadn't enjoyed lessons, but I made a grab for *The Catholic Book of Knowledge*. I had had to keep an eye on Monkeyface so often while the lads were in class, so now I could look through it, and I gawped at all those animals, whales and globes. I hid it under my pillow, though I ripped off the cover and tossed it on the fire. Later I put *The Catholic Book of Knowledge* under my tracksuit top... I spent the evenings poring over it and so protected myself from Monkeyface's face, until the Commander came in to tell his story.

Every day, old records turned into ash above our heads, then fell back down into our hair, and every day charred bits of pages floated down all around us. That was us clearing out the Home from Home.

One day I was standing there with the other Bandits (no-one was allowed near the bonfire on his own) when I was gripped with anxiety. I suddenly knew that nobody wanted to run away to join the Legion any more, so I would have to go alone, make my own way in the world, because I couldn't bear to stay in Siřem, because Monkeyface was there and because it had happened.

I tossed my pole away and left... The Bandits started shouting, but I went inside and I didn't care where Commander Vyžlata was, because he could be anywhere. I passed by the kitchen and round the bend in the corridor and down the steps to the cellar. The water made my feet cold. It splashed. I made my way to the cubicle and heard low, mumbling voices.

Šklíba was kneeling over Monkeyface's grave in a torn, dirty, black tunic and Martin was kneeling under the Cross in a crumpled, dirty, black tunic. Only two of the six little choirboys were kneeling there and they had just one tiny candle. Šklíba's face twisted with anxiety when he heard me. I gave him a fright! But when he saw me, his face was calm again... I went to take a look at the solitary cell and was amazed to see it had been repaired. I sat down inside it on a blanket.

In the silence the praying voices floated through all the cubicles towards me... but then I heard some quiet footsteps and before anyone spoke my short hair stood on end in horror. I could feel every single hair on my skull... I knew the choirboys couldn't hear the footsteps. When they prayed, they mumbled. And Commander Vyžlata said, 'What's this then?' After that all I could hear was him cuffing the boys and them yelling. I crept close to the cell wall. I could hear the boys sobbing, then Commander Vyžlata chased them out of the cellar and they screamed... but he soon drove them away.

Then I heard more quiet footsteps. He was going deep into the cellar. I found myself hoping he would fall – *plop!* – into some hole. There were supposed to be open drains back there, and huge rats. If you didn't have a candle or a torch they could finish you off. Commander Vyžlata wasn't afraid, but the Bandits wouldn't have ventured that far. Then the steps came very close. I yelped and the steps came my way.

The new boy, Margash, was out of puff as he sat down. He looked at me and said, 'I'm glad it's you.' Then he said, 'Yeah, I've been looking for you for ages. I didn't know you were here.'

'In the cellar?'

'That you're Czech and in Bohemia. It's a good thing the Commander didn't find you in the cellar. He hasn't much time to worry about us right now.' Margash tapped at the bars. 'Me and the Commander mended this on the first night.'

He raised an arm and grabbed the bars. I remembered Dýha and how he had ranted through them. The grille glinted in the half-light. I was happy there were puddles of underground water all around. If anyone came, we'd hear them. We spoke in low voices.

'I've been looking for you all this time,' said Margash. 'Everywhere.'

I was glad he had been looking for me, but it was a bit strange.

'I wanted to talk to you, too,' I told him. 'We're alike. We might come from the same country. Why do you hang around with the Commander?'

'That's just it,' said Margash.

I thought about Margash's dad.

'Did he really snatch you... from those horrible people? Did he? Why do you travel together?'

I liked us sitting there, looking at one another as if we had known each other for ages.

'That's not how it was,' said Margash. 'My dad's a wolf.'

'What?'

'Me and the Commander go everywhere together. And now we're here. I'm glad you're here too!'

'Right,' I said, already looking forward to showing him around all the hiding places in the Home from Home. I'd tell him everything there was. I'd always lived at the Home from Home.

'Kill the Commander,' said Margash

'You what?'

'You have to kill the Commander.' I must have stared at him, because he frowned and asked, 'Wasn't your dad a wolf, then?'

It crossed my mind he might have got some Czech words mixed up, so I said, 'I never knew him. I was very small.'

'I've often dreamed about you,' said Margash. 'I've often dreamed of meeting a boy who would be like me. You're that boy. Kill the Commander.'

I was lost for words. Margash pulled a long face. Now he was angry. It looked like he was cramming his eyes into slits. But he wasn't a

Chinky like some of the other boys. Now he looked more like some animal. I'd never heard of any wolves at Siřem, but there could have been some in Chapman Forest. I rolled my eyes a bit like Margash and thrust my chin down.

'Right,' he laughed, 'you kept turning up in my dreams.'

'What did you say about my dad?' I asked him.

'Was he a wolf? Because mine was. We might have the same dad, since you look like me.'

'Is it possible to have dads that are... not people?'

'Wolves we can.'

'Where are you from?' Again I remembered what Commander Vyžlata had said about Margash's mum and dad, and I had to laugh.

'I come from a wonderful country,' he said. 'No forests, grass everywhere, you can go wherever you like, on and on. Do you fancy coming home with me? I've got lots of brothers. Would you like to live with us?'

'You bet!'

'So kill him.'

'You want me to kill the Commander? You really do?'

'It's nice where we live, honest,' said Margash.

'But the Commander's really strong,' I objected, 'and he's got a gun.'

'So what?'

'Why don't you do it?'

'I can't,' said Margash. 'I dreamed that you would.'

'Couldn't someone else do it?' I was thinking of Karel. Margash shook his head.

'No. It wasn't anyone else in my dream.'

'I see.'

I remembered how Commander Vyžlata had cuffed the little choirboys. How he had sloshed quietly through the cellar water. And how he was in all places at all times.

'I dunno,' I said. 'I've never killed anyone before.' As I said it, I suddenly felt sick. If Commander Vyžlata could find the choirboys, he might also find the grave. I got up and went straight to it, and Margash followed.

It would be nice to go around together.

In the cubicle there were papers tossed everywhere and the kneeler was in smithereens. Commander Vyžlata must have smashed it against the wall. I did everything in one quick movement, like when you whip off a plaster. I shifted the papers, lifted the half-rotten board and tossed it aside. I raised the cover and there was the drain, very noisy, down below, and the stench and the cold rose up at me.

Margash watched as I told him everything. I also said that if Monkeyface was still alive and got cured, there'd be three of us.

'That's not gonna happen,' said Margash. 'But our little brother ought to be buried in our wonderful country!'

'Dead right!' I said. I looked around that squalid cellar in the gloom, and I dearly wished that Monkeyface could be out of there.

'We can do it, once my dream comes true. Shall we?' asked Margash.

'We'll move him, won't we?'

I was so glad to see Margash nodding. I couldn't stop myself from thinking how awful it would be if Commander Vyžlata found Monkeyface.

'Yep, we'll move him together,' said Margash. 'But you'll kill the Commander. If you don't kill him, I'm going to run away.'

'You can't run away now! You'd freeze to death in the forest. Or starve. And there are wild animals.'

'I don't care.'

'Okay.' I put the cover back and we left.

And the Home from Home was in uproar.

7

The Choirboys. New things. Knife, salt, matches.
Team commander!

The kitchen was full of crying longshirts begging for bread and tea.
Margash went into the command post, which Commander Vyžlata
had created in Sister Leontina's office.

Silva nudged me. He'd been chatting with the other longshirts.
'What's going on?' he asked. 'They've locked us in here.'

I said, 'Job assignments!' and Silva muttered, 'Bollocks!' But the
other longshirts stood to attention, then Silva took his place in line as
well... 'Quiet!' I shouted. 'Form a queue for bread issue! Form a queue
for tea issue!'

The boys I'd picked out hopped into position behind the bread
counter and next to the huge copper full of tea, complete with ladle,
and the youngsters started pushing and shoving, but when I bellowed
at them, they formed queues, and the bread was unbuttered and the tea
was cold, but that didn't matter. I'd noticed long ago that when they
were afraid or there was any kind of confusion, it was always best to
shout at them. Then they were less afraid, and the one doing the shouting also became less afraid. I sat down on a bench.

*

After a moment the door opened and I stood to attention to give my report, but Commander Vyžlata ignored me and everyone else... The order came for us to go to bed immediately. The Commander disappeared behind Margash and into the command post. The work teams were dejected and frozen stiff, but they hauled themselves off upstairs to the second floor without any fuss or noise. Only Mikušinec and Karel came back to help me chase the longshirts to their dormitory and the youngsters were playing silly beggars.

I went on upstairs and said to Karel, 'What was that about?'

Karel rolled his eyes and said, 'Phew!'

And Mikušinec whispered to me, 'Šklíba's in the shit. They was arsing about with Christ in the cellar.'

In the dormitory they were all talking quietly, and Šklíba was sitting on his bed in the corner, and next to him Martin. They were wearing black tunics, but no-one made fun of them. The moon was so bright we could see each other and we spoke quietly, because we had a sense that Commander Vyžlata wasn't going to be sending us off to sleep with a story today. I soon discovered that the Commander had blown his top because of the pious choirboys, and had burnt their stolen cellar Cross as a twentieth-century abomination, and made the two little choirboys trample on the Cross, and, to add insult to injury, the others had all laughed. But Šklíba insisted he hadn't stamped on it, even though Commander Vyžlata had ordered him to, and then the Commander had pulled out his pistol. But Šklíba refused to stamp on it anyway, to everyone's surprise. Now in the half-dark trickling in from the moonlight they were all debating the issue. What had actually happened?

'What was it like, Šklíba?' the boys asked. 'Were you scared?'

'I'd have been shitting bricks,' said Bajza.

'Don't be daft, you'd have stamped on it,' Chata said.

'And *you* wouldn't, you reckon?' Bajza replied, and they started fighting and Chata was suffocating Bajza with a pillow, but only pretending. Šklíba said nothing, though we all kept asking him, and Martin said, 'Shut up, the lot of you. He can't hear you anyway.'

'Aha,' said someone else, 'so he fired the gun right next to his ear, then the other ear?' And they went on and on, deciding that Commander Vyžlata had crucifixes and nuns on the brain. He was a nutcase, really. And all that stuff about the twentieth century. We didn't give a shit what century it was.

Then someone said, 'Did you stamp on it, Martin?' and Martin said, 'Yeah.'

The lads carried on chatting, but not me. I was thinking about what Margash wanted me to do. I couldn't let him run away. We'd get Monkeyface, then together we'd escape to Margash's wonderful country. I tried to imagine Margash. If I had a dream about him, we might talk in it again. I dropped off to sleep, then woke, because someone was standing by Dýha's bed.

I tried to blink my eyes open... It was Karel, Mikušinec, Chata and Dýha. I went over to them, barefoot. I could hear the breathing of the ones who were asleep, and someone in the corner was sort of squeaking, and the wind outside was going *whoo-whoo*, so the Bandits didn't hear me until I was right up close. Dýha put a finger to his lips and pointed downwards, so I dropped to the floor. The boards under Dýha's bed had been ripped out... They'd been putting little packets down there! Packets made out of old documents. I spotted the sharp blade of a kitchen knife, and there were more of the same. Mikušinec was just wrapping some candles.

Dýha pushed his lips towards my ear and whispered, 'That thing with the airguns, that's all crap. We don't give a shit about him and we're off to join the Legion. You coming?'

I felt like shouting out loud. I was suddenly so happy! But I just said, 'Yep,' very quietly.

Karel nodded. 'No-one messes with the Bandits!'

I reached in my pocket and handed Dýha my box of matches. He nodded and said, 'Fantastic!' and Mikušinec said, 'Good,' and wrapped them in paper. They put the packets down the hole and replaced the floorboards.

I crept off to bed. I was so proud to know the Bandits' secret. They had to tell me because I'd seen them. I was glad to be a Bandit.

I decided to tell Margash that he ought to join the Legion as well. We'd take Monkeyface with us and find some pretty spot on the way to bury him. I was really chuffed that Margash had said he had dreamed about me. I was so happy to have made an appearance in somebody's dream. I couldn't get back to sleep for ages, but I dropped off eventually.

Next morning we woke up like on any other day in our new life, but it was a completely different day, not just because of the evening bonfire and the fuss around Šklíba, but also because a car arrived bringing Commander Baudyš, so we didn't work at clearing out the Home from Home.

At morning roll-call Commander Vyžlata briefly introduced us to Commander Baudyš.

He told us that Commander Baudyš had been appointed to us by the Centre. He also said that we were to obey Commander Baudyš implicitly. Fair enough. But who was actually giving the orders? Sometimes it looked as if Commander Baudyš gave orders to Commander Vyžlata, and sometimes the other way around. Not that it mattered.

We formed a chain and started unloading mess tins and billycans and tracksuits and boots and boxes of airguns and smaller boxes of airgun cartridges and gas masks and green knapsacks and other stuff we'd no idea existed, and nobody talked about the Legion any more.

We were over the moon at all these wonderful things and several times whooped with delight. Commander Vyžlata smiled at our glee and put everything under lock and key. Then they handed out booklets that smelt of clean, new paper, but the lads just sneered – they couldn't stand it when the nuns used to try and teach them... My guess was that they'd soon have the booklets in tatters or lose them or not think twice about burning them, but I was thrilled by my first glimpse of *Fundamentals of Close Combat* and I looked forward to *A Manual for Saboteurs*. I also took a copy of *The Motorized Rifleman's Handbook* and hid it under my pillow.

I no longer wanted to go back to Shadowland, and Hanka had stopped coming to the Home. And so whenever I was snuggled up in bed, worn out from the day's work, and before Commander Vyžlata's footsteps came down the corridor, I would immerse myself in *The Catholic Book of Knowledge* or the new booklets. The other lads had had their chance to study, but not me. I'd had to clean the shit from Monkeyface's little arse and wipe the tears and spit and snot from his face! So the Bandits let me study now.

We knew we would see the things that had been locked up again some time. We would hold them and sniff at them, because lots of the things smelt different from anything we'd ever smelt before. These things were new, nobody had ever had them before us and they were for us.

Commander Baudyš had a whistle hanging from his neck. He wore a full tracksuit and he and Commander Vyžlata would call each other 'old warhorse'. Then Commander Vyžlata, in shorts and a T-shirt, showed Commander Baudyš all the limbering-up exercises, and Commander Baudyš said, 'This is going to be a super-dooper unit.' I was in one row and Margash was in the row behind me, and we were just doing a knees-bend and I whispered to him, 'The guy with the whistle, what about him?' and Margash hissed back, 'He wasn't in the dream.' Commander Baudyš was a huge man and must have been much, much stronger than Commander Vyžlata, so I was glad I didn't have to kill him in Margash's dream.

We didn't go off to join the Legion. We were thrilled by the airguns and talked about when we'd be getting the tracksuits and knapsacks and billycans, and Mikušinec said, 'With a billycan you can camp out in the woods.' Then Páta laughed, saying, 'You don't need anything to camp out in the woods!' and Dýha roared, 'With your prick you can camp out in the woods!' and they all laughed and laughed, and Chata said, 'Knife, salt, matches...' and then Bajza and Chata together started chanting, 'Knife, salt, matches...' Then Silva chimed in and some of the other little fuzzy-wuzzies, and they began pretending to attack Chata and Bajza, and they were all shouting, 'Knife, salt, matches! Knife, salt, matches!' and I found myself mouthing the words as well. Then Karel said, 'Spring's coming and you're all thinking of getting away...' We were standing in the snow, but there wasn't a frost and Karel said, '"Knife, salt, matches" – that's a gippo password... First time I escaped, I didn't have a knife or salt or matches... and I stayed hidden in the cemetery, but if ever anyone came there in the night, man! – I was scared... Then me and Páta ran into each other. That's how we met. He used to nick flowers from the graves to swap with the old ladies for an apple, and later we recognized the flowers – the old ladies would take 'em back. We got caught and they sent us to Siřem!' And I asked Karel, 'Can a boy have a wolf for a father?' When I saw the way he stared at me, I knew at once it wasn't possible in the twentieth century. Then there was a whistle blast, and commander Baudyš called, 'Line up! Equipment issue!'

One day, soon after our training started, I was taking the ashes out and Margash came down the corridor towards me, and he pretended to bump into me and whispered, 'Get it done soon!'

I gripped the ash pan and emptied out the ashes. They fluttered around my head in the morning air and landed in my hair. My fingertips tingled as I gripped the metal handle of the ash pan. I was glad Margash still wanted us to go with him to his country. But I had no idea how to go about making his dream come true.

The training days had begun and those of us who made up the combat unit came out of the Home from Home into the big wide world. We trained outdoors.

We ran across a field, hopping sometimes, because there was still snow here and there, but I kept being bumped into by flying beetles, then a bumble bee and a butterfly, and at first I tried to dodge them, then I broke away from the running line.

Commander Baudyš severely reprimanded me in front of the assembled unit, and the lads laughed at me.

After that I would run straight on, whatever came flying at me.

In the past, me and Monkeyface had been trapped indoors. Now we made up Fedotkin squads for offence, defence and sabotage. Under Commander Baudyš's guidance we learned how to protect ourselves from the most terrible weapon of the twentieth century: the atom bomb. We would lie flat, pointing away from the epicentre of the explosion, and cover our heads with newspaper. Except we didn't have any newspapers, so the documents from the upper floors served just as well.

During hand-to-hand combat I usually got beaten up, but I was absolutely the best at crawling, and Commander Baudyš took note of this.

I could creep up on an enemy patrol without a single twig cracking. I would think about the rat I turned into on the day they took the nuns away. I seized the enemy around the neck with my left hand and jerked his head back, while plunging my cold steel into his kidneys, then with an up-and-down flip I released my weapon from his body in such a way that the weight of the enemy falling could not damage my cold steel blade.

That's how it was described in the *Manual for Saboteurs*.

One time, I slipped past Dýha, who was on patrol, crept round Páta and Mikušinec and landed a fatal blow on Chata, who was standing around aimlessly, and I won.

That day, Dýha sang mockingly, 'No-one ever hears a sound when Prince Ratty comes around.' But the name didn't stick. Dýha and the others from his patrol were punished for being so useless. They had to clear a stretch of wood of every last fallen twig.

I was no longer the long-suffering little donkey the nuns used to call me. I really was more of a creeping, crawling rat. But the nuns didn't know that. And I didn't know anything about the nuns. None of us knew anything about them.

We all launched ourselves into the big outdoor world, which grew even bigger with our movements. I liked being in that world. I became a saboteur.

One part of the training of the Fedotkin squads was to spot and map all the bridges, big and small, in and around Siřem, as well as all the wayside shrines and triangulation points, and that's what we did, trotting this way and that the length of Chapman Forest. I mapped the area in pencil on documents gathered from the Home from Home. From signs and signposts we read off the names of the hamlets and farmsteads that lay all over the forest and I entered them in my maps made from those documents: Siřem, Ctiradův Důl and Tomašín, Bataj, Skryje... I never got a single thing wrong and Commander Baudyš commended me.

I carried my bundle of maps under my tracksuit top, and I kept rehearsing the various names the outside world had and thinking about them... Dýha told us that the town called Louny was huge – even bigger than Prague, the capital of Czechoslovakia, which was the country we were in – and that there were thousands of streets and thousands of paths and thousands of cars in Louny, and that there were huge numbers of people everywhere. He'd passed through Louny when the cops brought him to Siřem.

I would pore over the maps I'd drawn on the old documents and sometimes I closed my eyes and I could see Louny with its jumble of cottages and ponds and footbridges and shrines. I saw thousands of Mr Cimburas carefully lifting their feet, and thousands of Mrs Kropeks scrubbing floors, and thousands of Commander Baudyšes saying 'old warhorse!' and I saw myself, too, running all over the town, a thousand Ilyas, and we ran up and down the backstreets and dodged the traffic and the dogs and read hundreds of different names on signs and signposts, then suddenly it was just me and Margash there, and that was the best. We strolled through the streets and took from the cottages any food or stuff that we felt like, and then I could see nothing. I was asleep.

During our training we did a lot of marching, crawling or rushing along the fringes of Chapman Forest and forging deep into it.

One time we spotted some smoke and reported it to Commander Baudyš. We had found the spot on Fell Crag where the altar boys were camped out, but Commander Baudyš wouldn't let us attack, so we obeyed. What else could we do?

Poor lads, the altar boys, all ragged. They had to slog away in the field. They would have goggled at our weapons! An atom bomb would have killed them all! They didn't know anything! Ha, ha! we laughed. I carefully marked on my maps the spot where we'd seen the smoke.

Margash didn't gallivant around the fields of Siřem with us. He was Commander Vyžlata's main assistant in raising and training the long-shirts. The little choirboys were among the longshirts. They didn't wear their black surplices, of course. Martin and Šklíba stayed inside the home to be the Commander's aides. They both had to wear surplices. Commander Vyžlata meant to let them take their dirty surplices off when they came to their senses and recognized the truth about the nuns. They refused.

We were still cleaning the home out and burning bundles of paper. Part of our training was working in the village to 'win the trust of the wary population', as Commander Baudyš put it during the theory part of our training in the dining room, and that meant we would go out to do jobs.

During the theory part we read the booklets and revised from them. I took the cover off the booklet I was reading. I put it with *The Catholic Book of Knowledge* and my roll of maps and kept it under my tracksuit top.

One time Mr Kropáček needed us for a job in his barn. Páta kept saying dirty words, so we laughed a lot. Then Páta showed me how to wank, but I wasn't interested, and then Páta said that babies are made by a bloke peeing inside a woman, and we both laughed even more. But I didn't believe him. I thought it disgusting. I resolved never to do anything of the kind.

Mr Kropáček banged on the barn door and shouted, 'Shut your filthy mouths!' so we fell silent. It stopped raining. Mr Kropáček slung us out. Páta stole a cup with little apples painted on it and I took a cup with goslings painted on it. Unfortunately mine dropped out of my pocket in the yard and got broken. Mr Kropáček said, 'You of all people!' and he grabbed Páta and found the other cup. He whacked Páta across the face and said, 'Ungrateful little shit!' He didn't hit me.

Mr Kropáček reported the theft to Commander Baudyš, who came to pick us up with the others, and he wanted the cup paid for, but Commander Baudyš bawled him out: 'You must be joking! They work their hides off for you in exchange for dog food!' Mr Kropáček said nothing. Commander Baudyš was good at that sort of thing. He always took the part of us boys from the Fedotkin squads.

Whenever we ran up against the altar boys we would have a slanging match. We would throw sticks, stones, anything at each other. The worst thing that happened was when Dýha and Chata nabbed one of them on his own and stabbed him through the hand.

That time, Commander Baudyš lined us up on the village green and lots of the villagers gathered round and the stabbed altar boy's actual mother, Mrs Holý, gave Chata and Dýha a real good slapping, and in return Dýha kicked her in the ankle, and when the people saw that, they really started screaming at us, but Commander Baudyš restored order and promised to put things right.

He made Dýha and Chata step forward and so all the villagers could hear it said that they'd be going to jail, without further ado! And the lads had to say sorry to Mrs Holý, but not to the altar boy – he'd been taken off somewhere by his dad to be stitched up. But Commander Baudyš had only been pretending to bawl out Dýha and Chata.

Outside the front of the Home from Home he had us fall in again, and when he liked our lines he shouted, 'Karel!' then he made Karel an orderly. Then Commander Baudyš shouted 'Dýha, Chata, Ilya!' He appointed Dýha commander of the Fedotkin attack squads and Chata commander of the Fedotkin defence squads, and he made me commander of the Fedotkin sabotage squad! Margash heard it, because he was there with Commander Vyžlata and all the longshirts.

That was a ceremonial line-up.

Afterwards, they all surrounded us and congratulated us and Margash congratulated me as well, and he winked at me and shouted cheerily, 'It'll be a doddle now!' and I was the only one who knew what he meant.

We stood around in little huddles and were happy, because after the ceremony a special dinner had been announced. Our little group of saboteurs was joined by Commander Vyžlata. He was tottering a bit. He handed a bottle of booze to Commander Baudyš, then said to me, 'Well, my lad, how about I reassign you to the command post? You and Margash would have uniforms and you'd be a special unit. Guards!'

The boys were silent and so was I.

'Though in uniform or stark naked, few could tell you two apart, could they?' said Commander Vyžlata.

Commander Baudyš clapped him on the shoulder. 'Now, now, me old warhorse!' he said. 'You know what it takes to train up a saboteur and this one here's a natural. Off you go!' Commander Baudyš gave me a shove and our group broke up and mixed in with the other boys, and I fell in behind Orderly Karel, who was the tallest, and I had the Bandits around me.

In the dining room the tables were laid for dinner: huge quantities of frankfurters and bread and gherkins and jam for the longshirts, and not even the longshirts had to go straight to bed.

Commander Vyžlata started the dinner by getting up and saying, 'You can do all the fighting and bruising you want, my lads, but that ain't nothing compared to what the son of the regiment lived through.' Then Commander Vyžlata mopped his face clean of the tears that had gushed from his eyes and, before our hungry gathering, he spoke about Private Fedotkin, saying that not even in forty degrees of frost in the huts of the Vorkuta camp had he abandoned the son of the regiment, nor had the son of the regiment abandoned him. Not once!

Then Commander Vyžlata placed his face in his hands and peeked at us through his hands to check whether we were listening closely to his story... The Commander's tears dripped between the fingers of his clasped hands, then with his head bowed he kept on talking about Fedotkin and the son of the regiment, and me and the others couldn't help wondering how the story of Fedotkin and the son of the regiment ended. Would we ever know? But we were hungry and Commander Vyžlata was sobbing so much that between sobs you could hardly make out a word of the story.

Commander Baudyš slapped Commander Vyžlata on the back and said again, 'Now, now, me old warhorse!' Then Bajza punched me, saying, 'Me old warhorse!' so I punched him back. Commander Vyžlata fell silent and picked up a paintbrush. He turned to our squads as we stood to attention, then sketched in a new face next to Private Fedotkin's in the portrait. He glanced back over his shoulder and shouted, 'For your exemplary actions, I shall now paint a memorial to friendship, and to go with Private Fedotkin I shall paint in one of you, a Czech boy! At ease!'

We pounced on the food. Commander Vyžlata worked on painting the boy until the very end of the celebration, which came soon enough. In the dormitory I felt sick because I'd eaten lots and lots of jam, which I'd taken off the longshirts. I thought about being made squad leader. I couldn't get to sleep for sheer joy. But then I did drop off and slept until morning.

8

Work. Još. In the workshop

The days passed. Every morning we left the Home from Home and trudged off to the village, rather like when we used to go to church with the nuns.

Now it was Commander Baudyš leading us, assigning us jobs to do.

In the morning we walked through mist, then later the sun came out. During the day there was lots of light everywhere. The wind swept the snow, whined and skittered across it. The edges of the frozen snow crumbled away. The wind wooshed at the last snow frozen in tufts of grass. There was no snow left on the rooftops. There was snow left only here and there.

It was not a good time for burning papers! It was not a good time for training in the forest! It was wet everywhere.

The sleet froze us to the bone, even down by the footbridge. There was deep water under the bridge and some huge rocks.

'Right, lads, on this bank we're going to learn how to build levees and defensive ramparts,' said Commander Baudyš, pointing. 'Stay clear of the other bank,' he ordered.

All among the reeds on the bank opposite was the village rubbish dump. 'You get all sorts of stuff in rubbish dumps,' said Páta. 'But not in this one.'

In the frozen reeds there was a rotten door, a tyre, some rusting oil drums and scrap iron. There was lots of iron, its black outlines washed by the black water and overgrown by reeds. Páta said that where there were reeds there was mud. And leeches. We won't be going there, we told ourselves.

The longshirts stayed at the home. Studying and working. Šklíba and Martin were aides to the Commander. Margash too. Ah well.

My world in the village was vast. It had barns where we stored the tiles when Mr Moravčík stripped the roof off the cowshed, and granaries where we piled sacks, and yards that we cleared of dung and chicken droppings, and coal holes that we fetched coal from in scuttles, and sheds where we took bundles of wood that scratched our hands.

In my world there were cellars and stables and sheds full of animals, and there were pigs that would eat anything and nanny goats and billy goats that leapt up onto their shed roof after bits of green in the spring, and a huge bull and cows that kept curling their lips, and some of the animals were nasty, clanking their chains in the dark of their houses, because we didn't smell of the village, but of the Home from Home.

For our benefit Commander Baudyš set up jobs by the stream and in the workshop.

At the stream we worked with stones. The twisted ironwork in the rubbish dump, over which the black water flowed, looked like the skeletons of ghostly animals from the dawn of time, as pictured in *The Catholic Book of Knowledge*. I didn't tell the lads that.

There was a footbridge over the stream and under the bridge the water was deep. We picked rocks out of the stream, passed them to one another and built them into levees and defensive ramparts. That was one shift. The second shift was the reverse: we formed a chain and passed the rocks to one another back into the water. The rocks of the defensive rampart dried in the sun and wind. Until they dried out completely we did physical exercises.

Sometimes Commander Baudyš left us alone by the stream. He would go into the village 'to do some requisitioning', as he put it.

One day, just as he'd left us, along comes Još.

I was passing rocks and suddenly, from behind me, I hear Chata saying something in gippo to Još, an old gippo who had a cottage on the other side of the village, where more gippos lived. Chata and Bajza, and sometimes Silva too, would go there whenever they could... Now we all gathered round Još, who was carrying a sack... It was bulging and moving and Još hit it with his stick. I thought it might be a rat, but it was a weasel. Još told us this was what he did. They'd send for him from the village whenever weasels or martens were killing hens and chickens, and then, with their snouts soaked in blood, they'd eat all the eggs too. Još would lay traps for the weasels and sometimes even caught one... only sometimes! Usually not even the village dogs can catch a weasel! A weasel's fast! It fights like mad to stay alive! Often Još would be given a chicken, even if it was torn ragged and practically dead, and he could always get himself eggs – and that's not all! When he said that, we all laughed. Then Još shoved the sack with the weasel in it in the deep water under the bridge and held the sack down with his stick by the rocks, and the weasel was completely under water and thrashing about like mad. The sack bulged out in every direction and Još held his stick ever so tight in both hands. The weasel fought long and silently and furiously, then died. Još took it out of the sack. Its paws were sticking out sideways.

Chata and Bajza went to see Još at home and we had to work extra to make up for them, because Commander Baudyš knew how much time we needed to put the rocks from the defensive rampart back into the stream, and if we frittered away the time when we were alone, then we'd really find out what having a tough time meant! And we didn't want that.

During the damp and rainy days of the thaw Commander Baudyš found a new subject to add to our education: woodwork and metalwork.

In the early days of our training, Commander Baudyš slept upstairs in the nuns' dormitory, close to Commander Vyžlata and Margash's command post. Later, though, Commander Baudyš arranged things to suit himself, as he put it. He moved into the kitchen.

He had a bench and saws brought in from a van – tiny hacksaws and fret-saws, and a big saw for cutting beams – and he knocked up some shelves and filled them with little boxes of screws, large and small, wire netting and nails. And the fact of him showing us these things, that was part of our training. And because the ground around the piles of ashes left over from the burnt documents was soft now, some of us dug ash pits, while others, under Commander Baudyš's guidance, made wire-netting fronts for rabbit hutches or built shelves for jars of gherkins, tomatoes, sweet corn... whatever they wanted in the village! And Commander Baudyš also repaired locks and alarm clocks and pump motors, and could even mend snapped and rusted threshers.

After we'd done a repair job and returned it, Commander Baudyš received food from the villagers, and we all got to eat it, although any bottles of booze were for him and Commander Vyžlata.

We filled the breaks between jobs with lessons. What sometimes happened was that Commander Baudyš would call me and I'd take the bundle of papers out from under my tracksuit top and the boys gathered round and we revised the names of the hamlets and the positions of streams and triangulation points and committed them to memory. Commander Baudyš commended me. He was of the view that I should have a special leather case for my papers to wear at the waist, but that never happened.

It was soon certain that the lads would still be committing the world drawn on my maps to memory when the thaw came. Especially during the time of the thaw I worked busily at my maps. Sometimes I drew the world from reports by this boy or that. I found an old pillowcase. Then I carried my maps in it under my tracksuit top. At night I kept them under my head.

We worked and we learned things from the booklets and from Commander Baudyš's explanations. In addition to jobs to be done in the village we also worked on installations. That was one branch of workshop practice.

Outdoors it kept raining, and we couldn't practise crawling all day and every day in the soft mud with airguns and gas masks, though we'd have to in a real combat situation! So we would sit around the stove and watch Commander Baudyš's hands cleaning a watch mechanism or dismantling a gearbox or applying a soapstone coating to a piston with a fine cloth. In the kitchen-workshop Commander Baudyš never shouted; sometimes he even laughed. We never created mayhem. You couldn't with Commander Baudyš, but some of us did talk to him. And one evening, Páta coolly asked, 'Commander, why's the boy painted next to Fedotkin a Czech?'

And Commander Baudyš looked at Páta, who was both slitty-eyed and a darkie, and he said, 'Because we happen to be in Czecho. Don't you worry about it. But in the starvation huts of Vorkuta... that, my lads, was international, there you had every type of mug, like here.'

But Páta stamped his foot and said, 'Even so!'

And Dýha whooped, 'Ha, ha! The gippo cowboy!'

'Yob!' said Páta, and Dýha was about to lash out when Páta tossed a cloud of sawdust in his face. Without looking up from the huge bow-saw he was oiling, Commander Baudyš said, 'Orderly, discipline the men!' and Karel struck Páta in the midriff and stuck his chin out at Dýha, and the lads sat down.

When it rained we worked. We also learned things from *Fundamentals of Close Combat*, acting out the positions in the book's drawings. We were soon at the last lesson. We trained by the book both outside and in the kitchen-workshop, where it was warm because of the stove.

I did some thinking about whether I'd rather go with Margash to join the Legion, or to his country.

In Margash's country there would be no village houses in the sleet; no Chapman Forest full of animals just waiting to rip a boy limb from limb. It was a bright place, with grass everywhere. As I worked away at my the task I had been set I thought up ways to fool about in the grass: me, Margash and Margash's brothers. I enjoyed those workshop lessons held in the kitchen when it was raining.

One evening we learned the truth about Fedotkin. Commander Baudyš told us the story of the end of Fedotkin.

We were making a set of rabbit hutches and Commander Baudyš said, 'That's right, keep learning, lads. You know what they say: golden Czech hands. How could I have made it all the way here from that bloody camp at Vorkuta without 'em? That time we were freezing and helpless in the huts of the penal colony at the mercy of the cruel Soviet Russians. Yes lads, and if you think a Russian like that would sweep the flue of a smoking stove, bollocks! He'd just kick it. And when it was minus forty, who do you suppose sealed around the flues in the huts of Vorkuta to keep out the cold, eh? Aye, that was some cold, let me tell you, that time we set out from Buzuluk, meaning our entire Czechoslovak Army Corps... If you didn't wrap your foot-rags properly, you died in the ice and frost. And if a transporter got stuck, who was on hand? Or if a belt snapped and a half-track gave up the ghost, who did they call for, eh? "Baudyš, fall in!" So you see, you lot, learn how to handle a hammer, learn how to work. It'll come in handy one day, believe me!'

We did believe Commander Baudyš, and he was highly pleased and satisfied with us in our workshop lessons.

On many an evening he told us stories until we were quite worn out and until work ended, and in the dormitory his voice was replaced by the voice of Commander Vyžlata, telling the story of Fedotkin and the Czech boy.

That was how our commanders saw to our education.

Commander Baudyš told us how they, some Czech boys, had been called up by the homeland and how they had gone with the Czechoslovak Army Corps all the way from Buzuluk to Prague. In concert with the security services of the Soviets, our homeland had tracked them down even in the death huts of Soviet penal colonies. And Commander Baudyš talked himself hoarse about how the Czechoslovak Army Corps marched in concert with the Red Army from the icy wastes of freezing Buzuluk to the smiling face of Prague in May, and how they had cut down whole hordes of Germans on the way and saved hosts of women and children and defended the Fatherland... 'And now, Commander Vyžlata and I have been called up as educators,' he said, squinting into the fire.

'But then you know, boys, back at the Centre they had thrown in the towel as far as you were concerned. No-one wanted to come here. So for your benefit they enlisted us. The Party enlisted us – the obvious thing to do. And we'll make men of you yet. And when all's said and done, lads, I don't think you've done badly, getting us. Who better to nurture you, human spawn, than us old warhorses, eh? When the end of the world comes nigh once more, you'll be properly prepared. You know, Commander Vyžlata actually raised me, too,' said Commander Baudyš. 'We met each other in the hut for street kids at the Vorkuta camp up there in the Arctic. And Commander Vyžlata was saved, as a Czech boy in a burning village, by Stalin's Flying Brigade, as no doubt you know. The Flying Brigade! Now that, my lads, was a unit of Guards. They gave him an education, believe me. Then, as a foreigner, they shoved him in the camp, the way they used to in the Soviet Union. How I got there, I've no idea! I was little! Then we got hardened in combat, that we did. And now the ones who survived all that have been chosen to teach others. I reckon that's quite right and proper, I do. What do you think? Obviously, not all of us old warhorses who made it back to Prague could make a go of it as teachers. I mean, this war business. Some might've survived it – but without legs. Had 'em whipped off by a grenade – in seconds flat, right out of the blue. A bloke like that with no legs could hardly lead you lot through life, now could he?' said Commander Baudyš, and because he was checking the work we'd duly handed in and was satisfied with it, he was smiling.

And if one of us boys hit himself with a hammer and threw a tantrum or if someone got the shakes because one of his fingers had got frozen or he'd spiked himself on some wires in the mains supply, Commander Baudyš would cool him down – quick as a flash! – and say: 'Compared to the Soviet gulag, you're living in clover here in Siřem, believe me...' and Commander Baudyš used to smile fit to make his whiskers crackle.

And that evening we finally learned what had really happened to Fedotkin. That evening the Commander talked himself hoarse, and when his voice dropped to a low wheezing, someone piped up in a thin little voice: 'And Fedotkin? Did you know Fedotkin?'

'Oh yes, boys, I knew him.' Commander Baudyš fell silent, then he screwed up his eyes even more, because he was thinking so hard.

'And what was Fedotkin doing in Vorkuta?' the same little voice squeaked. I knew whose it was. It was Dýha. He was acting up and squeaking so that no-one would recognize him.

'Fedotkin was waiting for his court martial,' said Commander Baudyš, and we all – me and the other boys – pricked up our ears.

'But how could a war hero like Fedotkin get locked up?' someone asked.

'I never tried to find out,' said Commander Baudyš. 'You know, I was just a street kid, like you lot... and in those terrible camps at Vorkuta. But there you have it – see where I am now!'

'Commander,' Dýha began in his normal voice, 'did you know Fedotkin well?'

'Oh, yes.'

And we were all quiet. Anyone with a hammer stopped hammering, and the boys who were stoking the stove froze where they knelt. That's how keen we were to know, all of us who weren't outside raking ashes, because it happened not to be raining, and finally someone blurted out: 'So what did happen?'

'To Fedotkin you mean, boys? They shot him.'

And Dýha said in his normal voice, 'But why?'

'What's "why" got to do with it?' asked Commander Baudyš. 'That's irrelevant. And anyway, getting shot – that ain't too bad.'

We were all still. We had just learned how Fedotkin met his end.

9

And Fedotkin's boy? Liquidation. Šklíba

The truth is, sometimes we'd be waiting for Commander Vyžlata to tell us his Fedotkin story in the dormitory in the dark and he didn't turn up. That did actually happen!

But that day we didn't care that he hadn't come yet. We knew the truth about how Fedotkin had died. We'd heard it in the kitchen-workshop, and even those who'd been outside digging pits got to hear from the others about Fedotkin being shot.

And the boy? What about Fedotkin's boy? What became of him? Commander Vyžlata was not there to ask.

The truth is that when Commander Vyžlata came in, making the wooden dormitory floor echo with his footfalls, and when he told the story of Fedotkin and the son of the regiment, we did listen – we had to – but we slipped into sleep with our own thoughts in our heads and with endless images from all our training and working. The thing was that many of us now thought much the same about Fedotkin's story as Dýha, who had said, 'Sod it. He snuffed it anyway.'

We were all boys from defence, attack and sabotage squads, and Fedotkin's death by firing squad affected us.

I don't think we were quite so keen to hear the Commander's fairy story any more!

We had admired the undaunted Fedotkin and wanted to be just as courageous and ready to fight as his boy.

And Fedotkin's execution ordered by a court martial affected us, I can tell you!

We didn't want to hear about it!

After the news of Fedotkin's death many of us started talking again about escaping to join the Foreign Legion. I was one of the first.

Soon it was hardly winter at all. Then Šklíba disappeared.

Commander Vyžlata didn't like him. Neither Šklíba nor Martin took part in training exercises, and they didn't go to work either, being the Commander's aides.

But Šklíba did a bunk. He shouldn't have. After that things got a whole lot worse.

The alarm went off. First we gathered round to study the maps that I pulled from under my tracksuit top. I set out the parameters of the search. Commander Baudyš listened closely and sometimes gave a curt nod.

Then we quickly availed ourselves of the requisite arms and equipment, and Commander Baudyš read us our orders.

After Commander Baudyš had given us our orders, our squads began to fear the worst. I feared it too.

But it wasn't that Commander Baudyš didn't like Šklíba. He didn't actually know him! He was just doing what Commander Vyžlata wanted. That was the only reason why he commanded us to 'liquidate Šklíba with cold steel'. He didn't really mean it.

After the order had been given, our squads spread out in assault formation.

Šklíba was soon spotted. He hadn't even got as far as Chapman Forest, where he could have disappeared. But he hadn't made it. He was stumbling. Going slow. He couldn't go very fast in the muddy field full of slush. He didn't even try to avoid the wet stones. All shoes will slip on those.

'You, you and you! You will make the interception!' Commander Baudyš pointed at Mikušinec, Chata and me, and again he gave the order to carry out liquidation by cold steel without waiting for any signal. We set down our knapsacks and airguns and ran ahead.

Chata pretended to trip and twist his ankle painfully.

We ran on. As saboteurs we knew which way the wind was blowing, and that Šklíba could hear us and Commander Baudyš couldn't. Cautiously we called out to Šklíba. He didn't hear.

The shots from the Commander's gun close to his ears had burst his eardrums and he still had some dried blood in his ears even now. I saw it as I knocked him to the ground and pretended to pull my cold steel out of him. He gurgled, but he didn't spray snot all around him like Monkeyface, but dirty tears, yeah, he had those.

We raised him to his feet and took him to Commander Baudyš. We hadn't followed orders, but Commander Baudyš didn't say anything.

At the Home from Home Šklíba went straight into the solitary cell in the cellar, which they say is commonly the case with people who do a bunk at other Homes from Home for ne'er-do-wells like us.

Because we'd tracked down Šklíba so quickly, there was plenty of time left for jobs in the village.

*

Me and Páta were assigned to Mr Cimbura, who sometimes called me 'sonny', sometimes 'Avar' and sometimes 'goggle-eyed sprog', but I didn't care. If he called me 'shitbag' I only pretended not to care. I thought Mr Cimbura didn't remember who I was. I was wrong about that.

Even with me joining them, Chata was still the smallest Bandit. If anybody shouted or swore at him, he hated it.

Mr Cimbura's house was just beyond the village. By the cemetery. I didn't know if Sister Alberta sometimes lived here with him as man and wife. I wasn't bothered.

We wondered: 'Does the old boy keep gherkins in his cellar?' 'No, sweetcorn!' 'Could he have salamis?'

And we went to his cellar window and gawped inside: 'What's he got down there?' There were girls inside!

It was gloomy in the cellar and there were some girls there. All we could see of Mr Cimbura were his feet. He was sitting on something. The sun was blazing down on us, but the girls in the cellar were all wrapped up. They were wearing tracksuits or skirts and they had head-scarves on, so I couldn't tell if Hanka was there. How was I supposed to recognize her in the gloom? Now the girls were singing, so we listened to the song. It went something like this:

We're the girls of the village
and we're bringing you some flowers,
forget-me-nots
and everlastings
from that sweetheart of yours!

And then one girl started dancing in the middle of the others. It wasn't Hanka. And they had a portrait of Czechia in a big golden frame. They were taking the flowers to her. Bunches of flowers lay all around the painting. It looked as if they had painted over some Virgin Mary from the church and turned her into Czechia. The girls weren't topless, which made sense as it was so cold. Pity, I thought to myself, and I reckon Páta thought so too. Mr Cimbura was sitting down and his knees were shaking, though I couldn't tell if it was because of the song or old age. I looked at him and thought, 'It must be ages since I lived in the manor house. In those days Mr Cimbura's legs just wobbled a bit. I don't know how long ago that was.'

Then a different girl started dancing in the middle of the crowd in the cellar, wrapped up warm in her headscarf and fully dressed all over, no doubt because it was so awfully cold in the cellar.

The other girls were clapping. I could see pickaxes and shovels leaning against the wall and a pile of freshly dug soil. The girls were working in the cellar. And then someone suddenly gave me a shove. Páta was shoved too, making him yelp. Some big girls stood over us, swearing and chasing us away from the cellar window. There were two of them and they were a good match for us. They must have been in the cellar. They wore caps and scarves over their long hair, and aprons over their tracksuits and they were in wellies. I badly wanted to see what they were up to in the cellar and what they were singing, but I couldn't. The big girls were pushing at us and trying to chase us away from the window. I was glad nobody could see. If Dýha and Chata and Karel and the rest had seen those unarmed girls shoving me across that muddy yard, it would have been so, so embarrassing – a fate worse than death!

So we waited for Mr Cimbura by the fence. We fooled about, climbing on the fence and joking that it was nothing really, being chased by big girls, though actually we did mind. It was afternoon, the feeble sun had gone down. Páta pointed and said, 'Hey, Ilya. Those things I thought were thistles or something, they're crosses.' The sky was full of dark clouds and the snow that still lay here and there reflected no light, so the crosses in the cemetery on the other side of the fence weren't very clear.

Then we heard: 'That's right, young men, I've a fine view, no doubt about it. If you get up on your tiptoes, you can even see the tomb!' Mr Cimbura had toddled out to find us and was leaning on the fence. 'I often stand here doing nothing, keeping a lookout,' he said. 'But you quit snooping and get down to work. Go on, hop it!'

So we didn't even check in and set about our jobs straight away, and that day it looked as if things were going to be just like old times. But I was wrong.

First Páta spilt the grain for the chickens and Mr Cimbura gave him one hell of a whack across the face and yelled, 'You little brown shit! Who do you take me for? Some Cimbura Rockefeller, you brainless brat!' Then Mr Cimbura settled down in his chair and told us to light a fire with some green pine branches, which we broke down into small bits, and anyone who does that usually gets splinters all over their hands, but never mind that, and Mr Cimbura was drinking water from a big ladle, and he said to Páta, 'I know I can be a bit harsh sometimes. The hens would've pecked it all up, but you have to learn, even if it's the hard way, my lad... Just take it easy, no need to rush things... *slurp-slurp!*... and what's your dad do, by the way?'

And Páta said, 'My old man's a pilot.'

'Don't be stupid, lad,' said Mr Cimbura. 'No pilot would leave you in a rogues' orphanage. No, not a pilot... *slurp-slurp!*... I might even adopt you, but I know shit all about what you really are. You could have some bastard genes or something...' Then Páta suddenly yelped as if he'd pricked himself on the twigs, and he turned and was all white in the face (though he really is a bit on the sunburnt side) and he grabbed the ladle from Mr Cimbura and began laying into him with it, and Mr Cimbura tried to duck, but he couldn't get up on his feet, because Páta wouldn't let him use his arms to lever himself up. And Páta delved into the pile of greenwood by the stove with both hands and lashed at Mr Cimbura with some branches and bloody scratch marks zigzagged all over Mr Cimbura's old face, and Páta danced round and round him and kept on hitting him, and I said, 'Páta! Knock it off!' but Páta had gone crazy.

Mr Cimbura fell off his chair and I felled Páta from behind with a textbook move, and because he fought back I locked him in the best room. You could hear him making matchwood of the best room. But he couldn't get out.

Then I wiped Mr Cimbura's face, and it was like washing the shit off someone's old arse, but I washed the mess of blood and phlegm off his face and went down to the cellar.

There was no whiff of girls in it, just a smell of cellar and cold. If Hanka had been dancing there, I think I'd have recognized her smell.

It was cold down there. In the cellar wall there was a hole, a tunnel. Because I felt a gust of cold from the tunnel that cut right through to my bones, I realized that it led off to somewhere under the cemetery.

Mr Cimbura had just one shelf in his cellar. No decent stash! There were a few eggs, so I cracked one top and bottom and sucked it out... ugh, it was vile! My mouth was full of bitter, black muck. There were no good eggs, just these disgusting black things... I reckon he did it deliberately! My eyes flooded with rage as I spat out the eggy goo, then I smashed the rest of the eggs against the wall – ugh, the stench! They were all off... disgusting. There were some pickled ones in jars and I ate as many as I could, then I trampled on the rest and peed in some of the other jars.

I waited for Commander Baudyš.

A howling draught was blowing out of the hole. I went to the kitchen.

I thought I might have to treat Mr Cimbura some more, but I didn't. Mr Cimbura was sitting by the stove, sipping tea from a mug and his face was all wrinkly with age, but clean. And not a scratch on it, not a single one.

'Hmm, a nasty piece of work you've turned into!' he said the moment I entered the kitchen. I stopped where I was. The twigs crackled in the blazing stove.

'You handled that little brute nicely, though. That counts for something. You've grown. I never liked you much, no, but I never beat you.'

'And I didn't beat you neither,' I said.

'I should think not!' said Mr Cimbura. 'You've been snooping in the cellar, haven't you, my lad? I try to do my bit for the lassies, see. The country's going to the dogs right now. And the people's regime started out so well! The comrades wrung a few bourgeois necks and bent a few gallows, it's true. That counts for something. But now the comrades are getting all cosy with those Moskies. They don't love their country, bloody comrades. But Czechia will cleave them to her fine young bosom and crush 'em! Have you heard about the Moskies, sonny?'

'No, Mr Cimbura.'

'Our stout heroes have been giving the Jerries what for since the beginning o' time. So they'll deal with the Moskies all right too! Whoever heard of 'em before? They comes from Moscow. Russian Tatars, they are, but with their ugly mugs painted white to fool us, so they look like us. Siddown, lad! You used to get me bloody annoyed with all your sleeping. You can't do so much of that now, eh? I don't suppose you want to anyway. You've grown up. Have you notched up your first bird yet?'

I sat down, but I was really scared in case Mr Cimbura started asking about Monkeyface. I was relieved to hear Commander Baudyš's voice and Páta's hollering, because as soon as the Commander entered the hallway Páta started hammering away at the door of the best room, and when Commander Baudyš opened it, he jumped him, though it was pointless attacking Baudýš.

Although the lads kept a tight rein on Páta, he caused considerable confusion and no interrogation of Mr Cimbura or of me by Commander Baudyš took place.

We dragged Páta along and windows opened and mad dogs tugged vainly at their chains. Then our squad passed through the village towards the Home from Home, where we all spread out, because Šklíba had done another bunk – but this time he got away. I never saw him again.

Commander Vyžlata had us line up and Margash was still with him. The Commander was drinking some booze. He had a bottle in his hand and he said that something unfortunate had occurred, that one of us had left after having declined an offer of friendship. Commander Vyžlata shed a tear and bowed his head briefly, then wiped the tear away with a finger and flicked it to the ground. We said nothing... Then, gesturing with both arms, he summoned us into the dining room and we obeyed, because we were anxious, and there, painted on the picture of Private Fedotkin, was a Czech boy in a tracksuit with a green knapsack over his shoulder, and he was handing Private Fedotkin a gun belt. And we stood there in silence. We knew by now that they had killed the brave Private Fedotkin. And I looked towards Margash and Margash looked at me, and I got a shock, because Margash had a face as long as a fiddle, like that time in the cellar, and he was furious, but not in the way some of our lot sometimes were when we lost it a bit, us being psychopaths and all. When any of us got the red mist we looked different from Margash. And now I got angry as well, being full of hatred for Commander Vyžlata, because why should Šklíba have to wander alone through the snow and the forest just on account of the nuns? Why wasn't he here with us, like usual? Why was all this going on? Because of Commander Vyžlata! And it crossed my mind that if Margash said, 'Now!' I'd do what he'd already seen in his dream anyway. 'But how?' I wondered. 'How should I kill the Commander?'

Commander Vyžlata tipped back his bottle of booze and took a swig and flopped down on the floor. With him squatting down like that I could get at his neck. But the Commander suddenly stood the bottle on the floor and quickly stuck one hand in his pocket, making some of the longshirts squeal. Commander Vyžlata's eyes flashed as if he meant to spear us with them, but he stayed sat on the ground and I could have reached him, and the other lads would have helped me, I think... I glanced at Margash and nodded a 'Yes?' at him, but Margash shook his head, meaning 'No!' and that was good, because Commander Baudyš entered the dining room and said, 'Dismissed! Prepare for training!'

So we went outside the Home from Home and lined up in our shorts and T-shirts ready to train for whatever it was we had to do.

We used to train under supervision, under the commands of our commanders, but Commander Vyžlata wasn't training us this time. He was walking up and down our lines and talking about how he'd coped with other scum before this... like the guttersnipes of the Vorkuta camp... and he wasn't going to be put out by a handful of little jerks from Bohemia, so we should all bloody well watch it! That's what Commander Vyžlata said, keeping one hand in his pocket. Then he bellowed, 'Do you know what befell the son of the regiment, what they made him do?... They made an executioner of him, my lads!' The Commander smashed the bottle to the ground and the smallest longshirts squealed. Then Commander Vyžlata told us what it had been like in the freezing cold hell of Vorkuta... after the court martial! And how they had forced him, Vyžlata, to take up the murder weapon and finish off Private Fedotkin... thereby turning his – Vyžlata's – humanity inside out... but what else could he do? 'And what would you have done in the penal colony of icebound Vorkuta? Well?' All that was left of the son of the regiment's hand-sewn uniform were worthless tatters... The son of the regiment had finished off Fedotkin, the man who had been like a father to him. Yep. That's how it went at the snowbound camp in faraway Vorkuta. They saw things differently there.

Commander Vyžlata talked and ranted at us, but we cared sod all about what he was saying. We didn't want to hear any more about Fedotkin and we didn't want to be listening to our commander, because our mate Šklíba had gone.

In the evening we were alone in the dormitory. Commander Vyžlata, along with Margash, had stayed at the command post. Lots of longshirts came creeping into our dormitory, but we didn't chase them out.

The Bandits gathered around Dýha and Karel, and Chata openly took out some cigarettes. We sat there and stood about and our words flittered everywhere, and then we heard Martin saying, 'I'm leaving too!'

We said nothing and watched Martin, and Martin said, 'You lot know nothing. You lark about outside with airguns,' and he slipped off his bed onto the floor and curled up in a ball. We stood round him. Now he was blubbering.

And Karel shouted, 'Leave him be!' as if someone were doing something to Martin. Nobody was doing anything to him.

Martin got up and said, 'You lot know nothing. You haven't been locked up here with the Commander.' Then he goes on, saying that he really hates Commander Vyžlata, because Šklíba is wandering helpless among the ravening beasts of Chapman Forest and he might even be dead. 'I'm getting out of here!' Martin told us, though he'd already said it once, and he stood up.

And Chata said to him, 'And how are you gonna get past Vyžlata and the new lad?'

And Martin sat down.

And Páta said, 'Out of the window would work, with knotted sheets.'

No-one even laughed. I look at the moon, which had suddenly come out above the window, chopping the darkness into shadows. In the shadows that we cast on the walls we looked like grown-ups.

Then things went fast. Páta and Karel knotted some sheets together and Mikušinec gave Martin his sweater, and Dýha took a paper packet out from under the floorboard and Martin took it. I didn't know if my matches were in it, but there was a knife. Its blade glinted and someone gave Martin their tracksuit. Someone else even handed him an anorak and Martin tore off his black rags and got dressed.

As he climbed down the sheets I was afraid he might start kicking or shouting, or even drop down through the rubbish chute, so I didn't watch.

Páta told him what to do. He had already run away like this. When Martin was nearly down, Páta told him, 'We'll leave you some food in the cemetery. Hide in the tomb.'

'Which one?' Martin called back, quietly.

'There's only one.'

'Right,' we heard Martin down below.

And when Martin reached the bottom, Páta tossed him a blanket and Dýha also tossed him a blanket, because it was still very cold at night.

We got into bed and chatted for a while, and Bajza asked Chata, 'Did you give him any salt?' and Chata replied, 'Bollocks, let the old cheesecake cry himself all the salt he needs.' Only then did someone let out a 'Ha, ha!', and I decided to run away as well, then Margash's dream wouldn't come true, and I meant to run away after the others fell asleep, but I fell asleep too, and in the morning we went off with Commander Baudyš to shift rocks.

10

On the rocks and in the village

We were working away on the rocks. The sun blazed above us and jabbed at my head. It blazed above the rubbish tip on the other bank, drying out the reedbed. Water that had been locked in ice crashed into the pieces of iron and made the stinking things in the tip move about. In the winter the tip didn't stink.

Anyone who picked up a rock or a bit of wood with leeches clinging to it out of the stream and put it down on the grass would watch a while as the leeches shrank and dropped off in the heat. That didn't interest me. That morning we weren't sent to track down Martin. He wasn't on Commander Baudyš's list of squads. That morning, like many before, we worked on the rocks. But that day everything was different.

Commander Baudyš took a trolley to the stream. It was pushed by Karel, the orderly. The trolley was piled high with technical equipment from the kitchen-workshop. Commander Baudyš never let the trolley out of his sight, or if he did it was only to look at his watch. He was waiting for something or somebody. I wasn't really interested.

As always, we formed a chain by the stream. We heaved at the rocks and passed them one to another out of the water and onto the bank.

Chata held on to me. I pulled at the rocks that poked above the surface, all wet and jumbled. I was at the end of the chain, because I'm light... Chata suddenly pulled me over to him onto one rock and pointed under the footbridge and – oh dear – there trapped in the rocks was Martin's blanket. It was completely waterlogged.

I broke away from Chata and jumped off the rocks onto the grass, moving a little way off, then I curled up in a ball like some little kid. I suddenly felt sick. My head was full of the image of Martin lying motionless among the wet, black stones, water streaming over him. I wasn't feeling at all good. My life was not good.

Then Chata was right there beside me. He gave me a kick and said, 'Get up, man!'

A little way off, on the bank, stood Commander Baudyš, staring at his watch.

Now all the lads were scrambling onto the bank with the rocks. I got up and grabbed one where it was lying. We built them up into ramparts and in a low voice I told Karel about Martin's blanket, and Chata told Mikušinec. We didn't move our lips. The lads passed it on and before long we all knew, and the mist – chilly and clammy as it rose from the water under the footbridge where it was still cold – was like dark, choking smoke that made us cough as it swirled around, like church candles when someone snuffs them out after Mass. I had no idea I still remembered the candles. Commander Baudyš didn't know about Martin. We wouldn't tell him. He could kiss our arses now.

We were all lined up by the ramparts and defences and the squad commanders – me included! – were about to report, but... we could all hear it! We could hear this clattering noise, and it was the clatter of a pickup truck. The pickup was stopping! And some strange bloke hauled himself out! Hauled himself, because he had no legs! Not one! He held himself up on sticks, crutches. He held on to the pickup. None of us laughed.

Commander Baudyš went up to him and his face went from white to red and back. He went over to the stranger and he wasn't happy. He didn't like him.

But when he stopped in front of the stranger, he gave a smart salute, like soldiers do. Just like he'd taught us.

'At ease!' said the crutch man. It was interesting seeing somebody give Commander Baudyš orders.

They stood there gawping at each other.

Our ranks began to break up without Baudyš having stood us down. We broke up by ourselves.

'It's you!' said Commander Baudyš, and he stopped standing to attention and threw up his arms as if totally amazed. The man with the crutches just nodded.

'Where's the equipment?' he asked. Commander Baudyš waved to Karel, who went over to them, pushing the trolley full of wires and technical equipment from the kitchen-workshop. The guy on crutches bent down, holding on to the door of his pickup, and took a close look at all those wires and fittings, and the other stuff Commander Baudyš and Orderly Karel had piled on the trolley.

Then the man told us to step up. We didn't budge. Commander Baudyš glanced at us and you could tell he was glad. He was glad and proud that we were his. He gave an order. We shifted ranks, rearranged ourselves and lined up neatly. Karel took up his position as orderly. The stranger made a couple of swishes with his crutches, and now he was sitting on the trolley and upright he was quite tall. First of all, he said, he was called Major Žinka, but we should address him as 'Commander, sir'. He carried on talking very loudly: 'Listen, boys! It's said that you're the most neglected thugs in the country. Your commanders have turned you into a fine unit...' And so this Commander Žinka went on about all the stuff we knew, and behind me Bajza hissed, 'More vermin from Vorkuta,' and Commander Žinka said that the process of regeneration in Czechoslovakia was getting up the noses of the Soviet party bigwigs, and that hordes of Moskies wanted to crush Czechoslovakia under their boots.

I noticed that the sun was roasting and the clammy mist from the water under the footbridge had disappeared, and we were all exposed to the strong sunlight and had to screw up our eyes, and Commander Žinka went on and on about a spirit of defiance spreading throughout Czechoslovakia like a wildfire in the steppes, and that Soviet armoured corps might be lined up on the borders of liberal Czechoslovakia and that our freedom was in jeopardy, but we would not buckle! And I imagined that if hordes of jackbooted Moskies arrived, they might kill Commander Žinka, which would be great. Me and Margash would grab Monkeyface and beat it. And Commander Žinka was saying that he knew we would give a good account of ourselves, just like the boy soldiers of the Hussites. 'I was a boy myself once, lads!' he said. 'So I know that all healthy boys know how to fight and enjoy fighting.' Commander Žinka told us all this so we knew, but we couldn't give a shit. We were worn out from lugging rocks... and Martin! Oh dear. Without being given the order, we all sat down in the grass and started chewing stalks, perched on various rocks that had dried out in the wind and sun.

Commander Baudyš and Karel were fussing around the trolley, and Commander Žinka was still going on and on. We heard, but we didn't listen, until he said, 'While the representatives of a regenerated Czechoslovakia are defending socialism with a human face at the meeting in Čierna nad Tisou...', then Bajza got a fit of the giggles and started squirming, his lips twitching, and quietly muttered, 'Arsehole.' Commander Žinka leaned towards us from the trolley. 'You boy,' he said, 'have you got epilepsy?' and Páta roared, 'Nah, he's got syphilis!' and that was the end of Commander Žinka's speech. We got up, but something had changed.

Something had changed because Commander Baudyš suddenly turned to go. He looked back just once and ran an eye over our formation, which had begun to stand easy without being ordered to, and he just went... he was leaving. Just like that! Karel trotted after him and he was running, and we stared open-mouthed after our mate Karel, and when Karel caught up with Commander Baudyš he fell in two steps behind him with the easy stride of a detachment on the march, then both of them slowly disappeared from sight and we were left gawping at each other, and Dýha shouted, 'Hey! Karel! Come back!' and carried on like that, hopping up and down, but Karel couldn't hear him, or if he could he pretended not to.

And crutchy Commander Žinka watched it all, with his head held high and his chin stuck out, looking sidelong after the departing Commander Baudyš, and we all clustered round the trolley. Then Chata kicked me in the leg and Bajza tugged at my sleeve. I'm commander of the saboteurs! Chata and Bajza and me, we crawled under the footbridge, looking around the rocks, and poked at the dark water with sticks. All we could find was the blanket. No Martin. We were glad. I saw Chata and Bajza smiling and chattering away in their own language, so I told them to speak normal.

Bajza flung his stick in the water. 'He did the right thing,' he said. 'You have to dump stuff when you're escaping. 'Cause of dogs and things.'

'There ain't no dogs to chase escapees here,' I said, as if they didn't know.

'All dogs chase escapees,' Chata said.

'So where'd he get to?' Bajza asked.

'He doesn't know where the cemetery with the tomb is,' I said. 'He isn't one of us saboteurs!'

'Only a Whitey could escape down the main road,' said Chata.

'Hmm,' said Bajza, and I also said, 'Hmm,' though I'd never done a runner.

'He could still be downstream, couldn't he?' I said. 'Carried by the water, no?' I looked across the water, and it was washing over the scrap iron and other stuff in the tip across the stream.

They both laughed and went on in their own language. That pissed me off.

'The stones wouldn't let him pass,' Bajza explained with a grin, as if he were talking to some idiot, though he was smaller than me.

We clambered onto the bank.

The lads were now on the road by the trolley and the pickup. If our longshirts had happened along and squashed up tight, they would have all fitted on. We could all have gone somewhere. But that wasn't going to happen.

Commander Žinka sat in the pickup's cab. He had chucked his

crutches on the floor, and we could see his stumps wrapped in great big leather patches... As he sat there, we could see that he was huge, with paws like a bear out of Chapman Forest. He was explaining stuff to the lads and doing great things with his hands among the tools: 'And this is a loudspeaker, lads, and this is an amplifier,' and he kept pulling stuff off the pickup and more stuff off the trolley. The lads handed him at once whatever he pointed to, and he put it all together and then he was holding the loudspeaker with wires hanging from it... He had loads of these loudspeaker things on the back of the pickup... 'And you screw it together here, and so we've got a public address system and the revolution can begin any time you like, my lads.' Commander Žinka smiled at them and the lads were laughing too, having fun, listening... But I couldn't be bothered. I dunno what's wrong with me.

'Boys,' said Commander Žinka, 'we'll go into the village now and hang the wires and loudspeakers up, then we can inform the villagers about what's going on in Czechoslovakia!'

Dýha asked if we would be able to talk into a loudspeaker.

Žinka reached out a gigantic paw and smiled and patted Dýha on the shoulder, and he said, 'I like your initiative, boy. What would you say into it?'

'That altar boys are buggers, Commander, sir,' said Dýha, making such a funny face that we fell about laughing.

Commander Žinka said, 'No, that's not a good idea. But anyway, let's get going.'

Dýha and Páta led the procession, pushing the trolley along. The pickup followed them at a walking pace, and behind it there was us, the Bandits, and we were sorry we weren't on field manoeuvres. It would have been better to go into the village with airguns.

The pickup stopped outside the first farmhouse, belonging to the Kropáčeks. Commander Žinka pulled a stepladder off the pickup, opened it and swung himself onto it straight from the cab. He jammed his stumps between the rungs until his leather patches squeaked, helping himself along with his teeth. Then he fixed the first loudspeaker to the Kropáčeks' fence, and Mr Kropáček came out and said, 'What's all this, then?'

Commander Žinka handed him a sheet of paper. Mr Kropáček had to sign it and, syllable by syllable, he worked out that he was accepting material responsibility for the loudspeaker, and he gawped and said, 'And comrade, sir... erm, Mr Comrade...'

'Address me as "Commander."!' ordered Commander Žinka.

'Will you have a dram, Commander?'

'But of course!' said Commander Žinka. Grabbing the top rungs, he swung back a bit and launched himself into the cab. Mr Kropáček called his wife, and she brought out a bottle and a tray of glasses, and other people came along as well. We stood by the fence and were a bit surprised to see a couple of the altar boys arriving with the villagers, so Chata ripped a piece of wood from the fence, and Dýha and Mikušinec, who were behind us, picked up some stones and niftily slipped them to us in the front, but all the people from Siřem, including the altar boys, were just gawping at the pickup, and at the stranger, Commander Žinka, and at the loudspeaker.

Then we moved on again and arrived at the Holýs', where the stabbed and stitched-up altar boy lived, and Mr and Mrs Holý came out and Commander Žinka gave them a sheet of paper, and they signed it and they also fetched a bottle and poured a drink for

Mr Kropáček as well, and for anyone else who wanted one, but not us, and Mrs Holý was holding her hankie to her eyes and sobbing, and she said, 'So we haven't been forgotten by them in Prague! And how's that nice Mr Dubček?' And Commander Žinka had his stumps jammed firmly in the ladder, and he was attaching the loudspeaker wires with pliers, and he called down, 'Sasha Dubček's okay!' and they all shouted 'Hurrah!' and 'Hurrah!' and Mr Holasa's 'Hurrah!' was the loudest. He had brought a whole pail of sausages and frankfurters, and Mrs Holasa carried a tray full of bread!

Everyone helped themselves and Mr Holasa even came over to us – the Bandits! – and he said, 'All right, lads, you have some too... Today's a great day!'

Our front line swarmed around the bucket and cleaned it right out.

Then we moved on. The whole village was on the march and some people were waving Czechoslovak flags and red, white and blue banners, some of which had slogans like THE TRUTH PREVAILS stitched on them, and the old women of Siřem were at the church, but the church was closed. Father Francis wasn't there any more. Hadn't been for a long time. The church was all boarded up, and Commander Žinka ordered a loudspeaker to be erected in front of the church, and we helped him with it.

Dýha knew which wires he needed. Páta handed him the pliers, and Mikušinec the hammer. Me and Chata, we held the ladder... but I felt queasy.

It was warmer among the houses than down by the stream. The great big sun was unbearable, pounding away at the white walls of the cottages. The heat bore down on me and I didn't know whether I could take it. I felt hot inside as well. I was supposed to be holding the ladder while Žinka swung on it, but it felt more like I was holding on to support myself.

We were in the middle of a great free-for-all. We were surrounded by the entire populace of Siřem. I looked at the people between the rungs of the ladder, breathing the hot air. Over by the church I could see a girl in a yellow dress and next to her a girl in a red dress. They waved and their gazes cut right into me. I looked away and there was a girl in a green dress standing right by the ladder; we were so close that we could have touched cheeks. She was smiling at me, holding out a tray of little glasses. Men's hands immediately reached for the tray, so then all I could see were their sweaty vests and shirts and their sweaty necks, and then the girl slipped out of the circle of thirsty men, taking her tray with her, and she was gone.

I half-turned my head towards the church and glimpsed the fluttering red dress. It disappeared in the crowd and the fluttering of red, white and blue flags. I kept blinking, because of the glare of the sun bouncing off the church walls and all the white-painted house-fronts right into my eyes, and Chata thumped me on the shoulder, because I'd stood on his foot, and he said, 'Hold the ladder!'

This time there were far more people in front of the church than when Commander Baudyš was trying Dýha and Chata, and as Commander Žinka clambered down from the ladder one of the old village women knelt down and kissed his hand, saying, 'We've got our freedom at last!' and she was crying. In front of the church two old women were pushing Mr Cimbura along in a wheelchair, and there were more girls either side of him. But no Hanka! In no time at all, they had laid a plank across two crates and Mr Cimbura floated round to the other side of the plank, and he had something. A wodge of something or other, which he was handing out. I watched. The altar boys were milling around him, and Dýha! – Dýha as well – joined them, as cool as a cucumber. Mr Cimbura was handing out pictures of Czechia. Dýha was followed by Mikuš and then Mikušinec came back and showed us the pictures of Czechia! I wanted one too, but me and Chata were busy folding away the ladder, so I couldn't get one.

People were passing bottles around and eating, and gangs of Siřem boys were running about everywhere. Dýha was back with us. Us Bandits were together again.

Then Mr Dašler turned up and he had loads of tarts in the cab of his pickup. They were still warm. I know, because we got some as well. And Commander Žinka was sitting down and Mr Holasa and Mr Dašler and Mr Moravčík were standing up in the back of the pickup and chatting. Mrs Kropek was waving a banner saying THE TRUTH PREVAILS and Mrs Holasa and Mrs Dašler and other people were waving Czech flags and various religious banners like those I saw inside the church... And Commander Žinka told everyone there that the evil times under the scourge of Sovietism and bolshevism would never return and that our leadership with Sasha Dubček at their head ('Hurrah! Hurrah!' everyone roared at this point, even us Bandits) would never betray the people! Then Mr Holasa took the microphone and read from a sheet of paper, saying that it came from Prague, declaring the creation of the Siřem Autonomous Zone – Siaz! – and that in many places all over the country zones of resistance were springing up against the incursion of foreign troops. And everybody clapped like crazy, then Commander Žinka spoke into the loudspeaker and said that the Soviet Union was standing ready on the borders, but that this time the West wouldn't abandon us and that there would be no repetition of Munich! Then Mr Holasa grabbed the loudspeaker from him and bellowed, 'Just let 'em come! We'll give 'em what for!' and everybody clapped and shouted and rejoiced. People sounded the horns on their cars and tractors, which they drove around covered in flags, then they sang: 'Where is my home? Water murmurs among the meadows...' and so on. That's our national anthem. We used to learn it. And none of us was allowed to move, and I looked round and the ones who had been kneeling quickly got up and they'd all taken off their hats and caps, and some of them were crying, goodness knows why! Stupid buggers. Mikušinec and Páta also started snivelling, but they were just taking the piss... And then there was a moment's silence, so they could all wipe away their tears.

Then total mayhem broke out with shouts of 'Hurrah!' and 'Three cheers!' and hats and caps flying through the air, and the people with flags swished them this way and that. I was all agog, forgetting to keep my wits about me – then someone grabbed me and dragged me into a side street, and then I was lying on the ground and the altar boy Holý was standing over me and there were two others with him, and Holý said, 'Ciao, Avar!' and then they twisted my arms and dragged me off somewhere between the cottages.

11

Making friends. Nuns is nuns. Killing

They hauled me off into someone's backyard and there was Martin sitting there, lounging in the sun and munching something, and when he saw me he shouted, 'Hi there!'

I still expected to get a good beating, but the altar boys just stood around, so I said to Martin, 'Hi! Everything okay?'

And he said, 'Sure. You're going to be our negotiator, man.' Then he told the altar boys, as if he were pals with them, 'He's a saboteur, guys.'

Holý came over to me and said, 'So you're a Russian saboteur, are you? You Russian?

'Bollocks, man!' shouted Martin. 'That's Ilya.'

And the boy with freckles said, 'You a real Czech? Say something in Czech.'

'What?' I said.

And he said, 'Sing the national anthem!'

So I sang a bit of it, the only bit I could remember. Deep down I was thinking, 'Now you can start blubbering, arseholes!'

Then another of the altar boys said to Holý, 'Come off it, man, any

Russian saboteur knows our national anthem. It's the first thing they get taught, man.'

'That's true,' said Holý. 'I want Martin as our negotiator. The Russian guy can wait in the sty.'

'Ilya ain't no Russian,' insisted Martin. 'Wait here, will you?' he said to me. I told him I didn't care either way. He gave me what he had been munching on and it was a delicious-looking bacon and paprika sandwich, so I ate it. Then they shut me in the pigsty. There was no pig or anything, just a piggy smell and it was really hot. I was in there for a long time, but I didn't mind. Then one of the altar boys came in and said, 'I'm Pepper, 'cause I'm hot-headed. You Russian or not?'

'No.'

'So what are you?'

How was I supposed to know? 'I'm from the Home,' I said.

And he said, 'Come on then.'

We left the yard and went up the hillside, where more altar boys were sitting around and messing about with something by the glowing embers of a fire.

We sat down and from the feathers and the squidgy bits of mud lying around I could tell it was a chicken packed in clay, because Chata and Páta and even Karel and anyone else who's ever tried to do a runner had told us about it a thousand times.

'I know what you've got there, guys. It's gippo chicken! Have you got any salt?'

But they said nothing and just swapped glances, and then Holý said, 'We ain't no gippos.'

Suddenly we heard whistling and shouting – 'La-a-a-ads!' – and it's Martin with the altar boys behind him, and the Bandits!

They reached us and sat down around the fire, and you could tell they were all on speaking terms. They chatted away like normal, and Dýha had a picture of Czechia glued to his tracksuit. The altar boys extracted the chicken. Pepper tapped the clay with a knife and it fell away from the meat. It smelt great. I munched away at the bones and meat, and it was hot and good. Martin stood up and explained – chiefly to me, as he'd told the Bandits already – how the altar boys had met him when he lost his way in the woods, and they'd taken him to their den on Fell Crag and they'd made peace... And the blanket? The altar boys had rigged it up to look as if Martin had got away by swimming!

Then Freckles stepped up and said, 'I'm on guard and I see this ghost! And the ghost's this here borstal boy Martin and he's dragging blankets along! And he's blubbering. Yeah, you was, be honest! He sees me and he says, "Excuse me, which way is it to the cemetery?" Ha, ha!' Freckles laughed so much that he ended up on his back, kicking his legs in the air. 'Yeah!' and 'Sure!' roared the others and they laughed like mad... Then we talked about what would happen if the Russians stormed the country. There'd be a war, obviously, and the Bohemian Lion would roar! It'd be a right old ding-dong! Brilliant!

We sat in the grass and made friends with the altar boys, and talked about what fun we had when we were at war and reminisced about different events in that war, then Holý said, 'Peace can be fun as well!' 'Too right!' we all shouted. Then Pepper got up and said that they'd had their den, their defensive position, up on the crag, for a long time and that they could use a couple of extra hands. And we cheered and roared and Dýha shouted, 'Long live Czechia! Long live Siaz!' and everyone else joined in. I leaned across to Dýha and looked at the crumpled picture of Czechia on his tracksuit... And Dýha said it would be best to get a picture of Czechia permanently tattooed on our skin... Mikušinec explained that Czechia was depicted naked so that she could drag crying babies out of burning cottages and breast-feed them on the spot, at least that's what the old biddies at the church used to say, and Dýha told him, 'You're a baby yourself, man.' Holý said, 'Yeah, when we join the fighting, the nuns'll bring us food and medicine and ammunition up to Fell Crag. They could get past the patrols dressed up as crippled old women going out to collect fire-wood...' Then he went on to say that he respected us guys from the Home and that it was great that the guys from the Crag and the guys from the Home would make up a joint defensive force, but there's one thing he wanted to make clear to avoid any squabbling and ar-guments: 'Nuns is nuns, guys, right? And we ain't got no nuns.' We muttered and said things like 'Yeah!', 'Uh-huh', and 'Right!' Now we were all chatting normally again, so I asked Dýha, 'Where's that Bajza kid and Chata... and little Silva?' 'Those lads, they don't want gippos, and they preferred to go to Još's anyway.' 'I see,' I said, 'and there's someone else missing... Páta?' Dýha shrugged, saying, 'Dunno,' and passed me a bottle, and I took a swig and it was the first time I'd felt good all day.

When I woke up I had a headache. Little stars were crashing about inside my head and I threw up. All that was left of the bonfire were some smoking twigs and there was nobody around on the trampled grass any more... They'd cleared off. It was dark. I was chilled to the bone. My bones were all aching, as if someone had been tugging at them... I reached the church and kept to the shadows by the cottages and the village pond, and there were no dogs and no people anywhere.

I went down the hill towards the Home from Home and there were no lights on inside... I knew I was going to run away at last.

All I needed to do was tell Margash.

And I would tell him that I hadn't had his dream.

I got to the bottom of the hill and there in the grass... it was the whole gang of altar boys, and the Bandits as well. They were sitting on the slope, gawping at the Home from Home, and none of its lights were on and it was dark all around us and the moon was shining.

'Hi!' I said, but only Dýha turned round and said quietly, 'Ciao!'

I'm glad, because I thought they'd run away from me to Fell Crag, that they didn't want me in their den. Martin came over and said, 'Hi! They don't want you,' and I said, 'I know, but I don't care,' and Martin said, 'Liar! You do!' and I said, 'Wrong... I don't!' And then Dýha and Mikušinec and some of the altar boys came over, and Freckles said to me, 'Come up to the crag with us, but you must bring weapons and things.'

I ignored him. I looked at Dýha.

'Go on,' he said. 'Get some knives and stuff!'

And I asked, 'What's with the Home? What's going on?'

'Look, man,' said Dýha. 'They've taken the longshirts away! All of 'em! On lorries.'

That was quite a shock, because the Home with no longshirts... well, it was weird!

'We saw it. They took 'em away. They had their tracksuits and anoraks on, everything. The youngsters have gone!' Dýha told me, shaking his head as if he couldn't believe it himself.

'Some blokes shoved them on the back of the truck,' he said. 'We've combed the whole place in case any of the little 'uns were hiding, but no. Not one, man.'

We kept staring and we could hardly see the Home from Home in the dark, and it was full of silence. It *was* our Home from Home, and it *wasn't*. Something had changed. I could tell, and I didn't like it.

'And is Vyžlata there?' I asked, 'cause we both knew that was what mattered most now.

Dýha shrugged, 'We haven't seen him. Nor that new boy!'

The boys in the grass said nothing.

'You command the saboteurs,' said Dýha.

So I said, 'Yeah, but I've said all I want to.' I set off. Mikušinec called after me 'Ilya!' and someone else called out quietly: 'Ilya, kid, watch yourself!'

I pretended not to hear. I walked on quickly. If I turned back now and asked Mikušinec for the picture of Czechia, he'd let me have it. But there was no turning back. I was outside the Home from Home. I reached for the door handle. The door opened.

I peeked into the workshop-kitchen: shiny tools oiled and tidy everywhere. I drank from the tap, gulping down the cold water and remembering how I used to stand guard in there. Beneath me was the cellar. I felt sick. In my head and in my body. I must have been made ill by everything that had happened.

I went up the stairs, moving fast like a rat. On the first floor I almost tripped on a bundle of documents and broke my neck. There were still vast piles of this twentieth-century tat that we hadn't had time to burn. The beds in the dorm had no blankets, pillows, nothing.

I went on, invisible. There *was* someone in the Home from Home. I could tell.

I took off my shoes and tip-toed past the dining room. You can't hear me, I thought. I am a commander of saboteurs. Private Fedotkin was watching to check I didn't do a bunk. I wanted to get that stuff – the knives and things. I didn't know what was going to happen.

I slunk from step to step, and I was outside the shortpants' dormitory.

I slipped across to Dýha's bed, grabbed a floorboard, then another, and I stuck my hand in the secret hiding place.

The knives were wrapped in old documents. I crammed the matches, the ball of string and some other small items inside my track-suit top, stuffing them in there with my maps. The blade of a kitchen knife stuck out through the paper and was all shiny. I kept the knives in my hand and left.

I was about to slip out into the corridor, but I couldn't. I heard footsteps. It felt like the very worst moment in my whole life.

I leaned back against the door of Sister Leontina's study and I was in. I slithered backwards, tripped and fell – papers, candles and knives, the whole lot went flying. I'd tripped over Monkeyface's tub. I picked up some of the parcels, the rest I hid in various corners. My maps were safely in their place.

Commander Vyžlata had made Sister Leontina's study his command post.

I decided to try the nuns' bedroom. I turned the door handle and slipped into the gloom, blinking like a rat. That's how I could see in the semi-darkness... The door of the command post had just squeaked. Vyžlata had switched on the light, which shone on my feet through the crack under the door.

We were in neighbouring rooms. I crawled over to the door and peeped through the crack.

Margash was pouring water into the tub. He tipped buckets full of hot water into it. The steam made him cough. It was swirling around him. Vyžlata undressed and sat in the tub. Margash poured water over him. Vyžlata had his back to me. I had never ever cut anyone's throat, though they did teach us how to. I didn't know how I was supposed to kill him. I didn't know how I was supposed to get out of there. I waited to see what happened. Maybe something would happen by itself.

Vyžlata was wallowing in the tub and splashing.

I could see his back. He was washing with soap. It took ages. The steam kept rising from each bucketload. There were splashes on the floor all around the tub. Finally, Vyžlata got up. He came towards me. Towards my door. I crept under the nearest bed.

The door opened and Margash came in. He was naked. Vyžlata followed him. Margash lay down on the bed I was hiding under. Vyžlata lay down next to him. For a while they just lay there. I peeked out stealthily to see what was going on. Then Vyžlata hauled himself up over Margash and dropped back down. Like doing exercises. I could see the flesh on his belly wobbling, and I could see his neck and shoulders as he bobbed up and down on the bed... I closed my eyes and I could hear Vyžlata breathing heavily and Margash whimpering... and it was disgusting... I opened my eyes again and took another peek, and I saw Vyžlata's sweaty belly wobbling and flying this way and that, and the slapping noise it made... I shouted out... They couldn't hear me, because Vyžlata was wailing a terrible wail and it was all mixed in with Margash's whimpering... I started talking, so I didn't have to hear them, and I said all the dirty words the nuns wouldn't let us say. Then I ripped the paper off the kitchen knife and stuck it up under the falling belly. The belly speared itself on the knife, and I could feel its warmth on my hands... The belly reared up again, coming free from the knife, and now all three of us were shrieking, because the belly came hurtling down again onto the kitchen knife I was still holding. The blood squirted in my eyes. Then Vyžlata flopped sideways and spiked his hip on the knife as well... and it was over.

I crawled out. From the other side, Margash peeped under the bed, probably wondering what I was doing there... He scrabbled around under the bed, pulling out another knife, ripping off its paper wrapping, and stabbed Vyžlata in the neck.

I sat on the bed. Margash said, 'Quick!' He wrapped the body in a sheet. We were both splattered with blood, and I said as much. Margash glanced at me and said, 'Aha.'

We ripped the sheets off more beds and tossed them over the corpse.

We went into Sister Leontina's study and used Vyžlata's bath water to wash ourselves. There was no other water. We helped each other: 'There's some more here!' 'You've a spot there!' We helped each other, because we didn't have a mirror. So we stood facing each other and we were each other's mirrors, except that Margash was naked.

'Get dressed!' I told him. He put his vest and pants on, and a jumper and his tracksuit, which he had to hand. My clothes were bloodstained, but not much. Most of it was on my face and hands. I checked my pillowcase map. It was under my tracksuit. It had become part of my clothes. I wiped the blood from the knives as well. I spotted Margash wrapping a knife in a clean document, then keeping it, so

I did the same. I just stuck it behind me, inside my trouser elastic. Margash did the same.

'What now?' I asked.

'We'll take him downstairs,' said Margash.

'You glad?'

'Yeah. Very,' Margash said, and then we were emptying the tub together. We both had the same idea. We poured the water onto the bed, because the mattress would soak it up and there wouldn't be a telltale puddle. That was Margash's idea.

We picked up Vyžlata in the sheets and he was pretty heavy, and I remembered all those bundles of paper and scuttles of coal, and the rocks and sacks of flour and buckets of slops. Vyžlata was heavy, but we got him across to the tub. I wondered whether his arms had gone stiff like the weasel's paws. But they hadn't. They were flabby.

We put Vyžlata in the wash-tub, then Margash clapped his hand to his forehead and said, 'Hang on!' He nipped back into the nuns' bedroom. I was left alone with the corpse, and I didn't like it. But Margash came straight back. He tossed that big black pistol into the tub. I said nothing.

I went first and Margash held the back end of the tub. We made our way down the stairs, bumping on each one, then I heard a strange sound – *grx-grx!* – and Margash called out 'Stop!'

I put my whole weight against the tub and Margash explained that it was Vyžlata's teeth clacking. He wound a rag torn from a sheet around the Commander's chin and part of his head and we set off again, and this time it was okay.

Then one of Vyžlata's hands flopped over the edge of the tub. It dangled along the side, as if the dead man were trying to scratch the wall. I was glad when Margash tucked it back in and covered it up.

We carried on down past each floor to the dining room. There was someone there! We put down the wash-tub and went to see. Our knives were behind us, held in place by our trouser elastic. If you keep your kitchen knife like that, you know about it with every move you make.

Sitting on the table in the dining room was Žinka, dead opposite the portrait of Private Fedotkin and the Czech boy. He had an open bottle of booze. In one hand was a screwdriver and there was a big radio on the table in front of him. There was masses of technical equipment around. He must have brought it all in while the killing was happening. His crutches were propped against the table.

He gawped at us. He pressed down on the table and kind of got up, stretching. Suddenly he looked terribly pale! We could see his Adam's apple bobbing up and down. He was gulping. His eyeballs were popping. He stretched out a hand. His paw was aiming right at us. He was staring.

Margash tittered. I also laughed.

'Rascals!' said Žinka. 'There are two of you, aren't there?'

'Yes, Commander,' said Margash.

'Phew, that's a relief!' squawked the legless Commander Žinka, placing one paw on his heart. 'I was afraid I was seeing double.' He leaned over the table, grabbed the bottle of booze and flung it at the wall where it shattered. He would never have got away with making a mess like that with Commander Vyžlata in charge.

'Right!' said Žinka. 'My mind's made up: I'm not going to touch another drop ever again. Not until our final victory over the Soviets!

That was quite a fright you gave me, lads! Thought I'd got a touch of the DTs.'

We said nothing. I waited until Margash nodded, then I approached Commander Žinka. I kept one hand on the knife at my back. I was glad it was me who had the bright idea of where to keep a kitchen knife.

'I've had the DTs before, see.' Commander Žinka's head was nodding. 'Imagine, some vodka found its way into our block one day. No, you can't imagine it. I got so drunk I was seeing double. Double the number of huts in the penal colony, double the number of prisoners and double the number of butchers. Believe me, lads, it was almost more than a chap could bear.'

Commander Žinka fell silent for a moment, then started splashing his paw in a pool of alcohol on the table. We, too, were silent. Then Commander Žinka nodded towards the instruments on the table.

'The Radio Free Siřem transmitter... What do you think of that, then? And what about the good working people in the village? Marvellous, eh? Well, my boys! I'll be expecting you to be like the boy soldiers of the Hussites and fight to the last man!' This last bit Commander Žinka bellowed.

'Yes sir, Commander, sir,' we bellowed in turn, standing to attention on the spot. And Commander Žinka said he must arrange a meeting of all the commanders, and asked if we had seen Commander Vyžlata anywhere.

We fidgeted... In *Fundamentals of Close Combat* it says nothing about the combat situation where two boys are supposed to liquidate a legless giant squatting on a table-top, but Margash hissed and I made a move... Margash was almost beside the Commander. I was looking Commander Žinka right in the eye, my right hand on the knife inside my trousers behind me, and as Margash moved again I shouted, 'Up there!' to make Žinka look upwards, and as he raised his head I rammed the blade right into his neck. Saboteurs use this sort of trick all of the time, as we've been taught.

But Commander Žinka shouted, 'Aha, so he's up there, upstairs! Thank you, lads.' Then he reached for his crutches, slipped off the table, clipped his stumps into the leather straps on the crutches and sets off, as if nothing had happened. He left the dining room, banging away at the floor with his crutches, while me and Margash, we just stared after him... I was terrified he would find the body... and he did!

We heard a bang and a flop, and Žinka was lying there on the landing! His crutches as well! But all he did was shout, 'Who the hell left this wash-tub here, for crying out loud?' Then he grabbed his crutches and scrabbled his way up the stairs, groping step by step, rolling over the steps and slipping back down, cursing and swearing, and then he was over the top step and rolling around on the landing. He chucked his crutches angrily ahead of him and didn't even care whether he hurt himself on the floor – he was probably used to it. Me and Margash, we leapt up the stairs after him and when he entered the sisters' bedroom with a roar, Margash tossed one crutch in after him and we slammed the door shut and turned the key that was in the lock.

We leaned against the door to get our breath back, and I said, 'I'm glad we didn't kill him! He's not that bad,' and Margash said, 'You're right!'

We stayed for a while and listened to Commander Žinka roaring as he hammered away at the door. Then we grabbed the wash-tub and trundled it down the stairs so fast that Vyžlata fell out outside the kitchen-workshop and we had to stuff him back in, and he was all cold and slimy and disgusting, and it was a good thing that we did it.

In the passage to the cellar Margash told me to hold on to the tub, so I put all of my weight behind it, and I was alone again with Vyžlata. But Margash came straight back from the kitchen-workshop and tossed a huge saw and an axe into the tub, which was pretty heavy by then, bearing down on me as I struggled step by step.

We got the tub down into the cellar water, and then it was heavier than ever. Margash could only find two candles, so every few metres we had to go back and get them. We were dragging the tub along, bent over, and in the bobbing shadows on the wall we looked like hunched animals. Finally we reach the grille where the grave was. We removed the grille and pushed aside the mound of papers, and we were right next to the cover and Margash said, 'You go now!'

'What?'

'Go now!'

'But I wanna stay here with you!'

'You can't.'

'Bollocks... how come?'

'It wasn't in the dream.'

Margash braced himself against the tub and tipped it over, and the corpse in the sheet tumbled out, and its head slipped free and hit a stone on the broken floor, and the saw, which had also fallen out, also clanged against the stone.

The axe was in Margash's hand.

'You're not gonna cut me, are you?' I asked him, though I didn't really care.

Margash said, 'No! 'Course not.'

'What are you gonna do after I go?'

'Never you mind,' he said. 'Go now.'

I made my way through the cellar, telling myself that if he had cut me, it wouldn't matter. I went through the cellar and I couldn't see any shadows, because Margash had kept the candles so that he could see.

12

In the firing line

The Bandits weren't outside. I didn't care. My head was full of images of how we'd killed Vyžlata. Everything had happened so quickly that the images only started popping up now. If I stopped, the image in my head froze as well. I walked fast, so as to get through all the images as quickly as possible, so they'd stop coming.

Then suddenly I heard, 'Is that you, boy?' Mr Kropáček was holding a rifle and he said, 'Siaz! Now you say the password!' He'd said 'Siaz', so I said, 'Czechia!' and Mr Kropáček nodded and said, 'Follow me, boy!' and I followed him to wherever it was I was supposed to be going.

In the sitting room sat Mrs Kropáček and also the Moravčíks, and Mr and Mrs Holý and somebody else. They had the television on. Mrs Kropáček said they'd be only too happy to hear any orders I'd brought from the HQ of the Siřem Autonomous Zone, but for now I should shut up and wait by the wall, because they were watching the news.

Talking pictures went by on the television. I'd never seen this piece of technical equipment before.

'We have heard and seen that Soviet units have entered the Republic

and that the Czechoslovak Army has been offering heroic, sustained and effective resistance...' Mrs Kropáček was crying, and Mrs Holý blessed herself with the sign of the Cross and yelped, 'Our poor boys!' But Mr Holý roared, 'Ha, ha!' and thumped the table with his fist, and Mr Moravčík and Mr Kropáček kept thumping the table with their fists and laughing and shouting, 'Just you come and get it, you Russkies, you bastards! Ha, ha! The Russkies have arrived!' And Mr Kropáček showed Mr Moravčík his rifle, and Mr Moravčík said, 'Huh, all you kept hidden from the Commies was your poaching piece, while I – see!' and he held up a huge pistol. And then we all went out into the yard in the dark. The stars were out and Mr Moravčík and Mr Kropáček fired into the air, and in other parts of Siřem people had come out, the Russkies having arrived in Czechoslovakia, and they were blasting away at the sky. And suddenly all hell broke out in Siřem, and dogs howled and in the distance we could see lights all around and fires blazing all the way to the horizon.

Then we went back into the sitting room and Mr Kropáček poured everyone a shot – me too! – and he said, 'Right folks! I drink to the moment when Nato and the Yanks launch their bombers!' We drank up, then sat in front of the television again.

Now Mr Moravčík got up and looked at me, and said, 'And now, folks, permit me to drink a toast to this lad here!'

I was amazed that he was honouring me like this. They thought I was a messenger from the Siaz HQ, so they thought they were honouring the Siaz HQ. The men were smiling at me and the women were smiling, and they all drank another shot.

We stared at the box and the news was over. What was coming next? Mr Kropáček reached out towards me and thumped me on the back, and said, 'This'll be something for this young fellow here, just look at his ears twitching like he can't wait...' Everybody laughed – 'Ha, ha, ha!' – and Mrs Kropáček said, 'Leave the lad alone, Les. He's a courier and on duty,' and she took my glass away, but empty.

We sat and watched television, and the lady on the telly revealed the fairy-tale title of the next programme: *Enchanting River*! And at that very instant I must have gone mad, because it suddenly hit me how badly Margash had let me down. After all, I had hoped to leave Siřem for his country! That we'd bury Monkeyface in the sweet-scented grass of a wonderful land! I must have been mad. I was shocked by how much I loathed all of these people, these Siřem people who had called me a rat and an Avar and a filthy beast and a nutcase, and they had given me a stool to sit on to watch television, and they'd known they'd let me, the whole time I was there. Then they started nodding off on their seats and in their armchairs... I must have fallen asleep too. I dreamed about a chicken in embers and I was picking it out of the fire, taking it out of its clay and tapping it, and it was alive and we went off together into the big wide world... and then I heard giggling and loud laughter, and Mrs Kropáček saying, 'Les, you mucky pup! Get that kid out of here!' And there was a river on the telly with a naked girl in it. She was swimming and pawing at the water, arching her back in the water and looking straight at me... Czechia come to life, with long hair, standing in the water. I could see her breasts and her beautiful face... and the people in the room were like one big face, patted together out of a mound of flesh, and that fleshy mug went 'Ha, ha, ha!' at me. The stool tipped over and I jumped up and ran away, and I was suddenly outdoors in the dark and the cold, and, breathing as much air as I possibly could, I leaned back against the barn and wanked myself off and squirted my seed on the ground.

And before it even dawned on me that this was the very best moment of my life, it had passed.

Inside they poured me another drink. There was no girl on the television, or any troops, and me having had weapons training, I seized Mr Kropáček's rifle like a pro, but he slapped me on the hand and said, 'Now then, lad!'

I raised my hand to my mouth and bit it, quick and vicious-like, like a wolf, and suddenly I knew that no-one would ever dare to shout at me again. No-one would dare to slap me or call me 'animal' or 'filthy beast'. No-one would ever dare to pull my ear or bash me or call me 'little shit' or 'little bugger', because I could kill them – not with a rifle or my bare hands or a knife, but just kill them.

And Mr Kropáček suddenly realized all this too and he knew, and he looked at me and they'd all realized, they all knew, so they just gawped at me. 'What's coming next?' their eyes all asked.

'Nothing. I'll let you off for now,' I thought to myself, and out loud I said, 'I know a boy whose dad's a wolf. How about that?'

Mrs Moravčík spluttered and said, 'Sure you do, lad, and he was brought by a stork, just like you!' 'By a lady stork,' Mr Moravčík chipped in, poking her in the chest, and Mrs Moravčík went, 'Tee-hee,' and Mrs Kropáček said, 'A wolf? That's nothing, but how about a randy old goat?' and they all went, 'Yeah, a goat!' And Mr Kropáček said, 'Come, come, old thing!' and downed another shot and started choking, and Mr Holý shouted, 'You stud, you!' and Mrs Moravčík giggled and squealed, 'Goodness, you men! You're all goat here and stud there, but you're just filthy pigs...' and Mrs Moravčík took a deep breath, ready to say something else, but then we heard this almighty bang, then another and another, and suddenly there was light everywhere outside and the light smashed into the window, breaking the glass, which came flying in at us and we ran for it.

The sky was falling down! Giant storks were flying over the earth, flapping their wings, which were like sails of fire, and there were more great bangs, and the storks snapped their beaks – *tak-tak-tak-tak!* – and landed at somebody's feet, but I couldn't help laughing... Because in those fluttering shadows of the sky I saw pigs instead of clouds! The air was full of squealing piglets, and there was even a huge sow crawling across the black sky, and the shadows of billy goats and nanny goats leaping up high, dog shadows and cockerel shadows riding on the shadows of pigs! And a weasel with a bloody snout was begging on its hind legs in front of some hens that were miaowing like cats... It was great fun, all these rollicking shadows! And above the non-stop rumbling made by the heavens as they cracked open I could hear pigs grunting, goats bleating, and stallions and bulls stamping their hooves, making a throaty rattle, foaming at the mouth... Someone grabbed me by the shoulder and picked me up, and suddenly I was out of all that racket and chaos. Mr Moravčík and Mr Kropáček were standing together and looking up at the sky, as were the others. We stood in darkness. The sky was still thundering. Light still flew across it. But now it was far away.

'Christ almighty!' said Mr Kropáček. 'They're bombing Louny!'

'Shit!' said Mr Moravčík. 'So it can't be the Yanks.'

'They could've made a mistake,' someone said.

'The Yanks don't make mistakes,' said someone else.

For a moment we were all silent.

Then someone said, 'It's not Nato. That's not the Yanks. It's the Russians.'

Then some woman squeaked, 'Oh God!' But the others stayed silent.

'Where's the lad?' someone asked.

And someone said, 'Quick, find the boy!'

Mr Moravčík came towards me with his arms held out, and Mr Kropáček was also groping in the darkness. They were looking for me! I dodged out of the way and from the road a light whipped through the gloom. It rumbled and shrieked over my head. The Kropáčeks' cottage shuddered in flames and gradually collapsed. I could hear clanking and roaring coming from the road. There were some monsters by the bridge, crammed together. They had pointy beaks like storks, but they were tanks.

The air hissed again and I heard *vroweeee!* There was a flash of fire above me and a column of white smoke rose up in the darkness at the very spot where the people from the house had been standing. I took a step towards the bridge and went towards the monsters with my arms raised, outstretched. I went towards the shellfire, with my back to the people trying to catch me, and from the bridge it did it again: *vroweeee!* The air hissed and one of the tanks drove through the burning house. With a roar and a clank the tank stopped right in front of me, and rising up on top of it was the figure of a man in uniform, and he also raised his arms towards me, and I skipped up and over the tracks like a weasel and now I was on the tank with my dad. We tramp towards each other across the tank's armour plating, and we laugh for joy in the dark and the smoke and the thudding of shells. We rejoice and embrace! Otherwise I'd have fallen off!

Dad hugged me to him. I sank my face in his belly and I was amazed to have found my father exactly where Commander Vyžlata had told us. Shells whizzed past us. You could still hear shouting, but Dad held me tight, and I got this flash of an idea that even if this man wasn't my dad, it was definitely better to be standing on a tank than to be a corpse lying shot to ribbons under it. I guess that's obvious.

II
Tank Troops

13

And things started to happen! Sacks and violence.
The sweetness of the world. Dago

And that's how I came to know Captain Yegorov that night.

And things started to happen.

All I can remember from the succession of days that followed is the roasting, blazing daytime. It was very hot. We flew along, and the days and nights were coloured by the flashes that our column's weapons spat whenever the need arose.

Our isolated tank column criss-crossed the rebellious Czech countryside. The insurgents had torn down the signposts marking towns and villages, making it totally impossible for us to find our bearings in the open.

That much I gathered from what an orderly, Kantariya, said. As soon as me and Captain Yegorov, whose embrace had rescued me, jumped down off the armour plating of the lead tank, Gunner Kantariya and I unloaded the command tent for Captain Yegorov from the two pickups that made up our supply train.

I spent part of that night and the following morning answering the questions asked by the little band of tank crewmen and sub-machine-gunners. It was a friendly, informal interrogation. The experienced fighting men of the Soviet armoured corps were pleased to have met me. In the land of the Czechs they had grown accustomed to being sworn at, stoned and shot at by snipers. Whereas me, marching towards the tanks with my arms held high, I had seemed more like some boy fallen from the skies. They were pleased that I had greeted them in their own language. During the interrogation, not one of these smoking, smiling, fighting men had asked me about my parents. Later I understood that many of them saw the army as their family. I blessed all those at the Home from Home who had come from the Soviet Union and spoke their language, even though the nuns had tried to ban it. For it was only thanks to what they had taught me that I was of any use to my rescuers.

I spent that first night with Captain Yegorov in his tent, and when he ordered me to remove his boots I quickly understood that the trick was to kneel, grab one boot and hold it tight, while the exhausted captain levered gently against my shoulder with his other boot, gave a little kick with one leg and a jerk with the other and so liberated his leg from the boot's firm embrace. Only then did Captain Yegorov collapse onto his folding camp bed, while I wrapped myself in one of the many rugs that made up the soft, multicoloured floor of the command tent and fell asleep as well.

It happened in the morning, while we were drawing rations.

After answering all of the questions, I was assigned to the hull front of the lead tank in the column.

Gunner Kantariya brought me the bottom half of a tank crewman's uniform, while Gunner Timosha brought me the top half of a tank crewman's uniform, and we turned them up and pinned them.

As I was getting changed, the bundle of documents fell out from under my tracksuit top.

Gunner Kantariya tore one up and niftily rolled himself a cigarette, but when Captain Yegorov saw this he grabbed him by the ear and gave him a cuff.

Then Captain Yegorov pored long and hard over the maps I had drawn on the documents. During my explanation, he kept nodding in agreement.

I'd had saboteur training and now it came into its own. And if the Soviet soldiers still had any doubts that I'd been sent from heaven, now they were dispelled.

I described the world as mapped on the documents that had fallen from under my tracksuit top and Captain Yegorov listened closely. Then he clapped me on the shoulder and said, '*Molodets!*'

At the time I knew nothing about the special assignment of the 'Happy Song' tank column. I had no idea why we were cruising around the countryside and scouring it. I didn't know what or who we were looking for.

Nor did I know that the defiant Czechs had torn down and destroyed all of the notices and signposts and town and village signs absolutely everywhere, nor that Captain Yegorov's tank column, cut off for some strange reason from the main body of the Warsaw Pact troops, was wandering about the country lost.

That first morning of my life in the turned-up uniform of a Soviet soldier was spent watching Captain Yegorov and his taciturn band of tank crewmen and gunners study my maps long and hard. Then Captain Yegorov jabbed a finger into one of them at the point where the village of Tomašín was, and our column moved off.

And things started to happen!

*

I saw the world from the front hull plating of the tank, and I heard the world in the roar of its engine, and in the crackling and whistling of the radio, and the crackling of the transmitter inside the tank, and in the raised voices spluttering protests at the Soviet occupiers, crazed voices coming from the loudspeakers that had been erected in every village around Chapman Forest, just like in Siřem, and I also saw the world on the televisions inside captured but not yet demolished houses and cottages, but television held no more surprises for me. I didn't give a damn about it anyway, because there was never a naked girl on it. The television screens were just filled with newsreels from various battles, and you couldn't even tell which side was reporting, because the Russians often overdubbed Czech transmissions and vice versa, and sometimes the Czechs spoke Russian and the Russians Czech so as to confuse and frighten each other, and nobody knew what was really going on.

All the bonfires of the century converged on us, while the iron hammers of the age whizzed through the air above and pounded the landscape like an anvil. Hunkered down in my snug made from rags on the front hull of the lead tank, I realized that as interpreter to the 'Happy Song' tank column I had tumbled headlong into the greatest event of the twentieth century: the Czecho-Russian War.

It was summer and the land of the Czechs shuddered and shook under our tanks, and the horizon was filled with the smoke of fires. The armies of five nations of the Warsaw Pact, led by the Guards regiments of the Soviet Army, had attacked Czechoslovakia and an uprising had broken out.

Guiding the tank column around the Siřem area was dead easy. My maps perfectly depicted the landmarks around Chapman Forest.

Me and Captain Yegorov cruised the countryside aboard the lead tank, smashing pockets of resistance. We pored over my maps point by point, and my world became vast. I saw the world from the front hull plating of the tank, high above the heat-softened asphalt, over which the air quivered in blasts from our engines.

I surveyed all the footbridges and wayside shrines and triangulation points that I knew from our training sessions, and I guided the column safely. So we burnt down Tomašín, because some Czechs threw Molotov cocktails at us, and we fought doggedly against snipers hidden in treetops and barns. I pinpointed the last of them to Captain Yegorov with my arm outstretched and my thumb raised, and I estimated the distance with my fingers and reported it, exactly according to *The Motorized Rifleman's Handbook*, and when the barrel of our lead tank flashed and the sniper disappeared along with the treetop, Captain Yegorov put his arm around me and said to his men, 'That's my boy!' and the soldiers laughed, and Gunner Kantariya exclaimed, 'That was your first bag!'

And so on the squishy asphalt of Tomašín village we laughed for joy, because we'd destroyed a treacherous sniper. But we didn't laugh long, because we were attacked by members of the 1st company of the Jan Žižka Motorized Rifle Division of the Czechoslovak People's Army, and they didn't stop attacking us until we had killed lots of them.

And this was a new situation, since the Czechoslovak Army had joined sides with the rebels and therefore had betrayed the other armies of the Warsaw Pact.

I told Captain Yegorov what unit the dead belonged to after reading various papers taken from their pockets, and I translated their letters, but not quite in full because they began with things like

My love, I'm thinking of you... or *Hi Gran, I'm well...* Captain Yegorov just waved them away. But we didn't find any decent maps on the dead men.

And from the rasping transmitter in the tank and the radio receiver in the commander's tent I gathered that the Bohemian Lion had roared and the entire land was in revolt.

After we were attacked for the first time by a regular army corps, gunners Kantariya and Timosha, accustomed to killing cowards in cottages, sank into contemplation. Gunner Timosha said he couldn't understand how the Czechoslovak Army could take defensive action, betraying the armies of five nations of the Warsaw Pact, but Gunner Kantariya wasn't one for moping around, and with a whistle and a snap of his fingers he started dancing on the tank's front hull, as if to challenge the low, dismal clouds... Kantariya's dancing was a challenge to the land of the Czechs and a warning as well... The tank crews cheered him on, but I couldn't work out who had betrayed whom and where that left me. What would happen if I were spotted on the tank by, say, Mr Kropáček with his poaching piece or Mr Moravčík with his pistol? Who was that sniper we'd made mincemeat of? Was it someone I knew? And what would Dýha or Karel think if they could see me now? And I got the idea that from now on I would only look out at the world from my tank with my face blackened, and I was about to scoop up a handful of axle grease – a common subterfuge when you're in a hostile alien environment – when I heard a voice I knew well coming from the tank's radio down below, in between the whistling and crackling of the signal. And so, as swift as a weasel, I dropped inside the tank, and the clapping and whistling sub-machine-gunners who were still admiring Kantariya's dancing didn't find it at all odd: Ilya the interpreter was merely going about his work.

I dropped inside the tank and put on my headphones. The announcement – '*Hello, hello, Radio Free Siřem calling...*' – was followed by a terrible barrage of obscenities and profanities, many in Czech and many in Russian. It was Commander Žinka calling the people to arms and giving instructions on how to produce effective home-made weapons, as well as advice on the tactics of partisan warfare, including poisoning wells. He even talked about a scorched earth policy. Judging from the obscenities and profanities, I decided that Commander Žinka had not quite stuck to his pledge to give up alcohol, and I imagined Margash and me standing in front of Žinka with our knives down our trousers, still wet after washing off Vyžlata's blood, while he assembled the Radio Free Siřem transmitter. And I remembered the depths of the cellar at the Home from Home and what lay there, and I told myself that because of the rebels who listened to Radio Free Siřem and ambushed us and tore down signs and demolished bridges, we couldn't even get our tank column past Chapman Forest and leave Siřem far behind, and I was sorry that we, Margash and me, hadn't managed to kill Žinka in the end.

And so we cruised the countryside. Sometimes Czech bandits blocked our way with barricades, and in some places that we had previously driven through unmolested we met with gunfire. We were indifferent by then to the crack of hunting rifles and poaching pieces, but more and more we were subjected to volleys of automatic fire, and on the lead tank Captain Yegorov was frowning.

Sometimes, even during our evening halt and with his boots already removed, Captain Yegorov would listen to Radio Free Siřem.

During Radio Free Siřem's transmissions Captain Yegorov would drum his fingers on the top of the folding desk in the command tent, and I judged from his silence and the gloom that furrowed his imperious brow that the destruction of the Radio Free Siřem transmitter would make Captain Yegorov very happy.

But I didn't want to go into Siřem! I'd been using my maps to direct the tank column away from Siřem – as far away as possible.

Reading maps and using the Czech language were part of my job description. I only abandoned my snug on the front hull of the tank during battle situations, provided there was time. I was small enough not to restrict the movement of the tank's gun barrel, but I always wanted to be as far away from the cannon as possible. In battle situations I stuck close to the prudent Gunner Timosha and the roguish Gunner Kantariya, who never stopped cracking jokes, even in a blaze of shellfire. I was just following Captain Yegorov's orders. In the calm of evening, inside the command tent, me and gunners Kantariya and Timosha would see to the needs of our commander.

Kantariya and Timosha also looked after the supply train. They had the drivers and crews of both pickups in the train under their command.

It was like this: every time we destroyed a pocket of Czech resistance, Kantariya and Timosha would drive out in the two pickups. They would load onto them kitchen clocks, rugs, stag statuettes, church plate, wall decorations, and also selected fancy crockery and anything else that Captain Yegorov requested.

Money, jewels, watches taken from the dead and various other small items were stuffed in sacks by Kantariya and Timosha. It all belonged to Captain Yegorov.

At night it was me who guarded the sacks, but I wasn't allowed anywhere near the supply pickups. The two gunners made that plain from the outset. That was fine by me and I made no attempt to discover their secret. I had plenty of work of my own to do, thank you very much.

During that long succession of days, which were all much alike, I lived pressed tight to the tank's armour plating, snuggling up to the iron like a beetle mimicking the bark of a tree, and no-one ever called me a 'little bugger!' or a 'filthy beast!' or 'Avar!' or a 'poor slob!' Nobody there ever spoke to me like that. Bullets from the sub-machine-gunners' Kalashnikovs and the NCOs' side arms would have killed them on the spot if they had. Our column carried massive quantities of weapons and supplies and fuel, and nobody could touch us.

My task was to report everything I knew about my field training to Captain Yegorov. I reported where signposts were. I knew in advance where we'd get sight of a church tower, where there could be snipers or valuables, and only I knew which way and how to get inside grain stores, where there could well be pockets of resistance.

In the tank column I alone knew that barns also have small doors through which insurgent Czechs could cut and run for the open, and I alone knew that the cellars under the village houses were often linked by passageways, and where to look for them.

Yet I sensed that soon we would have covered the entire area marked on my maps, and then what would happen? I didn't want to go to Siřem. We trundled round and round in circles through the heart of Bohemia.

Commander Žinka and his Radio Free Siřem transmitter were to blame for that.

Following his instructions, people tore down the signposts and tried to lure our column into Chapman Forest with decoy fire.

We would come up to signposts and find them whitewashed out.

We criss-crossed villages and hamlets, and burnt down isolated farms with hostile people lurking in them, but nowhere were there any names for these villages, and the people we captured just shook their heads fearfully, and said in Russian, 'Don't know!'

In our entire column only I understood the Czech announcements that drifted our way from the loudspeakers in the villages just before we shot them to smithereens.

It was one of my jobs as interpreter to translate them.

I gathered that while in many places disorientated Soviet and other Warsaw Pact soldiers were sitting around in their barracks doing nothing, Czech units, armed to the teeth, were taking over arms factories, occupying airports and aerodromes, demolishing bridges and hunting down the Warsaw Pact armies.

The Warsaw Pact armies had been surprised at the stubborn opposition of the Czechoslovak People's Army and various armed bands of insurgents.

We had thought that the very first strike by our troops would bring the Czechs to their knees, and then the only people ruling in Prague would be traitors and collaborators, and the whole of Czechoslovakia would become a defenceless satellite of the Soviet Union. '*Obviously, that was their miscalculation,*' the radio announced.

Radio Free Siřem reported that heroic Sasha Dubček was leading the resistance of his people from somewhere below ground at Prague Castle and that the silver-flecked Vltava was awash with the corpses of occupying troops.

'*Following the attack by the invasion forces and the outbreak of a popular uprising, which has been given effective support by the Czechoslovak People's Army, the movements of Warsaw Pact troops within Czechoslovakia have been severely restricted. We've got the wretched Soviets in a clinch!*' the radio reported. Then, after its proud call sign ('*The Truth Prevails!*'), Radio Free Siřem usually played the song 'Arise, Ye Holy Warriors of Blaník', followed by the anthem 'Where is My Home?'.

The radio played these songs over and over again, and before long they even began to be whistled by the good-humoured Gunner Kantariya and other soldiers in our column.

Meanwhile, the number of sacks in the pickups continued to grow. They were hidden under tarpaulins.

The sub-machine-gunners and pickup drivers whistled merrily as they went about their tasks, because they didn't understand the radio reports.

The radio said that the land of the Czechs was undefeated, yet still more and more Soviet, Polish, Hungarian, Bulgarian and East German units came streaming in.

Also, the radio often spoke of the incredible feats of popular Czech outlaw-heroes.

It was then that I caught the name of Commander Baudyš.

The Soviet command issued an order for all radio transmitters to be destroyed, one by one, in any sector where their armies were operating.

On the day when the gunners and tank crews, headed by Captain Yegorov, heard a radio report that a Slovak national uprising had broken out and that the eagles of the Carpathians had swept aside the invading Soviet units, and that together with the lions of Bohemia they had the enemy in their clutches, Captain Yegorov ordered the radio to be switched off and no-one was allowed to listen to it.

He focused all of his attention on the Radio Free Siřem transmitter in our sector. But we couldn't put it out of action, because we hadn't found it, and I really didn't want to go back to Siřem.

'*Attention!*' shouted the radio, in Czech and in Russian, and the sound rumbled out of wirelesses inside every cottage, and the Czechoslovak People's Army fought hard and not one Czech or Slovak officer capitulated without a shot being fired, and the Czech voices coming over the loudspeakers were full of hatred, and the talking heads on television heaped abuse on the Soviet soldiers. '*Isolated groups are fighting their way through the countryside!*' they announced. '*Don't talk to the occupiers! Don't offer them a glass of water! Sit tight and await the arrival of the armed forces of the civilized world!*'

The Czechs we interrogated knew only one Russian word: '*Neznaju*', 'I don't know'. Yet those village loudspeakers emitted a constant stream of invective at the Russian soldiers, and walls were daubed with slogans and red stars intertwined with swastikas, and lots of the inscriptions were in Cyrillic, and our soldiers weren't interested in being offered water by the people we interrogated, but in knowing where we were, but the people didn't tell them.

And so we moved about according to my maps, eliminating any bandits in the sector.

We were at war and sometimes the movement of our column along the minor roads around Chapman Forest meant fighting for every square inch, at times relying on brute violence. We also tried to live a normal life, like drinking tea in the evening. Before joining the army, some of the soldiers and NCOs of the 'Happy Song' tank column had lived ordinary lives. But on the tanks we lived only violence. Living violence means that any single moment of one's life can suddenly turn into the violence that ends in death. That wasn't in the handbooks.

One morning I walked into the woods whistling a tune, just to... to squat down, to relieve myself like soldiers do. I went into the woods a little way from the tank, just two or three steps until I was hidden by a wall of greenery, the road well out of sight, then something cracked above me and a net fell over me, pulling tight, and a hand over my mouth stopped me from crying out.

They carried me in the net like a rabbit, deeper and deeper into the woods, where they shook me out onto the ground. There were four of them, armed with poaching rifles over their shoulders and knives in their hands.

'God, it's just a lad!' spluttered one of them in Czech.

'Who are you?' he asked me.

'I'm Ilya!' I blurted out, and to stop them killing me there and then I started gabbling about the Home from Home, Commander Baudyš, the tank column and all that.

'I see. So you're a Baudyš boy?' said one of the bandits, letting out a low whistle.

And then it started. They asked about the Russian column's fire-power, the names of the commanding officers, our numbers and the weak points in the column, like dented armour. They asked about the level of our stocks and fuel supplies, and you could tell from their questions that they had had some training, and I told them everything, even about Captain Yegorov's sacks. It was easy for me, because I'd been trained too.

And when I explained how I'd been guiding the tanks and the two pickups in circles round and round the area using my maps, their chief patted me on the shoulder and said, 'Well done, lad!'

They give me some tasty bread and salt pork, and I ate it, though I was far from hungry. Then their chief said, 'Okay, off you go...' and I said, 'What?' Having talked to them I didn't feel much like eliminating bandit gangs any more, but their chief said, 'You've got a job to do, haven't you?' Then he added, 'And you can always drop messages inside some roadside shrine. That'll work, the aggressor being illiterate and all, ha, ha, ha!' Then they vanished into a thicket. Since they obviously didn't want me with them in the forest, I stood up and headed back to the tank column.

I didn't tell anyone there about the interrogation. I'm not mad.

During the day I had plenty of jobs to do in the 'Happy Song' tank column. By night my job was to guard Captain Yegorov's sacks.

After a day full of the tensions of battle, the Captain enjoyed sitting in his tent and sorting out their shiny and precious contents. He soon realized they might be useful. For me there was the joy of pulling a little lever or straightening a bit of bent metal plating and setting an ancient silver watch bearing a portrait of Czechia going again. Captain Yegorov called this type of watch *'devochka'* – 'the maiden' – and he was fond of it. Many items were a bit sooty and battle-scarred. There was plenty of repair work to do. I remembered Commander Baudyš and mentally thanked him for all those woodwork and metalwork lessons when he'd taught us to respect the craftsmanship of 'golden Czech hands'.

Later, I was present at actions that presaged more spoils to come.

The church in the village of Bataj held many treasures, which the Captain saved from the flames that destroyed the church. Carved saints, pictures of the Madonna or Czechia, silver and gold plate belonging to the priest and to God. In the village of Skryje the priest buried the church treasures under the entrance to the vicarage. He only volunteered this information under interrogation. He was happy to hand over lots of gold and silver teaspoons as well.

The captain's sacks also accepted money. All currencies were welcome. After a string of interrogations, especially of cowardly non-combatants, we sometimes also found cute-looking money from those faraway, foreign Nato states Germany and America. Captain Yegorov took this as evidence that the bandit gangs were being financed by Western capital. There were many, many sacks.

It was a great honour for me to be allowed to assist Captain Yegorov during those peaceful evening moments, and sometimes I would tie up the sacks and sometimes untie them. The captain trusted me so much that he would even tie me to the sacks for the night. Having heaved his boots off by using me as leverage, he waved me away, and, tied to the sacks of valuables and money, I would snuggle down in my rugs.

Of course, after that Captain Yegorov carried on smoking, thinking or whistling on his camp bed. Sometimes he looked at his pictures. These came into his keeping after the capture of Tomašín and other pockets of resistance.

I must admit I was a bit surprised when, on one of my first days in the army, Captain Yegorov took me behind the tank and showed me these coloured pictures. They were images of sometimes comical animals from faraway places. He showed me a camel, a tiger, a duck-billed platypus, a kudu and other creatures, and asked if I'd seen any of them.

I assured him that, to the best of my knowledge, these animals didn't live in Chapman Forest.

Sometimes, during rare moments of leisure, the other men of the 'Happy Song' tank column also looked at pictures like these.

Once I caught Gunner Kantariya swapping a picture of an elephant for one of a zebra with Gunner Timosha, while they engaged in a light-hearted squabble accompanied by bursts of laughter. Gunner Kantariya had two elephants in his collection, but not a single zebra.

I knew all these animals from my nature lessons long ago, when the nuns had taught us. And I also remembered many of the illustrations in *The Catholic Book of Knowledge*.

At this time I didn't fully understand the ways of Soviet soldiers. I just assumed they were having lessons on the tanks.

It also occurred to me that they thought they were conquering Africa.

At the time, I knew nothing at all about the special assignment of the 'Happy Song' tank column.

That was soon to change.

That night I made the acquaintance of Willy. Willy Dagobert, the midget Dago.

I'd been crying in the night. I was lying wrapped in the rugs I was guarding, because it was the time of my guard duty, although after a day full of fighting I was in a kind of limbo, only then I wasn't in limbo, I was just blubbering.

All of us kids from the Home from Home had learned not only to speak without moving our lips during the endless roll-calls and lineups, but also to cry without making a sound, because if we'd disturbed the others in the dormitory, we'd have got a smack in the mouth; that's how things were in the older boys' dormitory, because one boy crying ruins everyone's sleep.

Blubbering in silence is easy, provided the blubberer learns to catch the snot and saliva and tears and keep swallowing them as he breathes in and out; the rhythm can even restore his calm and he can fall asleep.

I was blubbering then because there wasn't time to while our tank column pushed onwards or while we were conquering pockets of resistance, and above all there wasn't time to process the images that kept popping up in my head.

That day, me, Gunner Timosha and Gunner Kantariya made up the crew of the lead tank, and we had just captured a fragrant avenue of cherry trees, so we were celebrating noisily, reaching up to drag down the branches full of cherries that arched above our heads, un-picked, because the Czechs who had previously been stubbornly de-fending the avenue were now lying on the ground with holes in their heads and bodies or had fled into the fields. And a new watch on Gun-ner Timosha's wrist glinted under the blazing sun, and he was smil-ing, and Gunner Kantariya was laughing too, nudging me with his elbow and shrieking in Russian, 'Ilya, where are all the Czech girls?' We stuffed ourselves with cherries and our mouths were full of the sweet juice, and I was filled with the sweetness of the world, and I wanted the sub-machine-gunners to let me have a Kalashnikov as well, because I could handle a gun, they'd see! And I reached out for orderly Timo-sha's sub-machine gun, but his face suddenly hardened, as did Gunner Kantariya's face, and one said, '*Niet!*' and the other said, 'No you don't!', and I understood that even though I was one of them – that is, although I was the 'Happy Song' tank column's interpreter – in reality I wasn't quite one of them.

And I thought about what we had done to the Czechs who were defending the cherry avenue, and many others besides, and of course I wondered what the Czechs would do to me, despite my axle grease-blackened face, if ever I fell off the tank or something.

It was thoughts like these that troubled me as I cried silently among the sacks, and just before the darkness parted and I saw the midget Dago, Hanka kept appearing in my mind, I was back standing with her in the corridor, feeling her soft and firm and warm breast in the palm of my hand, and the image was so powerful and full of longing that I grew heavy and limp with all the sweetness of the world, which coursed in my bones as if through rigid pipes, and the image of Hanka flip-flopped with the image of the naked girl on television coming out of the water the day the Russkies came, and I nearly relived that very best moment in my life when I jerked myself off to my heart's content leaning back on the barn wall.

But I couldn't.

The thing is, in the middle of all that killing I couldn't.

So I wasn't like gunners Kantariya and Timosha and presumably all our other tank crewmen and sub-machine-gunners and pickup drivers, who went on about doing it with girls almost continuously both on the tanks and during rare moments of leisure in camp, talking like real blokes, in Russian.

I wasn't a real bloke yet. I was just a child, and I was sick of it.

And so I tried to do it, but I couldn't, and while the sweetness of the world drifted out of my reach, it was overtaken by a coldness and a futility that seemed to burrow deep inside me, as if driven by the chill wind blowing out of Chapman Forest.

And at that very moment the darkness seemed to part before my very eyes. A sack made the slightest of movements, and in the first glimmer of dawn I saw the strange face of the midget Dago.

14

We're on the run! Animals. Meadows. The first kurgan

He had slashed the canvas of the tent and stepped inside, then pressed himself against one of the sacks and in the half-light of daybreak merged with it.

I didn't know if he was a Czech sent to murder Captain Yegorov and steal his spoils of war or whether he was some bogeyman from Chapman Forest. My face was by his boots, but they weren't boots, more like bootees, and I could see that if this were a man he must be very small, and at first I thought it might be one of the Bandits, but I was wrong.

I attacked at once, determined to destroy the creature and forgetting that I was attached to the precious sacks.

We thrashed about in a screaming ball, and if he had wanted to stab me, he could have done so. I had anticipated that possibility, because in the tank corps I'd had some bad moments even on days that were otherwise glorious, and then I had hoped to be killed – those were my bad moments, which came from too much thinking.

But then I couldn't think. The little guy fought furiously and with skill, and while I was busy screaming, he defended himself without a sound. He had me flat on the ground, when suddenly I felt an excruciating pain in my side. A kick knocked me away from the creature, and I was staring up at the muzzle of Captain Yegorov's pistol, as well as the muzzles of the Kalashnikovs of gunners Timosha and Kantariya, while all around us were the other sub-machine-gunners, holding pistols and Kalashnikovs, and also knives and entrenching tools, and they looked so furious they would have killed us both if Captain Yegorov hadn't chased them out of the tent.

The gunners dragged me away by the rope that was tied to my ankles, cut me loose from the sacks and carried on guarding me outside, under the muzzles of their raised weapons.

Captain Yegorov stayed inside the tent with several NCOs, and the interrogation of the creature of the night began. I guessed as much from his howls. Finally I heard his voice and it was the voice of a man, and it was obvious that he was being interrogated. At one point the blows he received made the walls of the tent belly out, and you could see the outline of the creature's tiny body. He was smaller than the smallest longshirt at the Home from Home. Outside we all froze, because the stranger's howling inside the tent ended in the sort of plaintive whine that usually accompanies interrogations, then suddenly changed into a child's snivelling, and then something that cannot be described as anything other than the mewling of a baby. All was clear.

Willy Dagobert, known as Dago, was an East German comrade of ours. He was the only one who'd managed to fight his way out of enemy territory. The only man in the East German contingent who'd managed to make his way through Chapman Forest on foot, avoiding Czech patrols, and find our tank column.

So he wasn't really put out by his initial interrogation. The beating he received was more than compensated for by his joy at finding us, and discovering that he hadn't infiltrated a camp of Czech bandits by mistake, as he'd feared initially.

It wasn't long before he'd cemented his friendship with Captain Yegorov and all the tank column's NCOs and other ranks with the aid of several vodkas, and although he was bleeding a little from a few flesh wounds, he made light of them and gave an impromptu performance on the front of one of the tanks.

This was received with much enjoyment among the troops of the tank column. On Captain Yegorov's orders I also watched.

At first Dago just hopped up and down, but to the amazement and great pleasure of us all, once he got into his stride, he cut some capers on the tank, turning somersaults in the air, and it looked as if, under his tiny, sure feet, the tank was made of rubber and wasn't at all the murderous monster that crushed some men to pulp while providing a modicum of security for others.

Leaping high above the tank Dago turned somersaults, accompanied by all kinds of sounds coming from his tiny throat – deep, drawling groans and squeaky shrieks, and now and then even little tunes – and this medley of sounds seemed to converge on us from all sides until some of the gunners began looking about them in terror. Then with his little legs Dago did a pitter-patter run-up and started leaping from tank to tank, and in this way he cartwheeled and pirouetted his way around all the tanks in the column, and the soldiers' delight grew and grew, and then Dago executed the highlight of his turn: in the middle of a mighty leap in the air he made himself small, getting smaller and smaller, looking no bigger than a football. Rolled up like that, he landed in Captain Yegorov's arms, and now he mooed and whined and bleated like a baby, which was side-splittingly funny, because the baby in Captain Yegorov's arms had a moustache and the wrinkled face of a dwarf.

Roaring with laughter, the captain briefly dandled him in his arms, then kind of sniffed at his nappy and pretended to be fainting and gasping for breath, and we had never seen the captain so jolly and making jokes, so we clapped and cheered. Then he handed baby Dago to the NCO next to him, who also rocked him in his arms and to general laughter and amusement began pacing about like some village mother before passing Dago on. When Dago had had enough of this rocking and dandling, he suddenly leapt down, straightened his shoulders and stood there before us to acknowledge our applause and cheers, and Captain Yegorov was clapping, his eyes brimming with tears, and kept repeating, 'What an artist! What an artist!' and we all said it too.

Then Captain Yegorov bent down to the dwarf and shook his hand. We applauded, breathless with joy, and of course, Dago couldn't make himself any bigger.

That day we didn't determine our position using my maps. Dago the dwarf waved them aside and pointed to the spot on the horizon where the asphalt of the road seemed to merge into the trees of Chapman Forest.

Dago set our course and the column moved off to liberate the East German Hygea Circus, which was under siege by Czech bandits. He hoped that his East German comrades would be able to keep the rebellious villagers at bay until our tank column arrived.

That day, spirits were high. From Gunner Kantariya's silly jokes and Gunner Timosha's more earnest musings I gathered that my Soviet comrades loved the circus.

I still didn't know exactly what our 'Happy Song' tank column's mission really was, but from all the banter that rattled between the tanks to the rhythm of our progress it was clear to me that meeting a circus came as no surprise to Yegorov's sub-machine-gunners. On the contrary, it was supposed to have happened long before, somewhere in the Tomašín-Siřem sector.

But because of the uprising of the Czechoslovak masses and also the hostile operations of the Czechoslovak Army, the plans of the circus and our tank troops had been thwarted.

So it was no surprise that, as we travelled, feverish preparations were underway for a grand meeting. In a tank on the move there is no opportunity to wash one's clothes, so many privates aired the more neglected parts of their uniforms and underwear, at least perfunctorily, in the favourable summer breeze. Also on the move, they would rip fresh branches from the trees of Chapman Forest to make replacement camouflage.

Dago, safely ensconced between me and the gunners on the lead tank, never stopped chattering in his hard-sounding Russian, urging us to hurry. We especially thrilled to the things he told us about the girls of the East German Hygea Circus, who rode bareback and sang and flew on the trapeze. I also burnt with desire to see some of the mysterious, exotic animals I only knew from nature lessons and pictures, and Gunner Timosha didn't need asking twice to get out his set of animal picture cards. My delight knew no bounds when Dago dismissed the picture of an elephant with a scornful, 'Ours is bigger!' He said the same thing about the prairie dog picture, and the bear and the polar bear... The Hygea Circus seemed to be stocked with every conceivable animal in the world, and I couldn't wait.

And there was another thing. The circus might help me.

My days in the tank corps were mostly good, and no-one could get at me. But I sensed that no matter how many circuses we might meet, the uprising of the Czech masses would rage on. And what would I do if Captain Yegorov ordered me to start interpreting the broadcasts of Radio Free Siřem again, then ordered an attack on Siřem? How much longer could I use my maps to direct the tank column around and about Siřem, but not into Siřem?

It was clear to me that if Captain Yegorov realized that I was deceiving him, he would stop liking me. I didn't want things to go that far. It also occurred to me that I might fit in better at Dago's circus. Who so artfully dodged all those chain-clanking bulls? Who knew how to reduce a slavering village hound to groaning submission with a swift kick to the jaw? Who used to cart buckets of slops out to the sows that would eat anything? And who could communicate with a little horse harnessed to a sleigh? It wouldn't be work at all, dealing with animals again. I was desperately looking forward to meeting the circus. Everyone was.

But it came to nothing.

It was like this. Originally, the 'Happy Song' tank column simply put down pockets of resistance, then restocked with food from these captured positions. But things changed. Now we attacked every building we encountered, and because the Czechs wouldn't voluntarily give us even a glass of water, it was best to take everything they had.

We went straight in with the tanks, because the efforts of our supply squads had proved a failure. As far as I could tell from the level-headed musings of Gunner Timosha, the Soviet supply squads sent into the villages and hamlets of Chapman Forest often came back with less than they had gone with, and their haul might be no more than a couple of jars or tins, and it wasn't unheard of for them not to come back at all, and for the tank column to be surprised the next day by being cut off and fired upon by the valuable semi-automatic weapons taken from our dead soldiers.

Yet we had no way of stocking our field kitchen other than by stealing from Czech pantries. So our tanks always set an enemy building or whole village on fire first, then we would burst into the captured building or smouldering ruins of the village and grab anything that could be carried away, including water.

And we completely ignored the reports coming from the Radio Free Siřem transmitter.

And we also ignored the eyes in the forest, the entire forest having become bandit territory, and while we were still lords and masters of the roads and lanes, the forest was full of people who were watching us and meant us harm.

And we ignored the fact that painted on the white walls of houses and cottages, or on the tarmac of roads and lanes, were skull and cross-bones symbols smirking at us, and that we were also being vilified everywhere by signs and insults scrawled in Russian.

For Dago this was all new. Until the rebellion had begun, his circus had experienced only triumph and lots of bouquets and applause. The Hygea Circus had travelled from place to place as an ordinary socialist circus.

From what Dago said, I gathered that the situation had changed after the East German People's Army entered Czechoslovakia along-side the other Warsaw Pact armies to turn rebellious Czechoslovakia into a Soviet satellite. The circus, now under the protection of our East German comrades, headed for the Siřem zone, where it met with the full force of the uprising.

The migration of our column through the Bohemian countryside had been a battle. I've mentioned that often enough. But Dago was not used to a situation of relentless hostilities. I saw him cower in ter-ror when we had to abandon our cosy nest on the front hull as the shrapnel rained down, and we eliminated the bandits who had carried out the assault with a recoilless gun.

The village near to where we'd been attacked was marked on my maps as Luka.

I stayed by the cowering and ever-shrinking Dago, while our sub-machine-gunners burst into the village. Dago made more baby noises and the only bit of him I could see properly was his huge head. We waited on the tank for the marauders to come back. We had nothing else to do.

I swore a lot and thumped my fist on the armour plating. I had no Kalashnikov, nothing! Little Dago trembled beside me, and it struck me that whenever he was afraid he shrank, whereas I grew bigger. I was growing. Several times already I'd had to loosen the pins on my uniform. I was on military rations and I always ate everything.

'Let's run away!' cried Dago suddenly and, back to his normal small size, he slithered over the tank and entered the woods. I walked around the tank and set off after him, as if he were leading the way.

Was I pursuing a fugitive or doing a runner? That depended on who was asking the question, I decided. We walked quickly, very soon coming upon a footpath in the forest, and my heart pounded for joy at the prospect of having escaped at last.

We were in a clearing surrounded by the fence of an animal enclosure. We planned to dash across it and disappear into the forest. I was ready to strip off my Soviet uniform, because this was bandit territory.

I was about to clamber over the stakes of the fence – Dago was all right, he could crawl under them – when I stopped: the dwarf was kneeling in the grass, pointing at the fence.

The stakes looked a bit strange. The long spotted legs of some animal had been nailed to the crossbars of the enclosure, and I was staring at a nail in one of the hooves; another nail went through a joint in the long leg, and where stakes should have been there were a total of four long, weirdly twisted legs. Then I got a whiff of something: just a little way off in the grass there was the body of a large animal. I'd never seen one like that before. It was so huge that I might easily have mistaken it for a pile of blotched stones.

But it was a dead animal, covered in scars and scratches. I could hear birds scratching all over the wood of the enclosure, and because me and Dago were so still, the birds were climbing on the corpse, sitting on it and pecking at it.

Dago shuffled off and picked something out of the grass, then carried it back to me. It was a giraffe's head. He went back across the clearing and I followed. A giraffe's face is a bit like a roebuck's, though its ears are quite different, I can tell you.

We didn't speak. We went back towards the tank column. All we could hear was the odd round being let off, not sustained firing, and in no time we were back. We clambered onto the rags of my snug at the front of the hull, saying nothing. 'Did you know the giraffe?' I asked. '*Da*,' said Dago. We didn't run away that day after all.

Despite the success of the battle for Luka, the tank crews were glum, because the recoilless gun that had attacked them was part of the ordnance of the East German army.

Willy Dagobert was once again subjected to interrogation, but this time friendly and informal. Even I was present. Nothing new was discovered.

Dago talked at length about the charms of the bareback riders, and the grace and beauty of the circus girls, and he liked talking about the flowers and fruit showered upon him in the towns and villages that the Hygea Circus had passed through, and where he, Dago, had performed, although he was unable to give the exact position of the circus. He couldn't even provide a satisfactory statement of the manpower and ordnance of the East German People's Army units that were acting as the Hygea Circus's military overseers.

Whenever the amiable NCOs mentioned, in the course of the informal interrogation, the fact that the situation now involved fighting, Dago began squawking and crying, whining and shrinking into himself, making the NCOs less amiable. Dago refused to surrender the giraffe's head to anyone other than Captain Yegorov, biting and scratching several lower-ranking officers in the process. After which he was bound and left in my care on the front hull of my tank.

Earlier, during the interrogation, the giraffe's head had been entrusted to me. Under the watchful eye of gunners Timosha and Kantariya I had carried it the length of the tank column to the supply pickups. One of the drivers held the tarpaulin aside and I saw Captain

Yegorov's sacks, and I saw some corpses. The corpses in the pickup were in the same kind of sack as Captain Yegorov's treasures. The sacks kept the corpses in one piece. The soldiers of the tank column would put their fallen comrades under the pickup's tarpaulin for safekeeping. Gunner Timosha gave me a prod and I stowed the giraffe's head under the tarpaulin. So now the pickups with our fallen comrades were no longer a secret to me. I knew the Soviet soldiers trusted me.

We tried to live a normal life in Luka. My duties included feeding the troublesome Dago. I stuffed captured provisions into his mouth with my very own fingers. Shackled as he was, he amused both himself and me by cleverly shrinking and swelling. Slipping out of his bonds was child's play to him. I didn't report him, though I should have.

We were trying to live a normal life, but we weren't very good at it.

Under the command of Gunner Kantariya I went to fetch some water from a well in this newly conquered territory. It was guarded by our sub-machine-gunners. Gunner Kantariya winched up the metal bucket full of water, then he staggered and it went plummeting back down the well. Gunner Kantariya leaned on the wall of the well and puked.

I stared down into the depths, which were lined with cold, wet stones. Rays of sunlight danced on the metal bucket and illuminated the water that had been churned up by its fall, and I saw an animal's corpse. First I thought it was a gigantic, bloated pig, but in fact it was a hippo. The water wasn't fit to drink.

The Czechs were treating our tank column to scorched earth tactics.

During the night we made a barrow.

*

For once Captain Yegorov didn't need me on guard duty. No one in our tank column slept that night. Surrounded by a chain of guards, supported by a fan-shaped grouping of patrols, we soldiers of the tank column set out, under the command of Captain Yegorov, for the clearing in the forest, where we dismantled the animal enclosure. Then we dug a hole with entrenching tools, bayonets and knives. We worked quietly, the occasional clink when a spade hit a stone, or the noise of soldiers snapping or cutting through a root, didn't even reach the patrols. The work was hard, but we proceeded without a word, as silently as the leaves falling through the darkness into the forest grass. I carried the dug-up soil to the spot designated and soon it was a mound as high as a man. That's how to make a barrow.

At daybreak we placed the bodies of our fellow warriors into the excavated pit. I played no part in fetching their bodies from the two pickups; I didn't have the strength. The corpses in sacks covered the bottom of the pit. The soldiers aside set their spades and bayonets and stood there motionless, weapons in hand.

Captain Yegorov strode around the perimeter of the hole and called his fallen men by name one last time: Sergei, Abram, Ivan, Ivar, Volodya, Igor, Mikhailo, Maksim, Lev, Evgenii, Nikita – a long string of names. I only ever caught the first name, never the -ovich part. I can't remember them all. That wasn't my job anyway. My task was to gather the spades where they'd been dropped into a sack and drag the sack over to the black mound of excavated soil.

I was teamed up with Gunner Kantariya. We were standing beside the heap of excavated soil and waiting until Captain Yegorov had spoken to all of our fallen comrades. Roots and branches poked out of the heap of excavated soil, and pebbles glinted in the pale light of day. Gunner Kantariya wept. I glanced sideways: real tears. I pretended not to have noticed. If Gunner Kantariya had caught me watching him cry, things might have become awkward. I didn't want things to go too far.

The first to take up a spade and sink it into the pile of earth was Captain Yegorov. In total silence and with everyone looking on, he took it to the mass grave and tipped the dirt over the nearest sack. Following his example, the other soldiers of the column did likewise, one after another. I wanted to as well, but Gunner Timosha caught me by the sleeve and shook his head. I carried on guarding the sack of spades.

After every man had made a trip from the pile of earth to their fallen comrades, they came over to me, collected the spades and filled in the hole. The corpses were covered, and the soldiers went on heaping soil onto the grave. They worked hard and soon there was quite a hill rising over the corpses. To my short question, Gunner Timosha provided a terse answer: 'It's a kurgan, a burial mound.' Then we tramped this way and that over the kurgan, treading it down. That was something I could do. Then on top of the kurgan the soldiers tipped old, dry soil and twigs and pebbles and leaves. They used their knives to cut away all the bushes around and about, and turfs and saplings, and they set them elaborately on the kurgan. Soon the mound looked like any mound in Chapman Forest and not like a burial site of fallen Soviet soldiers. My handbooks had mentioned nothing about this.

On the way through the woods we soon spotted the tanks. We exchanged greetings with the patrols and the despondency with which I had learned how to bury people fell away... Gunner Kantariya and I got back last, because we were dragging the sack full of spades; the others were already by the tanks. Suddenly, in a crazy burst of noise, the forest around us changed. Bushes and grasses turned white and pink, and towards us and over our heads flew a flock of huge birds with gigantic beaks. The shuddering noise was the beating of their wings. Gunner Kantariya dropped the sack, which landed with a thump on my foot. He started pulling picture after picture out of his pocket, and when he shoved a picture of a flamingo where I could see it – a picture I knew from a section in *The Catholic Book of Knowledge* about the lives of the saints – he didn't wait for my verdict, but screamed, 'Flamingo! Flamingo!' Under the flying flamingoes we staggered along with the sack towards the assembled troops. Every soldier was following the stream of pink with staring, goggling eyes, focused solely on the flock as it vanished into the distance. If the Czechs had attacked us then, they'd have had us easy.

We had found the remains of the circus, that was more than obvious. And the murder of the giraffe and the hippo suggested that the Czechs had destroyed it completely.

A crazed Kantariya begged Captain Yegorov to let him skin the dead hippo, then cover the tank with its hide like a regimental flag, armouring our vehicle with animal skin. The hippo's head in particular, he insisted, would put the wind up the Czech bandits should they attack us, but Captain Yegorov forbade him to turn our tank into a hippo, and Kantariya came very close to ending up in shackles like Dago. Kantariya's railing merged with Dago's wailing, as he expressed his concern in German and Russian for the girls who had performed with the East German circus. His words filled us with dread, as we remembered what had happened to the giraffe and the hippo. 'It's hard to believe they'd let those wondrously beautiful creatures go free like the wild birds,' Dago moaned, and he banged his head against the tank's armour plating. 'They're bound to be languishing in the insurgents' smoke-filled cottages and underground bunkers, enslaved to those primitive yokels with no perfume or soap or applause!' Dago screamed and stormed and cursed, and we were glad he was tied up.

Captain Yegorov gave orders to bivouac in the vicinity of Luka and check for any trace of the vanished circus.

I continued in my role of interpreter and provider of intelligence.

After several early clashes, the Czechoslovak People's Army stopped attacking us. The actions of the armed gangs of Siaz also seemed to have come to a halt. The fighters had apparently withdrawn to the Prague–Beroun–Pilsen line, where the main offensive of the Czechoslovak People's Army against the occupying armies of the five Warsaw Pact nations was taking place.

I took off my headphones and handed a report to Captain Yegorov. My axle grease-blackened face didn't worry him. On the contrary. The forest seemed to be conspiring against us... in the area around Luka we were attacked by clouds of midges. The axle grease daubed all over my face didn't keep them away, nor did it relieve the pain of countless bites, but at least the insects stuck to my face and could be easily neutralized. The rest of the soldiers in our column also started putting axle grease on their faces. The black of their faces was blotched with the squashed and bloody bits of dead midges. The soldiers' teeth shone white, as did their eyes, otherwise their faces were a mask of blood and black. When captured bandits were being interrogated I discovered that it also had an undeniable effect psychologically.

Captain Yegorov decided to secure the entire area around the village of Luka. Interrogation of the captives would help us locate the missing circus.

And it began again. The sub-machine-gunners ran forward under cover of the tanks.

Shots crackled again in the village, where only dogs and cats were supposed to be still alive after the opening encounter.

The gunners plunged into the branching underground passages that went from barn to barn, attacked ostensibly invisible bunkers and sneaked up on concealed sniper positions, which they might never have found by themselves, and would have died in the crossfire one by one.

They were lucky that I'd been trained by Commander Baudyš.

Prisoners were marched straight to Captain Yegorov, and his axle-greased face was severe and grim, and all the NCOs wore severe, grim expressions, because the Czech insurgents spat in the venomously contorted faces of the Soviet occupiers, and had only one Russian word, which they repeated endlessly in answer to all questions: '*Neznaju.*'

And Captain Yegorov couldn't stand that.

Before long, all the houses in Luka were ablaze, along with the ruins of houses hit previously, and anyone who could, fled from the village into the forest. The rebels carried their injured away, but no-one could help those we had captured. I attended the interrogations, although *neznaju* didn't need translating. The last defenders were barricaded in a barn.

Later, I never wanted to talk about this. At the time, I had no-one to talk to. That could be why I picked up a pencil stub in one house and scribbled on my map documents everything about the interrogations and the fate of Luka. I covered lots of sheets. I even wrote down the names of the NCOs who conducted the interrogations. I wrote about everything I saw and everything I noticed.

I took the full sheets and hid them inside the wayside shrine, which by some miracle, perhaps, had survived the destruction. I weighed down the paper with a brick and placed it right at the feet of our Lord Jesus Christ.

Next day the paper wasn't there. I understood that there'd been further contact between me and the insurgents. I was very glad. None of the captives could say anything about me now, but I had no idea who might have seen me in Luka with the Russians.

15

Neznaju! Happy Song's mission. Captain Yegorov's concern.
Mermaid

When we had successfully mopped up the area around Luka, our
tank column moved on. We found no further traces of the Hygea
Circus and our tanks proceeded to the accompaniment of Dago's
swearing and moaning, shackled as he was to the armour plating of
the lead tank.

I had plenty of interpreting to do. I translated Czech news bul-
letins for Captain Yegorov, and when, bent over the tank's transmitter
or twiddling the knobs of the radio in the tent, I caught a hostile
Czech broadcast, Captain Yegorov would lean towards me, his care-
worn features creased with wrinkles.

The first evening after our column left Luka, Commander Žinka
addressed Captain Yegorov by name on Radio Free Siřem. He described the hopeless predicament of isolated groups of occupying
forces in the Siřem region, as well as the hopeless plight of the Soviet
parachutists fighting for their lives in the maze of little streets in the
capital of Czechoslovakia, Prague, since from the basement of Prague
Castle the heroic statesman Sasha Dubček had declared a nationwide
mobilisation, and the highland battalions of Slovak eagles together

with the forest battalions of the lions of the Bohemian Basin had the occupying armies in their clutches. Commander Žinka was jubilant and his voice thundered triumphally, and that evening Captain Yegorov punched the radio with his fist and made a particular point of asking me, 'Who's broadcasting this?'

'*Neznaju*,' I said.

I shouldn't have said it. It wasn't something Captain Yegorov liked to hear.

We listened to the news every day, and Captain Yegorov frowned and glowered, because the uprising was gaining ground.

Moravia and Silesia rebelled, and there was violent fighting in the streets of Brno and Ostrava. The focal point of the Brno insurgents was Petrov, which was transformed into a bastion of steel. Traditionally militant Moravian monks, released from Communist internment, teamed up with the people of Brno to form the Citizens' Company of Saints Cyril and Methodius, and were pushing the occupiers out of the city. The fighters collected mummies from the Brno catacombs and these mummies, armed with the most up-to-date weapons raided from munitions stores, were guarding barricades. By day and by night, illuminated by the flames of countless candles, they formed mobile battlefield altars.

The Polish strategic formations sent into Silesia refused to carry out the orders of the Soviet high command. The heroism of the Poznań Workers' Division shook the country. The officers were surrounded and, even after being bombarded for two days, refused to lay a hand on the military hardware and attack Czechoslovakia. Soviet *palachi*, butchers wearing leather aprons, decimated them.

Poland was on the verge of an uprising and a state of emergency was declared. Mass activity was being engineered by the workers' underground organisation *Produktiwita*.

There was so much news that all it did now was leave us confused. At times I couldn't care less. Captain Yegorov kept going back to the Radio Free Siřem transmitter.

Captain Yegorov decided to destroy the Radio Free Siřem transmitter.

Its broadcasts referred to our errant tank column quite often. They criticized our actions and spoke of our encounters as massacres. They also spoke of country folk being locked in barns, which then got burnt down. Captain Yegorov must have wondered where the insurgents got their information from. The broadcasts would also make mention of the hoard of gems, watches and church treasures in the captain's sacks.

I shouldn't have said *neznaju!* But what could I do about it?

I trembled at the prospect that one day Captain Yegorov would finally discover the truth about my various detours.

After all, we passed through some places more than once. After a long detour we reached Strabov again, already burnt out from the last time around, and we drove through Tomašín, herding the few people, bandits, who were still defending it into barns

Our errant column pottered about the countryside and the constant killing made us all feel sick. But what could be done? The Russians were alone in a foreign country, and I was alone among them. What could we do?

Dago's fetters were removed, but Captain Yegorov, infuriated by the dwarf's inability to offer any explanation as to the fate of the Hygea

Circus, kept him tethered to a rope. The end of the rope was entrusted to me.

We sat on the front hull plating, holding tight to the projecting metal and watching the landscape as it rolled by. We kept a sharp lookout for the circus, the soldiers keeping at the ready their picture cards of exotic animals.

It was only then that I learned about the 'Happy Song' tank column's mission. The Soviet military high command had entrusted Captain Yegorov with the special task of making preparations to meet the troops' needs for leisure and cultural activities in Czechoslovakia. In particular, he was to have created secure conditions for a model Soviet circus. His duty was to demonstrate to the Czechoslovaks and to the rest of the world that the Soviet invasion force was no barbarian horde, but in fact was a vanguard of the most sophisticated culture known to mankind. Project Socialist Circus was intended to prove that socialist circus performers are masters of their art, including the most humane taming and training of exotic animals.

'Obviously,' the dwarf said, getting excited, 'no-one can expect the Soviets to carry libraries on their tanks. But what better means can there be for educating the masses or filling their spare time than a circus?'

I didn't know. I'd never been to a circus, so I said nothing.

'Brilliant Soviet thinking is fed by the powerful wellspring of those Eastern philosophical systems that anticipate a worldwide dominion made up of the brotherhood of animals and men. The new world empire, whose vanguard we are, will also include machines,' said Dago, gently rapping the tank with his knuckles. 'In the world's new Eastern

Empire no-one will ever again humiliate or enslave man, beast or machine,' Dago continued, warming to his theme. 'And a big top's as good a place as any for the masses to swear their allegiance to the Soviet Union.'

I also learned that the East German circus had been the backbone of Project Socialist Circus. The zone secured by Captain Yegorov's unit was to have gradually become a home to circuses from all five of the states involved in the invasion of Czechoslovakia. The hippo found in the well was, for example, the first hippo to have been born in the zoological gardens of the Hungarian People's Republic, while the dead giraffe had once been the star attraction of the renowned Warsaw Variety Theatre.

The mainstay of the circus corps was obviously to be the East German Hygea Circus, with its bareback riders – 'the most beautiful girls in the world' – and its clowns, because 'German clowns are the funniest in the world, you know,' insisted Dago. 'But the cause seems to be lost,' he added, wrinkling his nose sadly. 'It looks as if the circus has been pulverized by Czech bandits. It's a great shame! These Czech diehards are their own worst enemies. They're depriving themselves of a magnificent, joyful show and they'll be the laughing stock of the entire civilized world. I'm so sorry for the performing animals, but also for the performers who will perish in this dreadful country.' Dago was least concerned for the Polish magicians, who probably felt quite at home in Chapman Forest, but as for the gorgeous East German trapeze artistes and bareback riders... every time Dago howled I had to choke him with a tug on the rope.

And I shouldn't have been surprised that Captain Yegorov had been so foul-tempered of late, because he was very worried, as Dago enlightened me. If Captain Yegorov doesn't execute his mission, he could be up before a tribunal.

'What?' I pricked up my ears, because I was quite familiar with the word 'tribunal'.

''Fraid so,' said the dwarf with a glum chuckle. 'He'll be sent to Siberia, the gulag. For twenty years, or life. Or he'll get a bullet.' And Dago fell silent. He craned his big head up on his thin neck, probably watching for signs of some animal moving through the bushes and undergrowth of Chapman Forest.

I looked at my legs dangling over the side of the tank next to his, and I squinted at the pinned and rolled-back sleeves of my tank soldier's jacket, hoping I might have grown a bit again. I must get over this childhood thing as soon as possible, I resolved as our tank trundled down the lane between Chapman Forest and a dust-covered field, where nothing grew that summer, and I clung to the tank's front hull and waited for my childhood to end.

Captain Yegorov was still in a bad mood. He still tied my feet together at night and untied them in the morning, but he treated me kindly, although he could be very sharp in the way he spoke to the sub-machine-gunners. He went on more and more frequently about the sorry state of our fuel stocks, and he constantly scanned the horizon with binoculars, and he also pored over my maps, and it became obvious to me that he was looking for Siřem, because the provocative Siřem transmitter was getting to him more than anything else.

Thanks to regular radio reports of our whereabouts we encountered plenty of graffiti in Russian, abusive and mocking, which wounded Captain Yegorov's pride, and it was solely due to these inflammatory broadcasts that we kept on being ambushed.

Then one day the cheerful Kantariya and the dour Timosha were sitting on the front of the tank, and Kantariya had just launched into a jolly song about girls. The sun burnt on our bare heads and the fresh breeze set up by the tank's motion cooled us, when suddenly, rounding a corner, we spotted two vandals.

They had just been vandalizing a white wall – black paint still dripping from their brushes. Above the unfinished sentence YEGOROV IS A THIEF AND MURD was a picture of Czechia, scowling at the approaching occupying troops, her unkempt hair leaping about the wall like living, burning snakes. The daubers might have had time to complete their graffiti while our tanks were still clattering down the road, except that this time the sub-machine-gunners had run on ahead of us in camouflage dress, darting here and there among the buildings, and they soon caught the two vandals.

I clambered down inside the tank to avoid having to interpret, but I couldn't get out of it.

The Czechs refused to speak, except when one of them shouted that he wanted to die for freedom, although Captain Yegorov hadn't asked him about that.

The Captain did ask where their command post was, how to get to Siřem and suchlike, but they said, '*Neznaju.*'

Then the other Czech ripped open his shirt and shouted that he wanted to die for freedom as well. Captain Yegorov nodded his assent, and the sub-machine-gunners led the vandals out into the yard and shot them.

The tank crushed the paint bucket under its tracks, and the paint on the brushes lying about on the ground dried hard in the glare of the sun, and it looked like tarmac and no good for anything.

The graffiti-vandalized building was a village school, its doors and windows knocked out. It looked as if there had been fighting inside. The ceiling of one of the classrooms had come down and there were piles of rubble all around, but the building was good enough for a short rest break.

In front of the school there was a statue of the warrior Wenceslas. He was armed and equipped in the old style, with a lance and a sword and a shield. He's our Czech patron saint, the champion of Christendom, as the nuns once explained to me. On the base of the statue the words LET US NOT PERISH, NOR THOSE WHO COME AFTER US were carved in large letters, and when I translated this inscription the Captain just shrugged.

The village appeared to be deserted.

The NCOs appointed patrols and anyone who could and wanted to found themselves a spot to sit down in the cool and shade of the school building.

I must have nodded off, because when I opened my eyes I was alone in the classroom with the collapsed ceiling, except for Captain Yegorov, who was hunched down on the dais in front of the board.

Lying all over the floor were books, torn exercise books, and in the corner a bundle of rags: red, white and blue Czechoslovak flags. It was like a den where someone's dossed down for a night.

The Captain picked a thick book out of the pile on the floor, flicked through it, then carefully and with interest studied every page in turn. His scowling and grease-blackened face began to bear the signs of a sad smile. Captain Yegorov tore out individual pages, crumpled them and threw them on the floor. He stood up and, although usually so swift, walked slowly out of the classroom.

The book was Brehm's *Animal Life* and each of those torn and tossed pages was a portrait of an animal.

I remembered what Dago had told me about what would happen if Captain Yegorov failed in his circus mission. I crossed the classroom and went down the corridor to the back, and through a little window I could see Chapman Forest. I could escape that way. I was only a stone's throw from the forest.

Dago had spoken about a military tribunal, and I recalled the old fairy tale about Fedotkin that our commander used to tell us, the commander that Margash and I had killed, and I told myself, 'Oh no! I'm not going to any fucking gulag with my captain, no way! When fathers fight, their kids have to join in, sure, but I've heard too much about the penal colony in freezing Vorkuta. I'm not going there for all the tea in China. I've got to get away!'

But if I did a bad job of running away from Captain Yegorov and we met again somehow, he wouldn't be kind to me any more, that was for sure. And once I was on the run I'd have to keep my eyes peeled for insurgents too. Yet I knew I had to get away. The problem was that I only knew the world of my maps. And I had no idea how to get out of it.

The rest break was suddenly shattered by the stifled shouting of the sub-machine-gunners and a weird grinding noise echoing through the previously calm summer afternoon. I dashed out of the classroom.

Our sub-machine-gunners were pushing two scruffy-looking guys at gunpoint before them. And a cabin on wheels pulled by a little donkey. One of the scruffs sat astride the donkey, which plodded happily along, despite all the noise around it. The other scruff was dragging the beast by its reins towards Captain Yegorov and a knot of NCOs.

The cabin looked a bit like a rustic outdoor toilet, except for being gaily painted. The NCOs, packed defensively around Captain Yegorov, lowered their side arms. We all stared. I could tell that the colourful scrawls covering the cabin were supposed to depict a seaside scene. I knew the sea and the seaside – sandy beaches and palm trees and monsters that peeked out above the surface of the water – from *The Catholic Book of Knowledge*. The cabin was covered in similar scenes, except that next to the palm trees on the beach was a naked woman. It was definitely not Czechia.

The donkey stopped short. The guy who was sitting on it jumped down, and the pair of them dropped to their knees before the erect figure of our captain, then raised their arms and started jabbering.

None of us would have been at all surprised if the Captain had suspected it was all a Czech subterfuge and had had the men and their donkey shot on the spot.

But Captain Yegorov smiled and asked, 'Are you circus folk? Is this a circus?'

And Captain Yegorov marched straight towards the slatted door of the painted cabin.

But the impertinence of the scruffs knew no bounds. They both kept waving their arms, babbling away, and politely, but firmly prevented the Captain from going inside.

'Ilya!' he shouted and I went to interpret.

But I couldn't understand a word! And they wouldn't talk to me anyway. They looked at me and I think they understood Czech, but they wouldn't speak it. So by snatches I tried this and that from what I remembered of the foreign languages the other kids would cry all night in at Siřem. And Captain Yegorov grew impatient and started tapping his feet. And it had all been going on for too long and I was about to throw up my arms and tell the Captain I didn't know their language, when the one who had arrived on the donkey, the one with a scar across his swarthy features, poked the other scruff and said, 'We can tell this one,' and to me he said, 'You from Siřem, kiddo? From the reformatory?'

I nearly fainted. That was how Siřem kids talked.

'You're from Siřem, aren't you?'

'Yeah!'

'So tell 'em we're Bulgarian. Go on, and in this cabin here we've got the Mermaid of the Seven Seas. For gentlemen, geddit?'

'Sure,' I said, and found a way to translate for Yegorov.

'Ah, my Bulgarian brothers!' The Captain was happy, and so were the NCOs, and they started demanding to see the mermaid, obviously.

And the Captain asked where the rest of the circus was.

And the two scruffs were grinning... They were no longer being held by the soldiers in camouflage dress, who had lowered their Kalashnikovs. The NCOs were tittering and sticking their side arms back in their holsters and sleeves and belts and boots, depending on where each one carried his. And the scruffs realized that things had taken a turn for the better, so they were happy. Scarface winked at me and started talking, and I translated and explained that the Bulgarian circus folk had fled in the face of an offensive by Czech bandits, and that they were now fighting their way across the heartland under their own steam. As to the whereabouts of their Balkan circus, unfortunately they didn't know and couldn't guess, but they were happy to be able to be of service to the heroic Soviet Army. Then Captain Yegorov stiffened ever so slightly, because the two scruffs began to explain that there was a charge to see the mermaid, and that they accepted marks, leva, zlotys, forints, roubles... any of the currencies of the five armies, they didn't mind which, and as for the mermaid, she didn't care about anything at all.

Captain Yegorov's blackened face went rigid, but only me and the NCOs could tell, not the scruffs, because of the axle grease he'd put on to stop the midges. Captain Yegorov had one more question.

He asked whether 'you, my Bulgarian brothers' knew the way to Siřem.

And the two scruffs started happily outshouting each other that 'yes', and 'sure', and that 'you're there in next to no time'! And would the officers, sirs, like to see their show now?

And I interpreted.

And Captain Yegorov was smiling again.

And I knew I'd had it, because I didn't want to go back to Siřem.

Now the scruffs, helped by the gunners, moved the cabin on wheels into the classroom, leaving the donkey outside, and the school classroom was apparently now the scene of some important preparations, and there, alongside the silent Captain Yegorov, the excited gunners kept nudging one another, overjoyed at having found another bit of the Socialist Circus. After all, around every corner of this Czech land our column had so far been met by warfare and more warfare, and suddenly there were the leaps and somersaults of Dago the dwarf, and now they even had a mermaid all the way from Bulgaria.

They were all looking forward to the show.

Captain Yegorov went into the classroom first. And he was there for some time. The gunners nudged each other, then one gave his army belt a polish, while another dragged a comb through his hair; one or two of the others even washed the axle grease and crust of dead mosquitoes from their faces, which, pink and smiling, they raised towards the sun... The ordinary servicemen were also full of anticipation. They knew that after the sub-machine-gunners it would be their turn... And the ones whose turn to mount guard had just come were making fun of those ahead of them... and in all the argy-bargy there was plenty of the sort of good-natured pushing and banter that were the norm in our tank column during those moments of relief when ordinary life briefly reasserted itself... And Captain Yegorov came out of the classroom, smiling broadly, and over his shoulder he barked an order to the gunners to find the Bulgarian comrades a place in the column once the show was over.

Then the NCOs went into the classroom, one by one, and they were inside, then they came out... They were in there a long time, so it was no surprise that the simple sub-machine-gunners and tank crewmen and pickup drivers were mad with curiosity and excitement, and they formed a queue and waited, and there were a lot of them. Despite our losses it struck me that there were still plenty of us in our tank column... but that was possibly because I was the very last in line.

Dusk was falling. It was gloomy inside the classroom. The cabin on wheels was open and all around it there was a lot of trampled mud from army boots. I peeked inside. I could see a girl in a bath full of foam. Her hair was all over her face. She was mumbling and groaning, apparently not at all happy to be there. I wasn't surprised... I got this idea that the girl in the filthy foam was a whore, and the lads at the Home from Home used to say that whores were the best thing for cuddling with, and I was astonished to find my cock inside my trousers was suddenly as big as that time by the barn... But when it dawned on me that my first time with a woman I'd be shooting my seed into a bath full of the seed of Soviet tankmen and sub-machine-gunners, my cock shrank back again. I looked at the girl in the gloom of the damp, filthy hut and she stared back at me, and suddenly my blood froze... If she had had a tracksuit on, and a scarf and cap!... and was running towards me across a yard in gumboots!... She wasn't wearing any clothes – not yellow, red, green – nothing at all. Only the cabin was a gaudy mess. She lay in the bath naked. I could see her shoulders and I tried to make out her hands, but they were tied... her arms were spread out and she was tied down in the bath, so she had to lie in the water...

What should I say? I didn't know. So I said, 'Hi, how are you?' In Czech, obviously.

She moved her head, which sent a ripple through the bath full of foam. I could see her lips moving. She was trying to say something, and at last a single word escaped her mouth, 'Siaz.' And straight away I said, 'Czechia!' and I dived at the bath and started dragging her away, but she was tied up. I scampered all around the classroom looking for something, but couldn't find anything, so I flew back to the girl and gnawed at the rope and bit it, and it worked! It was done! I undid the other one with my fingers. It worked! She could hardly stand. She was dripping wet and naked. I was embarrassed. There was no time... I grabbed the flags from the corner – there was nothing else! – and she wrapped one around her, and then we were headed across the classroom and down the corridor to the back, and there was the little window. I helped her. In the window she bent down and briefly rested her face against mine, and I blushed under the axle grease... I reckoned she would make it safely into the forest.

I went back to the classroom and the cabin, and Scarface was there. He was examining the ropes and looked depressed. He had just fetched a bucket of hot water to add to the bath. He poured it on the floor, turned the bucket upside down and sat on it, saying, 'You've gone and spoilt it!'

'I'll tell the Captain you're not Bulgarians, and you're for the firing squad!' I told him.

'You've gone and spoilt it, kiddo,' Scarface said again.

And something occurred to me, so I asked him, 'Do you know Još?'

'Of course we know Još,' said Scarface. 'We was on the way from his place when we got caught up in the war between all them idiots, so we invented a circus, because circus folk can go anywhere, and we're Bulgarian so we don't have to speak Russian or Czech. But what was that big-shot soldier guy saying about some great circus he's looking for? That'd be a godsend!'

I couldn't decide whether to mention the girl.

'We picked her up on the road,' Scarface said, without being asked. 'Some soldiers found some girls hiding, but this one escaped. So we saved her.'

'Saved, eh?' I said.

'Think what you like, kiddo. Now we've got to stay with this column. We'll say she's asleep, or sick like, we just won't let anyone in, see.'

So we were agreed.

And in the morning our column headed for Siřem.

16

A fantastic battle. Attack by demons. The egg.
Third World War and last television

If Captain Yegorov thought – having integrated the Bulgarians into the 'Happy Song' tank column – that his luck had changed for the better, I knew mine had changed for the worse. And then I had my work cut out with Dago, who kept shouting 'Bastards!' at them in Russian. He absolutely hated them. For him they were a disgrace to all circuses, while he was a credit to them. Perhaps he was remembering those glorious moments when the soldiers of the column had gaped in wonder at his somersaults, because now they ignored his protests at the Bulgarian circus folk. And Dago shrivelled up. He retreated deep down inside himself again and ceased to care what was going on, though we still chatted together.

The soldiers of the column were very happy with our Bulgarians, and most of all with the mermaid, that's for sure.

They attached the painted cabin to a tank at the safest position in the column, namely in the mid-rear, because they wanted to spare the mermaid as many of the consequences of any sudden attack as possible. They believed the girl was sleeping inside.

The two scruffs guided the column towards Siřem. They looked after the donkey nicely, it has to be said.

'I've already been through one war. I originally trained as a musician, see,' Dago told me during the easy ride of our lead tank along the tarmac road. 'This wasteland we're driving through' – his free hand swept the Czech horizon – 'is once more a battleground between East and West. I changed my name and profession in order to live again – too bad!'

I wanted to ask him what instrument he played in that other war, and who he was fighting and stuff, but he wouldn't let me get a word in edgeways.

'You might be little, Ilya, but you know lots of things. How old are you? You don't know? You understand, though, Eastern man holds his little hammer in high regard, but he's only got the one, its handle all shiny from use... And Western man has a whole cupboard full of stuff, all sorts of radios he's got, rockets and ballpoint pens, all those twentieth-century playthings and it's affected his brain.'

Now I had to laugh. I kept a few pencil stubs with my maps, and the odd Western ballpoint would have done me very nicely.

'You know it all, Ilya. I've been watching you. When Eastern people lose a million loved ones in the war, they tell themselves, "Oh well, can't be helped." They hold each other by the hand and they make a kurgan of packed earth... With Western man, one of his nearest and dearest kicks up a fuss and straight away it's on television, and there's a great hoo-ha and tears all round... so who will come out on top?'

'Well, who?' I asked him, just to see if he knew.

'Listen... You're a saboteur. I'm a spy, an animal spy, see? We circus

211

folk are close to the animals. We get these strange vibes from them...
Something's afoot. I think the Soviets, with things getting a bit tricky,
are going to try out some new secret weapon, and that'll really be
something!'

I hadn't heard about any secret weapon before then, so I let Dago
go on, just tugging on his rope now and again, because sometimes he
could get quite heated and I couldn't let him get too noisy.

'Listen, Ilya. We're both up this Czech end of shit creek, stuck in
this war between the Eastern Empire and the West! And you know
what we who are in the middle have to do, don't you? We have to
survive, understand? And that's not gonna be easy! If the armies of
the Eastern Empire use their secret weapon against the Western
forces of Nato it'll be Armageddon, an incredible battle! Do you
know what Armageddon is? No? Well, you'll find out soon
enough.'

I listened to Dago, at least it helped pass the time as we drove on,
and since he didn't get too excited I didn't even have to lash him with
his rope. All the way, Dago kept asking me riddles and inventing fairy
stories... I did think he might be showing off... A spy might be more
than a saboteur, but if either is caught behind enemy lines, they both
go to the wall, no questions asked... It says so in black and white in *A
Manual for Saboteurs*. So why was he getting so smart with me, this
midget? I'd no idea.

We were advancing on Siřem. Captain Yegorov didn't even look at me
as he tied me to the sacks that evening.

I had a dream about sea foam with a girl tied up in it, and in my
dream the foam in her bath changed into the tar water that the nuns

used to serve us in mugs and make us gargle painfully for lying and swearing, but through the dreamy waves of greying foam I also saw the beauty of Sister Dolores, so it was a nice dream... I woke up and immediately realized how close we were to Siřem.

I could never have guessed that our tank column would be attacked by demons, that Captain Yegorov's good fortune would rise again, and that the Third World War would break out.

That day we travelled through blazing sunlight and the battle-scorched land of the Czechs without a shot being fired, and we casually set up camp for the night in a village that we'd flattened only a few days before. It was only a stone's throw from Siřem, only twice the tanks' range from Chapman Forest, and Commander Baudyš used to run his field exercises all around here. Seated next to Dago and despite the fading light, I recognized the spot where Mikušinec and I had nabbed Šklíba in a wet field smelling of raw earth and handed him over for elimination. Oh dear. The forest track up to Fell Crag started here.

In the evening, we were allowed to make bonfires, and Captain Yegorov gave the order for Siřem to be taken the following day. His orders included the declaration that once Siřem had been captured work would begin on constructing a circus township and that the 'Happy Song' tank column's battlefield meanderings would come to an end, and so a joyful mood reigned in the camp.

Dago refused to climb off the tank and join us by the fire, which the two scruffs were stoking with branches from Chapman Forest, but he kept leaning over from his post on the front hull, holding out his mess tin... There was a bustle of joyful activity around our lead tank's bonfire.

Gunner Kantariya found a harmonica somewhere and, defying the censorious look of the dour Gunner Timosha, he uncorked a demijohn of meths looted from somewhere and probably kept for just such an occasion, and the sub-machine-gunners fraternized with 'our Bulgarian brothers', whose meths intake led to the revelation of such talents that now even the column's NCOs took a shine to them, and nudges and jokes and questions about the – as all the soldiers believed – peacefully sleeping mermaid came thick and fast.

'You're not gonna recognize Siřem, kiddo,' Scarface told me, though I hadn't asked him about it. 'The whole square is full of flowers, and there's beautiful wreathes and burning candles everywhere – like a cemetery, it is, but beautiful!'

'Come and join us,' the other one said, offering me a gulp from his mess tin, 'and you can stay at Jos's place, with them other kids of yours, like.'

'Our kids, you mean,' Scarface corrected him. 'And who are you exactly? You a Russki?'

That was a question I didn't fancy answering. I'd been going over what he'd said, that Chata and Bajza and perhaps a few more from the Home from Home were living in Jos's cottage somewhere in the forest. And to the doleful strains of Kantariya's harmonica it crossed my mind that I probably ought to make my escape then and there and find the lads. But I didn't do it, because our camp was attacked by demons.

Before we caught sight of their vile, diabolical snouts, and before the evening calm of our forest retreat had been riven by the horrible snorting and baying of these strange creatures, and our ears deafened by the clatter of their approaching hooves, something whizzed through the air and Kantariya's harmonica groaned and fell silent. The gunner leapt to his feet and yanked a long arrow from the instrument, its sharp tip glinting in the firelight. Obeying every instinct of a commander of saboteurs, I grabbed Scarface's full mess tin from him and poured it on the bonfire, which blazed up with a blinding flame, me knowing nothing of the properties of meths. Unfortunately, it looked as if I'd given our attackers a signal, and they were upon us.

Fearsome animals with wailing devils' heads spat gobbets of white foam at us. The warriors who sat astride the jagged backs of these monsters screamed deafeningly, but the sub-machine-gunners kept up their fire. With all the shooting we might have gradually killed each other. The enemy cavalry rushed past and over us, and in no time at all the thunder of hooves could be heard far away, towards Chapman Forest.

The bonfires were scattered on the instant and the darkness rang with the commands of the NCOs, and above all the smooth, perhaps slightly tense voice of Captain Yegorov. The tank commanders called in their positions, and in just a few moments the column had become a dark, silent wall of steel and armaments.

We might have held on like that until daylight, but after a short while Gunner Kantariya returned from a recce and, to the relief of all who saw him, the corners of his mouth were twitching mischievously. Gunner Timosha went along with him to report, and only when we saw his placid face and direct, proud gaze did we heave a sigh of relief.

Soon, from the obscurity over by Chapman Forest, we heard the odd clink, or possibly the sound of a pebble sent flying by a hoof, but the commands barked out in muffled voices by the NCOs kept us in the dark and silence. Snuggled up to Dago on the front tank, I listened out intently, when suddenly the night sky high above us turned bright.

Dago's cry of amazement was punctuated by a rapid *pop-pop-pop*...
the sound of flares going off, and the darkness ahead of us burst into a
myriad lights, Captain Yegorov having ordered the simultaneous de-
ployment of all the searchlights and floodlights and signal lamps and
any bright lights the tank column possessed. And we, thunderstruck,
were treated to an incredible sight, because approaching across the
field that in the darkness had merged into one with the rustling forest
came a great, jagged, un-horselike, cavalry monstrosity, high above the
beast's wobbling humps were two heads on necks that reminded me of
some fat snakes in *The Catholic Book of Knowledge*, but the really horrible thing was that little human heads were poking out everywhere
from the monster's body. I yelped and Dago shrieked, which wasn't
surprising, since we had no idea anything like that lived in Chapman
Forest.

The privates in our column were also all agog and sort of entranced.
You couldn't hear a single shout or shot as the many-headed creature
proceeded towards us in the blinding light, slowly and seemingly in-
escapably. I was all set to slip off the hull plate, and I would swear that
for the first time during our operations on Czech soil one or two of the
other men in the column were tempted to make a run for it... It came
towards us... The quiet that surrounded the slow march of the multi-
beast towards the tanks was suddenly broken when the dwarf Dago
let out a joyful yelp, and whistled and cried 'Hurrah!' and 'Bravo!' in
Russian, and our scouts Kantariya and Timosha now went among the
tank crews bringing calm and reassurance to the men, who were still
paralysed with fear... We'd only run up against more shattered remains
of the Socialist Circus Project: two riding camels and the Mongolian
boys who looked after them.

Illuminated by all those lights the riders dismounted from the camels, of which you could now tell there were two. They were young boys, no bigger than me, and as I saw them, one by one, surrounded by brightness, I remembered that vision of long ago, that night when Dýha and I and the little choirboys came out of the basement and stood face to face with Commander Vyžlata, and I first saw Margash.

The camel boys formed a circle around their snorting animals and tried to calm them down, since they evidently didn't like our silent wall of tanks.

And then I saw Captain Yegorov come striding along with the two gunners by his side. He had left the safety of the tanks and was heading straight for the lads swarming around their camels. Not bothering about Dago, I ran off after Yegorov. Exploiting my position of interpreter, I offered my services. Kantariya and Timosha seemed impressed by my bravery, but in truth I was dying to find out who these people were, and all about their camels.

Some of the boys gathered around the animals held bows and arrows, others had knives at the ready, and they all spoke Russian.

Yes, they were part of a broader contingent of the Socialist Circus Project, they replied to my first question. Asked why they had attacked us, they said that they attacked anyone and everyone.

Then Captain Yegorov barked out a command, and the camel boys fell sheepishly silent. He left them in no doubt as to his rank as commander-in-chief of the Socialist Circus Project.

The boys briefly discussed the matter in an unintelligible language, but they seemed to be convinced when they saw the pips on Yegorov's tank-brigade jacket, and also, more likely, by the fire power of his sub-machine-gunners. Their knives abruptly disappeared.

Then they unloaded a huge steel cage covered in skins from the back of one of the camels, and with the cage safely set on the ground they tore off the skins and we could see, inside the cage, an animal blinded by the blazing lights: a massive wolf with white fur.

Captain Yegorov snatched a riding crop from one of the boys and lashed the wolf across its snout. It gave a whine and pressed back against the mesh of the cage. Captain Yegorov inspected the straw the wolf had been lying on, then pushed both hands into it, while gunners Kantariya and Timosha aimed their Kalashnikovs at the wolf. Captain Yegorov held his hands aloft in the glare of all the tank column's lights, and we all saw that he was holding an egg.

It was a huge egg with a grey shell that looked leathery and was covered in cracks.

Captain Yegorov's face, his dust-covered face, gaunt and haggard with lack of sleep, his face on which fatigue and responsibility and privation had etched their maps, now glinted with a trickle of tears. I preferred not to look.

Another sunny day found me full of cares, sitting on the forward armour plate of the tank's hull.

We had added yet another circus contingent to our column, and all the signs were that Captain Yegorov's mood had improved again, and that we could take the shattered remnants of the Socialist Circus Project and at least make a half-decent variety show out of it, as the dwarf Dago put it.

However, Captain Yegorov failed to put in an appearance. That day I didn't even perform my duties as radio interpreter. Dago and I bounced along on the armour plating. He was still under my orders.

The pseudo-Bulgarians and their donkey kept to their position in the mid-rear of the column, their happy dispositions making them well liked among the privates. They dutifully kept the secret of the sea cabin, and surreptitiously took payments from the privates for first place in the queue. The camel boys spoke better Russian than me and before long they were larking about and discussing stuff with the soldiers up and down the length of the column.

When I saw them, it was just like the time I met Margash. Suddenly here was somebody who was like me. But they weren't like me.

It was my fault, and mine alone, that I had been through so much.

The more attention I paid to the camel boys, the more acutely I sensed the difference between us. I had almost grown into my torn and dusty tankman's uniform. At least at the points where it was pinned together. I couldn't mix with their happy band. Somewhere inside me I seemed to have stopped thinking about Margash's land. Inside me there were still all those things that had happened at Siřem.

That day I was summoned to a short conference of commanders.

Captain Yegorov remained in the bowels of the lead tank, nursing the giant egg on his lap. Gunner Kantariya told us that since the egg had been found Captain Yegorov hadn't stopped smiling at it. He hadn't been giving any orders either. The NCOs were of the view that we should press on against Siřem.

As the interpreter and an expert on the methods of saboteurs, I was invited along to a meeting about the Czech bandit gangs. The contingents of the Czechoslovak People's Army had apparently been redeployed away from the area of the Siřem Autonomous Zone, so we were being ambushed less often. Apart from Captain Yegorov's sacks our pickups were empty. We'd had next to no further contact with the enemy since executing those two vandals. The inflammatory radio transmitter appeared to have fallen silent. During our encounter with the camel team we had encountered sniper fire, but nothing had come of it.

So was it conceivable that the resistance of the Czech bandit gangs had been quashed? Or were they laying a trap? Such were the questions raised.

So it was decided that after a short rest, chiefly for the sake of the animals, which were now fully-fledged members of our column, we would carry on towards Siřem. Captain Yegorov would re-assume command as and when he saw fit.

A cheerful mood reigned among the soldiers now. They were all of the view that the capture of Siřem would not be difficult. And once the conditions were right for the Socialist Circus Project, we could all have a proper rest. Dago explained that the soldiers were relieved, because they no longer faced the more or less certain prospect of being sent to a Siberian gulag for failing in their mission. A question mark still hung over their commitment to a life of continual hardship in uniform, but they were used to that.

'Damn column!' Dago shouted down from the tank. 'Drifting column!' he muttered, yet he was happy at the rise in our numbers.

'The Mongolian camel riders,' he began explaining, 'could give the mess we're in a turn for the better. They're the real elite of the socialist circus. Ilya?'

I opened my eyes. I remembered how Mr Cimbura would also keep me awake with his endless cock and bull stories. But you can't really sleep on a moving tank anyway.

'It looks as if we've got it, Ilya!'

'What?'

'The secret weapon... the dinosaur egg from the Gobi Desert, hidden in the hot sand under which the mountains of the East are buried. Listen to me, Ilya! In the desert, nature cast a dragon, steeled by the fires of millennia. In its bowels the desert forged the dragon egg on the anvils of the ages in the farthermost wildernesses of the East... Ilya, look!'

I barely glanced up. We were passing a few bullet-riddled, burnt hovels. They might have been destroyed by us or by some other company, I couldn't remember. Dago poked me in the shoulder, and said, 'What the insurgents call the Sirem Autonomous Zone was meant to be the setting for the Socialist Circus Project, a joyous window display for the five nations... all our socialist animals and the men-in-arms of the five nations would have breathed in peace on the dragon's egg... but the Czechs shattered the alliance of the Eastern Empire and must pay the price.'

And then, through parched lips, Dago asked me to look about to see if there wasn't at least a drop of meths somewhere, because he had had a splitting headache since the events of the day before. And he remarked that whereas he had survived his first war thanks to music, this time it could be as a dancer, and next time he would certainly become a poet.

'Ilya!'

'What?'

'That is, if there is a next time!'

I looked at my fully grown arms and legs, remembering how, one winter, Mr Cimbura had regretted I was still a shrimp and that I couldn't go off through the snow to fetch him a bottle, after he'd talked himself hoarse with his yarns about Czechia...

'Yes,' Dago wheezed again, 'the dinosaur egg might save Captain Yegorov from being court-martialled... Since if the egg did hatch into a dragon it would be seen as a magnificent victory for the armies of the Warsaw Pact, and Communism in general. Yes, an actual dragon could turn the situation in favour of the Soviets,' the dwarf muttered, 'and... we might meet someone else. What do you reckon, Ilya?'

An order was given and we stopped in the middle of a sun-scorched field, stretching away from the road to the dark knots of forest trees. I slithered off the tank and left Dago to his own devices... He didn't know the Captain, but I did, so it was obvious to me that Yegorov had been puzzled by the egg and had picked it up for its very oddness, just as he picked up many other useless oddities from churches and cottages. He had subdued the little arrow-wielding boys with a command. Only if they gave him the egg would he accept them into the tank column. That's how it's done in an army. Dago's just ignorant... I was happy we'd stopped. I'd had quite enough of the tank's bumpy progress and Dago's endless wittering. But I would still look around for a nip of something for the midget, I promised myself.

I passed along the column and exchanged greetings with the servicemen, acknowledging their salutations and shouts, and the soldiers were tightening their belts, and those who didn't have helmets but caps on were mostly taking off their caps and putting on their helmets, because having your cap on meant taking a chance, and this close to Siřem no-one wanted to take chances. We expected that in a place where there was an inflammatory radio transmitter there'd also be armed men guarding it, and the soldiers in our column wanted to destroy that pocket of fanatical bandits once and for all. Many took advantage of the stop to put their arms and equipment in order, some were ambling about in the grey dust a few feet from the tanks, stretching their limbs, but they always remained vigilant. Unless the bandits had withdrawn for good... or perhaps surrendered to some other Soviet units... but we didn't think that was very likely... We knew by now that Czechs don't surrender. So we carried on as if they were all around us.

I got to the very end of the column, next to the cage with the wolf in it. This was where the camel boys were posted. That it was a wolf had been obvious to me when all those lights were blazing. I'd never have guessed that the first wolf I'd ever see would be such a wasted creature. It was cringing there on its pile of straw and blinking. I pulled a face at it, and narrowed my eyes to a squint and growled at it, but it didn't react. Its coat was all thin and moulted, and it probably couldn't care less that they'd taken away the egg it was keeping warm. Its eyes were all watery. I had to chuckle inside and thought to myself, 'So this is Margash's dad? And Margash's country where we were both supposed to go... it was probably about as beautiful as this here father of his was strong and mighty... ha, ha, ha!' I laughed at the wolf in a mighty voice, the kind of voice me and the boys had laughed in when we were making peace with the altar boys... Then one of the camel lads strolled over to the cage, and I pointed to the wolf and I said in Russian, 'Is that your dad?'

'Yeah,' said the lad, and made to push something into the cage.

'Is he the dad of all of you?'

'Yeah.' He nodded and looked at me, then he went off into some foreign language. He was younger and smaller than me. He had coarse black hair and his eyes were reduced to slits.

'I don't understand,' I told him.

'And who's your dad?' he asked in Russian.

'My dad's the military commander Captain Yegorov!' I said, and the lad pursed his lips and nodded, saying, 'Hmm...' and I got to thinking he was, like, envious of me. He stuck his hand through the bars and tossed a mouse into the cage. The wolf's mouth twitched. He bit the mouse in half and started chewing the spurting entrails and bristling skin.

I turned away and left. I hadn't found any meths. Dago was gonna have to get by without. Perhaps he'll give his tongue a rest, I thought to myself. If I'd had any inkling that I'd never see Dago again, I'd have thought something different.

I heard a shot, then another. Warning shots fired in the air. A group of women and children was coming towards us across the dusty field, their clothes grey with earth and dust... They were getting closer. Then they were quite close to the tank column. They were carrying sharpened sticks. They were poking in the soil... Captain Yegorov had probably left the egg in the inner recesses of the tank in the safekeeping of handpicked NCOs. He went up to the crowd of women and cowering children, looking around... and he was looking for me!... I crawled through a gap in the tanks and followed my captain into the field, my tankman's jacket flapping around me as if I were some longshirt, but I hadn't been a longshirt for a pretty long time now... I followed the Captain, and the women made way for us, and they weren't looking at us, and the Captain asked them things. He put the questions and I followed in his footsteps and said all the questions after him in Czech, which was dead easy. Captain Yegorov asked them,

'Where are your men? Where are the bandits?' and the women replied, 'Neznaju,' so there wasn't anything for me to interpret. And suddenly I was standing in front of Mrs Kropek, and she was so grey in the face I wouldn't have recognised her if she hadn't said, 'You poor blighter. They should've finished you off with a stick inside your mum's belly, you double-crossing Tatar monkey!' A girl stood next to Mrs Kropek, her face white and grey, and she was all haggard and worn, and I couldn't believe I'd once had her warm and soft and firm breast in the palm of my hand... Mrs Kropek carried on swearing at me, and some of the women had stopped retreating from us and our questions. They were laughing... 'You sodding treacherous little piece of Russian shit!' Mrs Kropek went on at me, and she gave me more of the same. I was looking over her shoulder at Hanka, who just stared at the ground and hid behind her mum. 'You twisted little rat!' said Mrs Kropek said. 'Go and die alone somewhere – and I hope it hurts, you filthy bastard!' That was a curse and they all knew it in Siřem, but they should never have used it... Captain Yegorov came over to us, asking what the Czech woman was saying, so I told him she was hungry.

Captain Yegorov gave an order and the field kitchen was brought from the supply train, and the women and kids got some army rations, today's gruel, and the whole grey crowd jostled around the kitchen, and we in the column were ordered back to our tanks, because Captain Yegorov had announced a midday break, and during the meal Captain Yegorov went about among the women and personally gave them second helpings, and carried on amiably asking his questions unaided, because the questions kept repeating themselves, the women already knew them, but they wouldn't tell him nothing.

While the mess detail packed the field kitchen away again, I sat behind the tank to check that my eyes weren't swollen or my belly dried out or my leg gone rigid – all of these could be brought on by that curse! But there was nothing wrong with me, so I gave a sigh of relief and got to thinking how good it would be if the mermaid were there among all those women and girls and kids! She'd tell them I'm different, that I'm a good guy... But I couldn't see anyone in the field wrapped in a blue, white and red flag, though I really strained my eyes. I went looking for Mrs Kropek and Hanka, because they must have finished eating by now, and Kantariya was dragging a girl out from the pack of women and kids who were still stuffing their faces. I couldn't tell it was a girl until I saw how she moved, lashing out with her bare knees when her dress rode up her legs, and also from how she shouted as he dragged her along. Another sub-machine-gunner had grabbed another girl from the crowd. He was pushing her ahead of him. If she fell, he picked her up. Then the women formed a wall around the other girls, who lay flat on the ground in the field, but for all their swearing at the soldiers and threatening them with sticks and fists, it did no good. The sub-machine-gunners dragged another one out. She twisted and turned and jerked her shoulders like she didn't want to go with them, but she had to.

I expected Captain Yegorov to bark a command and tweak Kantariya, who was dragging the first girl, by the ear and give him a slap, but Captain Yegorov did no such thing and Kantariya dragged the girl off behind the roadside bushes. The soldiers took away whatever girls they wanted to the same spot.

After a time, Captain Yegorov stood up, slid deftly from the tank and went into the bushes as well.

I was glad that Hanka looked so haggard and gaunt that they didn't want her. At least, I didn't see anyone grab her.

It took me just a few hops to get across the road and fly into the field. I dashed about looking for them. I knew I had to find them. If I didn't find Hanka, it would be terrible. I'd beg the Captain to let her come with our column. Hanka and the other girls might be able to perform in the circus, as Czechs. Why not? I roamed and ran about the field, looking for Hanka, but I couldn't find her. Had they run away while I was checking myself over behind the tank? I didn't know.

The women stared at the tanks and the tank men gawped back at them. It was quiet now. The almost still air was riven only by the loud wailing of some kid. The huddle of women, surrounding the one who was trying to soothe the bawling child, moved off towards the forest. Perhaps that was where they lived. Tank columns are equipped with lots of stuff, but nothing for calming screaming infants. The women left.

I never saw Hanka again. Or Mrs Kropek. They did a runner or something. That was the worst thing. I kept losing sight of people. Not like round a bend in a corridor or behind a tree. People were suddenly gone for ever.

The girls in the bushes came crawling out quite quietly. The soldiers were chatting very loudly, and they were laughing and dusting themselves down from top to bottom. The girls who'd crawled out of the bushes went and joined the others in the field. Then they all moved off, leading the children by the hand, carrying the tiniest ones, going further and further away into the dusty field, where there was nothing.

I returned to the lead tank. The ropes were there all right, but Dago was nowhere. He had gone. I was lucky nobody asked about him. After all, he'd been in my care.

The hamlet of Ctiradův Důl was the last stronghold before the final attack on Siřem.

The soldiers, excited by the women, were now hurriedly preparing their arms and equipment. We were about to break into Siřem and destroy all resistance, assuming there was any.

Well, I wasn't looking forward to that one bit. I wasn't feeling my best. After all, I'd lost Hanka again. And Dago, who was under my guard.

And to top it all, the Third World War broke out.

The Czechs unleashed it.

Once again, I heard about Commander Baudyš.

It was like this. Captain Yegorov and Gunner Kantariya and several of the NCOs and me were bivouacked in the only cottage that hadn't been burnt down, and where the Czechs hadn't even had time to switch off the television. And that, before we went on the attack, was something we welcomed, because the Radio Free Siřem transmitter had stopped transmitting and we lacked any reports from the Siřem military district.

On the Captain's orders, we surrounded the overheated television, each sitting or squatting down wherever he happened to be.

And we learned that the Third World War had broken out.

The Czech announcer said that the Czechoslovak people had been betrayed. He spoke of Czechoslovaks dying for the civilized world of Western Europe in an unequal contest against the Eastern hordes, all the while expecting that the former would come to their aid. They were standing up to an invasion from Russia's Asian steppes, just as their forebears had stood up to the invasions of the Tatars, and they were dying with their proud Czech or Slovak heads held high, having believed that the betrayal of civilized people would not be repeated, that there would be no repeat of Munich.

I translated and the NCOs muttered their displeasure and rolled their cigarettes, and then the news continued and now all the tankmen were cursing and swearing, and Kantariya even spat at the television, because it reported in words and pictures that many army corps of the Warsaw Pact nations had struck at the rear of the Soviet Army, alongside gangs of Czech bandits.

Many Polish and Hungarian divisions had torn up the Warsaw Pact and were engaged in battle with Soviet divisions. The numerically weaker Bulgarian and East German corps were fighting their way back to their own frontiers, or surrendering to the Czechs. But more and more new guards units of the Soviet Army kept rolling in and dealing severely with the betrayal.

Then we saw on the screen various army groups in various states of collapse and misery. We didn't find that funny... But then I stiffened and almost yelped, because there on the screen was a smiling Commander Baudyš!

He sat on a tank, waving a Czechoslovak flag on which was written THE TRUTH PREVAILS... and sitting next to him on the tank was Karel! I'd never have guessed I'd see one of the Bandits again one day.

It was Commander Baudyš and his partisan unit that had attacked West Germany. The thing was that Czech and Slovak partisans were impatiently looking out for the Americans and the forces of the Free World allied in the Atlantic Pact, Nato, and couldn't wait to get bedded down in suitable spots among the rocks and shoot down Soviet helicopters with American Redeye rockets, but the Americans hadn't shown up... The Americans and the forces of Nato weren't showing up... So Commander Baudyš had invaded West Germany to provoke a Third World War, at last giving the Americans and the Atlantic Pact a perfect opportunity and excuse for self-defence, and for stamping on the necks of the Soviet Communist hydra. And our heroic Czech and Slovak lads were making incursions across the western frontier on tanks and even in Soviet-made jeeps, carrying their recoilless Kalashnikovs, to tell the world about Communist atrocities so that the Free World would finally stir itself and not just stand by and watch Czechoslovakia's heroic resistance against the tide of brutal sovietization, but the world cared damn all and sod all and bugger all about Czechoslovakia.

The Atlantic Pact wasn't going to upset its tense relations with the Warsaw Pact over Czechoslovakia, so all sides agreed with all sides, and they hurled the rebels right back into the jaws of the Soviet hydra, and the situation changed for our Czech boys in the attack divisions that went into Germany. German bullets started whistling around their heads, and our boys tried in vain to show that their hands were up and that they'd come armed with nothing more than the Idea of Freedom... West German troops and the forces of the Atlantic Pact and American soldiers from bases in West Germany were now driving our boys back towards the Czechoslovak frontier – where, of course, the Soviets were waiting for them, as, having seized control of the situation, they had brought the rebellious Hungarians and Poles to heel. And our boys, who had attacked Germany to provoke a Third World War, were now being thrown back by the Germans towards the Russians, and the Russians were furious at their losses, so our boys really copped it, squashed between German and Russian millstones. The ones who weren't killed surrendered.

Only a single Bohemian lion did not surrender: Commander Baudyš and his division of specially trained saboteurs... After the renewed Soviet occupation of Prague, and the hero's death of the statesman Dubček, Czechoslovakia declared her unconditional capitulation, dictated by the supreme authorities of the Eastern Empire. Baudyš and his division alone did not accept it, and now he was hiding somewhere in the disorderly heartland of Czechoslovakia. And the guards units of the Eastern Empire, reinforced by Nato peacekeeping forces, gripped defiant Czechoslovakia in a ring of steel, and salvaged peace for the world and strangled the terrible Third World War before it was born... And the NCOs and Captain Yegorov cheered and clapped until the cottage shook, and they ran outside and gave the good tidings to the others – that it was the end... that there was peace at last!

The sub-machine-gunners shouted for joy and the ones who had steel helmets banged them on the tanks, and the ones who had caps tossed them joyfully in the air. The animals in our column added their neighing and braying to the jubilation, and the sub-machine-gunner standing next to me also tossed his cap in the air, and as he tried to catch it he staggered and I saw blood spurt from his neck, and then we heard a shot and another and then *Vrowwww!* and the cottage and its overheated television screen disappeared in fire and smoke. The cluster of cheering sub-machine-gunners was reduced to a jumble of crawling, groaning bodies... I looked for any sign of Captain Yegorov, but everyone had withdrawn to the tanks, and any minute now their guns would start spouting flashes, and I would be saved from the attackers, or torn apart by the gunfire... I jumped headfirst into the bushes, then I saw crouching shadows moving quickly around the ruins of the cottage, among the dead and injured. They must be the partisans who'd carried out the attack, but they didn't look like partisans and even in the thickening gloom it was obvious that they weren't soldiers of the Czechoslovak People's Army either... I propped myself up on one elbow and called out weakly, 'I'm here!'

17

Who got burnt? Hero in the hills. Czech sea. What's round the corner?

We were deep inside Chapman Forest. From the edge of the forest, where I sensed the tank column was, I could hear bursts of sub-machine-gun fire. And I could hear the lads chatting.

Martin said, 'It's that new lad. It's Margash, it is!'

But Dýha said, 'Bollocks! It's Ilya. I heard him say something.'

I sat up.

'Who are you?' someone asked, leaning towards me out of the darkness.

'Ilya.'

'And what's that stuff you're wearing, man?' asked Dýha. 'Russian clobber!'

They were wearing uniforms with the trouser legs cut off, and some had the sleeves cut off too, and they were all pinned up here and there, and some wore T-shirts and anoraks and trackies from the Home from Home, and various kids' clothes. But the main thing was how they were all hung about with weapons, sub-machine guns and Soviet pump-action guns, and almost all of them had knives. Not kitchen knives, but really nice knives, hanging from their belts in sheaths, like they should be.

Karel thrust his canteen in my hand and I had a drink. It was hard stuff. I didn't spit it out, but swallowed it slowly.

'What were you doing with the Russkies?' Dýha asked.

'Leave him alone!' said Karel. 'They probably captured him!'

I nodded and looked through the gloom. At the edge of the clearing was Freckles and some other altar boys. I recognized Pepper.

'Good God, Ilya!' Dýha exclaimed. 'If we'd known they was interrogating you in that cottage as a prisoner, we'd never have bazooka'd it, you know that!'

'We've been to Germany,' said Karel, sitting next to me. 'Do you want some chewing gum?'

We sat in the dense grass of the clearing, the tall trees around us looking like guardian spirits. It was still warm and the grass was teeming with insects. Suddenly I felt so tired that I stretched out on the ground. I lay in the grass, utterly defenceless, and took a close look at the boys' familiar faces. Some were missing, probably out on patrol. They were clutching their weapons, sitting and standing around me. Dýha, Karel, Martin from the Home. Some of the altar boys. They were lads that I knew – and they weren't. I was glad we were together. I think they were all glad.

Someone spat, someone else coughed, someone squatted down. I sensed that the tension there'd been in all of us had gone. It had been left behind on the path through the forest they'd dragged me along, and where we'd got stung by nettles and cut by the sharp tips of the long grass. The tension of combat sometimes falls away from men quite suddenly, like when you poke your head above water. The lads opened some tins and they'd also got bread. I had some as well, there was plenty of it. They nearly all had a canteen of water.

Dýha came and sat by me. 'We're drumming the Russkies out of the forest,' he said.

We were joined by Pepper and Freckles. 'Hi,' said Pepper. 'Hi there, man', 'Ilya, hi,' said some of the other lads as well.

'Hi, Martin,' I said. I only remembered him in a torn black smock, but now he was in camouflage gear. I used Czech. Talking Russian would have been stupid.

'I'm glad to see you,' said Martin. 'If you really are Ilya!'

'I am,' I said. 'Have you run into Šklíba?'

That was a stupid way to ask. I realized that at once, because Martin turned and left.

And then Dýha fell onto his back, he fell into the grass as if he'd suddenly been shot, but he was laughing. He'd made a lightning grab under my tank jacket, and from under the shabby trackie top I'd had at the Home he yanked a fistful of now well-thumbed documents with my maps on, which he must have spotted poking out. He was waving them around and through tears of laughter he said, 'Ilya's back... and his mission's accomplished! He's brought these!'

The lads started roaring and giggling, and some might have been imagining me disappearing through the door of the Home from Home to go on a combat mission... 'He has and all!... Accomplished his mission, ha, ha!' they laughed, and I hoped we were surrounded by really alert sentries, because that's how it has to be every time, even after a successful attack.

We sat in the grass together, just like old times, but there was no chance of making a fire, this was a powwow... There was lots of stuff I needed to know. I was pretty stunned to learn that Commander Vyžlata had been declared a national martyr, and it gave me quite a jolt that Commander Žinka had been executed for Commander Vyžlata's murder by the Home Guard, and that the Home Guard was made up of Holasa and Moravčík and Kropáček, and other Siřem men, obviously.

And Dýha told me that Vyžlata's body was lying in state on the square at Siřem surrounded by a wreath of candles that were kept burning and by a mountain of floral tributes, and I let out a little squeak of horror, which is something no saboteur should ever do... Dýha told me that Commander Vyžlata's tortured body had been found in a wash-tub by the new lad, Margash. Soon after that Žinka had confessed under some really tough interrogation, and because Margash had testified against him as well, Žinka was given short shrift by the People's Court. They shot him outside the Home from Home. It had happened fairly recently, which explained why the transmitter had fallen silent.

'The locals didn't want him as their commander anyway, see? They don't want anyone as their commander, see?' Dýha said. I nodded.

From the rest of our discussions I gathered that the lads were most concerned about the truce between the Nato forces and the troops of the five armies, now safeguarded by an army of new Russians of the Eastern Empire, a truce I only heard about on television in Ctiradův Důl, which was captured by the Soviets, then immediately lost again.

I was really pleased the lads were so full of their own adventures and so unconcerned about the details of my sojourn with the tank column.

'We were in Germany with the Yanks, like,' said Karel. I had swallowed his chewing gum ages ago, so he gave me another piece.

'And now the Nato lot's here and cosying up to the Russkies,' said Dýha.

'But our commander's never gonna give in to 'em,' Martin spouted.

'Nato's got men at all checkpoints along with the Russians, enough to make a decent chap afraid to poke his nose out of the forest,' said Karel.

'They're lookin' for weapons,' said Dýha. 'That's why they're turning over every chicken in the coop, and picking up every dog hair and stuff like that. They're scouring every village, man!'

'It's biological weapons they're lookin' for,' someone said.

'We'd have managed a war with the five armies by ourselves, us Czechs, with the Slovaks along as well,' said Dýha, 'but now the Russians have got all Nato on their side... well, who knows!'

I wanted to put my own oar in, and I couldn't carry on saying nothing, so I told the lads that some people in the tank column believed in a new brotherhood of machines and people and animals – and I was also wondering, since the war was over, whether we might not take care of the animals in the Socialist Circus Project. It was something we all knew about from working in the village...

'The brotherhood of people and animals? That was Eden,' said Martin. 'Nothing new! But with machines, man, that'll be Armageddon, believe me!'

'What's that?' I asked him, because I'd heard it before.

'The nuns taught us about it, man,' said Martin. 'You were always buried away somewhere with Monkeyface.'

I didn't want to hear about that, so I quickly started on something else... I told the lads about the wolf and the dinosaur egg, and they found it funny. They laughed, and I'd also found it funny when Dago told me about it on the tank.

So I told them all about the circus zone that was supposed to come into being under Captain Yegorov's command at this very spot, around Siřem. But the uprising had put paid to it!

The lads told me a group of Ukrainians had recently passed through with a dancing bear and that they'd let them pass. That could have been the circus.

Then the lads talked about running into a band of women one day in a forest clearing... They'd surprised the women in the forest, and a weird lot they were, because the women, wearing colourful clothes, leapt onto horses and charged off. I gathered that these women on horses had slipped past all five armies and the insurgents. The old people holed up in underground bunkers in the forest claimed they were wood nymphs and that it meant the end of the world, because whoever heard of nymphs on horseback wandering about among gangs of armed men?

That's what the lads told me, and I said nothing, though only I knew who those lady riders in motley circus attire were.

We simply chattered away.

'Say, though, Ilya, what did the wolf look like?'

My news about the egg and the wolf had provoked interest.

'I wonder if Nato and the new Russians are tightening the noose round Siřem because of the dinosaur egg.'

'Imagine,' said Karel, 'what a dinosaur attack could do to an American base! Reduce it to smithereens, I tell you.'

'But suppose it's not a dinosaur inside the egg, but something else. A secret weapon. Could be a live secret weapon,' I told the lads, and for a moment they were silent.

'Gosh!' someone gasped.

'It's something so terrible they thought it best to make a truce!' Martin panted.

For a moment we sat there saying nothing, then Karel ordered, 'To the crag! On your feet!' The lads stood up immediately, stuffed their spoons down their boots and the empty tins in their knapsacks, and cleared everything up, making it so tidy it looked as if no-one had ever even been there. Then Karel dived into the undergrowth of Chapman Forest, followed by the others. Only Dýha stayed seated.

'Look, the Šklíba thing,' he said. 'The altar boys that go and join their families in their shelters say that someone has seen a lone boy in the forest. What do you reckon?'

'Dunno.' I shrugged.

'And they say he was praying!' said Dýha. 'It could have been him.'

'Could,' I said and we both shrugged.

'Karel's an orderly, see,' Dýha added. '*I* should be the one with the higher rank!'

'Obviously!'

And I told Dýha that we needed to warn Commander Baudyš, because Captain Yegorov's tank column meant to attack Siřem.

'Hmm, well, that Yegorov of yours is in for a hard time. The whole area's being taken over by Kozhanov's 1st Tank Brigade of Guards, ain't that something?'

'Aha!' I said, though I hadn't a clue what he was on about.

'You're very lucky to be with us, Ilya,' Dýha said. We stood up and set off through the forest. I kept a close eye on the bushes and branches ahead of us, which were stirred ever so slightly by the lads who'd gone on ahead.

'Your pals in the tank column are headed straight for Siberia, you know, since they let their formations get knocked out by peasants,' said Dýha, and he laughed.

'What?'

'Yeah. The only ones in charge around here are gonna be Kozhanov's tank guards, and the Eastern Empire's new command's gonna sweep any other Russkies off to the gulag.'

For a while we just walked on.

'By the way, Ilya, that crap about dinosaurs and a secret weapon, that's just longshirts' horror stories. The Russians and Nato have reached an agreement. We're done with war before they do for us. The altar boys are gonna stay in the forest. They've got families here. But we ain't got no-one. I'm joining the Foreign Legion. You coming with me?'

I said nothing and kept walking.

'You left that paper in the wayside shrine, man,' Dýha was breathing down my neck. 'You did just the right thing! Baudyš was pleased. You're a great saboteur, man! But then if you weren't, we'd have done for you first, there on your tank, you realize that!'

'I'll report everything to the commander!' I said. I didn't want to say any more to Dýha. He was just like the soldiers on the tanks who liked their jobs in the column. He even smelt like them.

'You can't report anything to Baudyš.' Dýha laughed in the darkness ahead, where he had overtaken me. 'And what about the giraffe head?' he asked. 'Did it give you a fright?'

'Yeah!' I said.

'I bet it did.' Dýha was walking so fast I could hardly keep up, and he was carrying three Kalashnikovs, a full knapsack and ammunition. He knew the way, of course.

And then we were on Fell Crag. Part of the way we crawled up a steep hillside, and it was dead true that Dýha was a bright, nippy little guy, and as we crawled up through a cleft cut into the cliff overhang, I'd probably have got smashed up more than once without his hissed commands, like 'Toehold, man! Your foot this way!', and that wouldn't have been good for a saboteur redeploying to a new site. But I hadn't been waging war in the forest. I'd been on a tank.

Having climbed over the rocky ramparts, we were right there among the lads. They'd settled down on blankets and groundsheets around a little campfire, and those who wanted to were stuffing their faces again, and I said hello to Mikušinec. He gawped at me. Probably couldn't make up his mind whether it was me or not. The only one missing was Páta, but that our gypsies weren't there didn't surprise me a bit.

I'd been really lucky that they took out the cottage with a bazooka that day. It was their farewell night. The altar boys were off into the forest to their mothers and kid sisters, while Dýha and Mikušinec were already packed and ready to go off to join the Legion. I hadn't said yet where I was going, though I knew. 'And you, Martin? Karel?'

Martin told me he had one big task ahead of him still. Karel just sighed. There was water boiling in a battered kettle on the fire. Someone shoved a canteen in my hand, and I took a drink of hard liquor. I was to take part in the last night of the battle group, since Czechoslovakia, squeezed by the five armies, had capitulated, and I learned that the new Russians – that is Kozhanov's 1st Tank Brigade of Guards – would be here very soon to start picking up anyone who refused to lay down their arms, including recalcitrant Bulgarians and Poles and

Germans and Hungarians, and the old Soviet occupying forces who'd acquitted themselves badly, and so it really was time to do a runner, because anyone who stayed could expect to face a military tribunal! – and Siberia! – and that's if things went well! It's always been the same.

And the lads were earnestly talking about winding up their combat activities. Now and then they looked up towards the mountain high above our post with its defensive rocky ramparts, and some kind of saboteur's instinct told me that's where our Commander Baudyš was lurking. I wasn't wrong. In my mind I began to put together my report to him. I needn't have bothered.

The lads swished the liquor from their canteens into the hot tea, and reminisced about all the fighting. They were laughing and talking about people suffering in coarse, husky voices that broke now and again into a squeak like some mouse or bird, and again I was glad that Dago had done a bunk, disappearing before the bazooka attack, because he could easily have copped it... I wanted to tell the lads about the funny little dwarf, they'd like that!... But now wasn't the time, because Freckles, Holý, Pepper, all our altar boys were saying goodbye. We exchanged manly handshakes and, if we'd had stubble on our cheeks, furtive manly tears might well have run down it – that's allowed when the fighting's over! But our cheeks were still soft and whisker-free.

Now the altar boys quickly and quietly took off all the various bits of their uniforms and tossed them on the ground, and put on sweaters and trackies and other normal clothes which they had ready, so it took a while, and they also put their sub-machine guns and rifles and grenades and their cool knives in a big pile. Some had *Siaz* marked on them. Some were quite nice. Then one after another they clambered over the ramparts. It crossed my mind that one of them could be my lovely Hanka's brother, but I couldn't ask! I was just a reform school kid who'd skipped his tank unit! They didn't want me on the crag... I didn't dare risk it.

So I was sitting with the Bandits, just like old times, listening to all the tales about what had been going on. What surprised me most was the news that since his hero's death old Mr Cimbura had also become a superstar.

'What with Vyžlata being a martyr, that makes two Siřem saints,' Martin called out faintly. 'Think how happy that would make the sisters.' And in the glare of the fire he clapped gently, just patting his palms lightly, his cheeks ablaze.

Martin was glad I asked him things, so off he started and the other lads just chipped in now and then... I heard that the extraordinary wartime beatification of Mr Cimbura was decided by no less than the auxiliary bishop of Louny... and that the hero Alexander Dubček was still alive, and he'd sent a messenger to Siřem all the way from Prague with his personal greeting. After all, the entire Czechoslovak uprising – in the suppression of which the best combat troops of five armies were nearly bled dry – broke out in Siřem right after Cimbura's great act... 'Dead right,' the lads chimed in, and here and there one of them tossed a twig on the fire, and Martin handed me his canteen and carried on talking...

'First they wanted to turn Siřem into a model of collaboration, right? The Radio Free Siřem transmitter really got up their noses... In the five armies and all over Czechoslovakia people had heard about how brilliantly organized our Siaz was, and all zones in revolt looked up to us... We was held up as an example! So that's why the Soviets decided to bring Siřem to its knees,' said Martin, and the lads lapped it all up, and it crossed my mind that he wasn't telling this tale for the first time...

'The five armies' TV – the eyes of the entire world – were supposed to see us brought down and made powerless. There were platforms on the square in Siřem for all of them bigwigs and officers and top brass, and, just fancy, collaborators came up to them (they must have brought in actors or something, because a Czech collaborator? That don't make sense! They hired people) and the collaborators come up and they bring the keys of the town to them cut-throat generals with uniforms all covered with spangles, but it didn't happen, man... Siřem was meant to be a model of collaboration, but instead it came to symbolize nationwide resistance!' As he talked, Martin waved his arms about as if the words were straining to get out. He told his tale, but it was not like when Commander Vyžlata told stories to send us to sleep. It wasn't like Commander Baudyš giving instructions, and it wasn't like Dago's babbling on the tank. The lads hung on his every word...

'Suddenly, Cimbura rides into the square on his wheelchair, pushed along by some old woman. He's brandishing his crutch and he bellows, "To Moscow!" and he hurls his crutch and sends the collaborators' keys of the town flying into the dust, honest! And Cimbura wheels himself away from the old biddy, then pours petrol over himself and with everyone looking on sets fire to himself and rides straight at the platform and the platform goes up in flames as if hell itself had opened up!'

Martin spoke very fast, sweat streaming down his face. 'And so it started! People remembered their oaths and pledges, their dear Czech homeland, and the whole green rang to the tune of "Arise, Ye Holy Warriors of Blaník", and the Home Guard, headed by Holasa and Kropáček, and Moravčík and Dašler, got to work with a will, and before the anthem "Where is My Home?" came to an end all the Russians were gone from Siřem, at least the ones who were alive; the others were lying around the green in the acrid stench of the charred remains of the generals... The nation rose up after the great Cimbura became a living torch. I saw the live broadcast. The rest you know, eh, Ilya?'

They were all silent. I nodded earnestly, because what could I say? The tank column? Snipers? The gangs in our sector? There was no point.

I sat and watched... then I grabbed a handful of grass and rubbed the mask of axle grease and the blood of insects from my forehead and cheeks. The tea had gone cold, so I used that too... Martin tossed me a sweater he'd picked from the pile left by the altar boys. I stood up, pealed off my tank jacket and hurled it into the flames, then I wriggled out of my tankman's trousers and tracksuit, which was so covered in oil, sweat and blood (not mine) it was as vile as an old scab, and tossed everything into the fire. It was a good thing nothing was cooking on it.

Martin gave me a nice T-shirt to go with the sweater. I also got an army shirt with the sleeves cut back, and from the pile by the fire I chose other items, big and small, to cram myself into, and I was dressed like the other boys, and that was good. I kept the case with my maps, and the sad remains of the *Manual* and the *Book of Knowledge* and put them where they belonged. And when Dýha hung his canteen around my neck, the lads all laughed, and so did I.

Then a sound came down on us. My ears were muffled by that strange sound. I turned towards the heavy sigh that I could hear for the first time: *Ooaaargh!* And again: *Ooaaargh!*

It was coming from the mountain above us. I could have missed it, because Martin was talking. The hairs on the back of my neck stood on end, and a shiver ran down my spine. I glanced at the lads. They were all silent.

'They've got prisoners up there,' it crossed my mind.

'It's Baudyš,' Dýha told me.

'What's wrong with him?' I asked.

'He's groaning with pain, man,' Dýha told me. 'Moaning with the pain, our hero,' someone whispered. I was still shivering at the sound. 'The commander's studded with all sorts of injuries,' said someone else. There was another almighty sigh, so loud it seemed to fill the whole dark mountain above us, escaping like air from a giant balloon.

'We sank a shaft for the commander, just like he wanted,' Martin said in a whisper.

'We did it with dynamite,' whispered Dýha.

'And people decorated it,' said Martin quietly, 'with branches and flowers. The womenfolk swept all the odd bits and pieces of rock out, so it's all clean and cosy, like in church. You'd never believe it!'

'Kids took their toys to the shaft to honour the commander,' Mikušinec said.

'But now nobody's allowed near,' said Karel.

'At first,' Mikušinec said, throwing a few branches onto the fire, 'when our commander breathed like that, the whole mountain shook.'

'And even animals from Chapman Forest would come!' said Martin.

'I never saw none!' said Dýha.

'But I did,' said Martin. 'And eagles circled over the mountain.'

'Come off it, man,' said Dýha, 'where do you find eagles around here? Magpies maybe.'

'When our commander ordered us to dig out a shaft, there *was* birds circling over the mountain!' insisted Martin.

And again we heard sighs coming from the mountain. Now and again a twig crackled in the fire. I took a sip from a fresh brew of hot tea. All around, beyond the rocky ramparts, darkness was sinking into the forest. My old uniform on the fire had stopped stinking. It didn't stink for long.

'He'll let us know when we have to blow him up,' said Martin.

'You what?' I said, spilling tea all over my nice new clobber and scalding myself into the bargain.

'We'll blow him up with dynamite. So he stays up here for ever,' Martin tried to explain.

'So his hero's body can't never fall into enemy hands,' said Karel.

'So his hero's grave may kindle new resistance,' said Mikušinec.

'That was the Commander's instructions,' said Martin.

'That's right,' Dýha yawned. 'Our final mission, lads.'

'Yep,' someone else said.

Only after the sighs from inside the mountain had abated did we wrap ourselves variously in blankets and groundsheets, sitting or lying around the meagre flames of the fire, as if we wanted to protect it with our bodies from the damp and dark of the forest beyond the boulders all around our post.

I wondered about the watch rota, but no-one had said anything.

Mikušinec was repacking his backpack. He too was about to head for the Legion.

'You haven't got much with you,' I said for the sake of something to say.

'They'll give us everything in the Legion,' Mikušinec replied. 'The main thing is to get as far as the first port.'

'Where's that?' I asked, though I didn't want to go.

'On the edge of Bohemia,' said Mikušinec, 'by the sea.'

'Right. And where's Páta?' I asked, and Dýha said, 'He refuses to budge from Siřem cemetery. Likes the peace and quiet, he says.'

'Right,' I said again, and, even though as a saboteur I ought to have known, I asked him where Još's gypsy hut was, because that's exactly where I wanted to go once things were finished with on the crag, and Dýha told me.

'It's still odd, you know,' he went on.

'What?'

'Chata and Bajza and the other gippos tracked down their kid brothers, and are said to have carried out a raid on a children's camp to take them back to their shack. While we,' he propped himself up on one elbow and looked at me, 'we cared sod all about our long-shirts.'

'That's right,' I said, and in my mind's eye I could see the little mugs of the little lads, and I could see their feet, bare or in battered old boots, their white shirts flapping around their ankles. I thought of the long-shirts screaming in fear without the nuns, and padding around within the darkened walls of the Home from Home… I would sometimes remember them wandering around even during breaks in the fighting, if I heard tiny birds scrabbling about in the trees of Chapman Forest, and once, when I spotted some abandoned toys in one of the pockets of resistance that we smashed to smithereens, it crossed my mind that I could pick up the odd soft toy for the longshirts, but I had no idea where the little ones had gone.

'Gypsies,' said Dýha. 'Gypsies don't wage war on anyone,' he said, yawning.

Then I heard Mikušinec laughing quietly. He'd already snuggled down, wrapped up in blankets. 'That bear was so funny... me and Dýha here were in the forest and suddenly this bear! Made us jump, it did! And the bear gets up on its hind legs and sticks its paw out! Ha, ha! He were a performing bear, Ilya. You've never seen anything like it!'

'That's right,' Dýha mumbled, 'and he made you jump too!'

'Hey, Ilya,' said Mikušinec, sounding very sleepy, and suddenly I found it strange, all those years we used to chat together just like this in the older boys' dormitory, and I'd barely become a Bandit again, and it would all be over with on Fell Crag. Ah well... 'Ilya, kid, you noticed anything odd?'

'Like what?'

'You know, down in the forest. Like something's happened in the forest, man. Looks like the animals have done a bunk.'

'I haven't been in the forest much.'

'Right.'

Then Dýha chortled, 'Anybody would take fright at a bear. Anyone! But Mikuš here, he got kicked by a rabbit. Funny, eh? Ha, ha!'

Mikušinec was suddenly wide awake and said, 'But it was huge! A giant rabbit, man,' and he went on about rabbits the size of dogs that got up on their hind legs and tore through the camp when he was on sentry duty, and one of them gave him an almighty kick. It did!

Me and Dýha laughed until we howled, and Mikušinec said the giant rabbit that kicked him had a tiny little rabbit in its belly, and Dýha said, 'Now you're talking bollocks!' and I was watching the clouds as they crossed the sky, passing over the moon, which was dripping light. I was nearly asleep, but I still asked Dýha, 'What about sentries?' and he just mumbled that I could forget it. The Russians wouldn't venture into the forest. They were still scared of the Commander.

So we fell asleep, and that was a great mistake, because we were attacked in the small hours by the panzer grenadiers of Major General Kozhanov's 1st Tank Brigade of Guards, supported by the motorized riflemen of the 24th Samara-Ulyanovsk Division, and covered by the motorized riflemen of the 30th Irkutsk-Pinsk Guards Division, holders of the Order of Lenin and two Orders of the Red Banner; and we, up on our high point, were also pitched into by soldiers of the 1st Proletarian Moscow-Minsk Motorized Rifle Guards Division, holders of, among others, the Order of Suvorov (second degree) and the Order of Kutuzov (second degree); and on top of that the assault lines of those sent to butcher us were reinforced by observers and specialists from the Atlantic Pact forces. So we nearly missed blowing up our Commander.

Who the buggers were who were hell-bent on killing us that day I only discovered later. Early that morning there wasn't much time to find out. It was all I could do just to survive.

The first thing I'd seen at the dawning of the new day was Dýha's face, so screwed up that it scared me.

He was holding a finger to his lips.

It was quiet, not a bird tweeted and mist was rising from the woods beneath us, creeping towards us from the treetops, dribbling towards us over the rocky ramparts and through all the cracks in them. I saw all this because I'd rolled over on my front. The canteen Dýha had given me was poking into me. The lads were crouching behind the rocky ramparts, holding all their various machine guns and sub-machine guns and pump-action guns at the ready.

Me and Dýha crawled over to join them.

Down among the trees, amid the creeping shreds of mist, I caught a glimpse of something moving. It could have been a hind, but it was this guy in a black uniform, and behind him were others in camouflage gear. They were hopping through the mist, jumping between the trees and getting closer by leaps and bounds.

The forest was full of them.

Yet it was quiet. I turned to see the Bandits. They were kneeling, ready to shoot. The mist swirled around Martin's body. In no time he was just a black silhouette in white milk. The rock was digging into my knees. The last time we'd knelt together like this was in the gloom of Siřem church amid the acrid smoke of candles. Dýha was next to me, smiling. I thought he was enjoying himself.

And it was cold, just like in the church. When the rocks got warmed up in the summer's heat, they'd be riddled with bullet holes. I was unlikely to see that. I didn't care that I didn't have a weapon. In the first sunlight, I saw in the forest below us those familiar glints and it dawned on me that there were so many weapons down there that whatever we had we were done for. And I'd seen no sign of a bazooka or any other decent bit of kit among the boys. They'd probably squandered everything worthwhile back in Ctiradův Důl. If I hadn't burnt my tankman's uniform, I might have been mistaken for a prisoner of the Bandits.

Then I started to hear sighs from the mountain again, and suddenly I couldn't give a damn about anything. I think I just wanted everything to end.

In the quiet of early morning, the sighs and groans from the mountain sounded louder than in the evening. The Commander's breathing thundered and whistled in the stone throat of the shaft, and all those cut-throats and sharpshooters down below couldn't fail to hear it. The sighing and groaning inside the mountain went on and on, as if someone was being interrogated by mountain goblins. The Commander must have been in great pain from the wounds covering his heroic frame. For an instant I had this notion that the Commander's agonized breathing would sweep the attackers back down the hill, but that must have been my mind wandering off into some fairy tale.

Karel crept across to us, dragging a pump-action gun behind him over the stones with his left hand, which struck me as not very careful. In his right had he was clutching a thin black flex. Dýha turned away from the rock embrasure, and he said, 'Now?'

Karel nodded.

Martin peeped out of the mist, pulling a silly face, and with his mouth agape he silently asked the same question. Mikušinec came crawling through the mist to join us, pushing ahead of him the backpack he'd got ready to take to the Legion, and to his questioning expression Karel whispered, 'Yep!'

The flex in Karel's hand was fitted with a switch, something I knew about. So I waited for the big bang, and just hoped the lads had made a first-class job of laying the mines.

We waited. The men down below didn't. Now and again we caught a jangle from the equipment of some careless twerp, or twigs cracking. These were no performing bears or jolly kangaroos climbing up to inspect Fell Crag, no sir!

But Karel suddenly whispered, 'I can't do it!' and to my amazement I saw our orderly quietly blubbering.

'Well I can!' said Dýha, and he reached for the switch... One mighty sigh from the bowels of the mountain had just turned into a groan, as if the Commander was spurring us on... Suddenly this fire came hurtling at us out of the forest, igniting the air above our heads with a deafening crash. Around and above us, rocks were flying and stones smashed into boulders on every side, splitting into bits. I couldn't hear a thing in that hail of stones. I could only see that Dýha was no longer next to me. Part of the cliff had broken away and collapsed into the mist. I couldn't see anyone or anything. I lay down for safety and covered my head, the canteen digging painfully into my chest. I thought it was the canteen, but then I saw it was the black switch, and I'd rolled onto it by accident, and so it had come about that our Commander, and with him the whole of Fell Crag, was in all likelihood blown up by me.

I didn't worry about it. I dashed into the dark of the forest under-growth, which, as I have already noted several times, surrounded our post on Fell Crag.

I can't relay much about my wanderings in Chapman Forest. Stuff grew in some places, but not in others, and although I wasn't hungry, I was plagued by the most embarrassing gastric problems, and that's bad form for any fighting man. All I had was my full canteen. I didn't drink hard liquor, not till later, when I was talking to the gippos.

How I broke out of the encirclement and found myself alone in the forest, I've no idea. I could have fainted and lain in some thicket long enough for the soldiers to have withdrawn. It's hard to say. It did cross my mind to let myself be found by the soldiers. I knew how to cope with that by then. When all's said and done, I was just a poor orphan and I'd lost my way. But I gave up that idea after I saw the villages. I reached the villages later.

Moreover, I'd been engaged in battle in a combat unit. They'd be able to tell that from the way I moved, the way I walked, from all the things I did and knew. They'd ask questions. To be under interrogation on the opposite side from before wasn't something I fancied.

In the thicket where I came round, I inspected the terrain, sniffed the air and also hoped I'd meet one or two Bandits. At that point I'd have welcomed an invitation to go and join the Foreign Legion. But none of the lads showed up.

Just like a Soviet scout, I looked closely at the colour and humidity of the grass, and at everything else that was there, to see if the rocks were big and without odour and scarring or, conversely, riven by ancient waters and sweetly scented. I even scrutinized the heavy clouds that merged with the waving motion of the trees. So it wasn't at all hard to find the brook. Beside it I counted up my aching bones and I drank from it. I ate frogs and stuff.

Then I started having more dreams about Hanka. Her battered body came back to me, and with it a thrill. I imagined her wandering around Siřem, and I grew tired of life in my forest hideout. It was my first time alone, and I talked and snuggled up to Hanka all the more. It was nice in my dream. But I knew I'd have to leave.

I decided to find the gypsy shack and become a gypsy. I guess anyone who had spent part of their life on the front of a Soviet tank with his face blackened with axle grease would think that was a good idea. I knew that Još's valley was not far from Siřem, where the old buzzard often went in search of work.

When the lads were working on the rocks by the footbridge they would disappear to his shack. And Dýha had told me which way to go. So I followed the stream. It would bring me to the bridge, as I believed, but I mustn't turn off into Siřem.

The stream led me to some forest ground covered in dark green, dense tussocks of grass, and the forest moss became springy underfoot. At the Home from Home we used to while away our childhood telling spooky tales about various villains who'd met their end by wandering off the poachers' paths and getting swallowed up by the mire, so I took extra care. It was good to know that wherever I could wade through, any army vehicles, or even a pursuit platoon of giant paras, would nosedive into a deep squelching hollow of ooze. The forest was a safe place to be.

Then I saw the women trees. The frog zone had come to an end, but I was still hungry, and I had this idea that since I was so small it would also be all right to eat the smallest animals, but those ants were evil. They stung the inside of my mouth and throat real bad. Gargling with tar was nothing compared to that onslaught. I was at the spot Mr Cimbura had once told me about, or maybe I was just dreaming it, because of the ants' poison, and this spot had no mercy on me. Mostly I'd seen the face of Czechia, whether in pictures or my mind's eye, as lovely, but those masks of a woman's face carved into the hard wood of the trees were meant to scare the pants off you, and they did.

The Czechia war masks were cut into the trees at about my height. Perhaps the old people that carved them weren't very tall either. When I saw the first mask, I screamed and fell over, and felt a painful prick in my bottom. It wasn't another ant, but an ancient arrowhead, the sort of weapon foreign armies used to use. There was something about that in *The Catholic Book of Knowledge*, in the chapter about the boy Sebastian. If I stamped my feet in the nettles and thick undergrowth, I'd probably hear the crunch of the rotten shields of ancient marauders, driven mad by Czechia here in her grove. I looked back at the evil face of she who was supposed to bring comfort, and headed out of Czechia's grove, guarded by its tiny warriors. I was afraid I wouldn't get out of there, and I'd end up going round and round in circles, and then I'd drop down and die, but I managed. Czechia had recognized me as one of her fighting men. But I lost track of the waterway I'd found. Which is how I arrived at the villages.

The cottages in the captured territory looked like they were dying. Pockmarked by bullets, burnt. An isolated shot-up cottage at the edge of the forest resembled an injured cow. I'd forgotten if the signs with the names of the villages had been shot through by the insurgents to put the fear of God into us, or if we'd fired at them for the same reason.

A village always means noise. It's a living confusion of honking geese and waddling ducks, squabbling hens and ganders. But there was no sound. Not a hoof clip-clopped. There were no cats or dogs either.

The Bandits had talked about checkpoints, where Nato and the Russians inspected anyone left alive. I hadn't run into any such checkpoint, so I didn't know if the lads were talking rubbish or not.

I entered these villages by roundabout ways, across a field or through the forest.

The first one was a shock. I was following the route Skryje-Bataj-Tomašín-Luka-Ctiradův Důl. I didn't need to consult my maps. Our chain of tanks had rolled through this way. Someone had to have survived the passing of our column. There must be people somewhere in cellars, woodsheds, or the underground passages beneath the cottages. If I got collared now by someone who'd seen our attack or even spotted me scuttling off to report or something, that wouldn't be good. But there was nobody anywhere. I was on my guard. My nose sniffed the air, even while I was asleep. I couldn't smell either food or smoke anywhere.

The ruins had burnt out long ago. Things lay around here, there and everywhere, but only broken pots, smashed settees, general mess, rubble, rags, refuse. It looked as if someone had picked over things. The women with Hanka hadn't been carrying anything when we saw them in the field.

I picked up various rags and tatters, and made myself a snug for the night at the edge of the forest. I carried my rag bed on my back. The nights were cold. I wanted to get to Još's. And I don't mind admitting, I wasn't feeling my best. Which is why I drank that strong liquor one night. I was talking to the gippos. Later on, I heard about the women and saw some guys eating a guy. That was on captured territory. Oh dear!

In the evening I reached a school. It was the one where we'd met the Bulgarians with the mermaid. They'd guided us direct from there to Siřem. Somewhere in a classroom there must still be the pages that Captain Yegorov had torn out.

I sat down in the school entrance under the graffiti that got up

Captain Yegorov's nose. I started crying when dusk veiled the statue of Wenceslas, the patron saint of the land of the Czechs, along with its inscription.

I was wondering when my shitty childhood would come to an end, and what things would be like afterwards. I was disgusted with my own genes. I uncorked Dýha's canteen, saying, 'I reckon you're already with the Legion, guys!' and started drinking. I thought long and hard about the boys from the Home from Home, and then realized I was sitting bawling my eyes out on a war road, where there was no traffic and Chapman Forest all around me, and that I'd have to become a lone bandit in a region of Death. Death, who I'd tried my very best to keep fed with people. I tried to empty the canteen at the same rate as the twilight changed into darkness, and I cursed into the dark, and because I was trying to find the darkies, I spouted all the gypsy words I knew, and my swear words and foul curses were like the noise from the longshirts' dormitory when they were scared. But somewhere amid all the *dylinos!* and *degeshas!* I must have garbled some gypsy fairy-tale magic spell, because I was suddenly inside a gypsy shack!

It was Još's shack. A big place, full of rags and smashed crockery all over the floor, broken things, half-rotted straw. There was nobody there.

'So I've found Još's valley, and they're gone!' I said to myself, and I reached into the vast hearth, where there were a few scorched cans and masses of little bones, as well as a big pile of white embers, and it was completely cold. I leapt to my feet and started jumping up and groping behind the beams as well and sure enough they did have her there! But she'd been painted over. She had black hair and she was all swarthy, this Czechia of theirs. So I left her where she was behind the beam; I couldn't go around with one like this. I went outside and I saw Chata coming out of the forest towards me, and my hair stood on end, because it was Chata and it wasn't Chata.

And Chata said, 'What d'you want?'

'I've found you!' I said, and I wanted to go with him, but I couldn't.

'Listen Chata,' I said, 'I'd like to stay with your lot. Can I go with you?'

'Tricky!' said Chata.

'Dýha says you wanted to liberate the darkies... er... your brothers, who'd been taken prisoner!'

'Yeah,' he said, 'but that's the thing, we didn't manage to.'

'Listen, Chata,' I told him. 'I'm lost round here. Can't I stay with your lot?'

'Don't be stupid,' Chata said with a smirk.

And now old Još was standing next to him, and I could sense I couldn't go with him either. Još said, 'You wanna be with us because no-one makes war with the Gypsies, right?'

'Yeah.'

And old Još said, 'But they can kill us anyway, right?'

'Yeah.'

'So there you have it!' said old Još.

'Like I said, we failed. To free our brothers,' Chata said, pretty impatiently.

I'd completely had it by then. Još was old and the skin on his face was all crinkly like the crocodiles in *The Catholic Book of Knowledge*. I had a feeling he wouldn't laugh at me, so I asked him, 'And can I be all on my own for all time?'

"Course you can't,' said old Još.

'So, what am I supposed to do then?'

'Look, we've gotta get going,' said Chata. 'The brothers are waiting!'

Then they were gone. They weren't there any more. All I could hear was Chata laughing: 'Saying he wants to go with us... ha, ha, ha!'

I sat outside the school again and tried to put the stopper back in the canteen. I managed, then I started to fall over backwards, but because I'd got a bed of rags on my back, made up of stuff picked up at the cottages, I landed softly and was asleep in no time.

And that's how I was found in the morning, asleep, curled up like a dog, my thirsty tongue hanging out, by Peter, who was in charge of a machine gun-armed Soviet jeep. He was also inspector of reservoirs.

He kicked me in the leg and I yelped, and from his uniform and really weird Russian I gathered he was from the army corps of the Hungarian People's Republic. He wanted to know how to get to the Little Supremo.

I soon realized that Peter was crazy. In turn, he took me for some stupid peasant kid. He was quite happy to sit me in his jeep and give me something to eat and drink, and we chatted together. I picked up his semi-automatic from the back seat, and all he did was laugh and tell me to be careful, because it was loaded. I showed an interest in the two machine guns mounted on the back, so he explained how they worked, and he also boasted about the ones mounted in front. Next I wanted to examine his Nagant revolver and dagger, so he lent me them both and I laughed, because I assumed that was how a stupid peasant, especially one who's still just a kid, would laugh, and then I really was very happy, because this guy wasn't teaching me or training me or interrogating me, and if it came to that, well, he'd already offered me a way to take him out with a variety of weapons.

Peter questioned me as to what I was doing within the reservoir project catchment area. I told him I'd come out of the forest.

He nodded and said it was because of people like me that the Soviet command had appointed him inspector. He'd been driving around collecting leftover people, because here in the forest region even rural life had come to an end. But now he was looking for the Little Supremo. Otherwise there was nobody here any more. They'd all been evacuated.

I told him I'd noticed all the villages were abandoned and generally odd.

'Yes,' Peter nodded, 'this region is to witness the realisation of the ancient dream of the Czechoslovak masses. There will be a sea here. It will be the Czech Sea, as a gift from ordinary Soviet people to the ordinary people of Czechoslovakia.'

'I see,' I said.

'There will be this second Central European Balaton, which is why the main engineering works are being carried out by experienced Hungarian comrades – inlanders,' said Peter, and I didn't have a clue what he was on about, so I asked him where all the people had gone.

'Most of the population has already been evacuated,' Peter said. I didn't know what that meant, but it sounded pretty stupid.

'All around here will be flooded,' Peter went on, and he waved an arm, and that wave across the area around Siřem was probably meant to take in the deserted villages left over after the fighting.

Then Peter talked about women. He didn't mean the poor women that toiled in the fields, but described some gorgeous women on horses. He said he believed the riders were part of the Little Supremo's contingent. He talked about women jumping right over his armoured jeep on their horses – black, grey and piebald. He didn't manage to talk to any of the women and they rode off. He wanted to inform the Little Supremo about the reservoir project. He believed the Little Supremo and his contingent were detained in some inaccessible regions. He would be grateful, assuming I was a local, if I'd conduct him to the Little Supremo.

I hadn't a clue what he was on about, but I wanted to make him happy, since he'd found me, so I nodded.

'Be a good lad, Ilya,' he said, 'find the Little Supremo.'

Now Peter and me were sat next to the statue of the Czech patron saint, who was armed, in a village where some of the men had probably been killed and the women run away into the forest, and the remaining folk evacuated, whatever that meant, and Peter struck me as the craziest soldier I'd ever met. The thing about him was, he was happy. He was obsessed with finding the Little Supremo, who I knew nothing about. Peter said I seemed like a godsend, just when he needed one. 'Together, we'll creep our way through each and every army to the inaccessible regions,' he said, 'and we'll find the Little Supremo.'

I nodded. Then everything went so fast that I didn't have time to regret the brevity of our alliance.

I told Peter that I'd noticed the odd hoofprint from time to time in Chapman Forest, and once I'd heard female laughter. Peter was overjoyed.

We mooned around there, chatting. I translated into Russian the inscription LET US NOT PERISH, NOR THOSE WHO COME AFTER US on this statue of an older style of fighting man, and I told him that before long the only thing left of the Czech land would be its name, a fate that has befallen many other foreigners as well, as history shows. Peter started laughing and assured me I was totally wrong, then he span me such a yarn that if the nuns were around he'd have had to gargle a whole bucketful of tar.

He told me about the Little Supremo. His army corps' scouts had learned about the Little Supremo from their women prisoners.

Apparently, it was all about some new tactic in the fight against sovietization. 'It's the only way for smaller nations to prevent themselves from being totally submerged in the Eastern Empire,' said Peter.

When stories about the Little Supremo spread among the divisions, the number of deserters rose. After the Czech insurgency had crushed Peter's division, he decided to find the Little Supremo and offer him his services.

Peter had first learned of the Little Supremo from a female prisoner. She even came, apparently, from a place I'd mentioned – a Siřem girl!

'What did she look like?' I gasped.

'Pretty, young and wearing a tracksuit,' Peter said, but he didn't know her name. After the Siřem girl had filled the other prisoners' heads with silly ideas, talking about the Little Supremo, they escaped. All the women who had refused to be evacuated wandered off into the forest.

'What had she told them?' I asked.

'They call it the Prophecy of the Little People,' said Peter.

And off he went, though because he told me about the prophecy in Hungarian Russian, it's possible I didn't quite grasp it all. But what he said was roughly this. The heroic Czech men having fallen in battle against troops from the five armies despatched by the Eastern Empire, their womenfolk were left forlorn and weeping. They walked on and on through dusty fields on a terrible journey, attacked and violated by enemy soldiers. There was no-one to stand up for them. Then suddenly the women found their hero: a tiny man, who, all by himself, was pulling along a captured enemy tank on a rope. They were amazed at his strength and virility. He took pity on the women and went with them into the forest. Since that day, the bellies of the widows of those heroic warriors, as well as the bellies of young maidens, have been growing and rounding out, and many of them will soon bear little warriors. So little that it will be easy for them to slip between the checkpoints of the five armies and continue wreaking havoc on the enemy until his total annihilation. They would dwell in caves and forest hideaways, and they would be impossible to track down.

Peter laughed, waiting to see what I made of it all.

'You've really never heard of the Little Supremo?' he asked, unbelieving.

I thought he'd been wandering about that deserted landscape for too long. He was hooked on a fairy tale. It was obvious what had really happened, although there is a big difference between pulling a tank along and jumping over it. But it was entirely possible that Dago had been snatched by the women.

Peter was still laughing. He was really looking forward to this Czech boy leading him into the inaccessible regions of Chapman Forest. He was a deserter. He had no idea that the Siaz zone was trapped in a ring of steel by the armies of the new Russians. If I'd told him, perhaps he might not have bled to death later on my shoulder. After all, I liked being with him. I wanted to go on further with him. It had also crossed my mind that our progress would be safer in an armed jeep. Except I was wrong, as so many times before.

Peter slept in the jeep, between the machine guns, me with my bed-roll at my back. I went behind the school, not wanting to be too close to the road.

Somewhere in the grass, among some titchy little apple trees, I curled up in a ball and fell asleep. When I opened my eyes again, there beyond the school orchard I saw the flames of a campfire flickering and, because I'd had the training, I was wide awake at once and crawled silently towards it.

Unfortunately, what I saw was the ghastliest thing I've ever seen in my life: two men were carving up a third, who lay on the ground.

These guys had sticks, on the ends of which were chunks of meat freshly cut from the carcass. I could only see the outline in the grass, dancing in the glimmer of the fire. They didn't speak Russian or Czech, but something similar. I could understand them. It was how Mikušinec or someone used to witter on in the night.

They were just saying that a bottle of something with a bit of a kick to it would slip down nicely with Teddy.

Then one of them took a pinch of ash from the fire and scattered it over the bedarkened grass that lay all around, and said, 'We thank thee, Uncle Ted!'

The other did the same, also thanking poor Ted, who was lolling about in the grass, but also disappearing inside their bellies.

And they stuffed themselves.

Perhaps my tummy rumbled or I made a bad move or they'd had the right training, but suddenly they were beside me and dragging me, unarmed, across to the fire. Their grip loosened and I sat on the grass right next to what was left of Ted, and they observed, in Russian, that I was only a boy, and heaved a sigh of relief. I probably startled them, and I heard myself saying, '*Tovarishchi kanibali, ya ne vkusnyi malchik*,'* which was supposed to mean they were to leave me alone, because I wouldn't taste nice.

They were big men in rags. They must have got what they were wearing from around the villages. They were scruffy, unshaven. It crossed my mind that these forest folk were following in the wake of the tin armies of the new Russians, and that they just ate Czechs. That would have crossed the mind of anyone in my situation.

One of them lunged towards me, and there and then he had my canteen in his huge paw. He opened it and took a gulp, and I was so glad, because I couldn't drink that stuff.

I was sitting between them and to my amazement I heard them muttering something quite friendly. Then one of them knelt down next to Teddy, or what was left of him in the grass. A knife flashed through the air, and he offered me a stick with a chunk of meat stuck on the end. They didn't give me back my canteen.

I just sat there, saying nothing. I well remembered what Sister Alberta used to tell us: the Devil's most evil magicians eat human flesh and have yellow wolf's fires – lamps of the Devil – instead of eyes. It wasn't just the campfire that blazed in the eyes of these two. I was

* 'Cannibal comrades, I'm not a tasty boy.'

watching the chunk of meat roasting in the flames, when suddenly darkness around our campfire was illuminated by a powerful light and the furious roar of an engine. It was Peter, who had found me and was charging to my aid with might and main and the thunder of his machine gun-armed Soviet jeep. He felled a couple of the apple saplings.

In an instant he was in front of us, and the two men had their hands up, a machine gun pointing at each of them. Peter jumped up and with a gun in his hand he came running towards us, asking if I was okay. I said nothing, because in the brightness of the jeep's searchlights I could see in the grass a big bear's head with its fangs bared. I had run into another bit of the Socialist Circus.

We made friends with the two Ukrainian circus bear trainers. We heard their tale of woe concerning their journey through Chapman Forest, and the fate of their bears. 'Some of them might have fought their way through the battle lines and could be free by now, others were not so lucky,' said Vasil, the manager of the bear menagerie.

'Ted here,' said Grishka, indicating the creature on the grass, 'couldn't go on. He wanted us to carry him. He missed his native forest so much.'

'Now he'll become us, and with a bit of luck we'll travel back home together,' Vasil added, stroking his paunch and handing Peter a chunk of roast bear.

Peter took the two bear trainers aboard his jeep, telling them it was their last chance of escape before the entire region was flooded. The whole area, he informed them, was to become the Czech Sea, but I knew that already.

As our little group grew in size, I was sure Peter thought it would make us more interesting to the Little Supremo. He also told us that in the event of an attack he would not be able to man all four machine guns alone, something he was sure we understood.

The elder of the two, Vasil, scratched his head and said that they felt better now, because they had been worried by all those empty villages. 'So you say there's going to be a dam here, comrade?' the bear trainer said to reassure himself.

Peter nodded.

'And where are the people?' asked the other trainer.

'They've been evacuated to the Soviet Union,' said Peter.

'*Dalshe Sibiri nepovezut*,' the older one said: 'They won't take them any further than Siberia,' I translated mentally.

And I really stuffed myself with bear meat. It was my first solid meal in ages.

But I kept glancing at the eyes of the two men, and I reckoned that the little lights that blazed in their eyes were brighter than any reflection of the red-hot embers in our kitchen fire.

The next day found us once more by the statue of the patron saint of the land of the Czechs. Peter had got into an argument with the two Ukrainians. He thought that the great pile of bear meat, stacked about the jeep, would prevent the machine guns from being used to best effect in combat.

The Ukrainians maintained that the most important thing of all was a good stock of food. They also had some sentimental reservations about leaving Ted behind. Peter was most likely reassured by the belief that we'd find the Little Supremo in next to no time, and that a mountain of bear meat couldn't fail to raise spirits in the women's camp. It made sense to him.

The Ukrainians settled in next to Peter. I had to fit in the back with Ted, and soon we were whizzing along under my guidance, down the tarmac road in the sector of Ctiradův Důl, Tomašín, Luka, Bataj... away from Siřem, and I could almost hear the splashing of the sea that was going to be there, and I tried to nod off and the sea obliged, rising out of images remembered from *The Catholic Book of Knowledge*, accompanied by the sound of the creaking wood of the cabin on wheels of the girl I'd seen naked, and I imagined Dýha and Mikušinec's amazement when, once they had recovered from their cuts and scratches, they stood on top of Fell Crag and the tide lapped at their feet, and they would probably steal a boat to take them to the Legion... But I couldn't nod off and dream in the jeep. I couldn't work out why Peter kept sounding the horn before every bend in the road, and sometimes a rat-a-tat came from the barrel of one or other of the machine guns. I thought he was firing at deer, but he was firing at the bends. It seemed to me like an invitation to any enemy waiting in ambush to make mincemeat of us, but Peter thought it would frighten them away.

I soon realized that Peter knew absolutely nothing about waging war, and for the first time I recalled with regret my snug on the lead tank, and also the soundless interplay of battlefield gestures as used by gunners Kantariya and Timosha, who, although they were practised killers, also excelled at saving their own skin. And mine too.

Unfortunately, we made frequent stops in the villages. Peter claimed to be looking for any trace of those mysterious women. I hated these stops in the shot-up villages and always volunteered to guard the meat. The Ukrainians searched the houses, even the lofts and sheds, and although they smiled at first and obviously looked forward to looting, and boasted about turning our armed jeep into a supply truck, they began coming back more and more downcast and showing their empty hands in disbelief, and saying they couldn't find so much as a snail... Then Vasil, the older of the two, said, 'It's not all that bad. There's plenty of grass and bark on the trees in these Czech villages of yours – the Soviets haven't taken that.' And Grisha, the younger one, said that the earth around the fruit trees wasn't that bad either, and that the people round here had been doing very nicely, because they could live like kings off the nettles, ferns and all the other weeds... We were having a longish break, eating Ted, when Vasil told me I hadn't been very bright, telling them that I wasn't a very tasty boy, because when a chap's starving he'll eat anybody. And then I knew for sure that those yellow wolf eyes came from more than the flashing of the fire.

Except... the longer they went on about the terrible famine that led to their villages being incorporated into the Eastern Empire, and the more horrors they described, the less I felt like listening to them. They talked about how troops had surrounded the starving villages, where eventually people even from the same family would eat each other... There is no way of shutting your ears to such things, and yet again somebody was telling me ghastly fairy stories... I tried to hide from those yellow eyes behind the pile of bear meat, and I stopped watching the road, which was a big mistake... And I made up my mind not to stay with them any more. That came about anyway. I would never have guessed that by evening we would be as far apart as it is possible to be.

Then we drove through Ctiradův Důl and in a flash I knew that Peter not only knew nothing at all about waging war, but that he couldn't even drive: he was accidentally going back on himself... The whole time I had been thinking we were going away from Siřem, but I was wrong... I raised my head, saw what was around the corner and shouted.

18

Scrap iron. Squire of Siřem. 'The wayfarer.' Margash's dream.
It is me, it isn't me

I spotted the tank guns the second we hurtled around the sharp bend towards the little bridge, and they weren't the guns of the 'Happy Song' column. They had to belong to Major General Kozhanov's 1st Tank Brigade of Guards. Peter, as was his habit, had been firing into the bend, so it came as no surprise that the tanks gave us a welcome of hot iron, as if they'd been expecting us.

The explosive shells hurled Peter backwards, away from the steering wheel. He landed right on top of me. Sadly, I could hear the bullets ripping him to shreds, but if he hadn't been there it would have been me who caught it. I rolled up in a ball under Ted.

The jeep smashed into some rocks – probably the very rocks I'd once carried this way, in and out of the water. It hit the dark surface under the bridge, bounced off the bottom, and, while the shouting sub-machine-gunners blazed away at the bear meat, and quite likely at the men who had called the animal Uncle Ted, I knew nothing about it, because I had got into deep water and was being carried away by the fast current. I tried to float and only just made it through the big rocks. Then I remembered that I couldn't swim, so I began catching my belly against more stones. It all happened so fast. I was in a reedbed. Something gripped my leg. It wasn't alive. I was caught up in the scrap iron in the tip. I banged my head against some metal sheeting, then fell back into the water. When I prised myself up again I was stuck there, held fast by the scrap metal, water up to my chin. I heaved my shoulders and arms into a space surrounded by metal walls with just enough room to breathe. I was just starting to fight for my life when I found myself among rotten branches and reeds that cut like arrows.

I could hear shouting and calling coming from the bank of the stream... It was probably the sub-machine-gunners leapfrogging from their posts behind the tanks to find out who it was they'd shot to bits. They were running up in an assault line to comb the bank... The reeds pricked at my belly from below. This was a shallow bit. From my waist up I was clamped in iron sheeting. I groped around among the reeds and branches, making myself some space. I could smell a lot and see a bit, so I quickly got used to being in that metal air-pocket in the water and reeds. I was scared of the men on the bank.

The moon shone through chinks in the twisted metal and was reflected on the water in which I quietly fidgeted. It occurred to me that I could be in the cab of some sunken truck. But trucks don't have wings. The wings were twisted metal overgrown by reeds. Wherever the reeds moved under the joint forces of wind and water, the metal surface gleamed. I'd never been in a plane before, I thought. This small, battered plane was the biggest piece of scrap metal in the tip. I'd sometimes seen its iron skeleton from across the dark winter water.

Now in the summer the reedbed was shallow. No doubt all the

shelling and numerous fires all over Bohemia had boiled away the water of the rivers and streams.

The seat was stuck fast on its side, crisscrossed by perished straps. Sunk in the mud and washed by the water, the plane was completely overgrown with reeds.

So I had plenty of fun fighting with the reeds as I waded through the cold water to the bank. I have no idea how long I stayed in that air-pocket. I waited for the sub-machine-gunners to finish their work before leaving to clear another sector. Then I made a move. I can always tell when a forward patrol has finished its task.

I scrambled onto the bank, slithering through the darkness. The cottages I could see didn't look battered. I heard a dog barking. A rooster swore at his hens, even though it was night-time.

In Siřem I wanted first of all to find an ally, so I set off for the cemetery using footpaths and detours.

I found Páta easily. I had just pushed through the large rusty gates, heading straight for the toff's tomb, which stood out white amid a field of crosses, when Páta jumped me and floored me right there among the graves, and we rolled about on the ground and neither of us had the smell of the Home from Home in our hair or on our clothes. So for a moment I worried that it wasn't him but a stranger. Wrestling in silence, one on one, we fell through the earth and I got a bash on the head. Only then did Páta recognize me by the light of some burning candles, crying out 'Ilya!' and that brought me round from my sudden descent into the bowels of the cemetery. Páta was glad to see me there.

And Mr Cimbura was glad as well. He lay in some blankets, and said straight away, 'Hi, sonny... you made it!'

He propped himself up on one elbow. I had recognized him in the flickering candlelight, even before he had spoken. So Mr Cimbura and Páta have made up, I thought to myself.

Then Mr Cimbura yattered on, 'So, sonny, you thought you'd escape from your very own village on a tank, did you? Just like your old man, though he tried it by plane.'

In the bunker-like darkness, relieved only by the candles, I checked again that it was Mr Cimbura that I was seeing and hearing. I clenched my fist. I didn't want to hear any more of his or anyone else's fairy stories... Then I saw that there was somebody else there... I was so glad to see Sister Alberta again. She was sitting in a snug of rags, looking at me. She was pleased too, I think.

'Well, here we all are, come together like one happy family,' said Mr Cimbura. 'You know, sonny, how I used to look after you as best I could, seeing as you're the bastard sprog of an aristo, but I couldn't look out for the little 'un, you know that yerself.'

'I saw it! I saw Monkeyface fall all by himself!' Páta blurted out, and I said, 'So did Karel!' and I stamped my foot.

'Ah well, we looked after you under all them bosses that evil times inflicted on us, sonny. Everyone in Siřem took real good care of you... but then, you're our lord and master, kid... We always kept an eye on you, ever since I dragged you out of that plane in flames as a screaming wee thing. The eyes of all us folk, Siřem folk, kept a close watch on you. I was afraid you'd never ever get over all that gormless gawping you did, but you have. Our Hanka used to keep us up to date! It weren't easy for her, obviously, to keep up with some neglected, delinquent kid. She's a lovely girl really, but then she had to see to the wellbeing of the young squire. She had that explained to her proper like!'

Mr Cimbura sat up. I could see his face was terribly burnt, the light from the candles gliding over the craters in its ancient skin. He was covered in filthy bandages, and though it probably isn't right to say this of an old person, he stank. No matter how many times I'd been in combat, I'd never realized that burns could smell so bad.

'Well, sonny, you never needed as much protecting as when them red communards betrayed the Czech people and threw in their lot with the Moskies. If you'd been a growing, aristo orphan, you'd have been for it. Much better to be a retard. That was a damn good idea we had! And the popular masses put the frighteners on the Muscovite and now our victory's in tatters, but we'll pull through. We'll lie low in our cellars and pull through. There's always someone survives, that's a known fact. So, sonny, you've grown into a fine upstanding son of Czechia, a stalwart soldier in the Czech cause. You didn't get far from your native Siřem on that tank. And now you're back with us. Welcome home!'

Sister Alberta was smiling, like she was welcoming me back too, and she pat-patted her ancient hands. Páta was laughing and invited me to sit. I sat down on a length of timber. It was the shelf which had collapsed that time when I kicked everything off it. Mr Cimbura struggled across to me. He was offering me something... and he straightened up and bellowed, like he used to in the square, when everyone gathered round him: 'Little Ilya's the squire now!' and Mr Cimbura spluttered with laughter as he spoke. He could probably see I was looking at him real angry, like, so he pretended to have a bad coughing fit. But he stuck a half-rotten cucumber in my right hand and a potato in my left, and he started messing about. He bowed to me like I was a king being crowned on the telly in some fairy tale for the masses. Páta was giggling and did the bowing-before-the-king thing after Mr Cimbura, while Sister Alberta kept on clapping, and then she said, 'Welcome, lad!'

'Your dad, sonny,' said Mr Cimbura, 'brought back from his travels this weird woman. God alone knows in what deserted wilderness he picked her up. Your mother was a vile-looking creature, I can tell you... Well, because of that ugly mug of hers, you and your kid brother turned out how you fucking did – not your fault, my lad... The Jerries wanted to chop your dad's head off, but he got round 'em by letting on about all sorts of secret hideouts. But he couldn't get round the Commies. They went after his aristocratic blood like leeches... So, now he's enjoying his eternal rest in his Siřem tomb.

'The truth is, your dad decided to make a run for it, but his plane flopped down into the mud, and the mud of Siřem and the water of Siřem put the flames out, and we, the people of Siřem, we pulled you and your kid brother out. Your brother came off bad, like, we know. Your parents died inside the plane. It ain't true they didn't give a damn about you. All they did was die, and that's all there is to it!'

There were masses of candles in the vault. It had been a long while since I'd seen people sitting in the half-light, their shadows flitting all over the wall whenever someone moved... The shadows were bigger than the people... My own shadow looked enormous above me the moment I changed position... It crossed my mind that as soon as I grew as big as that myself, all these fairy stories would finally come to an end.

'How come my dad crashed his plane?' I asked, putting on a really deep voice.

'Good question,' squeaked Mr Cimbura from his pallet of rags.

'Rumour has it that all the Siřem folk took it real bad that the squire wanted to do a runner and leave us here. That wasn't right, now, was it? So you see, it turned out we were right. He shouldn't have run away from his people... He came a cropper! It's possible someone drilled a hole in the fuel tank, making it burst, so the plane took off and fell right back down in a blaze... Who could have done such a thing? Wicked undercover fascists? Evil commies? Some local with a grievance?... But listen, sonny, that was all a long time ago!'

'How long?' I asked.

Mr Cimbura said that we were not going to argue over time. When the Good Lord – or whoever it was – had created time, He had made plenty of it, and Mr Cimbura went on to say that all that mattered now was that I had survived everything and that I was finally home, and when the Czechs were once more their own masters, I would be the one and only lord and master of Siřem – me and me alone. 'And that's exactly what we're celebrating right now, sonny,' said Mr Cimbura.

I was squatting on the collapsed shelf, the cucumber in one hand and the potato in the other... and Mr Cimbura bowed to me again, as if to his lord and master, and giggled, though I well remembered how he had always hated the nobility... I didn't believe a word Mr Cimbura said. I wanted to get away.

So I didn't toss aside the things they had used for my mock coronation, but I placed them on the ground next to me. Páta handed me a jar of sweetcorn. They had tomatoes and bread and salami as well, so we ate.

I put some salami and lots of bread in my pockets. I watched Páta while I did it. He gave me the nod. So they had plenty. I grabbed the cucumber and potato while I was at it.

Once we had finished eating I asked Mr Cimbura, 'Where are the girls?'

'This here is the girls' bunker, sonny,' he said, 'but you went and frightened 'em off, staring in on 'em like that, just as they was working on it.'

'Where are the girls?' I asked again, because he hadn't answered. Obviously, I had only one girl in mind.

'Every decent village built shelters like this one for the protection of young girls – they've done it ever since the Tatars invaded,' Mr Cimbura muttered, 'but these Russians with their modern spy satellite technology, they can ferret out any woman anywhere, even underground. Never used to be like that, no sir! This time we failed, that's all there is to it!'

'So the Russians found 'em?'

'Some they found, some they didn't, sonny. This time we just failed,' said Mr Cimbura.

Páta said it was not a bad place to live, here in the girls' bunker. He'd known worse... and he and Sister Alberta tended to Mr Cimbura's wounds, since a symbol of national resistance like Mr Cimbura should never fall into Soviet hands!

'And what about the sisters?' I asked Sister Alberta, and she murmured that the Lord of Heaven is competent at His job, and every peasant is mindful that 'dust thou art, and unto dust shalt thou return', and so the Lord returns human lives to nothing, as He sees fit.

I hadn't a clue what she was on about.

And Páta said that only Sister Alberta had come back to Siřem, because she was a local and her papers said that she was a resident of the village, so she had to wait there to be evacuated. And Sister

Alberta said she couldn't care less about any evacuation – that there in the vault they made up the last cohesive Siřem family, taking turns to tend to the old man's wounds. Mr Cimbura would only emerge into the light of God's day when he was fully fit again, and as a symbol of national resistance his miraculous appearance would provoke another uprising. All three of them said this at once.

Then I told them about the villages with no people in them, and I asked, 'Where have all the people gone?'

'Look,' said Páta, 'when I saw you up top, I attacked you... I thought you'd escaped from a train. I'm sorry I went for you like that. Those runaways steal all the time, because they don't have nothing... and there isn't room in the girls' bunker for everyone... I didn't know it was you. I'm sorry, okay? You forgive me now, don't you?'

'What are those train runaways running away from?'

'Don't you know?' asked Páta, amazed. 'Everyone who lived here has been put on a train to Russia. Everybody from the insurgency zone. They say you get given a new cottage and stuff, but I'm not so sure... I don't wanna go!'

'Me neither,' I said.

'So stay,' said Páta, and lay on his back. Then we were silent. I lay in some rags, the steam coming off me. It was hot in there. The candles flickered. I lay still and dried out. I didn't think about what Mr Cimbura had said about my parents. I was thinking about what he had said about those Russian satellites. Maybe they can't see Mr Cimbura and Sister Alberta because old people don't have as much body heat. But they could pick up me and Páta. A platoon of Soviet paras could burst in on us at any moment. I wasn't going to hang around. I didn't care what Mr Cimbura said about my parents. Not one bit!

Now I sprawled out in some comfort. I heard Páta yawn. It was a good thing the girls or someone had brought in so many blankets. Down here you couldn't even hear the shellfire or anything. If the new Russians had joined Yegorov's tank column, we knew nothing about it.

I looked at Páta and remembered: Gypsy cowboy. I couldn't help laughing.

'What's up?' Páta said.

'Oh, nothing.'

Then Mr Cimbura piped up, and I, just as I had in my childhood long ago, ensconced in empty tar-soap boxes, listened, half-asleep, to Mr Cimbura's fairy story. In those bygone days we weren't hiding in a vault in the cemetery, while tanks and planes bent on our destruction rumbled overhead. I listened to the story of the dragon's egg for the first time.

'So, lads, I'm going to tell you how this Siřem of ours came into being, and who founded it hundreds and hundreds of years ago,' said Mr Cimbura. 'I'm telling you so that our squire here and his most esteemed delinquent brother know about it. Seeing as all the other locals have gone, you two stalwart sons of Czechia are the only ones left to keep alive this ancient legend... So listen carefully and stop fidgeting. Bullets are whizzing about outside and disorder reigns, but we're here, tucked away in our snug little hole, so I'm going to tell you about the wayfarer...

'Once upon a time, long, long ago, the wise men and militant boyars of the czar of the Eastern Empire decided they weren't going to leave the world until it was all theirs. So they sent out this wayfarer to

find the weapon with which they could subjugate the whole world...
And the wayfarer rode away, until he came to a soot-stained signpost,
on which it said: CAUTION: BOHEMIA! Well, the wayfarer wasn't
afraid, so he spurred on his horse... After travelling far across the
wilderness, he came to a cottage, see? Inside it was a man and a woman,
and their son, a chubby little lad who was a delight to behold.

'And who else does the wayfarer see? A beautiful girl... She's got
these great big eyes, the skies float in them; her hair shimmers halfway
down her back; and she's got this gorgeous figure, a neck as white as
snow, full breasts rising under her blouse, and a throat of radiant al-
abaster... She's the purest of maidens... but then, there are no blokes living anywhere nearby, because they've all killed each other fighting or
gone away or something!

'The girl was sitting on a little stool, sewing. She was embroider-
ing a white shift, and that shift was for her wedding day! Well,
they welcomed him in: "A wayfarer's arrived!" The girl gave him
something to drink, and they all said, "When Grandfather returns,
he will rejoice!" And the wayfarer learned that the old man had been
in the forest for two days, hunting a wolf, but was expected home
soon.

'After dinner they went to bed. They all slept in the parlour, though
they let the wayfarer have the lumber room, him being a guest. Only
the little lad slept in the lumber room, and he didn't disturb anyone,
he just whistled gently through his little nose.

'Well, that night the wayfarer's mind turned to that gem of a girl,
but he was all worn out from his journey and fell asleep.

'Next day, they were working in the fields and the wayfarer helped
out. They appreciated his strength and skill, which was good news for

him, because a powerful love was growing in his heart for the beautiful daughter!

'That evening, the wayfarer played with the little boy, and he was full of high spirits, and they all appreciated how good he was with children, which was more good news for him, given as how all he could think about was that girl!

'Well, there they were, having dinner again, only in silence. And when the meal was over and they had blessed themselves with a crucifix, the wayfarer took the Cross and put it outside the door. Then they told him about the grandfather.

'The old man had said that he was going after a wolf. "If I'm not back by nightfall on the third day," he had said, "or if I've been at all mauled by the wolf, don't let me in. It'll be me, but it won't be me."

'"I see," said the father, and he picked up a wooden stake and started sharpening it with his knife.

'Come the next evening and they heard this scratching at the door, and the little lad jumped up and said, "Grandpa's back!" and they heard the loud voice of the old man saying, "Open the door!"

'And the father said, "You're too late, Dad."

'Well, the woman and the boy begged him to open the door, as Grandpa was only a teeny bit late for dinner! He'd been chasing a wolf for three days! He was worn out!

'The father half-opened the door and said, "Show us the wolf's head, Dad!" But the moment the door was open the old man came inside.

'The father said, "Where's the wolf's head, Dad?" The old man let out a terrible groan – "Ooooaaaaaaa!" – and lifted his head, and through his whiskers they could all see his mangled throat.

'The father grabbed the stake and took aim at the old man – his very own dad! And the grandfather ran out of the cottage and was gone. So they all went to bed.

'Well, the wayfarer tossed and turned in bed, and told himself he'd be better off getting out of there, but then he remembered the beautiful girl. Then he heard a sound – *tap!* –at the window. The little lad sat up in bed. It was the old man tapping at the window, and he was ever so pale, and he said, "Grandson, come out to play." So the boy climbed out of the window. This family is weird, thought the wayfarer to himself.

'In the morning, the lad couldn't walk straight. He was all pale and he picked up the sharpened stake and tossed it down the well, making a splash. Then the boy died.

'"There's something odd going on here!" the wayfarer told himself. He wanted to leave for the Eastern Empire and go back to his czar – without the weapon – but he also wanted the girl. He asked her to come to the lumber room, just for a quick word.

'The girl came and the wayfarer prevented her from leaving. She stayed there all night, and in the morning the wayfarer left.

'He travelled home, and stood before the czar, who commanded him, "Come thou not back without the weapon!" So back went the wayfarer.

'The land was dark. The villages were deserted. Not a dog barked and no bird sang. The wayfarer met a priest, who asked him where he was going. The wayfarer told him he was going to Bohemia.

'"Turn around and go back!" cried the priest, but the wayfarer said he wouldn't. So the priest blessed him and gave him a crucifix. The wayfarer hung it around his neck, then off he went.

'He heard wolves howling, and by now it was getting dark. He arrived at the cottage and there was nobody anywhere. He entered the building and behold: the girl was sitting on her stool, sewing, but what was she sewing, what was she mending? A shroud made from the pelt of a wolf. Strong was the odour of wolf from the skin.

'The girl smelt strange, she smelt earthy. She stood up at once, opened her arms to embrace him, and drew him to her tight. The wayfarer couldn't catch his breath!

'And the girl said, "Come, my dear, our little one is crying." She led the wayfarer into the darkened parlour. And what was that in the cradle? A dragon's egg! And the egg was making a tapping sound and changing colour.

'And at once the wayfarer knew that this was what he should take to the czar. He grabbed the egg and wrapped it in the wolf-skin shroud. He no longer wanted the girl. He was in a hurry to return to his native soil, to his czar.

'The girl was pale. She asked for a kiss. Her lips were motionless and her face cold, as if she were not alive. She held the wayfarer tight in her embrace, and then she said, "They're here!"

'The wayfarer looked and behold! Outside the window he saw the old man, his son and daughter-in-law, and his grandson as well. They were scratching at the windows with their nails. They wanted to come inside. And they were all dreadfully pale.

'The girl hugged him so powerfully that she was crushing his ribs. "My name's Czechia," she said. The wayfarer grabbed the crucifix at his throat – the priest's gift – and the girl leapt away, as if cut by a sword.

'The wayfarer rushed out of the cottage and he jumped on his horse and galloped away.

'Soon he heard pounding footsteps behind him, and he heard wolves howling. They were all running after him: the old man, his son, the woman, the boy and the girl called Czechia. And now the grandfather had overtaken the horse and was blocking the way, but the wayfarer rode over him! He clasped the dragon's egg, our wayfarer! Then the father leapt at the wayfarer, who knocked him down, his horse stamping at the dust. Then the woman grabbed her little boy, whirled him round and around in the air and hurled him. And the lad went flying and landed on the horse, and sank his teeth in it. The horse shook the lad off and stamped a hoof, then galloped onwards. And now the lad's mother came flying through the air, howling like a she-wolf. She leapt towards the horse, but it ducked and she smashed her skull on the ground. Finally, the girl called Czechia came flying through the air, descending on the horse's rump, just behind the wayfarer! She bit the wayfarer and the horse dropped, breathless, to the ground, followed by our wayfarer. And he clutched the crucifix at his throat, but the girl had gone. The horse was dead. And the wayfarer's hand leapt away from the cross of its own accord – the flesh was burnt!

'The dragon's egg in the wolf-skin had gone! He had lost the love of Czechia, and the czar would chop off his head. He was all alone in that ill-fated land.

'The wayfarer thought, "Am I still me? After all I've seen?" He didn't know. And at that very spot he pledged to erect a church.'

I was glad he'd finished! Páta was too, I reckoned. But Mr Cimbura went on, 'And I've honoured that pledge. Fair busted my guts on that church, too. Anyway, it's Catholic now.'

Then he started mumbling something into his blankets, and

grunting and groaning, and it would have been nice if he'd been quiet at last, but on he went: 'The shooting's died down outside, right? There, we've come through safe and sound.'

I looked at Páta, and Páta looked at me.

'Okay, lads, you might be thinking I've been making fun of you! I'd happily show you the scars where that girl bit and scratched me, but here's the rub – my flesh being burnt, you can't see 'em.' And Mr Cimbura raised himself up on one elbow on his couch of rags.

I sat down. I looked at Páta. Had he heard? Cimbura had said that he was the wayfarer: non-human, tooth-marked. It crossed my mind that we ought to kill him straight away. Then it occurred to me that if Mr Cimbura was the wayfarer, we couldn't kill him anyway. It wasn't going to be easy! Anyway, he was probably just talking rubbish again... I glanced at him. He was staring at me too – staring right into my soul through the candles. It gave me goose pimples all over. Mr Cimbura knew what I was thinking. He didn't want to bite me, though he could have long before now! A thousand times. Yet he used to look after me so nice, like, when I was a defenceless kid. That was ages ago!

Mr Cimbura dropped his sharp gaze, lay back, wriggled a bit in his blankets and carried on talking: 'Right then, for crying out loud, you black-arsed moo, get a move on with them last rites!' And Sister Alberta stirred, though not towards Mr Cimbura; instead she came and sat with me, as if nothing had changed since the days of the soap store, except that now Sister Alberta was horribly fat and old. I was older too. I was so big I wouldn't fit in her arms any more. 'God brought you to us,' she said, 'let's have a cuddle the like of which the world has never seen!'

Afterwards she stood up and went over to Mr Cimbura.

There was this huge silence throughout the whole cellar, because nobody was talking. Páta was also next to Mr Cimbura, and he knelt down beside him. Mr Cimbura was lying there and he was quiet, which was one for the record books. I stood up and made a move into the darkness to where I remembered the door was. I went through it and climbed the steps, along the passage and past the kitchen and the best room and, hey presto, I was outside.

Mr Cimbura's storytelling had crumpled time. The thing is, he had us caught in his fairy story as if in a noose. This explains why I ran back out into the night. Was it the same night as when I was hiding in the plane? Or the next one? I didn't know.

There were no lights anywhere. I spotted a cat on the roof of a house, which was odd. They don't like to be seen. The cat shrieked and knocked a big black tomcat off the roof. He fell on the hard soil, leapt sideways and vanished into the weeds that propped up a fallen fence... Otherwise, not a soul in sight, but it was obvious there was life in Siřem... The tanks of Kozhanov's army had to be around somewhere. I sniffed the air for a whiff of petrol and listened for the growl of engines. If I bumped into the guards unit's sub-machine-gunners, running bent double with their Kalashnikovs at the ready and clearing the ground for a tank assault, that would be the end of me. All I could do was advance by leaps and bounds between the dark cottages, and so I got to the square, which is where I wanted to be.

Candles flickered in the wind. Lots of them had burnt right down. Some had been snuffed out by the wind.

A pile of wreathes reached up to his knees. I still remembered him in the wash-tub. The coffin stood propped against the church door.

The church rose black above him, the whole building. It looked like it had been lowered down from heaven, as if hanging from the pitch-darkness. Commander Vyžlata was tied to the coffin. The lads hadn't told me that. Perhaps they didn't know.

His arms were spread out, tied to the coffin at the elbows. His fingers were all sticking out. So Kozhanov's guards hadn't been here. They'd never have left him like that, like some Lord Jesus Christ with his arms outstretched! I'm pretty sure they don't like that kind of thing, any religious stuff. No way! They'd have taken him down, dead or alive, with the first volley, they wouldn't care. So they were behind me, somewhere.

I didn't look into Vyžlata's face. Didn't want to. But then it was inside the coffin and it was dark. All I needed was to know he was there, because apart from me there was only one person who knew where Vyžlata had been before: Margash. And only Margash knew who and what were still in the cellar.

I detached myself from the coffin's shadow, so as to slip into the mightier shadow of the church, and scuttle down the few streets to the pond, then make myself scarce somewhere in the countryside around Siřem, but then I heard them... First, a distant grinding noise and then the rumble that tanks make as they rip up the ground. They were getting closer... Now I was being chased to the Home from Home by the tanks of Kozhanov's army. Fortunately for me, they hadn't sent out a scouting party on foot. On the other hand, that meant they were on the attack.

I ran past the dark and silent farm buildings that marked the end of the village, immersing myself in the slow breaking of the day, as if I were carrying it. Next I ran past a tank. Its tracks were done for. It was burnt out, sadly. It smelt of burnt flesh and vomit. I knew it was part of the 'Happy Song' column... The Home from Home was surrounded by a solid wall of tanks. The 'Happy Song' tanks had formed a circular defensive line the whole length of the hillside, and beyond the tanks with their red stars pockmarked by bullets from all the village Home Guards in the sector that went from Tomašín, Luka, Bataj and so on, there's this barricade, a long inner defence barricade.

There's a lot going on between the Home from Home building and the barricade. Behind the barricade – piled high with bundles of paper, school desks, chairs and anything else that could be dragged outside the Home from Home – giraffe heads perched on long necks were waving; and beyond the barricade, which in the grey light of dawn seemed to be getting higher and higher, 'Happy Song' soldiers were flitting about, dragging bundles of paper and various other things. I couldn't recognize their faces at that distance. All I could see beyond the rampart were vague flittering figures in uniform. Crouching low I carried on... and I had to slip past the first tank of the chain of defence that had lined up ready to fire. They must have been able to see me! So I walked on slowly, just walking... At the very moment when I felt a gun barrel in my back, I heard, '*Eto Ilya* – it's Ilya!' Timosha looked closely at me from under his tin helmet. He was worn out! A second gunner in a raggedy sailor shirt and camouflage dress was just as tired-looking. They stared at me, but without really trying to work out where I'd been all that time... 'Great to see you! Off to the captain with you!' said Timosha, severely. He was staring at my tracksuit top. Perhaps he wondered why I wasn't wearing the tankman's jacket that he had pinned me into with his own hands. With a wave of his gun he chivvied me round behind the tank in the direction of the barricade.

The other one never opened his mouth. They were saving their breath, and saving on movement. I knew this kind of stiffness. They could scent battle in the air, and wanted to be prepared. I went where they told me.

The first light from the sky had diluted the shadow of the Home from Home into wisps that the gunners shredded as they moved around in it. They were pouring water onto the bundles of paper they'd piled up as defensive mounds – a burning barricade is hard to defend. Also on the barricade they'd put the stove from the kitchen workshop, and piles of wood from the cellar. They'd gone and chopped up the cubicles! There were all sorts of boxes and piles of bricks. They must have gutted the insides of our poor Home from Home... I walked slowly over to the barricade, walking as tall as possible, so as not to be mistaken for some enemy saboteur on a recce and killed by a burst of gunfire. But the helmeted gunner on sentry duty just waved to me. He recognized me... I skipped over the paper bundles in his sector and there I was, standing outside the Home from Home.

In my head I sorted out what I was going to say to Captain Yegorov. It was obvious from the unit's combat situation and the dead tank that the Bandits hadn't been fibbing: the new Russians didn't want this lot.

It crossed my mind that the 'Happy Song' tankmen and gunners were digging their own graves, and that inside the barricade, surrounded by the winds around the Home from Home, I was about to enter my own grave. The poles we had used to break cinder strips into crushed ashes, and to catch flying scraps of charred paper with, had been used to reinforce the barricade. I stepped aside for some soldiers, getting a nasty bang on the knee when I tripped over the wash-tub... The company sergeant, whose face I couldn't make out in the morning mist, gave me an earful. Accompanied by two gunners, he was dragging the tub along, filled with broken bricks, to add to the barricade. The bustle of work was mixed with the cries of small and fully grown animals, and it was obvious that more refugees from the Socialist Circus had arrived. I really wanted to take a good look at the animals, but there was no time, because I wanted to get inside and straight down to the cellar before daybreak, when everything is visible.

I edged at a snail's pace through the pushing and shoving mass of bodies. The soldiers were getting on with building the barricade, and the animals kept getting under their feet. I edged towards the front door of the Home from Home, stepping over and sometimes tripping on the hosepipes they were using to fill some buckets with stinking water, and then I realized that they were dousing the barricade with water from the cellar... They had even chopped up the Bulgarian seaside sideshow and tossed its painted planks on top of the bundles of paper. The camels were hobnobbing with some other animals, including the seaside donkey – well, that was no surprise! There were some big fat does, too, like I'd never seen running around here. They were gobbing at everything and lashing out with their feet. Some gunners were dragging them along with ropes behind the Home from Home, and I heard a sharp burst of automatic fire, followed by another. I had barely got a decent look at them and they were already being executed. Tough luck. Nobody took any notice, and they didn't take any notice of me either. How come, when I hadn't been with them for so long? They didn't care a damn about me... Then suddenly I heard 'Ilya!' and again 'Ilya!' and there was no mistaking the voice of Captain Yegorov. I stiffened to attention, then the cloud of dust kicked up by the fat deer in the haze of daybreak dispersed, and right there in front of the door of the Home from Home I saw a knot of people, and my captain was calling me from the middle of it! Soldiers were jammed around the wolf's cage, which was wide open, and the wolf was just lying there on its side. He was huge, lying there as if at death's door. I stepped forward, since it was my captain calling, then suddenly I was overwhelmed by an image that escaped from my head.

I saw myself in my torn tankman's jacket. I was running out of the door of the Home from Home in answer to my captain's call. I dashed outside with a kitchen knife in my hand, a great long carving knife pointing down... 'Ilya!' Captain Yegorov called again, and at last I saw him, squatting down next to the open cage. Margash came running from the kitchen to the wolf with a knife, and before the other soldiers gathered round the cage blocked my view, I saw Margash lift up the wolf's head. I saw the wolf's tongue flop out of its mouth, and I saw Margash cut its throat. But everyone thought it was me doing it...

I got past them easily. I slipped inside the Home from Home. I ran alongside the hosepipe that was snaking down the steps. I ran into the cellar. I was there in no time.

The hosepipes had sucked gallons of water out of the cellar. Footsteps echoed down there, as if you were not alone. I didn't need a light to get to the grave cubicle. The grating was down on the floor. Little Monkeyface lay under a dreadful, grubby sheet on the iron manhole cover. He was completely covered up. I could hear a droning sound. It was the wind from the bottom end of the cellar, where there were more cellars. I reached out and touched the sheet, and I was glad it was too dark to see.

I wasn't thinking about anything. My head was full of the churned-up leftovers of everything I'd been through. Yeah, I got the idea of staying there with him. But then I made up my mind to live as long as possible instead. I decided to wait until I grew up and to see what it was like. In the meantime, I'd gone there to hide with Monkeyface, because there was nowhere else in the world for me to go. Then the drone of the wind was interrupted by some volleys from outside. The walls of the home shook. Bits of plaster fell into my hair. Kozhanov's army had attacked.

I patted the sheet in various places to find where his foot, shoulders, knee were. I was with him. He couldn't forgive me. Nobody could forgive me. I could have waited until the end of the battle, then turned myself in for them to execute me, though they would probably just finish me off without any fuss. There wasn't any point in that. I went back to him. I was guarding him, my little brother, keeping a lookout in the dark. What more could I do?

Then some more volleys cracked. They were coming in waves. They were probably still blasting away at our tanks in the circular defensive line. Then, in a break between volleys, I heard him. But he only made me cross. Considering everyone in the column thought Margash was me, he could at least have learnt to move like a saboteur! He blundered through that cellar as if he owned the place. The camel lads were close on his heels. Some had torches. We could see each other.

He stood in front of me in a tankman's jacket that really belonged to me! He was covered in blood, breathing fast. I was surprised he was not surprised to see me. They must have come to get Monkeyface. They had hauled him out before, after all! Now two of the camel lads pounced towards him, but I wouldn't let them near.

'Ilya!' said Margash. 'I'm glad to see you! It's great you're here.'

'Sure,' said I. 'So you're off to that beautiful land of yours now, are you?' I said it to show him I hadn't forgotten anything. I spoke Russian so the camel lads – the cellar was full of them – could understand. Margash wasn't carrying a knife this time. But he took off his jacket and handed it to me.

He stood in front of me, stripped to the waist. He handed me the jacket and tugged at my tracksuit top.

'Quick,' he said, 'we'll take him away!'

'You're takin' Monkeyface away?' I shouted back, because the cellar walls were shaking with further bursts of shellfire.

'Yeah!' shouted Margash, because now the pounding was non-stop. Some of the camel lads were over by Monkeyface, and I couldn't stop them doing anything. I turned round quickly, because they had whipped the sheet off him and were covering him with some skins they'd brought along. And Margash tossed one big hairy skin right in my face. It was the wolf.

'I had this dream, listen!' shouted Margash.

'No!' I shouted.

'You're gonna kill Captain Yegorov,' Margash said in his normal voice, because the tanks had stopped spitting shells. Outside there was just the crackle of light arms and the chatter of machine guns, so we could hear each other... If he had told me this in some sun-dappled clearing in Chapman Forest, or even in my dreams, say, I'd have laughed, but he was telling me back there in that cellar, and my whole body was covered in goose pimples. The Home from Home was shaking from shellfire and my tank column comrades were dying.

'You said your dad was a wolf!' I said to Margash, hurling the wolf skin back at him. 'Why did you do this?'

'Captain Yegorov ordered me to,' he said. 'You've got to kill him.'

The camel lads were saying something to Margash in their incomprehensible lingo. They gently raised up Monkeyface. He was still lying on the floor. Five or six of the camel lads picked him up and set off out of the cellar.

Margash was buttoning up the tracksuit top I'd given him, and explaining that they were going to take Monkeyface to that wonderful land where there was lots of grass and where all boys are brothers.

'Are you glad?' he asked.

I nodded, because I did want them to take Monkeyface away, and I put on the tankman's jacket. It had splashes of wolf's blood on it, but that would soon dry out.

'The Captain's waiting for you,' said Margash.

He stooped, shifted the iron plate over the former grave to one side, fished down below, and handed me something wrapped in a rag: it was Commander Vyžlata's black pistol.

The camel lads were going down the passage ahead of us. We had become Monkeyface's funeral procession. We were taking him outside. I stuffed the pistol in my belt. I had no idea what would happen next.

We've came out of the dark of the cellar into the daylight. We stood outside the Home from Home, blinded and deafened by the explosions. The 'Happy Song' servicemen lying or kneeling inside the barricade were blasting away with their guns. I could tell the circular defensive line of tanks beyond the barricade hadn't been broken yet, but it wouldn't be long, because assault tanks were rolling towards the

Home from Home from all sides. The mist had cleared. The light falling out of the sky onto the fighting men was dotted all over with pinpoints of smoke, and those manning the barricade were setting off yellow and dark-blue smoke flares to make themselves less easy targets. So I was coughing, defenceless and exposed to the gunfire, but what happened next?...

If I were being told this by some stranger – even one who knew all about combat scenarios – I'd laugh in his face. I would know that telling lies in childhood had never led to him gargling vile, dark tar... but this is what happened: there, outside the door of the Home from Home, despite the clangour of battle and in the very thick of it, the camels calmly stood, all harnessed up, gently bobbing their heads, and then, right there in front of Margash, the lead camel, a truly gigantic beast, knelt down and Margash hopped onto its back, and the camel lads passed Monkeyface... his relics... up to him; then they calmly took up their positions on the wooden seats, and the kneeling camels, laden with lads, got to their feet and towered over everything, ignoring the shooting, the shouting and the choking of the injured; they ignored the bits of iron whizzing through the air; they walked on as if they really were part of one of Margash's dreams and not reality... I had an idea that Margash was dreaming right then, and that the dream was happening. But I wasn't dreaming, so because of the whistling bullets I hurled myself to the ground. The camels walked on through the shell-fire. Suddenly part of the barricade was ripped out by an explosion. I could see and hear soldiers screaming. Just a few paces from me one of them reared up, but it was not Kantariya! He dropped his Kalashnikov and fell headlong into a sack of paper. Shrapnel and odd bullets drummed into the barricade, into the paper saturated with cellar water, and now blood as well. I could see that the fat deer had been killed by the defenders, who had used their bodies to pad out the bulwarks around a machine-gun nest. The camels walked on through it all, slowly up the hill, striding along serenely with their load of lads, and I got this idea that of all the people there I was the only one who could see them, so I was becoming part of Margash's dream... The camels strode uphill, unnoticed by the fighters. Untouched by any of the projectiles, they vanished in the clouds of smoke.

I had no idea that instead of instant death – and with it the kingdom of heaven – camels were capable of passing through sustained fire into a dream landscape of peace and quiet. I was glad. I never saw them again.

I was floundering about outside the Home from Home with the bloody wolf skin in my hand, and because the gunfire had eased up briefly, again I heard 'Ilya!' It was my captain calling. I went looking for him.

I hoped little Monkeyface would be safe in the saddle of a dreamworld camel. I hoped he would travel all the way to a wonderful land. Then I resolved that another of Margash's dreams would come true, and I pulled out the pistol. I released the safety catch and went in search of the Captain.

Captain Yegorov loomed in front of me so abruptly that I dropped the raised gun. Then Kozhanov's lot started firing again. Captain Yegorov stood there as if there was nothing going on. He looked at me, fixing me with the searching stare of a seasoned, frontline warrior.

I hoped that the Captain would attribute any small differences between myself and Margash to the rapid changes that come about during an adolescence spent under fire... I half-crouched and tried to protect my head at least. The Captain stood motionless. He glanced at the wolf skin I was clutching, and his lips rippled into a tiny smile... He was glad he had found me! Shots crashed all around us, taking splinters out of the door of the Home from Home. We were veiled in a cloud of smoke, this time from a red flare. The Captain made a move towards me, not bothered by the black pistol I was offering him. My captain hugged me briefly, clutching me to him... It was just like that moment when the legend of Fedotkin and his boy came to life and Captain Yegorov embraced me on the burning tank... I couldn't bring myself to squeeze the trigger. The Captain took the wolf skin from me. I stuffed the gun with the safety catch back on down my trousers, and ran after the Captain. The wolf skin full of its gobbets of dark blood led me through the smoke of the flares as I chased after him.

We ran around the Home from Home and came up against a funeral pickup. Gunner Kantariya was gripping the steering wheel with white knuckles. Gunner Timosha stood on the runner, his submachine gun slung across his back. He was holding a sheet that had probably come from some nun's bed. At a sign from Captain Yegorov, I swung onto the back under the pickup's tarpaulin and landed on something soft. It was the entire wealth of the supply train they had there. I recognized the carpets I used to be tied to at night, and the grandfather clock and statuettes, and the washstand and mirror, the piles of knick-knacks, sacks full of watches and church treasures. Captain Yegorov's entire wealth, the column's treasure trove... And then the Captain knelt in the middle of it all, and right there on that mountain of carpets he spread out the wolf skin and ever so carefully placed the dinosaur egg in the middle of it. It was bigger than my head. He flipped the corners of the blood-soaked pelt over the egg, tied it into a bundle and carefully stowed the egg away... He had put his most treasured possession onto the pickup, and he had chosen me to be there! The pickup gave a jolt and I collapsed on all fours in front of Captain Yegorov, banging my head on the grandfather clock. Luckily, I caught it as it fell... Yegorov thumped on the cab. Kantariya tapped back and the pickup's engine roared...

Around the gap blown in the barricade, our sub-machine-gunners stood and knelt in various firing positions. Some of the injured ones had got stuck in the barricade, and as I looked about me, two or three were completely lifeless... Animal legs poked their hooves up into the sky from where a machine-gun emplacement had been camouflaged with bundles of paper. We set off through the gap and in no time we were passing our tanks. The chain of tanks in the circular defence line was unbroken, although a few machines had come off their tracks and one tank had had its turret blown off. Gunner Timosha was holding the sheet, which was blowing in the breeze, and the sub-machine-gunners and tank crews looked at our white flag and raised their arms to greet us. They were glad we had come out to negotiate a truce... Bodies in black tank troop uniforms lay in the grass on the hillside. The canvas tarpaulin covering the back of the pickup flapped in my face. I kept a frantic hold on the bench-seat – we were driving across the wild terrain of the slope, over potholes and the pits left by shells. Captain Yegorov let out a shout of rage, because the big mirror on the washstand had cracked. He was cursing and clasping the grandfather clock to protect it, and he only fell silent when we were brought up short by the barrels of Kozhanov's tanks.

The whole hillside was rippling with the activity of the sappers. Whole squads of motorized riflemen were scurrying into position. We passed by the dark-green wall of tanks, each protected by its red star. The tanks overshadowed a host of men toiling away with their entrenching tools, urged on by roaring NCOs. We passed all those new Russians in the trenches and gun emplacements, and I could tell they were in spanking new camouflage gear. Their trenches were bristling with weapons, light and heavy, and they struck me as rested, not worn to shreds and all battered and bruised like the 'Happy Song' men... It cheered me that along with Captain Yegorov we were off to negotiate a truce and the redeployment of the 'Happy Song' soldiers under the banners and battle colours of the new Russians, because what other option was there? We drove slowly through an armed human anthill. They reinforced their positions during breaks in the shelling, and there was no point trying to count the number of machine-gun nests. I had almost given up trying to keep such data in my keen saboteur's head. Instead I was more concerned about getting myself a new tracksuit top to wear under my tankman's jacket, so that, in the event of our making a move to clear Czechoslovakia of criminals, should the need arise – like if bandits launched an offensive – I could become a young country bumpkin, someone's prisoner or something. It crossed my mind this would be a good preparation for the next stage of my wartime life. But I was wrong again.

Vyžlata's pistol was digging into me and having such a thing on me could arouse suspicion, so I shoved it in among the carpets on the pickup. A swift kick sent it sliding as deep as possible into the

Captain's treasure trove. Not knowing where it was made me feel better straight away.

The shellfire of the 'Happy Song' tanks has wreaked merry hell, and not just with the terrain. We drove through a veil of insects. Armour-plated bluebottles and greenbottles were even getting in under the tarpaulin. We passed a dressing station. We could hear sighs, groans and weeping, and sometimes the occasional scream. It all came drifting through the air. It was the way they say things always are at dressing stations, especially at the front. I got that from the other soldiers of our column. We didn't have one. But then, one tank column doesn't make an army corps.

We came to a halt above the dressing station. We were at the top of the hill. If I stood on tiptoe I could see the whole village. We clambered out, the Captain first.

The command post was made up of a black awning on stakes. So the officer in a black uniform spangled with decorations had to be none other than Major General Kozhanov. I gathered that the numerous lances stuck in the ground were the battle colours of his unit. I got a bit of a shock, because women's hair was attached to the lances, blowing in the wind whistling up the slope. There was fair hair and dark, and it had all been twisted into thick plaits. As we got closer it occured to me that they might be horses' tails instead. I was right, they were horsehair.

Kozhanov was tall, taller than Captain Yegorov. Outside the tent on a folding desk there was a pile of maps – real maps, not like mine.

Captain Yegorov gave his name, but I didn't. Nobody expected me to. Timosha stood to attention on the pickup. Kantariya got out only when the Captain barked the order at him.

Kozhanov was standing in front of us, and for a while he didn't budge. Then he snapped his fingers and suddenly there was a line of paras behind us. I recognized the uniforms. They were from the regiment of guards, not just any old squaddies, and they were all huge.

'Someone kill that kid and the two drivers,' said Kozhanov, and I heard the paras release the safety catches on their rifles.

'No, hang on. Don't kill 'em just yet,' said Kozhanov. 'Let 'em say goodbye to their unit.'

Kozhanov waved an arm and we turned around. We looked at the massed tanks just crossing the barricade under continuous shellfire. From this distance and facing downhill all we could see were the tanks. The actual battle looked like ants scurrying about in the flames. I knew the barricade was there, with men and animals in it.

Then Kozhanov came over to my captain and hugged and kissed him.

The Captain ordered me onto the back of the pickup. It felt good to have at least the tarpaulin between me and the paras. The Captain ordered me to fold it back.

Kozhanov and Yegorov climbed inside, and Kozhanov patted the sacks full of watches and valuables. He even gave one large glass stag a slap of his hand. Looking around in the gloom he said, 'Souvenirs, hmm...' He caught his foot on the cracked mirror with washstand, cursed, then bashed it with his fist and shouted something, and a couple of the paras came towards us. Kozhanov pointed to the sacks and they picked them up and offloaded them, taking them away somewhere... And all Yegorov had left in the pickup was three sacks, which wasn't fair, anyone could see that. So Kozhanov hollered and the paras put a sack, the smallest one, back under the tarpaulin. Then Yegorov handed Kozhanov the wolf-skin pouch, undoing it to show the Major General the dinosaur egg, his most prized possession.

Kozhanov stroked the wolf pelt, and said, 'Very good, comrade. This'll make some excellent wolf-skin caps for our Russian winter. Very good.' Then he ran a finger across the rough surface of the dinosaur egg and said, 'This is an outstanding souvenir, comrade. Take good care of it... Of course, you don't need the drivers, or the lad!'

Timosha and Kantariya were hunched under the pickup's tarpaulin. I stood to attention. Captain Yegorov placed a hand on my shoulder, looking down at his feet, at the carpets we were trampling on, and said, 'This is my son. All his companions died in battle.' And Captain Yegorov gave a little snivel.

And Major General Kozhanov said, 'Ah, comrade of mine! Such is war, motherfucking bitch that she is!' and he also started snivelling. Then he said, quietly, 'Keep the lad then, and fly to safety! Fly like eagles!'

Kozhanov suddenly squatted down among the carpets and produced a flask from his coat pocket, uncorked it, took a swig, then passed it to Yegorov, who also squatted and drank. The Major General stroked the wolf skin and said, 'Go ahead and make a nice warm cap for yourself, and one for the lad.'

After a while, Kozhanov said, 'Well, we've had a little sit-down before the journey,' and he stood up and climbed out, followed by Captain Yegorov. I hopped out as well, the tarpaulin clipping me across the head.

Major General Kozhanov was smiling now, and he told us, 'The way is open, but just wait a moment...' He disappeared under the black tarpaulin of the command post and reappeared almost at once. Inside he had taken off his flat officer's cap and replaced it with a helmet with a metal spike. The helmet, decorated with a red star, looked old-fashioned and it was all shiny... 'Nice, eh?' Kozhanov laughed in our direction, but his paras weren't laughing. They were rigid, holding their rifles. The horses' tails on the lances were flapping in the wind, and Kozhanov said, 'Kill just the drivers.'

There was a burst of gunfire, then another. They merged into one. I didn't turn around, but out of the corner of my eye I could see two paras dragging Kantariya by the legs. He had a hole in his head, his arms trailing across the ground. Then I heard a revolver crack. That was them finishing off Timosha. It made me feel sorry.

Captain Yegorov felt sorry as well. Anyone could see that. Major General Kozhanov put an arm around his shoulders, gave him a bit of a shake, and said, 'I know what you're feeling, dear comrade. Your unit's been destroyed. I've been through all that several times... See it as a necessary rearmament of our forces. We won't be lacking tanks any more anyway. All around here,' he swept his arm over Siaz, 'will be one big storehouse for our nuclear arsenal.'

We sat in the driver's cab, the steering wheel still warm from Kantariya's hands. We would soon be beyond the sectors I had described and drawn in my maps. We were waved through crossroads and junctions by traffic controllers with signal flags, and here and there I spotted boards nailed to trees saying *Louny* in Russian letters, and an arrow marked on them, so I reckoned that was where we were headed, and I thought of Dýha and that I was also seeing this part of the world from a truck, and like him I was sort of under escort, though not with some Czech coppers! I was with a Soviet captain, not going to some sort of young offenders' dump, but to a real home, if Captain Yegorov was really going to take me as his son.

But I couldn't ask the Captain about anything. I clutched the shaggy wolf pelt tight around my knees, doing my best not to get covered in blood, which had already clotted in parts and was flaking off under my fingers; and because the skin was so very shaggy, I couldn't feel the rough, crinkly egg through it. The Captain said we were going to fly like eagles to a faraway and glorious country to the east, a country so glorious and vast that I couldn't begin to imagine it... but then I got pissed off with the Captain going on and on! It sounded like yet another fairy tale and I was too old for fairy tales. But I couldn't tell the Captain that, could I?

Then the Captain started singing, tooting his horn and generally carrying on. He stamped his feet – all to show how happy he was! His singing grated on my ears, deafened by countless battles, and on my guts, which were empty except for hunger. Then he was chattering on about some Katyusha bird, most likely some cuddly whore, creeping about somewhere on a river bank. Then in his deep voice the Captain started singing about a glorious, faraway land, a homeland full of dense forests and stuff. Next he was cursing Chapman Forest, this murderer of his own men, who sold them down the river so that that other murdering bastard, Kozhanov, would let him keep his trophies – stolen, regrettably, with my help, from ordinary village folk... I was just thinking his face was dripping with sweat, when I realized my captain was crying – and laughing at the same time. It crossed my mind to jump off the pickup, but that wasn't a good idea, because we were moving fast on a tarmac road. I'd never travelled so fast! Riding on a tank was nothing compared to this!

It could actually have been the speed that made faces in the landscape flash past the cab window. They kept surfacing in my mind. I was getting all of the people in my mind mixed up with real people. Soon we were passing just the odd, isolated traffic controller, which meant the fighting was over! Otherwise they wouldn't be standing there on their own! The bandits would have liquidated them! We flashed through some village where there was a herd of pigs rootling around in the puddle on the green and all the windows were curtained. I was beginning to see that my Czech homeland was truly massive! Much bigger than the piddling area shown on my maps! We passed other traffic, military vehicles with red stars and tiny private cars full of Czechs gawping, and they gave us some real dirty looks, I can tell you! But they didn't say anything, didn't even sound their horns when they got a sight of Yegorov's tattered, battled-soiled uniform, and mine too perhaps! They were frightened, these civilians... Then the Czech countryside was flashing past again, in various degrees of sludginess and batteredness. So I shut my eyes tight and over the Russian chit-chat and Captain Yegorov's singing and shouting I saw the faces of the people from the village... and I could see the men of the Home Guard, and the faces of the nuns, who were probably all dead. And I could see other people from the village. Some of them waved to me as if I were leaving for ever and running away, and they were happy! I could go, for all they cared, and they made it obvious they would never ever forgive me for what I'd done... I saw the faces of the people of Siřem that I used to know – who are probably all in Hell by now, or on their way there – being evacuated. They were lurking behind every tiny little stone in this Czech land that we were passing at a fiendish speed, and they were shouting at me, angry and spiteful... Everywhere I saw the faces of those people who were cowering in the barn, anywhere in that sector Tomašín, Luka, Skryje, Bataj and the rest... They shouted out how much they hated me and that they would never forgive me. Then we started down an avenue of trees, but there weren't any heavy branches flapping about laden with this summer's sweet cherries – no, they were women trees and here were the frozen masks of Czechia that ancient savages had carved in the trees in the days when Chapman Forest was everywhere. They were the battle colours of hate... The women trees vanished and suddenly I saw Hanka. Her lips were moving and she wanted to tell me something, so I leant across to her and bashed my face on the glass, because the pickup had stopped and I woke up, and Captain Yegorov tapped me on the shoulder and said, '*Bystro!*' We had been in some hurry to get away from Hanka's country.

We unloaded the trophies from the pickup, dragging the few sacks that were left. We had driven into some hangar, and Captain Yegorov stopped shouting and singing, and he wasn't crying either. He was making out that he was strict and tough, as a commanding officer should be... From under the limp tarpaulin I dragged out his pictures of stags and his statuettes of stags, big ones and small ones, and a hip bath and those carpets, lots of carpets, and I took it all away and stacked it up and crammed it into this small plane! So we must have been at our airfield at Louny.

Captain Yegorov was cramming even the cracked mirror with the washstand into the plane, but it just didn't want to fit! So, following the Captain's orders, I rearranged the sacks of money and watches and the carpets – but the mirror still refused to fit! We would have to leave it behind. Captain Yegorov kicked it to pieces.

He ordered me to climb into the plane's cargo space on top of the pile of carpets and other trophies, then he passed me the wolf pelt, ever so carefully. It was on my lap and the wolf hairs tickled my throat, but I held on tight to the egg... The Captain put on his pilot's helmet with lots of attachments sticking out, then he strapped me to his belongings! He must have lost the ropes that he used to tie me up with at night during some battle somewhere, or maybe he'd forgotten where he put them... There were these straps hanging from the sides of the cargo space inside the tiny plane, and it was these my captain tied me up with... I was already half-choked by the pile of carpets around me, and with the dragon's egg on my knees I was coughing up wolf hairs... and he still had to tie me up! A fine start to my new life, I thought to myself... The little plane set off at a crazy speed, and with the engines roaring we rose up and then hit the ground with the wheels again. We did a hop. My captain couldn't hear me, though I was shouting and hitting my head on the steel walls. The wolf pelt slipped off me, the egg rolled out and it was bashing against the walls of the plane, bouncing like a ball. My brain had almost turned to porridge when the egg came flying past me. With my free hand I dipped into the sack of watches to throw handfuls of them at the Captain's cabin to get him to stop – to get him to tame the egg! The other trophies also put my life at risk, the biggest stag with its massive antlers shattering against the walls of the cargo space. I kept dodging the bits and pieces flying everywhere like exploding shrapnel. I spotted the pistol that had slipped out from under the carpets somewhere: now it lay at my feet. I couldn't cut through the strap with a broken piece of the stag, but I did manage to snap it bare-handed, such was my strength born of sheer terror at the way the plane and the flying egg kept leaping about. I wanted to warn

the Captain, the confusion being the same as if we were in a battle...
Over all the noise the egg made as it banged into the walls – destroying a trophy here and there – the Captain couldn't hear me shouting...
only after a deafening gunshot did Captain Yegorov look back... and
just then the little plane left the ground and we were flying straight
into the sun... Captain Yegorov shouted something, leaning back towards me into the cargo area. The egg ricocheted off the wall and
bopped me on the head, and then there was another shot... Regrettably, I had shot my Captain Yegorov right between the eyes. He must
have fallen backwards onto the plane's control stick, though I didn't see
that, because soon afterwards we crashed.

When I came to, it was night. My captain and the entire cargo lay in
the wreckage of the little plane. It was easy to yank off a bit of twisted
metal. Then I started digging.

I spent three days and three nights making a kurgan for the Captain
and the plane. I had some provisions from the wartime shelter. Once
they had gone I stopped eating.

After I had trampled down the earth all around the kurgan, disguising it with turf and young saplings, I lived there for a while. I might
have been guarding my captain. I might have been on the lookout for
some new army to join. Then I realized I had to go. I consulted my
maps. I began writing.

When it comes to the writing, it is me and it isn't. I've written over
the maps and pages torn from books. I've written down the truth
about everything I've been through. I've written about the war of the
Czechs and Slovaks with the armies of the five states, and it's all true.
There isn't enough tar water in the world for me to gargle if I told a

single lie. I covered every bit of paper with my truth, and then I set off for Siřem.

Only I know where the kurgan – my captain's grave – is. And where the egg is. I haven't marked it on any map. I'll put these pages I've written inside my parents' tomb. Maybe someone will find them one day. Maybe someone will still be able to read Czech.

I'll also take a look at the wartime shelter, to see whether the last Siřem family is still living there. I'm just about to set off.

I'm going home.